CALIFORNIA SON

A Liam Sol Mystery

Timothy Burgess

Novels by Timothy Burgess

The Never-Ending Swell

California Son

CALIFORNIA SON: A Liam Sol Mystery
Copyright © 2018 TIMOTHY BURGESS

Cover Design: Iram Shahzadi
Interior Design: Crystal Watanabe

Printed in the United States of America.

ISBN: 978-1723045097
ISBN: 1723045098
First Edition
10 9 8 7 6 5 4 3 2 1

For Hayley and Kinsey
Thank you for making me a better man

PROLOGUE

La Bolsa, California, 1969

Julio Garza stood alone on the street in front of The Alamo bar. Patches of fog drifted through the neighborhood like wandering ghosts.

He didn't like the name the gringos had given to this part of town, *Baja La Bolsa*, the Mexican part of town, as if it were a foreign country.

The people who lived here worked in the fields, they worked in the kitchens, they worked in the yards of the white people, they cleaned the homes of the rich, and they fought in Vietnam for the American way of life. Yet, when they ventured into the *right* part of town, or set out their towels on the beach to soak up the sun, the locals looked past them as if they didn't belong. He laughed. A town with a Spanish name that wanted nothing to do with those who spoke the language.

But Julio wanted to belong. He hated himself for it, yet he couldn't lie: He wanted to live the lives they led. He knew that not all Mexicans were looked down upon in La Bolsa. Some had found some magic ingredient that allowed them to be part of the city, but they, too, looked down on people like Julio. Julio had been born in La Bolsa, but his mother was an immigrant, and that, he believed, proved to be the line in the sand.

He glanced at his watch. It was after two in the morning. His contact, the key to his future, was late. He wondered how long he should stay there. People said it never got cold in Southern California, but the bitter chill of the late November night seeped into his bones, and he began to worry if he was doing the right thing. He thought about his home and knew his bed was safe and warm, his mother asleep in hers. He heard the low rumble of a car engine. Julio stepped out from the fog and into a clearing in the street. He waved so the driver could see him.

The car crept toward him and Julio felt a sense of relief. He told himself he was doing this for his mother, but he knew she would never approve of his actions. But this was a one-time thing, and then he would go back to being the kind of man his mother raised him to be.

The car came to a sudden stop. Julio stepped toward it, his heart taking on extra beats. He wanted to get this over with. Then the car began to move toward him, almost coasting. Julio stood still, waiting for the car to pull up next to him. The driver jammed the high beams on. Julio put his hand in front of eyes, shielding them from the sudden glare. Then the driver punched the gas. Julio heard the tires cry out and saw the car zeroing in on him. He tried to run, but it felt as if his feet were stuck to the asphalt. He waved his arms and tried to scream, but all he heard was the roar of the engine. *This can't be real*, he thought. But when he saw the driver's face he knew he had gone too far, that he had been stupid and greedy, and he wished he could take it all back. But it was too late.

CHAPTER ONE

La Bolsa, California, 1971

When I returned home from the war two months ago no one spit on me. No one called me a baby killer. No one called me a murderer. No one accused me of crimes against humanity. No one called me a name of any kind. I'm not saying these things didn't happen to other soldiers when they came home, but they never happened to me.

Still, I found that some of my old friends and acquaintances would look into my eyes to try and see if I had changed. They wanted to see for themselves if I was someone they should be frightened of. They wanted to know if this war, unlike the other wars, had turned soldiers into monsters, and if we had brought home some new kind of evil.

I got used to the look, but not the apprehension they felt when they came across me, though, to their credit, they did try to hide it. There were times I wanted to look into the mirror to see if I could see a change, yet even before I left for Vietnam, I had quit staring at my reflection for very long. I knew that whatever darkness may have been hiding in my soul should remain untouched, buried and alone.

But in some god-awful way, Vietnam turned out to be an escape for me, from what I had left behind in La Bolsa. A lot of blood was shed in that town because of me. Good people died in that town because of me. My family was torn apart because of me. The nightmares I had of Vietnam paled in comparison to the ones I had of La Bolsa. But I came back because it was home and I had no place else to go. Yet I would soon find myself walking into another battle, and once again, more blood would be shed, more lives would be lost, all because of me. All because I refused to leave well enough alone.

CHAPTER TWO

It was just past sunrise. Wyatt Ford and I were lying on our boards, the water undulating beneath us. An onshore breeze left the swell flat and lazy. Spring had settled in and the warmth of the early morning sun felt good on my back. I'd been home for a couple of months now, trying to adjust to my new life. I'd learned not to be restless about matters of nature. The waves would come, maybe not this morning, but perhaps tomorrow or the next day. I could wait. It only mattered that I was back in the water.

The sun, the sand, the air, the ocean, all the elements felt different here, unique. If you blindfolded me and sent me to different beaches around the world, the one place I could pick out from my senses alone would be La Bolsa. There was no other place like it. How the sun touched my skin, the way it reflected off the water at sunset, the taste and scent of the salt air, the rhythms and flow of the ocean, it all felt different here. It all felt right. Yet, something in my bones kept whispering to me, telling me that I never should have come home.

We were south of the La Bolsa pier, away from the younger, more aggressive surfers. The culture had begun to change, due, in my mind, to the competitive nature and corruption of the soul that surf contests brought. Surfing became a sport, with winners and losers, no longer about being at one with the ocean and the elements that brought life to the planet, or achieving a sense of nirvana or salvation, or even the thrill you felt riding an epic wave. I hoped it was just part of a cycle, like a bad weather pattern, but I had my doubts.

Wyatt turned over on his back and stretched out on his surfboard. He scratched his chin and it appeared as if he were looking straight into the sun. Back in high school we used to joke that Wyatt was a stoned version of Maynard G. Krebs.

"Something doesn't feel right, Liam," he said.

"What do you mean?"

"Everything's changing, man," he sighed. "I can hear it in the wind."

That's how it was with Wyatt. He had the ability to spit out complete bullshit and still make you wonder if he were on to something.

And maybe this time he was.

Because today was the first day I wouldn't see Catalina Garza. Each day for the past two years she'd stood in front of the La Bolsa Police Department, holding a sign that read *Justise for Julio*. She would continue her vigil, rain or shine, until she felt justice had been served for her son. Until then, it would be just her and her sign, begging for justice. Begging for her son, Julio. When she first began her protest, many of those who passed her, whether by car or on foot, laughed at her. Catalina was an easy target. She had the dark skin tone from her Mayan-Mexican heritage. She had a thick accent and was overweight and illiterate. She wore what would charitably be described as secondhand clothes. But Catalina Garza had become part of the landscape now, as invisible as a Yield sign. But today she wasn't at her post, and I wondered if my article on her had anything to do with it.

Ben Daniels, my editor at the *La Bolsa Tribune*, had been adamant that I shouldn't chase an old story. It was a tragic hit-and-run, he said. No witnesses, no clues, no leads, case closed. But there was a dignity to Catalina and I wanted to know more. And I wanted to know

Julio's story as well, so I tried again to make my case.

"She's been out in front of the police station every day for two years," I told him.

"Which means nothing, Sol. We covered that case. The police covered that case. Neither of us found any leads. None. You're not going to come up with anything new."

"Let me talk to her. Maybe the story is about her not giving up, the enduring love of a mother."

Daniels sighed. "As long as you stick with the human-interest angle, you can go with it. Don't dig up shit where there is none."

Then he looked at me as if he wondered why he had ever hired me as a reporter.

Shortly after returning home I landed a job with the *La Bolsa Tribune*. Right before my first tour in Vietnam ended, I found I wasn't ready to go home, but nor did I have any desire to get back to combat. My CO referred me to the Office of Information out of Saigon, where I was assigned to write for *The Observer*. When I asked him why he did that for me, he said that I wrote good reports.

"That's it?"

"You need another reason?"

"No, sir," I replied. I found him to be a good commanding officer, though you could tell the war had gotten to him, how it had taken its toll. I couldn't count the times I'd heard him mutter to himself "What a waste. What a goddamned waste."

Writing for *The Observer* didn't involve much real reporting; it was mostly rewriting PR statements or highlighting the success of our troops in combat. I'm not sure how effective we were, or how good I was at it, but I did manage to write a few articles that I was proud of, pieces that I felt mattered. Overall, the work kept me busy and I found Saigon to be a place that, at least then, suited me well. Most of my assignments kept me out of the mud and the jungle and all that came with it. It was this experience that landed me the job at *The Tribune*.

Catalina Garza had agreed to meet with me at Bud's Coffee Shop on Ocean Avenue, not far from the police station. She was insistent about staying at her post until 5:00 p.m., as if letting go of it before then would be a signal to the police that her resolve had weakened.

"You no speak Spanish?" she asked. I told her I didn't. Because of my complexion and my last name, most people presumed that I spoke the language, but even though I was half Mexican, I knew very little Spanish. My father had forbidden us to learn the language. "We are Americans," he told us.

I knew it would have been easier for her to speak in her native tongue, but her English was better than I had expected. Catalina didn't tell me anything I didn't already know from reading the stories in *The Tribune* archives. Julio was out late at night. The fog was thick, and it was debatable as to whether the driver even saw Julio. And if they did, they never stopped. The police kept tabs on local body shops, figuring maybe the car had suffered some damage, but nothing came of it.

I wanted her to be comfortable, so we started off talking about her experiences when she arrived in California, normal background stuff. Catalina said she'd come from Tepic and after arriving here, she found work at a chicken processing plant in Santa Ana, where she disassembled chickens, preparing them so they could be shipped to restaurants and supermarkets. She described the grisly process to me and noticed my reaction. "It was work, you know." She shrugged. "So I could live and raise Julio." She told me that after Julio was killed, she had to quit her job at the plant so she could protest outside the police department. "I do this for my son," she said. "I must not give up." Catalina took a job at night doing janitorial work in local office buildings so she could pay her rent.

After a while I asked about Julio. She smiled. "Oh, he had big dreams, you know? He tell me one day he will buy me a big house. I tell him, just be good, Julio. Just be a good man."

Catalina shook her head. "Why Julio out so late in the night, I don't know. But he act different then. He always on the phone, whispering, not talking. Like he don't want me to hear, you know?"

I nodded. "Did you tell the police this?"

"Si. They say he just talking to friends, probably, but I don't think that."

She wiped her eyes and then took a sip of her coffee and looked out the window at the passing cars.

"I still don't go to his bedroom. He should be there. He should ..." Her voice trailed off.

I could see that her heart didn't just break but had shattered. I thought of my ex-girlfriend, Dawn, and knew there were pieces of my heart that I could never put back, but the only thing Catalina had left were those missing pieces, and as broken as they were, they kept her going.

"You said that Julio was acting different. How? Was he happy? Sad?"

"He was happy, but also ..." She was searching for the right word. "... nervous? Yes, nervous. And happy, so happy."

And then she began to cry. Tears cascaded down her cheeks and as she tried to catch her breath, she asked, "Will you help me?"

I didn't know how to respond. She grabbed my hand and I looked into her bloodshot eyes. "Please," she begged. "Please."

"Yes," I said. "I'll help." I immediately regretted my answer. I wasn't much of a journalist and didn't know where to begin.

Catalina refused when I asked her if she wanted a ride home. "I walk." She said it as if she had already asked too much of me.

I watched her walk away, carrying the sign over her right shoulder like Jesus carrying his cross. It was the last time I would see her alive.

CHAPTER THREE

I lived in the same tiny one-bedroom house as I had before I left for Vietnam. It sat on the corner of Pacific Coast Highway and Golden Sun Road, right across from the ocean. It was the only house around for blocks, a lonely outpost surrounded by vacant lots and oil fields. On most days, thankfully, the coastal breeze kept the scent of crude and sulfur at bay.

When I returned from the war, I was surprised to find the home in disrepair. I could hardly see it from the street, almost lost among the overgrown bushes and towering weeds that had spread out over the years like a cancer. Vagrants had camped in the place. Scrawled writing and crude drawings covered the walls. My favorite old leather chair sat near the window, torn and slashed as if set upon by a gang of Jack the Rippers.

There were other places I could have lived since I was working now, but as shabby as the house had always been, it had been my home and I wanted to bring it back to life. I wanted to make it better than it was before. The house was owned by my family, and when I last lived here my father had never charged me rent. I was surprised that my sister Marie had let it go, but perhaps the house represented all she wanted to forget and maybe she hoped the house, like her memories of me, would get buried and lost in the dust of time.

I was sitting on the front porch with one of my old friends, Lonnie Reaves, who was helping me fix up the house. It was livable now, though it still needed paint. I had the leather chair reupholstered and now it looked brand new, which wasn't what I wanted. It had a history and I wanted to keep that, but it was close enough.

Lonnie had been back from Vietnam for a couple of years. A bullet had caught him in the leg and he walked with a distinctive limp, but that didn't keep him from surfing. Our friend, Hike Harkins, was stationed in Honolulu and still with the Navy. He knew he was one of the lucky ones. He landed a cushy position and lived a nightmare free life.

"You going to try and come out to my church this Sunday?" Lonnie asked.

Lonnie was a pastor now. He had found God after a brutal firefight with the Vietcong. "The rice paddies were dripped with the reddest blood I'd ever seen," he'd told me shortly after I'd returned to La Bolsa. "It didn't look human. I swear to you I saw the devil himself dive into the earth just a few yards ahead of me. He smelled like burnt flesh and napalm. I chased after him, but he vanished before my eyes. In its place was the most beautiful baby you ever saw lying there like an angel, looking just like the baby Jesus in the manger. I saw a tiny red spot where a bullet tore through his heart. Then just like that, the gunfire stopped and both sides walked up and stared at him. We'd seen dead babies before, but not like this. Nothing like this. No one said a thing and then we collected our dead and moved on."

He'd told me the story a few times since I'd been back. Each time it had changed in subtle but tangible ways. I knew he was wrestling with the truth, struggling between what had really happened that day and the tale he needed to tell himself so he could get on with his life and still be able to look at himself in the mirror. I didn't know if the truth or the fiction would win out, but what happened over there had changed him and I knew he needed to prove to himself that he was a good man.

"I saw God in that baby, Liam. Every time there's a war, we kill a piece of God. If we don't stop these things, we're going to kill him. We're going to kill God."

Maybe we already killed God, I thought. Not once during my time in Vietnam had I ever felt God's presence. Not that I didn't pray. I prayed a lot, being shot at will do that. And while I came out okay, others, who were much more religious than I, had their body parts spread out over the rice paddies and elephant grass, right alongside the mutilated bodies of the atheists. Bullets and bombs didn't discriminate.

"I'm not sure I believe in Him, Lonnie."

"When was the last time you went to church?"

"I haven't stepped into a church since my father's funeral. And I don't see myself going back."

"Well, the offer stands. The door will always be open for you."

I nodded my head and took a sip of beer. Lonnie's congregation was a strange one: Misfits, druggies, drunks, old surfers, as well as a good number of veterans. Most everyone in town thought he was a little bent in the head since returning, but to me he was saner than the ones who laughed him off. And he was there for his followers, and they came every week. Some came every day just to seek his counsel. Every day, just like Catalina Garza with her sign in front of the police station.

"What do you think of the woman who's been protesting outside of the police department?" I asked.

Lonnie ran his hands through his long hair. "I read the paper, you know. You wrote a good story. She seems like a good woman, not the crazy lady everyone says she is." He patted me on the back, which surprisingly, made me feel good. "You can't do what she does unless it's the truth. Can't stand up there day after day for a lie."

"That's what I think," I said.

It had been three days since I had last seen Catalina Garza. And two days since my article had been published. Maybe she just felt feel too exposed and wanted to hide out from the public for a few days, but that didn't sound like the Catalina Garza I had come to know.

I looked out to the ocean and witnessed a blood-red sun descend into the blue Pacific. A cold breeze blew off the water and chilled me to the bone.

"Did you feel that?" he asked, wrapping his arms against his chest.

"No," I lied. "Didn't feel a thing."

The next morning, I drove by the police station to see if Catalina Garza had shown up. A city crew was trimming the bushes where Catalina had stood guard, but she still hadn't shown up. Something didn't feel right, so I decided to pay her a visit.

I sat in my red Karmann Ghia across from Catalina Garza's home. It was in a rough section of La Bolsa, home to a lot of poor Mexicans, or "wetbacks," as my father had referred to them. A car was parked in front of me, a navy-blue Impala lowrider that gleamed under the noon sun. An ornate script on its rear window read "The Bad Boogaloo."

As I looked around the neighborhood I could see it wasn't scary at all, just poor. And now, very quiet, kids at school, fathers at work in the factories or in the fields.

Even though I was half Mexican, I was still out of place in this world. I came from money and privilege. I didn't speak Spanish, and I felt no kinship to anyone here. And they felt no kinship toward me. Before leaving for Vietnam, and while growing up here, I felt the daggers from their eyes and what they revealed: *You think you're better than us?* And what I heard whispered to me when I passed by any of them: *Fucking puto.* But they never threatened me, nor did they fight me. They feared my father and what he would have done to them had I ever been hurt. I didn't know it at the time, but they had every right to fear him.

Catalina lived in a rundown little cottage. The paint was peeling, but the yard was immaculate. The grass had recently been cut and rosebushes ran along both sides of the property line. I had no idea how she found the time to keep her yard looking so good.

I climbed out of my car and crossed the street to her house. I peeked into her mailbox and saw that it was full. I knocked on the door and listened for any sign of life. Nothing. I knocked again, louder this time. Again, no response. I tried the door, but it was locked. I stepped off her porch and tried to peer through the front window, but the curtains were pulled tight. I decided to look around back. Next door, I could hear a woman singing in Spanish, her voice off-key, but the sound of her sorrow was unmistakable. A fellow soldier once told me that Mexican music could tell no lies. There were no lies in her voice, just the kind of deep pain that was universal, but only truly understood by those who had lost someone they once loved.

I opened the rear gate and crept into the yard. The back door to the house was open. My radar came on signaling to me that something was wrong.

"Mrs. Garza? It's me, Liam Sol. Are you home?"

I pushed the door open and peeked inside. A wave of noxious odor rushed over me. I pulled out my handkerchief, covering my mouth and nose. The neighbor's song hit a never-ending note of heartbreak that Catalina Garza would never hear. She lay on the floor on her back, her mouth open, her tongue, swollen, sticking out, the telephone cord wrapped tightly around her neck. Her body had bloated up and her skin had turned a grotesque shade of purple. I stepped outside and tried to catch my breath. I'd seen much worse in Vietnam, but seeing Catalina Garza's lifeless body on the floor of her own home was a punch to my soul.

I took a deep breath and ran to the neighbor's house to see if I could use her phone. She was singing a new song now, still in Spanish, but she stopped after hearing me knocking on her door. I noticed an American flag posted in her window, indicating she'd lost someone close to her in the war. The woman was younger than I had expected, in her early twenties. Too young to be a widow. Too young to have a flag in the window. I didn't tell her what happened, only that I needed to use her phone.

As I called the operator, I noticed some framed pictures of what must have been her husband. He looked so young in his Marine dress uniform. So proud and handsome. One of the photos read "Private First Class Antonio Garcia." I wondered how he was killed, and I was sure it wasn't pretty. There was nothing pretty about dying in Vietnam. I glanced through her front window, and I could see that the Impala was gone. Only a puddle of leaked oil had been left behind, which looked like a small pool of wet blood.

CHAPTER FOUR

You've been gone a few years and everything here is nice and quiet. You're back, what two months, and we have a murder, and look who's right in the middle of it." Detective David Greene glared at me as he if he'd caught me kissing his mother.

"Well, they put you on the case," I said, "so I guess they don't want the killer to be captured."

We were in Catalina's back yard. The coroner was inside examining her body for evidence, while a photographer snapped pictures of Catalina from various angles. It looked like a macabre version of a fashion shoot.

Greene moved closer to me, perspiration forming on his upper lip. His red hair was parted in such a way that I wondered if he was trying to cover up a receding hairline. He studied me for a moment, then took a step back.

"Just don't try solving this yourself. We do that, not you. You understand?"

"Where's Branch? I can't believe he left you to handle this all by yourself." Detective Branch was Greene's senior partner back when the two of them had arrested me on a bogus murder charge.

"He's living out in the desert. You know, he retired after your case. After dealing with you, he'd had enough."

"Branch already had enough of it, Greene. He was just going through the motions. I bet at one time he was a good cop. What's your excuse?"

"Just back off, Sol," he said.

He slid by me, careful not to touch me as if I were contagious.

I shouldn't have gotten into it with him. I couldn't make it personal. I had a job to do. And as much as I disliked Greene, I needed to work with the police.

When I first met Detective Greene, he took on the role of good cop to Branch's bad cop. Ironically, Branch, as much as he hated me, was, in his own way, trying to do the right thing. He had saved the life of my ex-girlfriend when she was just a kid. But Greene? He was overplaying the tough cop role. I'd seen it in the war, officers going overboard in an attempt not to have their authority questioned, not to be exposed as a fraud of some kind.

"Hey, Lombardo," he called out. "Can you deal with this ... this reporter?"

Detective Lombardo stared at me like I was a Kleenex tissue that he had just sneezed into. As much as I hated the thought of it, I was going to have to play nice with this guy.

He looked like he was a former wrestler or football player. At first glance, you'd think that he'd been born without a neck. His slicked-back hair was slathered in Vitalis. He appeared to be close to my age, late twenties, I guessed. "I just need to ask you a few questions," I said.

"You need to ask me questions? You write a story about this woman and then you come to her house and find her dead? From what I hear, you seem to have a knack for getting people killed."

Lombardo gave me the once-over, then looked away. "They tell me you just came back from 'Nam."

I nodded. "You serve?"

He shook his head. "I was number 365 in the lottery. February 26th."

The draft lottery. A cockeyed system that determined where you landed in the draft by your date of birth. The lottery had been televised and the nation had been glued to their sets, seeing where either they or their loved ones would land. I remember a fellow soldier telling me about it.

"September 14th," Private Draper said. He looked like a high school freshman. "Number one. The only time I'd ever been number one in anything and it was the goddamned draft." Draper turned out all right and made it out with barely a scratch.

"You were lucky," I said to Lombardo.

He shrugged. "I would have gone, but I still feel I'm serving my country as a police officer." I didn't care if people served or not. To me, it was their own damn business, but that didn't stop some from needing to justify their avoidance from serving. Justifying to whom, I always wondered.

"Anyway, right now it looks like a burglary gone wrong. The suspect probably thought the Garza woman wasn't home, that she'd been out doing her little protest." Lombardo looked at me as if it was my article that caused the would-be burglar to make that assumption. "She's probably been dead a couple of days, at least."

"Lombardo, can you come over for a moment?" It was Greene. "Sol, you stay there. We still have questions for you."

Lombardo strutted over to Greene and the two huddled together with a few uniformed officers. I was sure they were getting an earful about my past life here, how I got one of their own killed and how I got my ex-girlfriend killed and now, maybe, Catalina Garza. This wasn't going to be easy for me. I didn't want to relive the past. I held tight and tried to look like I knew what I was doing.

I could see her body through the back door. Two uniformed cops were having trouble turning her over. It looked like a bad Laurel and Hardy routine. No matter what kind of life you've led, how good a person you were, death can transform you into some kind of grotesque caricature and the dignity that carried you throughout your life vanishes in an instant, turning you into a sick joke for the world's idiot brigade to enjoy. The two laughed as they tried to turn her over.

"Come on, Mamasita. Come on, señorita," one of the cops said. "If you hadn't eaten so many beans this wouldn't be so hard." He resembled one of the Blockheads from the Gumby show.

I watched as they were finally able to turn her onto her stomach. After they turned her body over, they began waving their hands in front of their faces. Pent-up gas had accumulated in her body. Moving her like that had probably caused it to release itself.

"Oh, señorita, don't you know that 'beans, beans are good for your heart, the ...'"

My stomach began to lurch, and I turned away and walked down the driveway before the asshole cop finished his little song.

Greene screamed at them. "Knock it off! Don't fuck with the evidence."

Catalina Garza had been instantly reduced from victim status to merely a piece of evidence. I leaned against one of the patrol cars. Somehow, I was able to keep my guts from blowing out of my mouth, though the taste of vomit had settled in my throat like bad mouthwash. Catalina was right. I could see by the way they treated her body that the police could not have cared less about what happened to her son, and now, probably to her.

Catalina had been dead at least a couple of days, most likely killed after my article had been published. I thought about what Lombardo said to me. Maybe he was right. Maybe I did have a knack for getting people killed, at least here in La Bolsa.

The thing is, my story didn't reveal anything new about her. It concluded that Julio's death was probably never going be solved, that whoever had run him over would remain a mystery. Still, something in my bones told me that Catalina's murder wasn't random nor was it a burglary gone wrong. My bet was that someone had been searching for something. Something they believed could tie them to the hit-and-run murder of Julio Garza. There was a killer out there. They killed Julio and they killed his mother. Though I had only spoken to her a couple of times, I found that I liked Catalina, and more than that, I had respected her. I wanted to find her killer, though I had no idea where to begin.

CHAPTER FIVE

W e can't print this!" Daniels screamed.
"Why not?"

He was pissed that I'd included the cops' racist comments in my story. I knew he'd edit them out, but I had to get their bigotry and cruelty on paper.

"It's not relevant to the murder," he said.

"It shows how little the police care about her. They're going to investigate Catalina Garza's murder as much as they did her son's, which means they're not going to do a damn thing."

"It's your job to keep them honest, but we can't print that. The police will never talk to us again. We can't have that."

I stared at my typewriter. "I guess there's only so much truth you can put into a newspaper story," I said.

Daniels gave me the once-over. "You still have a lot to learn, maybe too much."

He had a way of making me feel like I was the missing eighth dwarf in *Snow White*. Dumbass.

Daniels tossed the copy on my desk. "Fix it," he said. "We're on deadline."

I typed up the story the way he wanted me to. I could do this with my eyes shut, just like the stories I wrote when I worked for the Office of Information in Saigon, when I reminded our soldiers they were fighting for the American way of life.

Wyatt and I sat on the sand, letting the late afternoon sun dry us off. We'd just come out of the water. The waves had returned, three feet high coming out of a southwestern swell. Still, the ocean couldn't rid me of the guilt that had set in.

Wyatt stared at me like I was a puzzle and he was wondering where to place the last of the pieces. "What's eating you, man?"

"I think the story I wrote got Catalina Garza killed. But there was nothing new in it. It just talked about her life. Other than that, it was just an extended version of the sign she held outside of the police station."

"Nothing occurs without cause, Liam. Storms create waves."

I considered what he said but found it difficult to process. I'd written a damn human-interest story, not an exposé.

"It doesn't make any sense," I said.

"I know, man. Nothing does. It's not like yesterday."

Yesterday was a time and place known only to Wyatt. Some peaceful bliss he'd let slip away long ago that continued to haunt him like a recurring nightmare. I suspected it all had to do with his long-standing rift with his father. They had been very close until Wyatt's parents divorced, after which he chose to live with his mother. After graduating high school, he dropped out of Stanford and traveled to India, returning with a different view on life. It was clear that he would never become the type of man his father wanted him to be; in fact, he became the opposite. Something I understood. But his father never forgave him. Wyatt had delved too deeply into drugs and it had messed with his brain. He saw things others couldn't. Whether those things were real was a matter of debate.

The next morning Daniels called me into his office. It was a mess of a place. Copies of *The Register*, the *L.A. Times*, the *Herald Examiner* and even the *New York Times* and the *Washington Post* sat scattered about the office. He had a few framed pictures of him and his buddies from the Korean War, and one picture of his wife, who looked like Elizabeth Montgomery from *Bewitched*. He'd been divorced for two years, but he kept that picture on his desk, right where he could see her. I wondered if seeing her face all day gave him warmth or filled him with anger and regret.

"I have another story for you." He put his hands on his hips. "I don't have anyone else available, I'm sorry."

"What is it?" I asked, thinking it would be another ribbon-cutting ceremony or something equally asinine.

"Glenn Frost is announcing his candidacy for Congress tonight. He's going after Luther Bennett's seat. I want you to be there. Cabot called in sick. You're the only one I have."

"Are you kidding me? Glenn is married to my sister, Isabelle." Glenn and I had a mutual hatred of each other. He was a piece of shit. On top of that, I had been estranged from my family since before I left for Vietnam. "Isn't there a conflict of interest here?"

"Yes. And we'll disclose it in the article. You're not covering the rest of the campaign, just tonight's announcement."

"Isn't this early? The primary is over a year away."

"Luther Bennett's been in the house since Truman," Daniels said. "It's going to take a lot of time and money to unseat him."

"My family's going to be pissed when they see me there."

"I cleared it with them. They're looking forward to seeing you."

I wasn't. I hadn't seen them since I'd returned. What Daniels didn't know about my family would have been a banner story. Isabelle, the middle child, murders her father to protect her brother (me). Marie, the eldest child, unleashes a pale-faced psycho on said brother to scare him off from discovering the truth. Along the way, the psycho killed a cop and my ex-girlfriend, Dawn. We were able to keep our family's involvement secret, as we were the only ones who knew the truth. There was more, but I refused to think about it. I had no interest in dragging myself back into my private hell. I'd done enough of that already.

"There's no one else?" I asked.

Daniels gave me a smirk. "Seven o'clock tonight at The Beach Club. Wear a tie."

This was just getting better. The La Bolsa Beach Club was the last place I saw my father alive, when I told him that I didn't want to be anything like him.

I slumped into my chair. I thought about Vietnam and what I'd be doing there if I had re-upped. Writing puff pieces and drinking too much, I guessed.

Then there was Jackie Minh. Another failed relationship. Jackie was born in Vietnam but educated in France. She had worked as a translator and analyst for the American Embassy in Saigon. She made me laugh and smile and, most of all, forget. I didn't love her, but I needed her as she helped keep the devils at bay.

You could see that Saigon was once a beautiful city and we were treating it like an adult playground. Like "Alice's Restaurant," you could get anything you wanted in Saigon. Hell, you could do what you wanted there, too. You could fuck girls of almost any age, sometimes getting them pregnant, then leaving them alone to raise your baby alone in a war-torn city. Forget what you were fighting for, whatever ideals you believed in were soon lost in certain parts of the city where you could indulge in whatever your dark heart desired. American ideals in action. And we were supposed to be changing hearts and minds? Who were we kidding?

"Answer your phone!" a voice yelled out.

I realized the phone had been ringing for a while.

"Sorry." I answered it, but before I could say hello, a man's voice on the other end said, "We need to talk."

The voice didn't sound familiar. "Who is this?"

"I have information regarding the murder of Catalina Garza."

I grabbed my pen and reporter's notebook. Whoever it was, his tone was overly formal, as if he were attempting to hide an accent.

"No names. We must first meet."

"Have you gone to the police?"

"The police cannot be trusted."

"Are you saying the police killed her?"

"I'll be at The Alamo tomorrow at noon."

The Alamo was a bar that sat on the edge of Baja La Bolsa. Julio Garza was run down in front of that very same bar.

"I'll be there. How will I recognize you?"

"You won't. But I know you, Mr. Liam Sol."

"Have we met before?" But there was no response. He'd already hung up.

CHAPTER SIX

To me, wearing a suit and tie was equivalent to wearing a prison uniform. I also felt like a fraud. The suit declared that I belonged in places like the La Bolsa Beach Club, that I was one of them. I wasn't. I was as far from being the man in the gray flannel suit as I was from being an Apollo astronaut. Even when I came to the club with my father, who had been a founding member, I didn't belong. I was a surfer, not someone caged in by corporate walls and I didn't want to be any part of a building that divided the haves from the have-nots.

I waited in the valet line in my 1967 Karmann Ghia, the top down. A soft breeze blew in from over the Pacific and I didn't want to shut it out. Some bubble-gum crap song I'd never heard before came on the radio, so I turned it off. I knew a lot of good stuff was starting to happen on the FM dial, but for now, anyway, all I had was an AM radio. I'd thought about installing an eight-track tape deck, but since the tracks would sometimes change in the middle of a song, making you wait a moment or two before it came back on, I decided to pass. Good songs should never be interrupted.

I looked around the parking lot. The cars waiting in line in front of me were shiny new Cadillacs and Lincolns and similar cars, preferred by the wealthy elite of Orange County. A few had patriotic bumper stickers that read "America, Love it or Leave it" or "Nixon's the One." I was surprised that the valets didn't direct me to where the help parked. It's not that my car was in bad shape, it's that it didn't scream money; it screamed kitchen door. This was the first time I had ever been on my own, without any financial help from my family. Yeah, I had a small trust fund, but I wasn't touching it—not now, maybe not ever. It was strange feeling the difference. I was now, as my sister Marie liked to put it, "one of them."

The Beach Club looked the same. It was a modern design: lots of open space, a large dining patio overlooking the water, and floor-to-ceiling windows. Yet with all the sleek touches, all the openness, minorities, as far as I could tell, were left to prepare the food, park the cars and clean up after the members. It was something that had always confused me. My father, a man of full-blooded Mexican descent, but a proud American, had wanted to keep Mexicans out. He was the first and last minority admitted. He knew he was a member only because he owned the land on which it sat, land which he later donated to the club. My father knew the other members regarded him as less than them, but they feared him, and because of that fear he knew he could control them.

After his death, it was back to an all-white club—an all-white male club of which State Senator Glenn Frost was a proud member. A good Protestant married to a Catholic, a half Irish, half Mexican one at that. Glenn had tried to talk Isabelle into changing religions, fearing that her being a Catholic would hurt him in the heart of Orange County, but my sister, who had always been accommodating, would have none of it. And since the events that surrounded my father's murder and after her stint in a mental hospital, which no one outside the family knew about, Isabelle had determined that she would no longer be pushed around. How and where she found that strength, I didn't know, but her Catholic faith must have been a factor.

Yet she and Glenn made a beautiful couple. He was handsome in a West Coast preppy way and Isabelle was stylish and stunning. And that, he knew, outweighed any of her perceived political liabilities.

I stood in the check-in line behind an older couple who reeked of too much pipe tobacco, Brut and Chanel No. 5. The wife looked up at her husband and straightened his ascot.

"Did you take the spare change out of the car?"

"Yes, dear," he said as he eyed the well-shaped ass of the lady in front of him.

"Even the ashtray? You know how those Mexicans are, honey."

"I don't keep money in the ashtray." He glanced over at his beige Caddy. "They better be careful with it. You ever see their cars? It's obvious they can't drive worth a damn."

"I don't know why they can't hire ..." She looked around and saw me, and then whispered to him, "white people."

The man followed his wife's eyes and he paused when he saw me, not sure what race I was. My skin tone was naturally olive, but the sun had turned it to a dark brown which, other than a few sun streaks, matched my hair. My eyes were blue, though, and that confused him. He smiled politely and nodded his head. He turned back to his wife and put his arm around her, inching her up in line as much as he could to increase the distance between us.

It was a strange feeling. My family had pretty much built this town after my grandfather naively purchased property in La Bolsa that appeared to be nothing more than useless marshland. Useless, that is, until oil was discovered there. After my grandfather died of a heart attack, my father took over and expanded the reach of Sol Enterprises and proved to be as ruthless as any land baron California had ever seen. But because of him, people here chose to see us differently, as pillars of society, all because we had money and influence. Growing up wealthy, I never got the snub. In fact, most everyone went out of their way to be nice to me. I liked them. They gave me smiles and pats on the head and said the world could be mine. But now I saw them for who they were: The people who looked down on everyone else, the ones my father did business with. These were the same people who sent us to war and who barely tolerated those who looked different than them.

In Vietnam, there was an unofficial segregation among the soldiers, sometimes by class, but usually it came down to race. It wasn't uncommon to hear blacks talking about having to fight a white man's war. While at times there seemed to be an invisible wall separating us, there was also a gate which we crossed daily, where we bonded, laughed, and shared our stories with each other. The unease became more apparent when, consciously or unconsciously, we segregated into racial groups. After Martin Luther King was assassinated, the tension began to heat up. At times, it spilled over into fights. Yet it never impacted us while we were under fire from enemy combat. There we had each other's back; there we were one. It wasn't until I enlisted in the Army that I saw America how it really was, a country somehow both united and divided at the same time.

I remember a fellow soldier once asked me, since I was half Irish and half Mexican, what I considered myself to be. I told him that I considered myself to be an American. He looked at me as if I didn't understand his question. "You have to choose sides," he said. I didn't know then that everyone eventually chooses a side. And if you didn't choose one, one was chosen for you, whether you wanted to be on that side or not. Once I never noticed race, but since returning from Vietnam, I couldn't help but notice it everywhere.

"Liam? There you are."

My body flinched at the sound of her voice. My sister Marie sliced through the crowd like a knife through a cake. She was all smiles as she hugged me. She smelled like jasmine and champagne. Her long dark hair was touched with a brush of gray. A little premature, but I knew it couldn't be easy being the bully of La Bolsa.

"We've missed you, Liam. I'm so relieved you came back in one piece."

She let go of my hand and looked up at me, examining my face. Her eyes were moist, and she brushed a strand of hair from my eyes.

"Dear, dear Liam," she whispered.

I waited for the backhanded compliment, but she never served it up.

"I've been meaning to phone you and have you up to the house for dinner, but I didn't think you'd want to come. I understand, of course, but Brona misses you so."

She still referred to our mother by her first name, and after all these years, it still bugged the hell out of me.

"She's not feeling well, so she won't be able to attend tonight, but you must see her, Liam. It would mean the world to her."

I knew that in her own way my mother loved me, but I didn't miss her. How could you miss someone who fed you to the wolves? When I said my goodbyes to my family, I thought it was for good. I wanted it to be for good, but maybe I came back to La Bolsa hoping that we could be one again, or maybe I was just a masochist who needed an unending supply of pain.

"It's good to see you, Marie," I said, confused whether my response was a truth or a lie, but it was the only thing I could think to say.

She took my hand and squeezed it gently and held it as she led me through the crowd, greeting donors along the way, yet not introducing me to any of them.

"I hate these things," she said, "but it's how politics are done, I suppose."

I wanted to laugh. She lived for these nights, exercising her power, working the strings behind the stage, a sinister version of Geppetto.

"I know you're here to report on the campaign, so if you need to interview Glenn, let me know. I'll make sure the two of you get some privacy."

"I don't think we'll need a private room," I said, as I felt my free hand ball up into a fist. Too many emotions ran through me. I was surprised to find I still had any affection for Marie, yet I felt fearful and distrustful of her at the same time.

I let go of her hand. I could feel her trying to reel me in and if I didn't pull away from her now, I wasn't sure I'd ever be able to.

"It was good to see you, Marie. I'll get up to see Mom soon, I promise. I'm on a tight deadline though, so I'd better get to work."

Marie looked hurt, as if I had just called her a bad name. She quickly composed herself and gave me a hug, my heart beating against hers. Then she looked at me. "Get the story right, Liam. You'll do that, won't you?" She smiled, and for a brief moment I saw the real Marie. I continued to walk away from her, trying like hell not to run.

I headed straight for the bar and ordered a beer. I wanted something stronger, but knew I had to keep a clear head. As more people arrived, the room turned smokier. I took my beer and stepped outside to the patio. I leaned against the rail overlooking the Pacific. The sun was beginning to set. Streaks of reds and yellow painted the western sky as the golden ball of the sun came closer to touching the horizon. Southern California sunsets were beautiful and full of promise. Yet it was an illusion. It was the smog, the very poisons that crept into our lungs that created these breathtaking sunsets.

"Shouldn't you be inside pouring drinks?"

I turned to the voice and saw a woman about my age. She was pretty, very pretty, and obviously of Mexican descent. She had a lovely smile and her black hair had been pulled up in a bun. I could tell that she was pleased with her opening line.

"I'm on strike," I said. "What's your excuse?"

"I'm with the band."

I didn't know if she was joking or not. She held a glass of white wine and her red dress was doing a fine job of framing her body, which was impossible not to notice, but I did my best.

"I'm guessing you're the singer?"

"No. Just a lawyer. Elisa Vargas," she said, extending her hand, which was soft and welcoming.

"Liam Sol."

"You're Marie and Isabelle's brother, then? The prodigal son?"

"That's what they claim. So, what really brings you here?"

"I'm the legislative advisor for the Frost campaign."

My heart sank a bit. "Well, no one's perfect," I said.

She laughed. "Funny. You're not a fan of your brother-in-law?"

"I know him too well, but tonight I'm supposed to be neutral. I'm covering the event for the *La Bolsa Tribune*."

"You wrote that profile of Catalina Garza, right?"

I nodded my head.

"It was good. It really brought her out."

"You knew her?"

"No. I meant your article made me feel like I knew her. It was tragic what happened. I wonder about this world sometimes, you know?"

"Yeah, I do know." It felt good that my article touched her. "I'm not done with her story. I'm going to keep pushing. I owe her that much."

"I'm not surprised," she said. "I can tell it's important to you."

It wasn't until that moment that it hit me that my job mattered. That what I did meant something.

The band started playing "Happy Days Are Here Again." She looked inside. The crowd pushed its way closer to the stage. "That's my cue. He's ready to announce."

Elisa's eyes lingered on me for a moment, and I'd be a liar if I said I didn't want to get to know her better, despite who she worked for.

"I hope we can talk some more, Mr. Liam Sol."

"I'd like that," I said.

She placed her glass on the table, a hint of lipstick kissing the rim. She smiled and walked inside and into the music, the gentle sway of her hips tugging at me. Yes, I thought it would be nice to get to know her, yet I knew I'd find some way to screw it up and leave her, or me, with a long list of regrets.

I finished my beer and watched the last of the sun sink into the ocean. I looked out over the never-ending water, the horizon lost in mist and twilight. I heard Marie's voice through the loudspeakers as she spoke to supporters about our family. The myth we all bought. And Marie could sell it well. Sweet, beautiful lies which I still wanted to believe. But the lies proved to be deadly, though they still had the power to lure me in.

The crowd cheered when Glenn took the stage. I pulled out my reporter's notebook and followed his voice inside, placing myself among the adoring crowd. Isabelle stood behind him, looking as radiant as ever, though I knew she hated every moment in the spotlight. Isabelle was the only one in my family who wrote to me while I was overseas. She was the one person in the family who tried to understand me. Isabelle was the one person here I wanted to talk to. The one person I was truly happy to see. When our eyes met, I gave her a small wave of my hand and smiled. She shook her head slightly and then proceeded to look right through me as though I were invisible. It felt like a bayonet had been rammed through my heart. She put her head down momentarily as if in prayer and then looked up at Glenn, a frozen smile pasted on her face.

The wind picked up and blew through the open doors. It was a warm breeze, yet it made me feel cold, exposing me to the one truth I didn't want to face: I was all alone in this world. And it was my choice and I had to live with the consequences.

A young blonde, who looked as though she were still in high school, passed out copies of Glenn's prepared speech. She looked uncomfortable in her red, white and blue cheerleading outfit. It was much too tight in the chest and occasionally she tugged at her short skirt to keep from showing too much leg. She handed me a copy of the speech and shrugged as if to say, "It's a job."

I should have been taking notes and interviewing guests, but I decided to frame the article around his speech and add a few lines about the enthusiasm of the crowd. The story didn't require much in the way of reporting.

The cheerleader stood near the corner of the stage, talking to Archibald Roth, my father's former business partner. He whispered something to her. Her cheeks burned red, as if she'd been slapped. She folded her arms in front of her chest and slinked away.

Archibald Roth was "a man who got things done." He was someone who thought he could outsmart the devil and he was probably right. He was facing the stage now, as if the exchange with the girl had never happened. He was nodding his head and wore his ever-present cowboy hat, his teeth clenching a smoldering cigar.

My mouth felt like sandpaper and I was having trouble breathing. I loosened my tie. I hated being stuck in this place with Marie and Glenn. And I couldn't get the way Isabelle had looked at me out of my head. The room began to close in on me. It was as if I'd been held down under a wave for too long and didn't know if the surface was up or down. I took in one last draw of my beer and then headed for the exit, trying to leave the ghosts of my past behind, but knowing I would never escape them.

CHAPTER SEVEN

He greeted me with a nod. A copy of the *La Bolsa Tribune* sat on the bar in front of him. My article on the murder of Catalina Garza was face up and in clear view of anyone who might pass by. He introduced himself as Charlie Moran. He was a short, thin, middle-aged Mexican man, and it looked as if he'd been ironed into his suit.

I took the seat next to him, glancing at the empty shot glass in front of him. He motioned to the bartender and she poured more tequila into his glass. She was muscular, not bulky, but strong and rough around the edges. I asked her for a Tecate.

"You know, Mr. Sol," he said. "Most people think that all bars smell the same. They don't. Each one has its own particular scent. Many things come into play: the location, the characters they attract, what they drink, smoke, what kind of work they do, how much blood has been spilled, do they clean the floors with just soap and water or something stronger. The combinations are all different, all unique."

The bartender put the bottle down in front of me and asked if I wanted a glass. I told her I didn't. She stared at me a little too long, as if she were trying to place me and then she walked to the far end of the bar and picked up a book, *The Drifters* by James Michener.

"What does this bar smell like to you?" I asked.

The little man breathed in through his nose and held it a second before exhaling.

"Loss," he said. "This place smells like loss."

"I think that's true of most bars."

He stared down at his drink. "Not like this one."

He picked up his glass and put it to his lips and paused before downing it.

"A boy was run over in cold blood just outside of this bar. The police do nothing." He shrugged his shoulders. "If a Mexican kid is killed, the police find it difficult to care about who murdered him."

I recalled how the cops treated Catalina Garza's body. I took out my notebook. "Are you saying the police didn't bother investigating his killing?"

"I am not saying that."

"But they know who killed him?"

He responded with a shrug.

"And why are you so concerned?"

He pulled a card from his shirt pocket and placed it on the bar in front of me. It read, *Charles Moran, Attorney, Chicano Legal Rights Association.*

"I paid a visit to Mrs. Garza the day before she was murdered," he said. "I offered to represent her. I thought she should bring a suit against the La Bolsa Police Department."

"And if successful, you'd get a nice paycheck."

"The Chicano Legal Rights Association represents people free of charge."

Sure, I thought, but I bet they planned on taking a big slice of whatever settlement they came to.

"Did she hire you?"

"Mrs. Garza told me that she wanted to talk to you first."

"She said that?"

"It appears she trusted you a great deal."

I felt a stab to my chest.

"I'm not sure why you wanted to meet," I said. "Did Catalina tell you something new?"

He reached into his coat pocket and pulled out a badge and handed it to me.

"It seems that Julio Garza was working for the La Bolsa police."

I examined the badge. It was from the La Bolsa Police Department's Explorer Scout program, where high school kids who wanted to become police officers would help out during citywide events and occasionally participate in ride-along programs with officers.

"Catalina never told me about this."

"It was a surprise to Mrs. Garza, too. She had no idea. I asked if I could look in his room. I found the badge under some comic books tucked into his dresser drawer. He seemed to have a fondness for the *Silver Surfer*."

He looked at me as if I had some knowledge of the comic book. I didn't. I hadn't read one since junior high.

"If he was with the police, why would they cover up the murder?"

"Yes, that is a very important question," he said.

"Have you asked anyone at the department about this?"

"I have a contact there, but he has proven to be unreliable, perhaps even untrustworthy. So, Mr. Sol, I am requesting your assistance. You are a reporter. Your job is to uncover the truth."

I didn't want to go up against the police, but I owed it to Catalina to do whatever I could to find the truth. "I'll see what I can do," I said.

Charlie Moran smiled and stood up. "I'll be in touch." Then he walked outside and into the blinding midday sun.

I glanced at the bartender who was lost in her book.

"Have you worked here long?"

She raised her index finger at me, indicating for me to wait a moment. Then, she dog-eared her page and placed the book on the counter.

"About a year," she said. She headed my way and then poured a cup of coffee for herself. She looked at my notebook.

"I'm a reporter. Just following up on the killings of Julio and Catalina Garza. Julio was run down in front of this place a couple of years ago."

On closer look, she was younger than I'd thought, maybe in her early thirties, but the years had been rough on her. A thin scar rode down her right cheek like a jagged highway. Her smile revealed a chipped front tooth. I could see that something other than the years had been rough on her.

"I was in Corona then."

"What's in Corona?"

"A prison." She took a sip of coffee and raised her eyebrows. I was surprised at her openness.

"Is this where I ask what you were in for?"

She looked me dead in the eyes. "Killing my husband." She saw my expression. "You asked."

"I did."

"And your next question is ..."

"Am I that easy to read?"

"It's a normal reaction."

"I'm sorry, you don't have to tell me, it's not my business."

She gave me a long look before responding. "It was self-defense. My husband liked to hit me, and I finally had enough of being beaten. The state called it murder, the jury settled for manslaughter. They gave me five years and I got out in two." She held up her coffee cup as one would hold a champagne glass in a toast. I picked up my bottle in the same manner. I could have told her that I knew all about killing in self-defense, but I was in an unending battle to distance myself from my past.

Her face clouded over, and she looked at me as if she had said too much and headed down to the other side of the bar. She grabbed her book and went back to reading. There was something tender about her, though I had a feeling she'd never let anybody see that side of her.

"Is there anyone who still works here that was here back then?"

"No. No one stays here for very long."

I nodded. "How's the book?"

"It's assigned reading for a class I'm taking at Golden West College. I'm going for my Associates Degree. It makes me want to visit Spain." She shrugged. "Who knows, right?"

"I've never been. I'm Liam Sol, by the way."

"April Fairchild."

It was a pretty name and I wondered if she'd had a pretty life before her husband. Or was he just another wound that she couldn't shake free from?

Before I made it to the door, she said, "You know that guy you were talking to?"

"Charlie Moran?"

"I'd be careful around him."

I didn't let on that I was thinking the same thing. "I'll watch my back."

I put on my sunglasses and drove to the Beach Reads Bookstore. There was a novel I wanted to pick up.

CHAPTER EIGHT

Back at work, I called Detective Greene, but was told he was out of the office. The cop who answered the phone asked why I wanted to speak to him.

"I'll call back later," I said. I hung up before he could ask for my name. I didn't want to give Greene any time to prepare a response. I wanted to see how he reacted when I told him I knew Julio Garza had been an Explorer Scout with the La Bolsa Police Department.

I thumbed through my notebook to see if I had missed anything. I had a lot of questions beyond who killed Julio and Catalina Garza. Why were they killed, why didn't the police investigate Julio's death more deeply, especially if he was an Explorer Scout? One answer that came to me was an obvious one: He knew something about the police he shouldn't have known, so they killed him. Then why kill Catalina Garza two years later? I didn't have a clue.

I went back to perusing my notebook where I noticed something. The Bad Boogaloo, the lowrider that was parked across the street from Catalina Garza's home. I'd told Detective Lombardo about it, but by the time I'd seen it, Catalina had been dead for at least a couple of days, so he didn't think it significant. And it may not have been, but it was all I had. It would have been great if I could look up The Bad

Boogaloo in the phone book to find out who owned it. I knew where I had to go. I just wasn't looking forward to it. My Karmann Ghia looked out of place among the sleek and shiny cars parked in front of Delgado's Car Repair and Detailing Shop on Sandy Hook Road. A Chevy Impala sat on a lift and Hector Delgado was studying the underside like an art critic appraising a painting.

My family and the Delgados had a history of sorts. Back in high school, Hector's brother, Hugo, asked my sister Isabelle out on a date. Isabelle was all smiles waiting for him to arrive. She picked out the proper dress to wear and Marie helped her with her makeup. I couldn't remember a time when I had seen Isabelle so excited, so hopeful. She had just turned seventeen and I was fifteen. When Hugo arrived at the front door, he came face-to-face with my father, who collared him and dragged him back to his car. I watched in horror as my father told him he had no right to go out with Isabelle, that he should stick to going out with girls from his own neighborhood.

Hugo protested. "I like Isabelle, Mr. Sol," he said. "I think she likes me, too."

"I know your kind, sniffing around, trying to mark your territory."

"I'm not like that, sir."

"Yes, then maybe you want my money? Get married to Isabelle and think you can sit on your lazy, wetback ass all day?"

"Sir?"

"If I see you around here again or with Isabelle, it will be the last thing you'll ever do, I promise you that."

My father grabbed him by the throat, pushing him against the car door. He whispered something to Hugo that drained the color from his face. Hugo nodded and scrambled into his car, then tearing out as if a bomb were about to explode.

"Why, Dad, why?" Isabelle asked, sobbing.

My father took Isabelle by the arm and pulled her upstairs.

"You will go out with who I say you can go out with. Do you understand?"

Isabelle continued to cry and then I heard a door slam upstairs. Tears flooded Marie's eyes. She headed for the stairs, but stopped, and then ran out of the house through the back door. Some force led me outside. I hurried down the driveway and kept going until I reached Coast Highway where I hitched a ride to Dawn's. She knew something was wrong, though I didn't say a word about what had happened. She made some popcorn, and we sat on her front porch, drinking Cokes, looking at the night sky and talking past midnight.

The next day, everything was quiet, as if nothing had occurred. It was never spoken of again until years later when Isabelle told me the history of her and my father and how he had sexually abused her. I can't believe how deliberately ignorant I was back then, but I had always been good at turning a blind eye to things I didn't want to see.

Hugo came out all right. I'd heard he earned his degree in engineering from Cal Poly Pomona and was living in San Jose with his wife and three kids. But Hector never forgot what happened to his brother and carried the grudge like a sword.

"I smell a *pocho*," Hector said.

I guess he'd seen me coming. *Pocho* was akin to being Mexican on the outside and white on the inside.

"Hola, Hector," I said. As soon as it came out of my mouth, I knew I had chosen the wrong word.

Hector came out from under the car grinning like a Jack in the Box clown. He was shorter than me, but he had the body of a bull. He responded to me in Spanish, a language that, except for a few choice words and phrases, was foreign to me.

I put my hands out in a "come on" gesture.

"What? You can't understand your own language?" Hector seemed to have developed a slight accent since the last time I spoke to him. "Oh, that's right, you're whitewashed."

I didn't want to ask him for help. Maybe I should let the police get the information from him, but no way was I walking away from him. I nodded to him like I got the joke.

"I was wondering if you could help me out."

"What, your rich family can't do that?"

"Not with this."

"It's a Mexican thing, huh? I read in the paper that Isabelle's faggot husband was running for Congress."

"Yeah, I know. I wrote that story."

He smiled. "All in the family, huh? Must be nice. So, why do you need the help of a—what is it again?—oh yeah, wetback?"

"I'm not close to my family anymore," I said, not wanting to go down that road. "It's just a question or two."

"I have all the time in the world, *pocho*. You notice I run my own business now?"

"Yeah, I'm impressed."

"I don't give a fuck what you're impressed with."

He wasn't going to let up. I needed to get the information and get out of there.

"You do a lot of detailing and a lot of work on lowriders."

Hector bit his lip as if to keep from laughing. "Yes."

"You ever work on a car called The Bad Boogaloo?"

"The Bad Boogaloo?"

"It was parked out in front of a crime scene—where Catalina Garza was murdered."

"That *loca* bitch?"

"Just wondering if they saw anything."

"Because Mexicans must know everything about crime in this city?"

His accent was wearing thin. "Do you know the car or not?"

"Freddy Alvarez drove that car."

"Do you know where I could find him?"

"San Quentin."

"He's in prison? For what?"

"Burglary. Can you believe that shit? You think a white guy would go to Quentin for burglary?"

I nodded my head, pretending to understand him.

"I did the detailing on Freddie's car." Hector went on to describe every inch of the Impala.

"Thing is, Freddie was a good guy." He gazed up to the sky for a moment. "Prison is going to fuck him up, but good."

"You know who's driving it now?"

"I don't know. I haven't seen it around. Maybe the police confiscated it. They like doing shit like that to us."

I thanked him and headed back to my car.

"Don't use my name in your story, Liam," Hector yelled, his accent now all but gone. "I don't want my business tied up in any murder. I don't need that shit in my life."

CHAPTER NINE

Back at the office, I was surprised Daniels wasn't in his office. He prided himself on being the first one in and the last to leave. The man bled black ink. I stopped by our receptionist's desk to see if Detective Greene had returned my call. He hadn't, but there was a message from Elisa Vargas.

"Did she say what she was calling about?"

"No. She just wanted you to call her." Helen Morrison was pushing fifty, but her passion for gossip was that of a fifteen-year-old girl. "She must be cute." Helen gave me a wink.

"Why would you say that?"

"Because your face just turned all kinds of red, hon."

"I'm not a blusher, Helen."

"Of course, you're not, Liam." She gave me another wink.

I headed back to my desk wondering why she had called. I figured it had something to do with Glenn's campaign for Congress. As I dialed her number, I noticed that my hands were trembling slightly. Elisa answered on the second ring. There was a lot of confidence in her greeting and I found that my stomach was trembling as well. It was as if my teenage self had inhabited my body.

"It's me. Liam Sol. Returning your call."

"Hello, Liam Sol. What are you doing tonight?"

She didn't mess around with small talk.

"Nothing set in stone," I said, trying too hard to sound casual, which I found annoying and adolescent.

"I'd like to take you out to dinner. Seven o'clock sound good?"

"You know, I'm not covering Glenn's campaign for Congress. We have another reporter who I can—"

"It's about a date, *stupido*. Would you like to go out with me or not?"

I felt myself smile. "I'd like that," I said.

"Good answer."

"I'll pick you up," she said. "Where do you live?"

"You'll pick me up?"

"You have a problem with that?"

"No." I gave her my address and she told me she was looking forward to tonight. I'd never had a girl ask me out before, let alone have her pick me up in her car. Women seemed to have changed a bit since I'd been gone.

It was 4:30, and I didn't feel like hanging around waiting for Greene to call me back. In fact, suddenly I was in too good a mood to want to hear from him. I grabbed my sport coat and strode out of the office.

Elisa arrived right at seven. I took one last look around my house to make sure it would pass a basic inspection and then took a glance at myself in the mirror. I felt stupid and self-conscious, but I couldn't help myself. I wanted her to like me.

As soon as I opened the front door, she asked if I was ready. Her hair was loose, parted down the middle, and fell past her shoulders. She wore denim bell bottoms and a suede leather jacket, and she smelled of summer. This was obviously the relaxed version of the corporate-looking Elisa Vargas I'd met at Glenn's announcement.

"Let's go," she said.

I followed her to her red Alfa Romeo Spider, admiring the view.

She drove fast down Pacific Coast Highway. Not like she was in a hurry, but because she liked the feel of the speed. The top was down and her hair blew freely in the wind. Elisa knew how to handle the car. She read the traffic around her like Dan Gurney in the Indy 500.

"I hope you like Irish food," she yelled over the roar of the highway.

"I haven't had much of it."

She gave me a look. "My father banned it," I said. "He always said that Irish food was for the dogs. That and my mom wasn't the best cook in the world."

"You'll like this place."

She shifted into the next gear and floored it, leaving those behind us in the proverbial dust.

The Donegal Man was a tiny pub in Pacific Harbor. Elisa told me John Wayne was a frequent visitor. It was where he hid out when he didn't want to be bothered.

We took a seat at a booth along the back wall. There were pictures of Ireland and a few of John Wayne in *The Quiet Man* but no sign of the Duke.

We engaged in the usual first-date small talk, but I couldn't ignore the fact that part of my heart had begun to creak open for the first time in a while. There was something about her, something I felt I could trust. I didn't know if it was due to vanity or pride or what, but I sensed a mutual attraction.

The waitress came by and asked if we'd like a drink. Her voice carried a soft Irish lilt.

"I'll have a pint of Guinness," Elisa said.

I told the waitress that I'd have the same.

"Have you ever been to Ireland?" she asked.

"Other than serving in Vietnam and taking one of my leaves to Australia, the only times I've been out of the states were trips to Mexico."

"What did you do there?"

"Surf, mostly."

"Mostly?"

I shrugged my shoulders.

"You mind me asking how you handled being in Vietnam?"

I'd received similar questions about my time there from a number of people, both from those I knew and others whom I didn't know. I never knew what they wanted to hear. The fact is I did my job. I didn't like it, but other than the drugs, which I avoided, there weren't a whole lot of options over there. But the way Elisa asked the question, her tone, her expression, indicated she wanted to know more than just how I dealt with being in the line of fire day in and day out.

The waitress returned with our pints. Elisa ordered a Guinness stew and I asked for the shepherd's pie. I took a sip of the dark stout.

"There were two Vietnams for me," I told her. "I got the Purple Heart while being in the infantry, then I was stationed in Saigon where I worked as a reporter."

"You were shot?" She reached out and held my hand.

"I wasn't shot. I was hit with shrapnel from a grenade."

"Where? Was it bad?"

"It hurt like hell, but it wasn't bad. Nothing like what other soldiers got over there. I caught it in the ass. A couple of VC were tossing grenades at us like they were playing three flies up. We fired back, but they answered with more grenades. They must have stolen a crate of them. There was no place to hide. They were exploding all around us. We couldn't see where they were coming from, so we all ran for cover. I caught some metal scraps in my right butt cheek. Getting a medal for running away isn't very noble. It would have been funny if we hadn't lost anybody."

"Were you friends with the soldier who died?"

"Not really. He was new to our unit. He caught a grenade. I mean, he literally caught it in his hand. We all yelled at him to get rid of it, but he just stared at it, wide-eyed, realizing his life was about to end and there wasn't a single fucking thing he could do about it."

Truth was, I knew him fairly well. I couldn't tell Elisa the whole story, because I knew I wouldn't be able to keep it together. We all liked Jeff Burke. He may have been a fucking new guy, but he hit it off with us right away. He wanted to fight the bad guys, but he was no fool. Jeff was eighteen and he hadn't ever been laid, hadn't even been in love yet. I remembered trying to stop the bleeding from his wounds, but there were too many, he wasn't even whole, his arm was gone and so was part of his face. I couldn't believe he was alive. He pleaded with me, but I couldn't help him, no one could. He died with one eye open, staring at me as if I'd let him down. The fear, the stench of human waste, the smell of gunpowder, the screaming, the sounds of choppers landing, the intense heat that seemed to rise up from somewhere far beneath hell, and the mildew growing everywhere around us, the whole mess of war, came back to me in waves, waves that I tried to hold back for much too long. My eyes pooled up with water and then tears fell like rain.

"I'm sorry," she said. "I shouldn't have asked."

"It don't mean nothin'. That's what we'd tell ourselves. It don't mean nothin'. Jesus Christ."

She squeezed my hand and reached over with her other hand to wipe the tears from my face.

"I don't know why we're there. The locals had to play both sides just to stay alive. You march into a village of frightened people who don't speak English and then try ordering them around. You start to hate them for no reason, calling them gooks and shit like that. We were in their country. They didn't attack America. This wasn't like World War II. They just lived there, and here we were, ordering them around in their own homes, just huts, really, pointing our guns at them and threatening them. We were scared. They were scared. They were terrified of us and they were terrified of the Viet Cong. They just wanted to live. That's all. Sometimes the VC were there, sometimes they weren't. We never knew. Sometimes the villagers didn't even know. So, we just scared the fuck out of them because we were scared shitless, too."

I took a long drink of the Guinness.

"I come home and turn on the TV and Walter Cronkite's reporting on the daily body count. It's bullshit; it's all such bullshit. We aren't going to win this thing. There's nothing to win. Either we stay there forever or we leave. Either way we lose, and a lot of innocent people are going to continue to die." I wiped my face. "Does that answer your question?"

There were tears in her eyes now. Elisa opened her mouth as if to say something, but the words wouldn't come.

"I think it answered mine," I said. There were more questions, but I couldn't deal them now, so I cast them back into the darkness where they belonged, knowing they would return when I would be least prepared to face them. I realized I had built a wall of lies around my experience in Vietnam. I was good at building walls, but now the cracks were revealing themselves to me.

We sat in silence for a moment, her hand still resting on mine. "I'm sorry," I said. "I haven't thought all that much about the war since coming back."

Elisa smiled at me. "I'll be right back." She walked over to the bar and spoke to our waitress. I felt foolish and exposed. I had let my guard down, and I didn't like it. Elisa returned with a large doggie bag.

"Let's go," she said. "I know a place."

Her apartment wasn't far from the water in Corona Del Mar. The windows were open, and I could hear the waves slapping the sand while a soft breeze found its way inside. We had finished eating, yet most of the food was left on the plate. We were drinking Tecate and listening to Rod Stewart's "Every Picture Tells a Story". A couple of Diego Rivera prints adorned the walls, along with a psychedelic peace poster and hand-drawn poster of a closed brown fist surrounded by the words *Brown is Proud*. Elisa lit a couple of scented candles and sat next to me on the couch.

"When I first came up to you, I thought you were shy," she said.

"But you're not. You're quiet, but you're not shy."

"I think too much," I said. "At least that's what my friends tell me. I'm not so sure, though."

"You do, I can tell."

I reached out and held her hand, her touch pulsing through me, my heart opening up against my will.

"Why did you come up to me at The Beach Club?" I asked.

"Truthfully, I liked the way you looked. You're cute. And I liked that you weren't comfortable there. They weren't your people."

"No, they're not. But you knew who I was, too."

"Marie had us keep an eye out for you. I'd seen your picture at their house, and how Isabelle spoke of you. Okay, I wanted to meet you."

"You're not shy."

"No. I'm not. Shyness rarely gets you what you want in life. I used to be, though. When I was little I hardly ever spoke outside the house."

"That's hard to imagine."

"I know, huh?" She laughed. "Now I'll talk to anyone—even you."

"What changed?"

"Everything. I was born in Tijuana and lived there until the first grade. My mother worked in a little tourist shop on Avenida Revolución. The shop catered to Americans and they would come to bargain. It was all a game, of course. People would ask how much and she would give them a high price and let them bargain down, let them think they won."

I knew what she was talking about. We'd drive down to Tijuana for great deals on leather goods, like huarache sandals, and then we'd get drunk and bet on jai alai matches. I hadn't been down since arriving home, but from what I heard, Nixon's war against marijuana made border traffic back into the US one long nightmare.

"Most of the Americans acted very nice around us," she said. "They saw us as quaint little figures that weren't quite real, as if we suddenly appeared just for their amusement, like the Seven Dwarfs at Disneyland." Elisa shook her head. "Of course, they ignored the very poor children and looked at us as if we were creatures who had crawled up from the sewers. But they looked down on everyone. Stupid Mexicans, we would hear that a lot. Mostly because we played dumb when bargaining, and of course, we spoke broken English with thick Mexican accents. When they walked away, I could hear them laughing at us. My mother told me to ignore them, that they were foolish people. But they had money, nice clothes, and drove nice cars. They had to know something I didn't. I figured if I kept quiet, they would have no reason to laugh at me."

Even though it was warm in her apartment, she wrapped a blanket around herself. I wanted to take her into my arms but held back.

"What brought you to America?"

"My father was a policeman in Tijuana. What a thankless job. Frat boys, teenagers, and servicemen from the US would come over, to our town, and cause trouble. He tried stopping them, but he was not a big man and usually there were too many of them. They would push him around and laugh at him. They came to our town and treated it, and us, like we were nothing. Like they owned us, and who was he to tell them what to do."

I looked out her window to the lights reflecting off the water. I was one of those people once. I would drive to TJ with my friends, and we drank too much and chased the women and puked and pissed in their streets. We never considered the fact that people actually lived there, or that they tried to raise their children there or that they tried to live a decent, normal, and moral life. That was what we did in Southern California. Tijuana was our playground and to hell with everyone else.

"One night, my father came across a group of American teenagers urinating on a man who had been begging for money. The man was too weak to protect himself. My father stepped in and ordered them to stop, but they beat him up. The man who was begging helped my dad get back to his feet. He said the kids ran away and got into their car. My father chased after them on foot. They drove down a dead-end street, so they had to turn around. He stood in the middle of the road to stop them, but they ran him down and left him to die there as if he weren't worthy of their help."

Hit-and-run, I thought. Just like Julio Garza's killer.

"They were never caught." Elisa wiped her eyes. "My mother said that Tijuana was no place for us to live. She had a sister who lived in West Covina and we moved in with her, in an apartment right across the street from a Catholic church. My mother liked that. She cleaned houses in the day and at small shops at night. She couldn't afford to send me to Catholic school, so I had to go to public school. I was so scared because my English was horrible. My second-grade teacher, Miss Spadano, took special care of me and taught me how to speak and read and write in English. She also taught me how to stand up for myself."

"It must have been rough on you."

"Yeah, it was at times. But the strange thing is that the Americans treated us better here than they did in Tijuana. I never understood that." Elisa regarded me for a moment and shrugged.

"Why'd you become a lawyer?"

"To get those guys, the ones who killed my father. I mean, I knew I would never be able to bring them to justice, but others like them. That was my goal, anyway."

"What happened?"

She laughed. "The money, that's what happened. First, I worked in corporate law, but that wasn't a good fit for me—I really needed to get out of there. Then this came up. Glenn pays well, not as much as my last job, but I can still take care of my mom, so she doesn't have to work as hard." She wiped her eyes again. "She never complained a day about how hard she worked. I like that she's proud of me. And with Glenn in Congress, we can get a lot done to help minorities in this county."

She turned to me and touched my face with her hand. "This isn't what I had planned for tonight. I'm sorry. I was never good at dating." She smiled. "I hadn't talked about my childhood since ... well, I can't remember the last time. It all seems so long ago."

I pulled Elisa close to me and felt the warmth of her body against mine. I wrapped her blanket around the two of us. We stayed there, huddled together, and tried to keep the bad memories away until we both fell asleep.

I was on my back, riding along the lip of a beautiful wave, but I wasn't in control. I was letting the wave carry me. I didn't know where it was taking me, but it felt good. My hands gripped the rails of my surfboard and the water undulated beneath me to an ancient beat. Then I dropped down into the wave in a free fall, but there was no bottom. I kept dropping into the wave and I didn't want it to stop. Then I heard myself moan and I found I was having trouble catching my breath. I opened my eyes and the ocean had vanished, but Elisa had appeared and she was naked and had taken me into her mouth, her tongue and lips performing a slow and seductive dance. I reached down and gripped her long, dark hair and closed my eyes and I was back on that endless wave and letting it take me. Dream and reality were alternating, flowing back and forth. Then I felt her weight on me and her mouth on mine and we kissed, long and deeply. Her fingers ran through my hair and then moved down to my pants, pulling and tugging, and I helped her take them off, and then the wave opened up and I was naked, riding in the curl of the wave. Elisa climbed on top of me and took me inside of her. Our bodies moving in time with the flow of the ocean. She pinned my arms over my head and I felt her breath in my ear. She let out a soft moan and freed my arms and arched her back, her body moving with the wave, her hands caressing her breasts. I rose to meet her, and we pushed our bodies against each other in a pulsating rhythm, trying to inhabit the other's skin. We were caught in a current that took us further and faster out to sea. I buried my face into her neck and ran my tongue along the nape and she tasted like honey and salt. Elisa whispered my name and then she wrapped herself around me tighter her fingers digging into my skin, the water rolling beneath us, surging faster and harder, the current pushing and pushing until the ocean opened up below us and we fell, breathless and drained into each other's arms, our lips barely touching, mouthing unknowable words.

Sometime during the night, we must have moved to the bedroom as I found myself in her bed when I awoke the next morning. Elisa was still asleep, both of us lost in a tangle of sheets. I watched her as she slept. She was lying on her stomach, her face peeking out from under the long strands of her hair. Her brown skin contrasted nicely against the white of the sheets. The feelings from last night were still electric. Elisa opened one eye and gazed at me for a moment before breaking into a smile. She raised her index finger in a "come hither" motion and then rolled on her back. I leaned over to her and we kissed, slowly this time.

"I need to ask you something," I said. "I should have asked last night, but you kinda caught me by surprise ... umm..."

"Yes," she whispered, "I'm on the pill."

"That's a relief," I said, kissing her breasts. "Because I'm too exhausted to make a drugstore run right now."

"Yet, you don't seem too tired for this, do you?"

"Yes, I'm much too tired for this," I replied.

"Really?"

I ran my lips over her body and then back up to her mouth, where we kissed again. "Much too tired."

"I like this kind of tired," she said.

"So do I."

After we made love, we took a quick shower together. Elisa got out first, and I let myself linger there a while longer, letting the hot water run over my tired body. I thought I was in shape, but I guess some kinds of exercise are different than others. I had recently hit twenty-nine and wondered if that had anything to do with it. *That's right, Mick,* I laughed to myself. *What a drag it is getting old.*

Usually, after having sex with a girl, I'd head out before falling asleep. I hated the awkward feeling of seeing the person the next morning, trying to act as if everything were normal. But now I wasn't acting. Being with Elisa felt natural. I liked being in her bedroom. I liked being in her house. I didn't feel trapped, nor did I feel like an unwanted stranger.

I walked out to the kitchen when I heard a man's voice. It was a familiar voice. I peeked out and saw Elisa at the breakfast table with my brother-in-law, Glenn. My stomach dropped, and I felt the bile building up in the back of my throat. My right hand instinctively clenched into a fist.

"There you are," Elisa said. She looked uncomfortable. "I have coffee and toast for you." She nodded at the place setting across from Glenn where my breakfast waited for me.

Glenn smiled at me with his perfect white teeth. "Good to see you, Liam," he lied. He stood up and extended his hand. I wasn't about to respond in kind. "Fair enough," he said, his hands raised in a surrender gesture. Glenn sat back down as if this were his apartment. He wore tan khakis and a navy blazer over a white polo shirt. He was obviously going for the Kennedy weekend look.

I glanced at the two of them and all sorts of thoughts and images ran through my mind, none of them good.

"I better move on," I said. "I'm working on some stories with a hard deadline."

Elisa rose from her chair, her eyes pleading. "Liam, stay."

"I hope you're not leaving on my account, old sport," Glenn said.

Did he really just call me that? He'd gone from Kennedy to Gatsby in the blink of an eye. Glenn turned his gaze from me to Elisa. He looked at her as if he knew her body by touch. Maybe it was just an act, a way to get to me, or maybe there was hidden knowledge behind the look. Glenn was not a loyal husband to my sister Isabelle. I recalled the moment I saw him in a very intimate way with Marie.

I felt my heart starting to tear. I didn't want to feel like this, I just wanted to leave. I realized that my car was at my house, but I had to get out, even if that meant hitching a ride back to my place.

"Liam is good at leaving, Elisa. It's something you should know about him."

My hand gripped the doorknob, squeezing it hard as if it were his neck. He was right, though. I was good at leaving. It was what I did. I looked back and saw Glenn's smug little grin and then I saw the look on Elisa's face and I wondered if she were daring me to walk out. Maybe this was a test for her, to see what kind of man I was. I didn't give a shit about what Glenn thought, but I did, I discovered, care a lot about how Elisa saw me.

"Work can wait," I said, as I took the seat across from him. I crinkled my nose at the overpowering smell of Glenn's cologne. It was like sitting next to a dying pine tree. "Can you pass me the butter, Glenn?"

Glenn forced a smile and studied me for a moment before handing me the butter plate.

"Speaking of work," he said, "I know you must not have been thrilled with having to cover my announcement for Congress, but you did a fine job."

I wanted to hit him, hard. "Wasn't much to it," I said.

"I see you're also covering the killing of that Mexican woman. Any leads?"

"You'd have to ask the police."

"I'm in touch with them," he said with a knowing look.

"Did you know Catalina Garza?"

"No. I never had the pleasure, but I've received calls from some of my constituents. As you must know, crime is always at the top of their concerns."

I had no interest in discussing anything with Glenn and I had no idea why he decided to engage me in small talk.

Elisa came up behind me and put her hands on my shoulders, trying to calm the tension that had been building up inside of me.

"Did you need anything else, Glenn?" she asked. Then she kissed the top of my head.

He took a sip of his coffee, then placed the cup carefully back on the saucer.

"I need that brief by the end of the day."

"It will be there."

Glenn nodded and sauntered to the front door. "So glad you're back, Liam," he said, his teeth gritted together as if stuck together by glue.

After he left, Elisa apologized for his intrusion.

"Does he come here often?" I asked.

"If you're asking if Glenn and I had a relationship, the answer is no. Why he felt the need to come over this morning, I have no idea."

"How can you work for him?"

"Have you read his platform, Liam? Have you?"

"No," I admitted.

"It's good. It's really good. Did you know there are high schools in this district where colleges don't even bother to visit? Where the only ones who show up to meet the students are recruiters from the armed forces. You want to guess why?"

I told her I knew why. Those high schools were predominately Mexican, and colleges just passed them by as if they didn't matter. I'd heard about it from guys in my unit. While some of the students were eager to enlist in the military, others thought they had no choice.

"He wants to change that. He wants to provide more options for them."

There was no way Glenn came up with that idea on his own. I knew Elisa must have talked him into it.

"He never served, you know. Glenn let others do the fighting for him."

Elisa bit her bottom lip. "He hired me, Liam. No one else wanted to hire a Mexican to help run their campaign. He did."

"You shouldn't trust him, Elisa. Be careful, promise me that."

Elisa looked out the window. "I will," she said. "I promise."

She put her arms around me, holding me tight. But even in her arms, I had to fight the urge to walk out. I hoped that she was strong enough to keep me from leaving.

CHAPTER TEN

La Bolsa was in the process of building a new police station next door to the present one. The new one was a long rectangle; the existing one was a big box. You gotta love progress.

Greene never returned my call and I was tempted to phone him again, but I knew what Daniels would say. "Phones are for pussies. Get off your butt and go to the police station." He used that word a lot, pussy. I had to wonder if he liked the term or was just mad that he wasn't getting any.

The station smelled the same, a mix of cigarette smoke, puke, dried sweat, bad coffee, and Comet. Maybe the new building would have a new, modern scent, one that didn't make you think of diseased microbes hovering around you like house flies.

I sat on a metal bench that looked as if it had been made from old jail cell bars. Greene poked his head out and waved me back to his office.

"Sorry I haven't returned your call. It's been busy here," he said. Not too busy, I thought as I watched a handful of cops sitting around, drinking coffee from Styrofoam cups, trying to stay awake. While there had been an increase in crime, La Bolsa was still a relatively peaceful town. I wondered if the police secretly wished for a high crime rate. It must get boring just randomly harassing surfers and Mexicans for no good reason because there wasn't enough for them to do.

Greene's tiny office looked crisp and clean. The furniture appeared to be brand new and paintings of seascapes adorned the walls. It was all very neat and orderly, everything in its proper place. In fact, everything in his office looked like it belonged in another building, like a bank. Everything but Greene. He looked like a cop: slightly disheveled and overwhelmed. But I found him to be insecure and someone who wrapped his identity around his badge. It gave him power and he liked that. He let out a sigh as he sat in his chair.

"So, what can I do you for?" He asked it like he'd rather be getting a dental exam.

"How's the Catalina Garza case going? Any progress?"

He smiled as if I were a child. "The case," he said, "is progressing."

"What does that mean?"

"It means we're on it. You have something you'd like to share?"

"Yes. Why didn't you tell me that Julio Garza was an Explorer Scout with your department?"

Greene's smile disappeared like it had been slapped off his face. His eyes narrowed, and he looked around the office as if searching for a life vest. Then he tried to relax, but it didn't work.

"Where did you hear that?"

"Is it true?"

He hesitated, and I knew I was on to something. He stood up from this chair.

"Who did you hear this from? I want to know."

"What does it matter? Was he an Explorer Scout or not?"

"Liam, I need to know who told you this. You can't hold back evidence."

"Evidence? You're the one holding back. He was working with the police or he wasn't."

"Are you going to put this in the story, because I'll deny it."

"So, he wasn't an Explorer Scout."

"No," Greene said, clearly flustered. "He was, for a brief time, but then he quit."

Greene was on edge. I wondered why he had been reluctant to admit the truth.

"But you knew Julio, right?" It was a guess, but I think I knew the answer.

"I knew who he was, yes, but I didn't know him."

"You think both killings are connected?"

"I know how to do my job, Sol. After Catalina Garza was murdered, I looked into her background and checked out Julio's file. At this point, the deaths look unrelated. A random hit-and-run and then two years later a burglary gone bad. I don't see how they could be tied." Greene looked like he was regaining his footing, the color returning to his face.

"Anything else?" I asked.

"Just that both cases are still officially open." He paused for a moment. "Now I have a job to do, so if you don't mind." He opened a manila folder and pretended to read the contents.

I stood up and stopped at the door of his office and stared at him for a moment. He looked up at me. "What?"

"I want to find out who killed them. I just hope that we're on the same side."

"Don't put anything in the paper that you can't back up. Watch yourself."

When I got outside, I took a deep breath of the fresh salt air. Greene was hiding something, something big. I saw it in his face. I didn't peg him as a killer, though. But maybe he was covering up for someone else. That, I wouldn't put past him.

I sat in Daniels' office. He was going over my notes, shaking his head. "Your handwriting is shit, anyone ever tell you that?"

As hard as I tried, I couldn't improve it. I was the victim of an Irish-Catholic mother. As a toddler, I tried to use my left hand to color or to pick up toys. I say tried, because according to my mother, she'd slap my left hand and put the pencil or the crayon in my right hand. "The left hand is the devil's hand," she told me much later when I had asked her about it. "There will be no left-handed people in this family. The devil can find another family to infect." Little did she know that the devil had already found a home with her.

So, I spent my life writing with the wrong hand. I don't know if that's why my penmanship was so horrible, but it sounded to me like a reasonable excuse.

Daniels glared at me from behind the reading glasses perched on his nose. The glasses looked like they were considering jumping off at any second, to go in search of someone who might not fling them across the room in a fit of rage. "Christ," he said. "Jesus Christ."

He handed my notes back to me.

"It's good. From what I could decipher from your infant scrawl. You raise some good questions."

"Thanks."

"Have you looked into this Moran guy? You should. This could be something. Keep going, you'll get there."

I let out a deep breath and stood up to leave.

"I was called to the mountain top yesterday afternoon," Daniels said.

"What the heck is the mountain top?"

Daniels gave me the look. The one that said, "How do you even survive in the world?" It was a look I was getting used to. I talked to some of the other reporters and they told me that he gave them similar looks.

"Your house. Your *casa*. Your hacienda, whatever the hell it is."

He was talking about my family home, where my mom lived with Marie, Isabelle, and Glenn. It was situated on top of a big hill, surrounded by orange groves and it overlooked La Bolsa and the Pacific Ocean.

"Who wanted to see you?"

"Marie. You want to know why?"

I didn't want to know, but he was going to tell me, anyway.

"She wanted to know how you were doing."

Some would have found that touching, but I knew better.

"She wanted me to take you off the Catalina Garza story. Said she didn't want you covering murders, said it would look bad for the family and for Glenn. And she not too subtly reminded me that she was very close with the owners of this very newspaper."

That sounded like the Marie I knew. She wanted to control everything. She wanted to control La Bolsa and she wanted to control me.

"What did you say?"

"That I didn't think the story was going anywhere."

"What are you telling me?"

"As of last night, I thought the story was a dead end."

"But it might not be now," I said.

"Good thing I didn't know that last night."

"I don't want to cause trouble for you. What will Marie say when she sees my follow-up stories?"

"First, I haven't seen a follow-up story from you. Second, if you're worried about causing trouble, then you shouldn't be a reporter."

Even when I was younger, I was never one to make trouble. I surfed, I chased girls, and even when I was looking for the person who killed my father, I naively tried to avoid any conflict. A lot of good that did me. But this wasn't going after trouble for trouble's sake. This was about finding the truth. This was about not letting my family control me. I again questioned why I ever came back home, but then I thought of Catalina Garza. I thought of her son, Julio. And then I thought of Elisa. They weren't the reason I came home, but they were the reason why I was going to stay.

"Are you still up for this?"

"I am, but what about you? Marie's going to be pissed off and you could lose your job. I think I know my sister better than you do."

I was serious. As much as I wanted to tell Marie to shove it, I didn't want anyone to lose their job because of me. Marie could be wicked in more ways than I could count.

Daniels seemed to consider my words, then he took off his reading glasses. "To paraphrase Marie Antoinette, let them eat shit."

I stepped out of the office to get some fresh air. I had a lot to take in. Some part of me felt abused, as if Marie was still trying to pull the strings and I was only under the illusion that I was on my own. Marie, it seemed, could not leave me alone. I couldn't tell if she did it out of spite or fear. Perhaps it came from love, I didn't know, but then, a lot of bad things are done in the name of love.

I headed toward the beach. I always headed to the beach when I needed to clear my head. "Back to where we came from," Lonnie used to say. "The water is always calling us back."

CHAPTER ELEVEN

It was a warm spring day and people were out enjoying the sun and the fresh breeze that blew across the ocean and into town. I hustled across Pacific Coast Highway and onto the pier. I realized this was my first time there since my battle with the pale-faced man. I later learned his name was Matthew Baker. It was a nice and common name. His parents were schoolteachers in Seattle. They had three children, two were normal and they were now raising their own families. Matthew was different, his mother said. "He was born with the wrong kind of feelings. It's hard to believe he came from my womb. Hard to believe he came from anybody's womb."

You never know, I thought. Some people just come out bad.

I stopped in front of the Sea Legs Bar, in the same spot where I had my encounter with the pale-faced man. The same spot where he tried to kill me, but where I ended up killing him. I recalled the color of his eyes. They were as black and as vacant as death, not a trace of light in them. As I stood and looked at the spot, it felt like a cold hand had come up from my gut and had grabbed my heart. I steadied myself and took a long, deep breath and continued walking toward the end of the pier.

I'd come across a few head cases when I served in Vietnam. They gave off a certain energy that alerted a primal trigger that screamed *stay away*. Though I called myself a Catholic, I wasn't sure if I believed in God or not, but when I came across these people, it sure as hell made me believe in the Devil.

I looked out to the ocean. There were no surfers out as the water was flat as a lake, just ripples. Two pretty girls in bikinis waded slowly into the water. I could see they were locals, their skin already tanned into a dark brown. When the water got to their waists, they dived into it and came back up strong, pulling their wet hair from their smiling faces. They turned on their backs and lay on the water, feeling the sun's rays warm their bodies. There was not a note of self-consciousness about them. It was just them, the sun, and the water.

When I reached the end of the pier, I stood at the railing and stared at Catalina Island and the unending horizon beyond. A few feet from me, a father was teaching his son how to fish. The boy looked as if he were around five years old. They had just reeled in a Pacific mackerel, about a foot long, and put it in a bucket. The fish flopped around, trying to get out.

"What's it doing, Dad?" the kid asked.

"Don't worry about him. He'll be dead soon."

"I don't want him to die, Daddy, he's pretty."

"Just let him be, Danny."

Danny looked up at his father, trying to understand why he wasn't bothered by the fish struggling for its life in the bucket.

"Let's see if we can catch another one," his father said.

While his father was putting the bait on, Danny placed his hands on his hips and stared at the fish. Then he looked at his dad, who was still fiddling with the lure. Danny took a closer look at the mackerel and tried to calm him down. "It's okay, Mr. Fish," he said. Then Danny picked up the bucket and tried to raise it over the rail. His dad saw what he was trying to do.

"Danny!"

"I can't let him die, Dad, I can't."

His father let out a deep breath. "Hold on."

He took the bucket from his son and dumped the fish back into the ocean below. Danny had a big smile on his face.

"Thanks, Dad. You couldn't let him die, either, could you?"

"I guess not," he said. He knelt down and gave his son a big hug.

His father caught my eyes and gave me a "What are you going to do?" look.

The boy looked up at his father. "I wonder if he's going to tell his friends what happened to him. I wonder if they'll believe him."

"They probably will," his father said. "I tell you what, let's get our gear packed up and I'll buy you lunch in town."

"Can I have fish sticks?" Danny asked.

His father let out a short chuckle. "Whatever you want, little guy. Whatever you want."

I couldn't help but smile. When I was a kid, my father and I had similar moments. The kind that make you into the person you'll become later in life. I thought he was the greatest dad ever, and then I learned differently. I watched them as they put their rods away. As I headed back to town, I thought that Danny's dad looked like a good man to me, but I guess you never know.

Every now and then a chilling thought seeped its way into my consciousness. What if I was destined to turn out like my father? I saw no trace of it, but maybe I wasn't looking hard enough. I witnessed my father go out of his way to help strangers in need, pick up trash on the sidewalk, carrying it until he found a trash can, and countless other examples that taught me what a man should be. But then I learned how ruthless he was. It was as if two different people had inhabited his body. I couldn't help but fear that someone else lurked inside of mine, someone evil. He just hadn't introduced himself to me yet.

What I did know was that I hadn't been able to shake my family's influence from me. I worked at a newspaper whose owners certainly listened to them, and they owned the tiny house I rented. My home seemed to fit me and I was beginning to like what I was doing at the newspaper, but was I so naive to think I could make my own life in La Bolsa and still be free from my family's grip? Probably.

When I crossed PCH, I noticed the marquee for The Gold Coast. Linda Ronstadt and some group called the Eagles were playing tonight. I walked down Main, past the Belly of the Whale bar, the stench of beer and tobacco wafted out through the big open window, where the guys liked to catcall the pretty girls who strolled by. There were a couple of new surf shops, a headshop with black light posters in the front windows, the Crest Theatre, where two surf movies were playing, *Cosmic Children* and *Pacific Vibrations*—"Like Woodstock on a Wave," the poster cried out. The Driftwood Café was still there, as were Western Auto and Pacific Shells, a souvenir shop that sold postcards, seashells, Coppertone, and a variety of other beach accessories to wandering tourists. Main looked tired and worn, but maybe that was how it always looked, and I just never noticed until I came home.

I took a left on Orange. And across the street stood the building that was once Dex's Bar or, as locals called it, the DMZ. The bar was a haven for those who had secrets or just wanted to forget. It had been owned by my friend Dex, another victim of the pale-faced man. It was now the site of Lonnie's church, The Church of the Innocent Child.

I hadn't been here since Lonnie had converted it into a house of worship. The bar had been moved to the rear of the space and now served as the altar. Handmade crosses constructed of old driftwood stood on either end. The burning of incense candles failed to mask the decades-old scent of beer and cigarettes that inhabited the walls.

Above the makeshift altar was a mural of the baby Jesus lying in a nest of dried elephant grass. Three American soldiers, M16s strapped to their backs, all of whom had the faces of the three wise men, were on their knees, praying over him.

Benches, bar stools, and chairs were lined up for the worshippers. It was empty now, except for Lonnie, who was kneeling at the altar. His was not a face of peace, but one of anguish, as if God had told him things he didn't want to hear.

I didn't want to interrupt him, so I took a seat in a foldout chair along one of the aisles. It made perfect sense for Lonnie to use a former bar as a church. Both places catered to lost souls trying to find refuge from the storm. When it was the DMZ, I had come here a few times to forget as well. I closed my eyes for a moment and said a silent prayer for Julio and Catalina Garza, then one for Dawn, and finally, one for my father, though I didn't think my prayer for him would do him any good.

"Liam, so glad you came."

I opened my eyes and saw Lonnie walking up to me with his ever-present limp. He wore faded Levi's and an old Hawaiian shirt, and I noticed that he was barefoot.

"I was in the neighborhood," I said.

He took a seat next to me. He had a weary look, as if he'd been through a rough battle.

"Everything all right?"

"It's a struggle," he sighed.

"What, believing in God?"

Lonnie smiled. "That's not the struggle. I believe in God, but sometimes I don't like him very much."

"There's a lot of bad shit in this world, Lonnie. Why do you believe in Him?" I asked because I wanted to know. Maybe I wanted him to convince me of something I couldn't convince myself of: That there was a reason for all of this, a reason for all the bad.

"I know this may come across as strange to you," he said, "but I believe in God precisely because the world can be so cruel and awful. You hear about a child that's been killed and you question that if God exists, how can He allow that? But when a child is killed, that makes me believe in God. I hate him for what happened. I can't lie. But don't you see that if evil exists, so must God. That people who suffer wounds from war, or from cancer or from anything else, that cruelty, that suffering, their deaths and we think that's the end of it?

That doesn't make sense. There must be more." Lonnie paused for a moment. "God holds them in his arms, Liam. He holds them in his arms. While our hearts break and we can't find a reason why these horrible acts happened to our loved ones, God holds them. We're left behind with the pain, but God takes care of them. He takes care of them."

"But not the living?"

"No, not us. We're on our own."

I looked around his church. "Then why all of this?"

He rose from his chair and patted me on the back. "Have faith, Liam," he said. "Have faith. I have a sermon in a few minutes. You should stay."

Lonnie walked into the small room that was once Dex's office and closed the door behind him. I sat there alone and stared at the mural of the baby Jesus. I heard movement behind me. A few people were making their way into the church. A few bums, some who looked too broken to ever be fixed, a few vets, and others who looked as normal and sane as anyone. They all quietly took their seats and put their hands together in prayer. I didn't belong here. I got up and walked outside.

In the distance, I could see the fog rolling in, pushing the sun and the light and the warmth of the day aside as if they were only an illusion. Then, for reasons I could not begin to explain, I stepped back inside and stood in the doorway and listened as a vet confessed his sins to the congregation. "I was only following orders," he said, his voice quivering. "I thought we were the good guys." He paused, the congregation quiet, the only sounds I heard were my own breaths, shallow and quick. "I'm not even sure there even is a right and wrong, or good and evil. There's only what you can live with and what you can't, and that's all we have. And I'm not sure I can live with what I've done."

"Take my hand," Lonnie whispered to him. "Take my hand. God will forgive you, but you need to forgive yourself. Can you do that?"

"No," I whispered to myself. I slipped out the door and into the fog and hurried back to the office, feeling the ever-present weight of all those who had died because of me.

CHAPTER TWELVE

Wyatt was already out in the water by the time I hit the beach. Shards of sunlight slashed their way through the morning fog, creating a dreamlike effect. I sat in the sand and watched him work the waves. They were three feet high and coming in on a southwestern swell. Wyatt was a mad poet on the water. Some guys rode the hell out of waves as if they were to be conquered, others took what they were given, some glided, some danced and still others used the waves as an artist would use a blank canvas. But Wyatt interpreted the waves. He read between the lines and saw what others were unable to see. The water spoke to him in ways that I couldn't conceive. He was not the most talented or athletic surfer, but he was the most unique. In his words, his goal was to become what the wave wanted him to become. Each wave was different. Each wave asked him to become something new. He said he always left the water a different person than when he entered. Most mornings, he left a better person, but sometimes, rarely, he emerged from the waves as someone he didn't recognize, someone he didn't understand. Sometimes, he told me, he left with a darkness in his soul that he couldn't comprehend.

I'd woken up before first light this morning. Elisa was already in the shower. I wanted to get her day off to a good start, so I made breakfast for her, my take on Joe's Special.

I set out the plates and silverware on the small dining table just outside of my kitchen. It was in the corner against two windows, one had a view of one of the oil pumps that sat next to the house, and the other had a view of the Pacific Ocean. It was too dark to see the water right now, but anything was better than looking at oil wells.

"This is so cool," she said after greeting me with a kiss.

"Wait until you try it. You might think I'm trying to kill you."

I pulled out the chair that faced the ocean and poured her a cup of coffee.

She smiled at me and took a bite. "I like it!"

"Don't sound so surprised."

"It's good. It has a nice Mexican touch to it," she said. Her fork cut through the scrambled eggs and ground beef, revealing spinach, onions, sliced tomatoes, green peppers, ancho chiles, and salsa. "What else do you cook?"

"My fish tacos aren't too good, but pretty much anything with eggs I can do. Machaca, huevos rancheros, chorizo, that's about it."

She took another bite of her food and then tilted her head as if she were studying me.

"What?" I asked.

"It's funny, that's all."

"What is?"

"It's all Mexican food. Your father said he never wanted you to think of yourself as a Mexican, but all you make is from south of the border."

It was something I hadn't thought about. "We had a Mexican housekeeper, Graciella. She cooked most of our food. I guess I ended up learning from her without really thinking about it."

"Do you think of yourself as Mexican?"

"Not really, no. I don't feel Irish, either," I said. "I'm an American. I know it's more complicated than that, but that's how I feel."

She narrowed her eyes, continuing to study me.

"Aren't you going to ask what I consider myself to be?"

I looked out the window and tried to see the ocean through the darkness.

"I don't care what the answer is, Elisa. Why would it matter?"

"That's good to know, Liam. I'm a Chicana. I'm a citizen here now, but I feel just as Mexican as I ever did. That doesn't mean I want to go back there and it doesn't mean I don't love this country."

"I told you that I don't care."

"Would your father have approved of me?"

"Not that it matters, but he would have loved you. You're successful, pretty—he liked pretty."

"And Mexican," she said.

"But not too much of one."

"What's that mean?"

I walked into that. "I don't know. This was his view, not mine. My father put people in boxes. And he was hard on Mexicans. There were high-class ones and low-class ones. I think he considered most to be low class and they embarrassed him. Listen, I don't want to go inside that man's head."

Elisa nodded. "But you don't think like him, do you?"

"No," I said. "God no." But I wondered if that were completely true. If Elisa had lived in Catalina Garza's neighborhood and had a thick accent and a menial job, would I have thought of her as just some Mexican girl who was nothing more than a potential one-night stand?

"You're a good man, Liam," she said. "I can tell."

Sometimes I wasn't so sure.

The phone rang, rescuing me from my thoughts.

"We need to talk," the voice on the phone said.

It was Charlie Moran.

"Yeah, I want to talk to you as well. How about your office?"

"Let's meet at our usual place. Say 11:00 this morning?"

"I can do that."

"I'll see you then." And then he hung up the phone.

"Are you okay?" Elisa asked.

I thought about Elisa's question as I watched Wyatt ride a wave into shore. I knew I couldn't trust Charlie Moran, but I couldn't ignore him, either. I had to see where he led me even though I wasn't sure I wanted to go there with him.

Wyatt had his board tucked under his arm as he came out of the ocean. I rose to greet him. "You looked good," I said.

He stared at me for a moment as if he couldn't quite recall who I was. "You going to the protest?" he asked.

"There's an antiwar protest going on?" I thought I would have heard of one.

"They're trying to develop the coast, man. We can't let them destroy nature. It's not ours to destroy. We're the caretakers, man."

I thought about Dawn and her efforts to protect the marshes along Coast Highway, even going up against my father. Dawn thinking of preserving what came before us, my father wanting to build on it and alter it forever.

"I have to work today." Though I knew that even if I were free, I would have passed on it.

"We have to fight the machine. If you're not against it, that means you're for it. You need to figure out which side you're on." He pulled on his Pink Floyd T-shirt and walked away.

I wondered if what he said was true, that life was all about choosing sides. I'd heard it enough in Vietnam, but it seemed so small, so tribal. Yet, as much as I wanted to, I couldn't dismiss it. I knew that Wyatt had experimented with every drug known to man and lived in a state somewhere between reality and illusion, but I respected him. Wyatt never burned his draft card and had dismissed declaring himself a conscientious objector. He was determined to serve, but he never made it past the psychological exam. Some, I knew, tried to fake it, but Wyatt was surprised that he didn't pass. He came to the conclusion that if the Army thought he was the crazy one, then in Wyatt's mind, that only confirmed his sanity. I didn't know about that. I'd encountered more than a few crazy-ass fucks over there, the God-and-country types, and I knew that while we all may have been on the same side, we weren't necessarily all fighting for the same thing.

Except for the bartender, whom I didn't recognize, The Alamo was empty. I was disappointed not to see April. I thought of her as an ally and when dealing with Charlie Moran, of whom I had a visceral distrust, I knew I'd want someone like her in my corner.

I asked the guy tending bar for a cup of coffee. He looked to be in his early forties. His hair was cut in a flattop and he wore a button-down shirt tucked neatly into his beige slacks. He placed the coffee on the bar.

"Is April Fairchild working today?" I asked.

"She has class now. She'll be here tonight." Class, I thought. Good for her. I didn't want her to give up.

"You new here?"

He smiled. "That obvious?"

"I won't tell," I said.

"I just got out."

"Where did you serve?" I asked, thinking he just got out of the military.

"Oh," he smiled. "Lompoc. I was in prison."

I tried not to act surprised, though I was.

"Javier, the owner, he hires ex-cons. Don't worry, I didn't kill anybody. I just fucked up a lot. He likes to call this place 'the saloon of second chances.'" He smiled again. "Your name wouldn't be Liam Sol, would it?"

I paused. "Yeah. Why are you asking?"

"A Charlie Moran called and said to tell you that he was running a little late. He apologized and wanted you to know the drinks were on him."

"Coffee is fine."

I sat at a table near the front door and waited. Despite having to meet up with Moran, I felt good. I'd only been able to hit the waves for about half an hour this morning but managed to catch a few decent rides. I don't think I left the water a better person, but as with most days surfing, I left feeling that the world wasn't such a bad place. Sometimes it's good to let the ocean fool you into believing things are better than they seem.

I looked at my coffee and thought a beer or a little tequila might take the edge off, but I wanted to be alert when dealing with Charlie Moran.

"Ah, Mr. Sol." It was him. He must have come in through the back door. "Please accept my apology for being late. It is good to see you again."

He took the seat next to me. He had on the same suit he wore when we first met.

"Why the back door?"

Moran shrugged and glanced at the rear entrance. Though he tried to appear nonchalant, I could tell he was nervous. The bartender came up to the table and asked him if he wanted something to drink.

"Tequila, please." The bartender looked at me and I told him I was fine.

Moran watched as he walked away.

"Everything okay?" I asked.

"Yes, of course. Everything is how it should be. So, tell me, what have you learned?"

I don't know why I was surprised at his boldness. He acted like I worked for him. Yet, I thought if I told him a little, he might respond with some information of his own.

"The cops confirm Julio was an Explorer Scout, but say he quit."

"Resignation by death, you mean."

He wanted to make this into a game, a game I didn't want to play. "You're holding back on me, Moran. What do you know?"

Before he could respond, the bartender arrived with the tequila.

"Anything else?" the bartender asked.

"Nothing, thank you," Moran said. Both of us kept our eyes on the bartender as he walked away.

"Because, Mr. Sol, Julio Garza was working for me."

I put my cup down and tried to take this in.

"Why didn't you tell me this before? What was he doing for you?"

"I wasn't sure how much I should trust you. I apologize. You should know the police department here in La Bolsa doesn't have a good track record when it comes to the treatment of Mexicans. That is what people have told me and what I have come to observe. What I needed, however, was proof. Julio was looking for anything he could find on them and their treatment of Mexicans. I was working on a civil rights case. I hadn't come close to filing it as it was only hearsay, but I thought Julio could dig something up. They have bad people on the force, Mr. Sol."

"What did he find?"

"More than he was looking for. Something he was surprised to discover." His eyes focused hard on mine.

"Like what?" I realized I was gripping the coffee cup as if I thought that someone would grab it, which didn't escape his eyes. All I could think was, does he know the truth about my family's crimes?

"You seem nervous, Mr. Sol. Why is that?"

"Quit playing games, Moran. Just get it out."

"Julio stumbled onto something and misplayed his hand. He wouldn't tell me much, but it sounded as if it involved not just the police, but people even more powerful than they." He paused, as if waiting for me to respond. I wondered if they taught the art of the dramatic pause in law school, because this guy had it down pat. "People like your family, perhaps."

It was a sucker punch and it missed. I kept my poker face. If Julio had learned the truth that it was Isabelle who killed my father and not the pale-faced man who we had blamed it on, then he certainly could have been killed because of that. And that thought terrified me. The police didn't know the truth about Isabelle. We kept it from them. I don't know how Julio Garza might have learned of it, but if he had, I was sure he hadn't told Moran, or he would have come at me harder. My guess was that Moran was throwing darts against the wall, hoping one of them would stick. Still, the need to protect my family was something I could never let go of, even though I knew it would eventually lead to my destruction.

Moran leaned across the table. "You know there is a client-lawyer confidentiality agreement, so if there's anything you'd like to tell me …"

If I needed someone to represent me, I thought, I could certainly pick a better attorney than him. "I'm fine."

Charlie Moran smirked. "Not the most forceful denial I've ever heard."

"I have nothing to hide. Did you ever think that Julio was killed because he was working for you, Moran? Maybe his mother was killed because of you as well. You ever think of that?"

He looked away, his eyes on the back door. "I am fully aware I may be to blame for putting him in the path of danger, but there is a killer out there, one who must be stopped."

"If what you say is true, aren't you worried that they'll try to kill you as well?"

"I am taking the necessary precautions," he said. But his face betrayed him. Small drops of sweat formed on his forehead. They appeared embedded like braille dots.

I wasn't sure what he meant by "necessary precautions," because he was starting to behave like a man with a target on his back.

CHAPTER THIRTEEN

As soon as I returned to work, Daniels called me into his office. I was still struggling with the notion that perhaps Julio Garza had stumbled onto the truth about who killed my father, and all the covering up that ensued. How, though, could he have learned this? Maybe it was something else, something that had nothing to do with my family. Whatever it was, it had cost him and his mother their lives.

"What do you have on the Garza killings?" he asked. "What did the lawyer have to say?"

I sat in a chair and crossed my legs and considered the best way to respond. I couldn't tell him the truth. But here he was, backing me up on the investigation, ignoring my sister's request, and putting his job on the line for me, and I was going to lie to him. Was it to protect my family? Was it to protect Isabelle? I couldn't be sure, but I had to contain the story until I knew that my family wasn't involved.

"Nothing. He wanted to know what I had. It's was a big waste of time."

He looked me in the eyes.

"There's more here, Sol. I can feel it. You're doing good work, but keep digging. Find another source in the police department. Go after this."

"You got it," I said, trying to act enthused.

I stayed home that night. Elisa was in Newport Beach working on another fundraiser for Glenn's campaign. I missed her, but I needed the space and time to think about what I had learned and what I intended to do about it. I couldn't keep lying to Daniels. I knew from experience that hiding the truth only sets you up for an ambush down the road.

I opened a Dos Equis and sat on a chair on the front porch. It was dark out and I could hear the waves crashing on the sand, and the lights on the La Bolsa pier twinkled in the moonlight. I closed my eyes and let the sounds of the ocean flow through my body, but I couldn't clear my mind.

Did I believe anything Charlie Moran told me? I had no idea what his motives could be, but I had to be careful that he wasn't setting a trap for me or my family.

Still, I had to go after this story. No one from the police department was going to tell me anything about Julio Garza's death. However, there was someone who might talk to me. I'd be the last person he would want to see, but there was a chance he could shed some light on Julio's death and maybe he knew something about Charlie Moran as well.

Detective Louis Branch, formerly of the La Bolsa Police Department, was now retired and living a peaceful life in Palm Desert. He had once arrested me for murder and blamed me, perhaps rightly, for Dawn's murder. Even though I killed the pale-faced man who murdered her, Branch never forgave me for her death, because it was me who had led the killer to her door.

The next day, I drove out to Palm Desert. He wasn't hard to track down. I called Information and that helped me narrow down the search. I could have phoned him first, but I doubted he would have spoken to me. I had to surprise him. He lived on a quiet street with the looming San Jacinto Mountains watching over the neighborhood. I stepped up to the front porch and rang the doorbell. I heard a man cussing inside and I knew I'd found the right place.

He opened the door and took one look at me, his face turning red. "What in the hell are you doing here?"

He wore blue plaid Bermuda shorts and a blue Hawaiian shirt. He looked like the kind of tourist you'd see wandering around Disneyland with a Kodak Instamatic camera in one hand and a melting ice-cream cone in the other. He'd taken on a few pounds since I'd last seen him, and his skin was the beige you'd find on a hospital wall.

"Did you get someone else killed?" he asked.

"Maybe."

Branch clenched his jaw so hard I thought his teeth were going to fly out of his mouth. "Christ. Come on in."

It was the kind of home that seemed to thrive in the desert. It had a sleek, futuristic feel. Isabelle used to call them George Jetson homes. I pictured Branch as more of a brown stucco box type of guy. The living room, kitchen, and dining room opened up into each other, and the back wall was mostly windows, giving him a clear view of the mountains. It was all perfect, except for the furniture, which was better suited for a rustic mountain cabin. It was as mismatched as the clothes he wore.

Branch had the radio on. Dick Enberg was doing the play-by-play for a California Angels game. Nolan Ryan was on the mound, which meant the Angels had a decent shot of winning. The dining table was covered in papers, and I noticed an application for the Palm Springs Police Department resting on top of one of the piles. A black jacket with a security guard patch was draped over one of the chairs.

"Get away from there. That's all personal stuff."

I told him I was sorry. "I don't want to take up much of your time. I just have a couple of questions."

"Oh, I'm not worried about that, Sol. I'll tell you when I've had enough of you."

"I don't doubt that."

"It's too stuffy in here. Why don't we go outside? You want

anything to drink? Coke, Dr Pepper? I don't have anything stronger. I gave all that up a long time ago."

"Coke's fine."

I opened the sliding glass door and stepped out to the patio. There was a small kidney-shaped swimming pool that was only half filled, and the water had a green tinge to it. Two wooden benches sat next to a wooden picnic table and a huge umbrella was positioned next to the table and benches. The furniture set looked brand new, the type you'd find at Montgomery Ward's.

He carried out two bottles of Coke and handed one to me. He took a seat on the other side of the table.

"You could have called," he said.

"I thought you'd hang up on me."

He grinned. "You got that right."

"Nice place," I said.

"I hate the goddamn desert."

"Then why'd you move here?"

"I thought I'd like it. Wide-open spaces. You'd think it would clear a guy's head, but it just reminds me of death and whatever comes after. Big mistake."

"You shouldn't have left La Bolsa."

"I had to." Branch eyed me like a boxer in a prefight stare-down. "Too many bad memories."

I turned from his gaze.

"Why did you go back?" he asked.

"It's home. That, and I didn't know where else to go."

"I get it. You need to know where you're going before you get there, or you could end up stuck in the desert." Branch took a sip of his drink.

I couldn't read Branch. In no way could I have imagined that he'd be sharing his existential life crisis with me. I guessed he was lonely and talking to me was better than sitting around doing nothing.

My mind drifted to the application form that sat on his dining table. "You enjoying retirement?"

He smiled. "Pension's great. Can't complain about that."

"What about being a cop? You miss that?"

He shook his head as if it were a preprogrammed response to a question he'd been asked too many times. And one he had no intention of answering honestly.

"What about you? Your family still paying you to surf so you won't get in their way?"

"I'm paying my own way now."

"Impressive, Sol. What are you now, a lifeguard?"

"I'm a reporter for the *La Bolsa Tribune*. That's why I'm here."

"So now you're getting paid to be a pain in the ass?" He picked up his bottle then put it back down. "Why the hell are you here, Sol? What do you want?"

I gave Branch the backstory of the murders of Julio and Catalina Garza, but left out the parts about Charlie Moran, and, of course, my family's involvement in the cover-up of my father's murder.

"So, you did get someone killed. That poor woman had no idea the kind of the shit you were going to bring into her world."

"Let it go, Branch. I want to find out who killed her—who killed them. And I'm getting the impression that Greene doesn't want me to know. Maybe he's involved in the murders."

"Watch what you're saying, Sol. Greene is a damn good cop."

"Then why he is stalling the investigation? Two murders and the police have done nothing."

"They're working on it, believe me. Maybe not as fast as you reporters would like, but they're doing the best they can."

"You guys never had a problem moving too fast before," I said.

"Yeah, and as you know, we got the wrong man. Let them do their due diligence."

"I'm making more progress than he is, and I barely know what I'm doing."

Branch let out a sigh. "He'll figure it all out. He's a good cop, Sol, believe me. And he's a good man. A damn good man."

We looked at each other for a moment.

"Anything else?" he asked.

"I don't think so."

Branch got up and I followed him through the house to the front door. I realized there was a question I forgot to ask.

"Do you know anything about the Explorer Scout program?

"I never got involved with them."

"Do you know if Greene was?"

"He started the program. His way of reaching out to the community, I guess. Why are you asking?"

"No reason."

I thought about Greene as I drove down the Ortega Highway. He was hiding something. Greene had been nervous when I brought up Julio's name. If Julio had quit the Explorer program early, what was the reason? I couldn't help but wonder why Branch was so protective of Greene, and why he was so insistent that Greene was, in his words, a good man.

I continued to drive down the Ortega Highway, through Santa Ana Canyon, winding past thirsty pine trees that, while native to the land, looked lost and out of place. Branch seemed like that as well. A man whose identity was so tied to being a cop, he couldn't imagine life without a badge. But he wasn't my concern. Assuming Greene had something to do with killing Julio, then why would he have killed his mother? It didn't make sense, but when it came to murder I've found that sense has little to do with it. And if Greene thought I was on to him, then I'd have to watch my back. A killer with the law on his side is no one I wanted to run up against.

A strong gust of wind whipped down the canyon pass, rattling my little Karmann Ghia. I grabbed the steering wheel tighter, which gave me the illusion of control. The sun would be setting soon, and the Ortega Highway wasn't the kind of road you'd want to be caught alone on in the dark. It had a history of fatal car crashes, and over the years, more than a few dead bodies had been found along the side of the road. I rolled up the windows, locked the doors, turned on the headlights, and focused on the road ahead.

CHAPTER FOURTEEN

I woke up feeling like crap. After a shower and a shave, I made a cup of instant coffee and brought it out to the front porch. Any thought that riding the waves might improve my mood was quickly dashed by a tranquil sea that sat motionless, barely a ripple to be seen. I sat in my chair and watched the cars cruising up and down Pacific Coast Highway. Most were driven by surfers, their boards secured in racks on their roofs or in the back of their trucks or perilously hanging out of their car windows. All of them searching for the secret spot where the waves might be breaking, a secret place that would cure them of their ills.

Elisa was in Sacramento and wouldn't return until later tonight. I missed her. It had been a long time since I felt that ache, that longing, and I wasn't sure I liked it. I didn't like feeling vulnerable. I wasn't sure I was strong enough to let myself go. I wasn't sure I was strong enough to quit being alone. But the truth of the matter was that I wasn't sure I was strong enough to have something to lose.

Surfing or being with Elisa would have made me feel better, but something was eating at me. Two people, actually. Detective Greene and Charlie Moran. Greene clearly didn't want me to know about his involvement with Julio Garza, whatever it was. Could that have been the reason Julio was killed? And Charlie Moran's involvement in this didn't make any sense. The obvious question I hadn't thought of until now was: Was he pointing me in the direction of Julio and Catalina Garza's murderer, or was he directing me away from them? It was time to learn more about Charlie Moran.

The Chicano Legal Rights Association was a hole-in-the-wall a couple blocks up from The Alamo bar. The neighborhood was often referred to as Baja La Bolsa, and not because of its geographical location. Marie had always referred to this area as *that part of town*. It felt like less of a beach town here. There were no surf shops, no souvenir shops, no stores with ocean-themed names, and no one wore a swimsuit or bikini. Few people were on the street and most were Mexican women carrying paper shopping bags filled with groceries. This was not a pretty part of town. Many of the storefronts looked old, cracking at the seams. I walked past a barbershop, a beauty parlor, a small restaurant and a grocery store with stands out front that were filled with fresh fruit. Across the street sat a liquor store, a bar, a discount store, a crowded laundromat, and a shop filled with both wedding gowns and brightly colored Mexican dresses. The La Bolsa Tourist Office didn't have brochures featuring this part of town, and I don't think many of the surfers who lived in La Bolsa ever ventured here.

The door to Charlie Moran's office was open. The reception area held a few metal folding chairs along with old copies of *Newsweek* and *Look* that covered a banged-up Formica table. It was just past ten in the morning, but no one was at the reception desk. I called out a hello and thought I'd heard some movement in one of the back offices.

"Hello?" I repeated. Again, no response.

I crept down the hallway. There were two offices; the doors were open to both, as well as what appeared to be a supply closet.

"I'm here to see Charlie Moran."

I caught the smell of a woman's perfume. It was strong and on the verge of being unpleasant. I peered into one of the offices. It was empty, but the office was a picture of disorganization, papers piled high on the desk and more stacks covered the small couch that was pushed up against one of the walls. As I turned back into the hallway, the smell of perfume intensified. I walked into the second office and stared right into the barrel of a gun. A woman with light brown skin held the pistol in her hand, though it wasn't steady I knew she wouldn't miss me from this distance. She was short, probably just a bit over five feet tall, well dressed, early thirties, and attractive. And she'd been crying.

Instinctively, I raised my hands.

"I'm looking for Charlie Moran."

She nodded her head. "He's not here."

Her voice struggled to remain calm, while the gun trembled in her hand.

"He knows me. I just want to talk to him. Who are you?"

"Ramona Ortiz. I need to see him."

"Was the office like this when you arrived? Unlocked doors, no one here?"

"Who the hell are you?"

"Liam Sol. Can I put my hands down?"

"I never asked you to raise them." She lowered her weapon. "I don't know where he is."

"Why the gun?"

"You scared me, that's all."

I wondered if she had a reason to be scared.

She narrowed her eyes. "You said your last name was Sol?"

"What about it?"

Ramona Ortiz let out a harsh laugh. "The Sols of La Bolsa. The hell with you people." She placed the gun into her purse. "If he comes back, tell him I need to see him." She looked at me, her eyes dark and focused. "He'll know what it's regarding." She pushed by me and stormed out of the office.

I didn't know what she meant by "the hell with you people," but when it came to my family, it could mean anything.

I decided that while I waited for Moran to return, I'd check out his office to see if I could find anything that might shed light on the Garzas. If he caught me going through his stuff, I doubted he'd turn me in. Charlie Moran didn't trust the police.

It appeared that the Chicano Legal Rights Association was a one-man shop. I started scanning through his file drawers, looking for anything with the Garzas name, anything to do with my family, or the police. I wanted to know for certain what he knew and see if I could figure out his real agenda. Nothing was in any kind of order, not alphabetical, not by subject, not by anything I could comprehend.

A manila folder lay on the floor behind his desk. I bent down to retrieve it and saw a shadow cast over me. Finally, I thought. I picked up the folder.

"I've been waiting for you," I said. "You really should keep your doors locked." I stood up and before I could see who was there, I felt a powerful blow to the side of my face. I dropped to the floor, the room suddenly hazy and misshapen, and then the room tilted sideways, and then I felt nothing.

I don't know how long I'd been out. The left side of my jaw burned as if it had just come out of the oven. I carefully placed my hand against it. It felt as if it had grown a few sizes. I slowly got to my feet and then I slumped down into the chair behind Moran's desk. I tried to assess the situation, but my thoughts were disconnected. Whoever hit me was most likely looking for something in his office, but what?

I picked up the phone to call the police but put the receiver back down. The cops didn't like me and I didn't want to have to explain to them what I was doing here. I thought about waiting until Charlie Moran surfaced to see what he could tell me. Unless, of course, he was the one who coldcocked me. There were no good options, and I knew I was in no condition to talk to anyone. I stumbled out of his office and headed for my car.

The one thought that popped into my head had nothing to do with Charlie Moran or the Police, but that Elisa was stopping by tonight. I hoped I could get the swelling down in my jaw before she arrived. No, I wasn't thinking very clearly right now.

After I made it home, I put some ice on the side of my face and downed some Tylenol along with some coffee. After a while the pain had started to subside, and my mind finally began to clear. Still the side of my face hurt to the touch, so I stayed with the ice.

I felt all out of whack, exhausted and jumpy at the same time. The initial rush of adrenaline came right after I got home. I replayed in my mind what had occurred—the violent assault, my complete vulnerability, and my utter helplessness while lying on the floor. Even if it's not your fault, you feel the shame.

I sat on the floor Indian style and tried to slow my breathing. Deep, slow intakes through my nose followed by slow exhalations out of my mouth. I did this for a few minutes while I pictured the beach at sunset. This was a technique I picked up in Vietnam after experiencing some intense firefights. I still felt a little agitated, but at least I could get myself back under the illusion of control. I might have to do this off and on for a while, but at least I knew I could manage the effects of another rush.

I wasn't sure when Elisa was due to arrive, so I grabbed a beer from the fridge, wrapped some more ice in a towel, and pulled out one of my Santana albums. I put the needle on "Samba Pa Ti" and sat in my leather chair. I looked out at the Pacific Ocean and let the song take me away. Halfway through the song, there was a knock on the door.

"What happened to you?" Elisa asked.

"I didn't think it looked that bad."

"What happened?" she repeated.

"Come on, in. I'll tell you all about it."

I didn't, though. I didn't tell her about Charlie Moran or why I had visited him. I didn't tell her the truth. I told her I had a bad wipeout while surfing this morning. Was I lying to protect my family? A family I never wanted to see again, and never wanted to have anything do with? Yeah, but I was also protecting myself. If I was ever under the assumption that I was the pure one in my family, then I was sadly mistaken.

I thought if Elisa ever discovered the truth about my family and my lies, I was sure she'd break it off with me. I guess that meant that now, whether I liked it or not, I had something to lose.

"Maybe you should see a doctor."

"I'm fine."

"You're an idiot."

"I was hoping for manly."

She shrugged her shoulders. "Sorry."

Elisa ordered me to sit on the couch. Though I insisted I was okay, she declared that we weren't going out for dinner and that it was not up for debate.

"I'll make us something," she said and ran off to the kitchen. I heard her open the refrigerator and then the cupboards. "Where do you keep the food?"

"It's in there, I think."

She walked out of the kitchen. "Peanut butter and jelly, no bread, but plenty of mustard, beer and instant coffee—that's it. Where did all the food go?"

"They went into that breakfast I made for you the other day."

"I'm going to pick up some groceries."

"I'll do that tomorrow. Let's just get burgers from The Driftwood." The Driftwood served as a hangout for surfers and fishermen, and they made damn good hamburgers. I got up from the couch.

"I'll pick them up," she said. "You stay here." She grabbed her keys and purse and headed out.

"Don't forget the fries and a chocolate malt. And a Coke."

After she returned, I set out the food on the coffee table while Elisa went into my room to change clothes. I lit a couple of candles and I put on Van Morrison's *Tupelo Honey*. I wanted to put on *Moondance* but didn't want to appear too eager. She came back wearing a yellow summer dress that made my breath stop. She sat on the floor next to me, her shoulder grazing mine, her perfume subtle, but inviting. We talked through the first side of the album, taking in small nibbles of our food. Every now and then she glanced at my face and asked if I was okay.

"I worry about you," she said. Her words dug into my heart.

"I'm fine," I said. I asked about her trip. She said that everyone she met who worked in the Capitol reminded her of contestants on "The Dating Game."

"They will say anything they think you want to hear. Anything to get you into bed—the political bed, I mean. They don't even realize that the only thing they care about is money. Truth, justice, and the American way is a foreign concept to them."

"The truth is big with you, isn't it?"

She looked at me, her brown eyes serious in the candlelight. "Yes," she said. "It's everything." She took a sip of her Coke, then bit the end of her straw.

"What is it?" I asked.

"Your family is hosting a big cocktail reception for Glenn Friday night. They want you to come."

My muscles tightened. "Why do they want me?"

She put her Coke down and reached over and held my hand.

"Your mom. She misses you so much, Liam. Listen, I don't know what happened with you and your family. It's none of my business, but your mom, she wants to see you. They thought if other people were there it wouldn't be so awkward."

"It would be horribly awkward for me, Elisa. I can't go. I can't do it. Besides with my face in this condition, Marie wouldn't let me in the door."

"It's the day after tomorrow. Some of the swelling should be gone by then. And Marie will be fine. Liam, it's also about Isabelle. She asks about you every time I see her. She misses you."

"She asks about me?"

"Yes, she does. Isabelle also told me that, well, she thinks ... she thinks that I'm good for you, and that you'd be good for me."

That was what she had said about Dawn and me. My eyes wanted to well up, but I forced the tears back. Isabelle was the only one from my family who I missed. She was the one I wanted to save from them, but I feared I was too late.

"Isabelle said that about us?"

"She did. Will you at least think about attending?"

"Okay," I said. "I'll go." Immediately regretting it. "You just can't leave my side. Promise me that. I'm not kidding."

Elisa took my other hand. "I promise."

She must have read something in my face. "It will be okay."

"You promise that as well?"

"I do." She nodded her head slowly and then bit her lip. Elisa had a way of looking at me that made me want to lose all my inhibitions—even those I didn't know I had.

"Liam, you're blushing." She leaned over and kissed me, and then her lips brushed against my ear.

"Ouch. Not this side, the other side."

"I'm sorry. I forgot."

Elisa let go of my hands, stood up and pulled off her dress, letting it drop to the floor. She wore nothing underneath. Her brown skin illuminated only by the flickering candle lights and the glow from the moon that slipped in through the windows. She turned and strolled toward the bedroom. "Oh, and put on *Moondance*. I know you wanted to earlier."

My hand trembled as I put the needle on the record. Was that because of what awaited me in my bedroom or the fear of facing my family?

Elisa called out from my room. "If you don't get back here now, Liam, I might just doze off."

"I'm on my way!" I made a mad dash to the bedroom, struggling to get my Levi's off. Friday night was going to have to take care of itself I thought. But nothing ever takes care of itself, and it was naive of me to think so.

CHAPTER FIFTEEN

I'd spent Thursday at home, nursing my jaw. I called in sick to work, which felt like I was playing hooky. But when Friday morning came along, I grabbed my board and hit the beach. Wyatt was already out in the waves. The saltwater stung my face, but I soon got used to the pain. It almost felt good. The waves were mild, but still rideable, though they made you work for it. Elisa had left the house early, eager to get to the office, but I milked the morning and the waves for all they were worth.

"Do you miss your father?" Wyatt Fordham asked me. We had just returned from the waves and we sat in the sand letting the morning sun dry us off.

We'd never delved into anything personal before and his question caught me by surprise. Our conversations centered on surfing, nature, and music. He had never asked me about the war or about my family. Our fathers' businesses were closely linked, though the two men never became friends.

Wyatt and I weren't close. He was a couple of years older than me, and while we attended the same high school, our paths never crossed as he hung out with an artier crowd. Our lives intertwined only on the beaches of La Bolsa. He hadn't even asked about my swollen jaw. He lived in his own world and that was fine with me.

I thought about how to respond to Wyatt. I didn't want to answer with the truth, so I just responded with a shrug. But at times, I found I still missed my father. He possessed a rare insight into people and their motivations, and while he had been a good father to me, his greed and utter amorality disgusted me, and, in the end, he got what he deserved.

"How are things with you and your dad?" I asked. Everyone knew about Wyatt's relationship with his father. James Fordham had essentially disowned his son after Wyatt chose to live with his mother after their divorce. James Fordham wasn't quiet about it either, mocking his ex-wife and son whenever the opportunity arose.

"He called me the other day. My roommate answered it. My dad told him that he'd like me to come over. He had a proposition for me."

"What was it?"

"Huh?" he replied after a moment, as if I had awoken him. "I haven't called him back. I don't know if I want to talk to him."

Wyatt had his arms wrapped in front of him, as if hugging himself. "Your dad was something else, man," he said.

I gave him a look, wondering where that came from and wondering, too, what he knew, all the while keeping my poker face on.

"What do you mean?"

"I had a big crush on Isabelle in high school. We went out a couple of times."

"Really?" This was news to me.

"She wanted to be an actress or a writer, did you know that?"

I did. I remember one afternoon Isabelle coming into my room and telling me she wanted to try out for the high school play.

"But daddy won't let me. He said it would be unbecoming of a Sol woman to pursue such a thing."

"Just do it, anyway," I told her.

She smiled. "You still don't understand him, do you, Liam?" Isabelle grabbed my hand and held it tight, her smile gone. "Listen to me. One day he'll try to get to you. He'll want you to work for him. But you need to live your own life. Be who you want to be. You understand? Don't let him change you into his image, Liam." She proved to be right. Years later, he gave me an ultimatum. An ultimatum I would never have to answer. Isabelle had made sure of that.

"She wasn't like the others, you know?" Wyatt said, bringing me back to the present. "She had her own thing going. I thought our heads traveled in the same clouds."

Back then, before Wyatt got into all the drugs, I could see it. In one awful way they had been alike. Emotionally fragile people whose fathers abused them, in different ways, yet it was still abuse.

"What's this have to do with my father?"

"He heard about it, man. He found me on the beach one day and told me that because I was the son of James Fordham he was going to let it pass this time. He told me to leave Isabelle alone forever. He said I had bad blood. And the vibe he gave out was ... I don't know, man, it was bad." He shook his head. "So, I just faded away like I always did."

Wyatt's gaze was still fixed on the horizon. His fingernails dug into his skin, carving marks into his arm.

"Wyatt," I said.

"What?"

"You're hurting yourself." I pointed at his arms. And then I saw them, the various scabs and sores that dotted his upper arm. I was surprised I hadn't noticed them before.

"Oh, yeah, I do that sometimes." He brushed the side of his arms as if they were covered in sand. "I'm going for a swim."

He ran into the water and dove under a wave, surfacing a few seconds later, before submerging himself once again.

I didn't know why Wyatt brought up the thing with Isabelle. I guess it haunted him, the feeling of cowardice, the what-ifs, which I knew all too well, or maybe he was clinging to something that was never there to begin with. Maybe he thought Isabelle could save him, keeping him away from the self-destructive road that he now found himself on.

Isabelle hadn't dated much, and after what my dad had done to Hugo Delgado when he tried to take her out, I could see why. In fact, I couldn't remember her dating anyone but Glenn. Their engagement hadn't exactly come out of nowhere, but their courtship had been brief. I recalled asking Isabelle about him and she told me that he was a good fit, someone she liked, and someone who our dad would approve.

Glenn understood the advantages he'd have by marrying Isabelle. While he came from a wealthy family, the connections and the influence the Sol family could provide him were limitless. And Isabelle's presence made anyone who stood next to her look a million times better.

One thing I knew about Wyatt was that money meant nothing to him. He lived in a garage apartment, which he shared with a roommate, and he had never taken a dime from his mother, whose second husband was another Orange County millionaire. He also told her to take him out of their will. They obeyed his wish, which wasn't known until the two died when their plane crashed last year while trying to land at the Catalina airport.

And then there was me, who, though I hadn't spent a dime of it, still collected money from a trust fund my father had set up for me. I didn't know what that said about Wyatt or about me, nor was I in any mood to contemplate it right now. Nor did I want to contemplate going to the cocktail reception at my mother's house tonight.

The afternoon dragged on as if held down by an anchor. I tried to keep busy, but everything moved in slow motion. It reminded me of high school when the clock ticked at a glacial pace. I thought about backing out of the reception, but I didn't want to flake out on Elisa. Her opinion of me mattered more than I had realized.

I picked Elisa up at her apartment. She wore a black Mexican peasant-style dress, but it looked elegant, as if it were designed with only her in mind. I had on tan slacks, a white dress shirt with a plain red tie, and a navy sports coat. I felt like I was dressed for an admissions interview at a New England prep school.

We drove down the coast toward my family's house. I wanted to arrive a little late, so I parked on a bluff overlooking the ocean. We sat on the hood of my Ghia and watched the waves break along the coastline. It wasn't a strong swell and the waves were only about two feet high, but I was able to show Elisa how the surfers read the waves. Why they paddled after some and let others go.

"What's he doing?" She pointed to a surfer who looked like he was performing a type of rapid soft-shoe routine, using the surfboard as his stage.

"He's hot dogging. Not too many people do that anymore. You should have seen Miki Dora work his board. He was something else."

"Can you do that?"

I shrugged. "It was never my thing."

Elisa smiled at me. "Not your thing, huh?"

She held my hand, and it felt nice, as if I was meant to hold it.

The surfer rode along the shoulder of the wave. Then he baby-stepped his way to the front of the board, placing one foot on the nose. After a moment, he brought the other foot over next to it. Then he held his arms over his head and rode the wave to the shore.

"There," I said. "He's hanging ten. See how his feet are on the nose of the board and all ten of his toes are hanging over the front? That's hanging ten."

"God, I feel like an idiot. I just thought it had something to do with the shirts, but now I get it."

I put my arm around her and she rested her head on my shoulder. We watched the surfers glide along the waves, the sun setting behind them, the sky a brilliant orange. There was no place else I wanted to be.

"We should go," she said. "I don't want to be too late. Remember, Glenn and Marie are my bosses."

"Not yet," I replied. "You can blame me. I just want to linger here for a while longer, okay?" That was what I'd learned after losing Dawn. Some moments you just need to hold on to for as long as you can.

CHAPTER SIXTEEN

We arrived at the house half an hour late. Still too early for me. As we walked up to the front door, I couldn't help but notice that everything looked the same. It wasn't all the same, though. There was literally something different in the air.

"You smell that?" I asked.

"Yeah, it's jasmine. It's all around the house."

Isabelle had once told me that it was our mother's favorite scent, though we never had it around the house growing up. I never knew why. She must have had it planted after my father's death.

Marie met us at the door. She wore a red dress that revealed more cleavage than I would have expected from her.

"Elisa, how good to see you. Liam, you're looking ..."

She stared at my bruised jaw. "Bad wipeout," I said.

Marie rolled her eyes at me.

"Same old Liam."

"I aim to please," I said.

Marie leaned in and gave me a hug, and whispered, "Best behavior tonight, Liam. Okay?"

"I'll do my best."

Marie reluctantly took my hand and led me into the living room.

"Look who's here!" she announced as if she were happy that I was there.

"Is that Liam?" My mother's voice was unmistakable, and I felt my muscles constrict. She would never let go of that Irish brogue of hers, as if it were the one thing that reminded her of who she once was.

My mother looked younger than when I last saw her. She also appeared to be healthier. A glow had returned to her that I hadn't seen since I was a teenager.

She held her arms out and marched up to me. "What on earth?"

"Surfing accident."

She smiled, and her eyes glistened with sudden tears. The emotion seemed genuine. "That's my Liam. Now, you may not want one, but I'm giving you a big hug."

I felt Elisa's hand move to the middle of my back, gently pushing me to my mother. "Hello, Mom," I said.

We put our arms around each other and I felt her body quiver, her tears warm on my neck. Images came to me like a home movie, the color faded, the memories fresh and raw. My mom holding me after I fell off my bike, trying in vain to help me with my homework, cheering for me at a basketball game in the La Bolsa High gym, teaching me to slow dance before my first sock hop, telling me how much she loved Dawn, and then serving me up to a cold-blooded killer, and, finally, the sounds of her wailing as I left the family home for what I had hoped would be the last time.

She let go of me, her tears now cold on my neck. I knew she was happy that I had returned, but I saw it, the tell, buried somewhere behind the blue of her eyes, the belief that I had betrayed her, that I had walked out on her. She had begged me to return, and I had turned my back on her, severing the cord that bound us. I knew I would always be on the outside and never truly welcomed back. That was what I wanted, to be on the outside, but still, I was surprised by how much it hurt.

"We're all out on the patio," she said.

We followed her onto a courtyard filled with the scent of money, tobacco smoke, competing perfumes and VO5, all lighted by rows of Chinese lanterns hanging gracefully over the patio.

It was an elite crowd, though the names of many of them escaped me. But Glenn was there, of course, though not Isabelle. She hated crowds and would probably slip in later in the evening. The lieutenant governor was there with his wife, who kept touching her pearl necklace as if she were worried someone might steal it. So, too, was Wyatt Fordham's dad, James, who was the head of Coastal Shores Oil and Gas. His company leased my family's oil fields. David Shaw, the mayor of La Bolsa, was there alongside Archibald Roth, and his date, Nancy Page, who I knew from high school and, who, rumor had it, had given Mr. Ranval, her history teacher, a handjob in exchange for a passing grade. Nancy caught my eye and gave me a shy smile, then quickly looked away. I noticed Neil Cook, chairman of the Orange County Board of Supervisors, who checked his breath by exhaling into his hand, while his wife, Teresa, an attractive woman who clearly had one drink too many, stared longingly at Glenn.

There were over a dozen other guests I didn't know and didn't want to know. Younger couples, the up and comers, mingled about, looking out of place. The women wore miniskirts and the kind of heavy eye makeup most women who lived at the beach would never wear. The men sported their version of long hair, letting it fall just past their ears, along with thick mustaches and sideburns, dressed in suits with colorful ties and flared pants, all in an attempt to showcase themselves as the new breed, while still desperately hoping for acceptance from the old guard. My stomach clenched, and I had serious doubts that I would make it through the evening.

My mother gave my hand a brief squeeze and then she walked over to James Fordham and whispered something into his ear. His face turned a soft shade of pink.

"Can we go home now?" I asked Elisa.

She handed me a glass of wine. "Stick with me, kid. I'll be your knight in shining armor."

"Is my mom seeing him?"

Elisa glanced over at the two and frowned.

"He has his charms, all right, but I don't think your mom is falling for him."

"Then what am I seeing?"

"I think your mom is playing the game."

"The game?"

"Yeah, the one your sister's gotten quite good at it."

I watched as Marie held court. It was an incredible act. She moved effortlessly from group to group, smiling, touching men's hands, flirting, laughing at their jokes. The men's eyes darting down to steal a glimpse of her cleavage and Marie knowing it and encouraging it. This was a Marie I'd never seen before, and she clearly liked being the center of attention. Though the two of us were never that close, I felt embarrassed for her. The Marie I had known got things done by brains, intimidation, and sheer force of will. It wasn't pretty, but it was her. The old Marie would have hated and mocked this new version of her, even if she was only temporarily playing the part.

She settled next to the mayor, nodding her head and holding his gaze until she noticed that something else had caught his attention. He peered over her shoulder and Marie's expression changed. She lost her glow and I saw her bite down on the inside of her cheek. I followed her eyes to Isabelle, who had just stepped into the courtyard. Everyone's gaze darted to Isabelle though she never made a sound. I knew she had tried to slip in undetected, hoping to get lost in the crowd, but it wasn't to be. She had that way about her. It wasn't as if she were more beautiful than Marie, both were stunning, but Isabelle had this gift, a gift she didn't want, one that drew everyone her way. She put on a good face, as if she were completely at ease being in the spotlight, but I knew she desperately wanted to be anywhere but here. Glenn greeted her with a kiss on the cheek, knowing he was a much more attractive candidate with Isabelle by his side.

The mayor whispered in Marie's ear, then left her to greet Isabelle. Marie shot a look of irritation toward my mother, who responded with a thin, almost bitter smile. Next to my mom was James Fordham, who was all hers a moment ago. His eyes bore into Isabelle as if he were undressing her and enjoying it. I felt myself wince and then I looked away.

Neither Marie nor my mother liked the attention Isabelle had commanded, as if she had diminished their own attractiveness. The attention would pass, of course, but every man at the party would occasionally try to steal a glance at her or try to find an excuse to talk to her, making their wives or dates unhappy, yet understanding, as they couldn't deny the attraction Isabelle held.

Elisa was true to her promise and kept me safe from my family, except for one moment when Glenn asked if he could speak to her.

"I'll be right back," she said.

I thought it might be the perfect time to talk to Isabelle. I scanned the crowd for any sign of her, but she must have been in the house. She liked to slip away from things like this just to find a moment or two of solitude before joining the party again later in the evening.

James Fordham gave me a wave and I nodded my head, hoping that would be enough. I saw the damage he'd done to Wyatt, and after the way he looked at Isabelle, I didn't want to be near him, but he headed straight for me, extending his hand.

"Liam, good seeing you."

I shook his hand. It felt like wet sandpaper.

"You didn't get that from the war, did you?" he said, examining my face.

I told him it was from a bad wipeout.

He gave me a look. "The waves have been on the small side lately, haven't they? You're better than that, I hope."

"I must be getting old." My eyes went from looking for Isabelle to looking for Elisa.

"Maybe you were surfing the wrong break?"

"No, same old break. The ocean can still throw out a surprise when it wants to. You can't predict nature."

"That's probably true. Unfamiliar waves can come out of nowhere."

"Do you surf?"

He laughed. "No, but I sail. Quite a lot, actually. You should come out with us one day."

"Us?"

"Yes, your mother and me."

What was going on between them? My mother hated the water. I couldn't picture her in a sailboat.

"I see you brought Elisa Vargas with you. You have good taste in women. You should bring her along. I'm sure she'd love to go sailing."

"I'll think about it," I lied.

"So, how is Wyatt doing these days?"

His question caught me off guard. "He's fine. He's doing well."

"He's a loser. He has too much of his mother in him and not enough of me."

I wondered for a moment if that was how fathers judged their sons. I didn't like James Fordham, and I felt compelled to defend Wyatt. "Maybe that's what makes Wyatt a good guy."

He grinned at me with what felt like contempt. I knew I'd hit a nerve, but I didn't care. I needed to get away from this guy.

"I have to go talk to someone. I'll see you 'round."

"Remember to be careful about surfing strange waters," he said. "The water has hidden dangers. You should only go where you know the territory."

"I'll keep that in mind."

"Let me know about sailing. I'm sure you and Elisa will love it."

I bumped my way through the crowd, wondering why Fordham had even bothered talking to me. And the way he said Elisa's name bothered me, how he lingered on the S sound in her name, almost like a snake.

There were only two people I wanted to talk to right now, Isabelle and Elisa, and neither were in sight. I headed to the bar and ordered a beer. I was getting antsy. Coming here had been a mistake.

"Ah, there you are, Liam. I've been lookin' all over for you." I started at the sound of my mom's voice.

"This is quite the party," I said. "I'm surprised Governor Reagan isn't here."

"Oh, Ronnie. We invited him, but he couldn't make it."

Ronnie. I wonder how she referred to Nixon.

"Let's go inside, shall we?" she said. "I want to catch up."

As we moved inside, I asked if there was anything she wanted to tell me about her and James Fordham.

My mother smiled. "Nothing to tell. It's all a game, Liam. I only wished I'd learned that earlier."

She led me to the kitchen. The quiet of the room contrasting with the noise outside felt oppressive, but that had nothing to do with the room itself, which I always felt at home in, but being alone with my mother.

She opened a cupboard and pulled out a bottle of Powers Irish Whiskey.

"Get some glasses, will ya?"

I grabbed a couple of small ones and we sat down at the kitchen table. She filled the glasses to the brim, not allowing for any ice or water.

She took a long sip. "That's good," she sighed. Then she took another drink, savoring it, smiling as it slid down her throat. I joined her, but I was never a fan of whiskey, though this wasn't bad, the finish a little lighter than other whiskeys.

"So, tell me, Liam, how does it feel to be back?"

"Back in La Bolsa or here at home?"

"You still call this home, then?"

I looked down at the glass, the whiskey a golden honey color. I took another taste and went to the sink, turning on the faucet, and letting a splash or two of water into the glass. I turned to her and leaned against the kitchen counter.

"I guess in my mind this will always be home."

"Did the war change you, Liam?"

I shrugged my shoulders.

"Going through something like that," she said, "I guess it makes you realize what's really important in life." She stood up and walked up to me. She was a tall woman, close to six feet, but I had a couple of inches on her. "Your family, your home, what truly matters in this world. Who you are, where you belong."

"The war didn't change me nearly as much as what happened here, Mom."

"Yes, your father was a monster, you know."

"I don't think he was alone in that."

She grinned at me. It was the kind of grin usually followed by an insult. My mother leaned against the counter, inches from me.

"You're not all that different from him, you know."

A wave of numbness flowed down my body.

"I'm not like him at all."

"You keep telling yourself that," she said. "There was a lot of good in the man, but he had a darker soul than anyone could imagine." She looked at me like that was something I had in common with him.

I took a drink of the whiskey. I never should have let Elisa talk me into coming here.

"Marie seems to have changed her outlook on life," I said, trying to change the subject.

"You saw how she was behaving out there, did you?" she asked.

"Yes, the new and improved Marie. I preferred the old one."

"You know in all those years your father was having his way with Isabelle, he never touched Marie. Not once. Just Isabelle. Marie never knew why, and it sounds crazy, I know, but she always resented Isabelle for it, though it horrified her to no end. It was hard on Marie, you know." She raised her glass. "It's good to see Marie flirting with men, her knowing that she's attractive, enjoying her femininity. He took that from her. Isabelle wasn't the only victim."

"Of course not. Is Marie still fucking Glenn?"

My mother glared at me. "That's over now, and don't bring it up with Isabelle. She's finally on the mend."

"On the mend? I know what you did to her. Electroshock? Christ, why didn't you just carve pieces out of her brain instead?"

She finished off her whiskey and walked to the kitchen table and poured herself another. "If it were only that easy. You don't know the half of it. But the important thing, Liam, is that you're home. It's been too long, but you're finally back where you belong."

Why was she trying to sell this to me? Did she think I couldn't remember the past? I felt the anger rise in me, and not just toward my family, but toward Elisa as well. She was the one who pushed me to come here.

"I'm not here for you, Mother. I came to see Isabelle. I don't know why I said anything about this being my home. It's not. I grew up in this house, but it's not my home."

I poured out the rest of my drink into the sink. "I should leave now."

As I headed toward the patio, my mother grabbed me by the shoulder. "I read them, you know. The letters you sent Isabelle while you were in Vietnam."

I pushed her hand away and faced her.

"I didn't know about your correspondence until I was in her room and found one of the letters you wrote to her. Very touching, indeed."

"Those weren't meant for you."

"No, they weren't, were they? You were going to come and rescue her from us and take her to some safe place far away from here. But then she said she was fine, that she was all better. You remember that?"

I nodded, recalling the letter.

"That wasn't her, you know. That was me who wrote that. After that, it was me you were responding to. Me, you were confiding to. Me, you shared your secrets to, and those were my words, my handwriting, that you were reading, not Isabelle's."

I felt my body shiver, my breath catching in my throat.

"You couldn't tell, could you? Her handwriting wasn't hard to copy. What you said about me, Liam. Was it true?"

"I have to go."

"Was it true? Tell me!"

"Yes, it was true."

"Then say it to my face, Liam."

I couldn't meet her eyes.

"Say it!"

"I hate you, Mother. I hate you." Tears welled up in my eyes, my heart pounding hard and in an unfamiliar cadence against my chest.

"I forgive you, Liam. I do. You'll be back, and I'll be waiting for you with open arms. I love you, Liam. We're family. Nothing will change that."

"Go to hell," I said. I stormed out to the patio, mad at the world, mad at myself for coming here, mad at Elisa for talking me into this. I tore through the crowd looking for Elisa, glasses clinking, whispers, cigarette smoke choking the air. I walked past James Fordham, who was laughing at someone's joke, his gaze following me, and Marie talking to the mayor, flipping her hair back, him blatantly checking her out. I went back into the house, past my mother, who looked at me with a pity I'd never seen before, and through the living room where I heard Isabelle's voice, restrained, but angry, probably going off on Glenn. I held back the urge to find out where they were and kick his ass just for the hell of it.

I returned to the patio. "Elisa!" I called, not caring who could hear me. "Elisa!"

I saw her through the crowd, moving quickly toward me.

"We need to go," I said.

"What's wrong, Liam?"

"Let's go."

She stared at me, confused. "Liam?"

Elisa followed me out to the car, the noise from the party floating over the grounds like an impending storm.

We rode in silence, neither of us saying a word the whole time. I pulled up to her apartment, the engine still running.

"Liam, what is it?" she finally asked.

I didn't know what to say. Part of me wanted to tell her everything, that Isabelle killed my father, the cover-up, all of it, but I didn't. I couldn't. I was still lying for my family, for me, and maybe even my father. But why did I feel the need to cover for them, especially after what had happened tonight between my mother and me? You'd think that after facing down a killer and getting shot at in a war that nothing would ever scare me again. Sometimes it's not the things that can kill you that you fear the most.

"You want to come inside?" she asked. "We can have a drink, hell, get drunk and you can talk about it or not talk about it, I don't care."

I didn't look at her. I concentrated on the dashboard as if it were a crystal ball that would magically give me all the answers.

"Liam, what is it? What happened tonight? You can tell me."

"No," I said. "I can't."

She reached her hand out and held mine. I felt a charge go through me. You can trust her, it said.

"I can't," I repeated.

Elisa released my hand as if it had stung her, and then opened the car door, the cold night air rushing in. She stepped out of the car and stared up at the moon a moment before looking at me. "I'm here, Liam. I'm not the one who's running away."

She opened her front door, pausing a moment before entering, then she went inside, closing the door behind her.

CHAPTER SEVENTEEN

I drove home with the windows open, the ocean air blowing through the car, Janis Joplin on the radio singing "Me and Bobby McGee," and me wanting to keep driving until the sun rose over the Pacific, with La Bolsa and all that came with it far behind me.

I grabbed a beer from the refrigerator. I wanted to forget about tonight. Forget all of them. Fuck 'em, I thought. I don't need this. I stepped out to the front porch and listened to the pulse of the ocean. It was soft out there, nothing you could surf. I didn't want my board anyway, I wanted to feel the water on my skin, with nothing between me and the ocean. I wanted to take deep dives into the dark sea and lose myself in the cold waters of the Pacific Ocean. I finished my beer and put on my swim trunks and crossed Pacific Coast Highway and climbed down the bluffs to the beach.

A group of college kids sat around one of the fire pits, the smell of burning driftwood mingled nicely with the scent of marijuana. They wore school sweatshirts less like uniforms, but more like letters of recommendation or stamps of approval. The Doors' "Riders on the Storm" played on their radio as they passed around a joint. I took in the scene, suddenly missing nights like this. The stars, the crashing of the waves, the flames, and the possibilities moments like this could bring.

"Hey," one of the guys said. "Come join us. We have plenty of wine and weed."

This wasn't my crowd anymore. I was about to move on when I spotted one of the girls smiling at me. I caught the glow of the campfire reflecting in her hazel-colored eyes, her blonde hair long and parted down the middle. She wore a blue Allegheny College sweatshirt, and her legs looked lean and tan in the firelight. She took a deep toke on her joint and then handed it to a skinny guy with a Dartmouth sweatshirt who sat next to her. He didn't appear too thrilled to see me.

"Sure, I can hang out for a little while."

The girl in the Allegheny sweatshirt made some room between her and the skinny guy.

The skinny guy tried to stare me down as I sat between them, but I shot him a look, knowing he wouldn't be able to hold it. It was a bullshit move on my part, but I was in a bad state right now, and I didn't give a fuck. He turned to the girl next to him and passed the joint, and his attention, to her.

The Allegheny girl's name was Julie. She was a year out of college and had been living at home in Meadville, Pennsylvania, saving her money until she could come out to California and follow her dream of becoming an actress. She told me a lot about herself, and I told her as little as I could about me. I knew where this was headed and didn't want her to know where I lived. I didn't want this to lead to anything more than what it was going to be. And while I didn't think she was looking for anything more either, I wasn't about to take that chance.

Julie and I kept talking, ignoring the others, though we did take hits of the joints being passed around. I noticed that she had inched closer to me, our thighs touching.

"I was going to go swimming," I said. "You want to come?"

"Isn't the water going to be cold?" she asked, not trying to hide her smile.

"Only one way to find out." I stood up and extended my hand. Julie took it and we held hands as we wandered toward the ocean.

"Have fun," someone from the group yelled out.

We got to the water's edge. The waves were long and soft and tender, not breaking so much as gently rolling to the shore. I pulled off my T-shirt and debated taking my trunks off. We were alone, and no one from the party had bothered to follow us. What the hell, I thought. I slipped off my trunks and tossed them at her feet.

"See you out there."

I ran into the water. It wasn't as cold as I expected, and after diving in and taking a few strokes, it felt good. I didn't see Julie on the beach, but her shorts and sweatshirt were piled on the sand next to my stuff.

She surfaced just in front of me, naked, beautiful. Not caring about my past or my future. Not caring a damn thing about me. She only cared about right now. And that was just what I wanted. No expectations from anyone, just the right now. She pushed her hair from her face, smiling at me, her breasts full and dripping wet. She glided up to me and put her hands on my shoulders.

"Hi," she said. "I'm not normally like this. I don't want you to think that I'm some kind of slut."

"I don't think that at all." I didn't know why she needed my reassurance, but it seemed to bring a devilish smile to her face.

"Must be the ocean air or something," she said.

"It can do that," I replied.

Yet, I could tell this was all new to her, giving herself permission to have sex, not out of love, but simply because she desired it. She was free and on her own, testing her limits and boundaries.

"And you don't have to worry, I'm on the pill."

"Good, I was about to ask," I said. Though, shamefully, it never even entered my mind, as I hadn't been thinking. I didn't want to think. The way the water and the moonlight played upon her body made her appear almost ethereal.

"Come here," I said.

I placed my hands against the small of her back and gently pulled her to me, our bodies responding to each other's, my hands sliding further down her backside. All I wanted right now was to lose myself inside of her.

"You feel good," she whispered.

Her hands slid down to my hips and she kissed me, her tongue finding mine. She pressed herself against me, harder, her body willing and ready. She let out a soft sigh and reached down and took me in her hand, about to guide me inside of her, and all I wanted to do was to push everything aside and take her, our bodies working together with the pulse of the ocean, slow and long and tender, tasting her, touching her, forgetting everything and just doing her until ... until Elisa stopped me. She wasn't at the beach, but somewhere inside of me. In a place I tried to keep hidden from myself, a place where Elisa had found a home. She was trying to keep me from once again running to the cold comfort of an empty wasteland that called out to me like the devil offering lost souls a place of refuge.

"What?" Julie asked. "Did I do something wrong?"

I backed away, not looking at her, but only at the water.

"No, Julie, you're ... I just shouldn't be here."

"There's someone else, right? Hey, I'm not asking for anything—"

"I think I am, though."

"This is a first," she said, her arms now folded across her chest.

"It's a first for me, too—and not without some regret."

"I hope you do regret it," she said, before turning her back to me. "I certainly do." I watched as she swam back to shore as if she were competing in a swim meet.

I stayed out in the ocean, letting the water work on me. I turned over on my back, the ocean keeping me afloat, and I stared at the crescent moon and the stars. The water covered my ears, silencing the world around me. Just me, the ocean, and the night sky. I needed to clear my mind of all the noise that I'd let in, but my conscience wasn't about to let me off the hook.

What the hell was I doing messing around with that girl? And why was I taking my family's madness out on Elisa? I hadn't felt this way about anyone since Dawn. What the fuck was I doing? Just being me, still running after all these years. It had become a way of life, something I didn't think about, but just did, and I was sick of it.

I hadn't let anyone get close to me for so long, and even then, I was too careful, too insecure to open up completely to anyone, including Dawn, who could see right through me. But I was too weak to let her all the way in. And I'd regretted it, but only after it was too late.

I swam to shore, feeling somehow stronger than before, knowing that I was going to tell Elisa everything. I wouldn't hold anything back about me or the family. And I'd tell her what I finally realized to be true, what I finally could admit, and that was that I loved her, and I wasn't going to run away. I put on my shirt and trunks, and veered past the campfire, the radio playing a song I'd never heard before, the scent of weed still hanging in the air.

I climbed the trail up the bluffs and crossed PCH to my house. It was too late to call Elisa. I plopped down on my sofa, cursing myself for being so stupid for being with that girl. I'd never met anyone like Elisa. She didn't play games, she didn't pretend to be someone she wasn't, and she was completely comfortable with who she was. The question that lingered in my mind was whether I deserved someone like her.

CHAPTER EIGHTEEN

The ringing of the phone woke me up. Before I could say hello, Doug Everly, the assistant editor at the *La Bolsa Tribune*, was already talking.

"Hey, Sol, you need to get to Sunset Marsh. They found a body and Anderson is on vacation, so you're on." He hung up before I could reply. I threw on some clothes, splashed water on my face, and arrived at the scene about fifteen minutes after the call.

Four La Bolsa police cars and an ambulance were parked on the side of the road. When I was a boy we used to play along the edge of the marsh. On hot days, the rotten-egg smell that hung over the water didn't deter us as we had too much fun running through the tall grass and along the muddy shoreline catching lizards and snakes. We quit playing there after hearing rumors that someone from the Alligator Farm in Buena Park had released live alligators into the marsh. We heard tales of random body parts, and the bodies of small boys, found floating in the shallow waters, covered in alligator bites. Today, under a gray overcast sky, it looked to me like a smelly swamp that cried out to be paved over.

Detective Greene met me at my car. He wasn't in a good mood.

"Follow me," he said.

"Who is it?"

Greene didn't respond.

Flies buzzed around the body, which was caked with mud and weeds. Ramona Ortiz looked as if someone had strangled her to death, exactly what someone had done to Catalina Garza.

"What's that around her neck?"

"A vine of some kind. We'll know more later. You ever see her before?" Greene asked.

"No," I lied. I wasn't about to explain my encounter with her in Charlie Moran's office. I had a habit of attracting dead bodies and I didn't need the police digging into my life again.

One of the uniformed officers handed a purse to Greene. Like the body, it, too, was covered in mud.

"Is that hers?" I asked

Greene nodded. "It's been in the water for a while, so we're probably not going to get any prints." Greene led me away from the body and we walked along the edge of the marsh. Though I knew the rumors of alligators were only that, rumors, I still felt uneasy.

Greene stopped and pulled out her wallet.

"We found this inside." He handed me a card. It was wrinkled and wet.

I tried to keep my hand from shaking as I held the card. *Elisa Vargas. Legislative Advisor, Glenn Frost for Congress.* What was Ramona Ortiz doing with Elisa's card?

"Do you know this Vargas person? She works on your brother in-law's campaign." My stomach tightened and I felt my heart drop. "Yeah, I've met her." I didn't know who I was trying to protect, her or me.

"We talk to her first, you hear me?" he asked.

My head was spinning, but I managed to croak out a yes.

"I don't know. Just because the victim had her business card doesn't mean she knows anything about this."

"We know how to do our job, Sol."

I looked back at the crime scene, focusing on Ramona Ortiz's lifeless body.

"Doesn't this look familiar?" I asked Greene.

"What do you mean?"

"How she was strangled. Just like Catalina Garza."

Greene sighed. "There's a similarity."

"It could be more than that."

I left Greene and went about my job. I talked to a couple of other cops and jotted down some notes, all the time wondering what Elisa had to do with Ramona Ortiz.

Daniels wasn't in when I returned to the office. He'd been bugging me about any leads in the Catalina Garza case, so I hoped this would please him. I wrote the story, mentioning that La Bolsa police Detective David Greene had noted a similarity between this murder and Mrs. Garza's, but had declined further comment.

After living through the last twelve hours, I was done. I'd ridden through a rollercoaster of emotions from wanting to declare my love to Elisa, to rejecting her, to loving her again, and then the police finding her business card in Ortiz's purse.

After my encounter with the blonde at the beach last night, I couldn't wait to see Elisa. Now, I wanted to avoid her. I wasn't good at love. My history proved that.

When I got home, I called Lonnie to see if he was up for hitting the waves. He no longer surfed every day. When he did surf, he never stayed in one spot, he liked to hit different breaks along the Orange County coastline.

"God loves you," he said, answering the phone. God sure had a funny way of showing love, I thought. Any more love from him was apt to be the death of me.

"Hey, it's me, Liam. You want to take in some waves?"

"Sure. I'm free. No one came today."

I asked him what he meant.

"Church. No one came this morning. I wondered why, and then

I discovered that I'd locked the door. People wanted to see me today and to be with God, but I kept them out. So, yeah, I could use a good wave or two."

To say that Lonnie was the walking wounded would be an understatement, but he was, in his heart, the same guy I'd grown up with. The war had taken its toll on him, though. A pacifist by nature, I witnessed him break up more than a few fights out on the beaches of La Bolsa, always putting himself in the middle, where he was at risk of getting punched out by both sides. When Lonnie was drafted he didn't object. He felt it was his duty. In his mind avoiding the service would have been unfair to all the others who had been drafted.

Lonnie picked me up in his 1968 yellow VW bus. He said he was fine surfing La Bolsa, but I told him I'd rather hit Salt Creek. I hadn't surfed there since I was in high school. It was a secluded beach, hidden under steep cliffs. The surf had a reef break that made for great rides. The locals there didn't like outsiders riding their waves, but since Lonnie surfed there occasionally, and I knew some of them, I figured we'd be fine. Just respect their waves and honor the lineup and everything would be cool.

We pulled off PCH and onto a dirt road and stopped at the tiny unmanned kiosk where Lonnie left fifty cents for parking. About a couple dozen cars were in the lot, many with "Save Salt Creek" bumper stickers. Developers had been eager to build a community for millionaires here, but locals fought back and so far, they had succeeded, though the fight would never be over. They had to remain vigilant, or the developers would get a good bite of the land and the beach here would be altered forever.

We carried our boards along a dirt path through a field of sage, wild mustard, and prickly pear cactus. A red-tail hawk circled above us hunting squirrels and field mice. We reached the cliff and looked out along the coastline. While Salt Creek was safe for now, other communities along the coast weren't so lucky. The once wide-open hillsides were beginning to be dotted with new, expensive homes.

"Paradise lost. Welcome to the new California," Lonnie said. "But this bluff, this view, the endless waves. All of this has been here forever. Think about it."

The deep blue of the Pacific Ocean lay before us. A gentle offshore breeze cleared out the morning clouds, leaving us with a day bathed in bright sunlight. The breeze also heightened the effects of a swell that seemed to rise out of nowhere. The waves at the point and the middles were waist to shoulder high and breaking like a dream.

"Makes a man believe in God, doesn't it?" he asked.

"Almost."

Lonnie knew I was a struggling agnostic and didn't mind giving me a kind God-shove when the appropriate moment arose. We headed down the dirt path to the beach; that was the easy part. Climbing back up after a good hard day of surfing when your arms and legs felt like noodles and your board felt as if it weighed five hundred pounds was going to be hell, but well worth it.

On the south side of the beach sat the point, which was crowded with surfers. They soared through long, glorious barrels, causing my heart to jump.

"Can we drop in?" I asked Lonnie.

"No way, man. Priority rules, you know that. They'll let us in the lineup, but we'd have to give up all the good waves to the locals. That would be like having Jennifer O'Neill tell you that she'll make love to you, but you'd have to watch her have sex with all of your friends first."

Lonnie shrugged and gave me his old smile. The war may have gotten to him, and religion had made its way into his soul, but the love of a pretty woman had always been his Achilles' heel.

We paddled out to the middles. Though not as intense as the point, the waves here were clean and strong and beautiful. We dropped down into adrenaline-laced hollow tubes, the waves roaring like thunder, the wind racing through our hair, the spray in our face, and the ocean welcoming us and challenging us at the same time.

No one dropped in on anyone else's wave. We were all stoked and in high spirits. The ocean vibe and the abundance of kick-ass waves put everyone in a sharing mood. There was less competition here than at the point and after my first ride I was happy with our decision to hit the middles. We surfed for a couple more hours and when the waves began to get choppy, we decided to head out on a high note.

On the drive back, we stopped at the Surf Shack, a small food stand that overlooked the Pacific Ocean. We sat on a bench with a great sea view and had tuna sandwiches, date shakes, and "Have'a Corn Chips," which local legend says were made by Hare Krishnas at their Laguna Beach temple, but I wasn't so sure if that was true. People believed a lot of strange tales out here.

Lonnie watched as a mother passed by carrying her infant daughter in her arms. The baby's eyes locked onto Lonnie's, but he quickly turned away and stared intently at the ocean.

"Thanks for coming out today. I really needed this," I said.

Lonnie turned to me and smiled. He took a bite of his sandwich and gave me a funny look. "Why'd you call me? I can tell you had more than surfing on your mind."

I didn't answer him. I wasn't sure how to begin.

"Is it about that girl, Elisa?"

"That obvious, huh?"

"I haven't seen you all torn up like this since Dawn."

"I haven't said anything."

"It's all over you, man. You didn't have to utter a word."

So I told him. All of it. And he let me ramble, pause and stutter until I revealed it all. No wonder strangers came to his church and poured their souls out to him. It was like going to confession but without the guilt and shame.

"Love is hard," he said. "It's certainly not for pussies."

"You're a pastor, can you say that word?"

Lonnie grinned at me. "I never told you this," he said, "but before leaving for 'Nam, Pam Clark and I started going out."

"Tuesday Weld?"

Lonnie laughed. "Yeah, her."

Pam Clark was from one of the better families in Newport Beach. She was a dream. It wasn't uncommon for people to ask for her autograph as she was often mistaken for Tuesday Weld.

"She heard I was going off to war and she suddenly clamped on to me. I didn't get it. My dad's a mechanic at the port in Long Beach, and we didn't make much money. I was just a surfer who worked in a surf shop. Why me? I thought. I'd chased her for so long and nothing. Then, suddenly, she gives herself to me. I had something to come back to. Something to hope for. Then I get my leg shot up and come home and she's not the same. She's changed. The world's changed. Pam's wearing peace signs, has antiwar stickers on her car and is organizing protests. Hell, I was against the war. I was just doing what I was supposed to do. I thought I was coming home to something special, and she tells me that she can't be seen with someone like me. Someone like me." Lonnie winced as if her words had cut into his skin.

I put my hand on his shoulder. "She'd be lucky to have someone like you."

"The point is," he said, "Elisa is into you despite the war, despite your past, and despite you being you. I mean it, Liam. Stop running away from the things that can save you."

CHAPTER NINETEEN

After Lonnie dropped me off at my house, I took a long, hot shower. The water felt good on my aching muscles. It was a good ache, the kind you get after a day of great waves, exhausted, but refreshed and alive. I called Elisa's apartment, but there was no answer. It was four o'clock and she was probably still at work. I phoned the office, but the woman who answered told me Elisa was in a meeting.

"Do you know how long she'll be?"

"It could be a while, sweetie," the woman said. Her voice had a soft, Southern lilt. She sounded young and pretty and I wondered if Glenn was messing around with her. I told her I'd call back later. I didn't know why Elisa had gotten involved in politics, especially working for Glenn. She thought he'd do a good job in Congress, but I knew how my family could bend whatever values he possessed into a pretzel.

I paced around the house, not knowing when I should call back. I wanted to see her and I didn't want to wait. I threw on some Levi's, a light blue Oxford shirt, and my desert boots, and drove down PCH toward Glenn's campaign office in Newport Beach. The ride down gave me a little time to think. There were several reasons her card could have been in Ramona Ortiz's purse, but I was curious about how she knew her—or even if she knew her. All that had to wait now. No more seeking out roadblocks. I only wanted to be with her and hold her in my arms.

I pulled up in front of Glenn's office, an ugly beige stucco box, which matched his personality. We were seeing more of these structures lately. It was as if every architect had just given up. I didn't see Elisa's Alfa Romeo in the parking lot, but Glenn's convertible Mercury Cougar was there. Maybe Elisa was already on her way home.

Back on PCH, I turned on the radio and KHJ was playing "Hawaii Five-0" by The Ventures. As corny as it sounds, there was something to be said for cruising down the Coast Highway while listening to surf music. I rolled down the window and took in the moment, the salt air, the sun reflecting off the Pacific, driving to my girlfriend's apartment. Yeah, life wasn't so bad.

When I hit Corona Del Mar, I made a right on her street. I thought that maybe I should have brought her flowers, but I didn't want any props. It had to be just me. I knocked on her door and waited, but she didn't answer. Her car wasn't in her driveway, but I strolled up her block to see if she had parked on the street. Maybe she stopped off somewhere on the way back to her house. I headed back to my car and waited for her to return.

And waited. A half an hour later and Elisa still hadn't come home. She was probably out with donors or constituents. Politics. I decided to drive home before one of her neighbors called the cops on me as I'm sure I looked suspicious. Along the way, I stopped off at a Gulf station and used the payphone and called her home one more time, but she didn't answer.

The sun had just begun to dip into the horizon and the sky over the ocean was a collision of pinks, violets, and dark blues. It looked like a gorgeous bruise. You live your whole life at the beach, and after a while, you take these sunsets for granted. Before leaving for Vietnam, I had taken a lot for granted, too much, really.

I wasn't in the mood to return home. On a whim, I decided to drive to my mother's house to see if maybe Elisa was there. I didn't pull all the way into the driveway, knowing I'd be too easy to spot. I pulled my car off to the side of the long driveway, just out of sight from the house, and, feeling foolish as all hell, snuck up on foot to get a good view. There it was, her Alfa Romeo Spider. I knew there could be many reasons for her being at the house—and even being out with Glenn—but that didn't make my gut feel any better as the image of him at her apartment that morning was still etched into my mind. I was going to have to try this trust thing out and do my best to ignore my jealous side. I trotted back to the car and sat for a moment. I still didn't want to go home, but I didn't know what to do next. I realized that I hadn't eaten in a while, so I thought I'd stop off at Rosa's Cantina for some Mexican food.

But I didn't stop at Rosa's. The image of Ramona Ortiz's body lying along the banks of the marsh crept its way into my head. Had she been murdered there or had her body been dumped?

I headed north toward the edge of town, where La Bolsa bordered Sunset Beach, and parked close to where Ortiz's body had been found. It was still early in the evening, so traffic on PCH was fairly heavy.

I grabbed a flashlight from the glove compartment. I didn't know what I was looking for, or what I thought I'd find, but I wanted to look around anyway. I walked over to where her body was found and shined the light, searching for God knew what. I spotted the footprints of the cops everywhere and wondered if they had covered the killer's prints. Knowing them, it was certainly a possibility. I searched the edge of the marsh until I heard a splashing sound as if something had just slid into the water. I stepped back, reassuring myself that no alligators lived here. Still, gators or not, there was nothing new here for me to find.

I was dead tired when I got to my house. I tossed my shoes and socks off and untucked my shirt. I felt more alone in my place now than I ever had before. It had only been a day, but I missed Elisa. I turned the TV on to *Hawaii Five-0*. Twice in one day. Maybe the gods were telling me to go to Hawaii. Who needed church when you had the radio and TV to guide you? I wasn't paying attention to the show and had begun to nod off when the doorbell rang.

"I came here to give you a chance to apologize," she said when I opened the door. Elisa wore a tailored brown jacket and matching skirt, her office clothes.

"I'm sorry. I never should have taken my issues with my mother out on you. I shouldn't have driven off like that. I'm sorry. I was wrong."

I took her hands and guided her to me and kissed her.

"That was easy," she said.

"I wanted to tell you earlier. I drove by your work, stopped off at your house—called your house. I couldn't find you." I didn't mention I saw her car at my mother's house. I don't know why, but I wanted her to tell me where she had been.

Elisa smiled. "You did?"

"Just like a real high school boy."

"I must be just like a real high school girl then. I drove by the paper. I drove by your house, and yes, I called you."

"We're a couple of losers. What did you end up doing tonight?" I asked.

Her fingers slipped through my hands. She cast her eyes down. "I dropped by your mother's house. Don't get mad, but I wanted to fix things with you and her."

"You can't," I said. The fact that she told me the truth about where she had been mattered a lot to me. There was no reason for her to lie, but I was still learning how to put my trust in someone.

She put her hands on my shoulders. "Well, I never got around to it anyway. They fed me, and then Marie wanted to talk about campaign strategy."

"Where was Glenn?" I couldn't help myself. I was testing her.

"He wasn't there. He left the office in a hurry and didn't say where he was going." She kissed my cheek and whispered, "I don't want to talk about him."

I pulled her to me, our hearts pounding in sync.

Her eyes met mine. Elisa wasn't looking at me, but into me, and I let her.

"I love you," she said.

"You do?" I asked, a wave of joy pulsing through me.

"I don't lie, Liam."

Elisa ran her fingers through my hair and kissed me on the check. I felt like the Grinch when his heart grew three sizes. Her words scared me, but I felt that maybe I was brave enough to be vulnerable again.

"I love you, too, Elisa Vargas." I didn't choke on the words. In fact, they freed me.

It was different this time, all laid out in black and white. I can't recall the details, but the feelings, the emotions, were fresh and raw. I wasn't hiding from her, but running to her, falling freely, knowing that she'd catch me.

We were in my bed. Moonlight reflected off the walls, the ceiling, the floor, and dripped down over the sheets, and onto us. Our bodies merging together, timeless. "Crimson and Clover" on the radio, over and over, as if we existed in a time and place separate from the rest of the world, some sacred space belonging only to us. Because there was nothing else, and there was no one else, only the two of us, moving together in rhythm, the earth turning with us, "Crimson and Clover," over and over, until we found ourselves bathed in the morning light. A warm breeze sailed off the ocean and blew through the windows, grazing our bodies. The future before us—our future—fresh, clean and new. Nothing concealed, nothing held back ... nothing that is, but the lies that I wouldn't reveal. The truth about Isabelle, the truth about my family, and the truth about me.

I caught Elisa staring at me when I woke up. She leaned on her elbow, smiling, her body against mine, her hand stroking my stomach and chest like a feather. Her long dark hair flowing over her shoulders, touching the tips of her breasts.

"I like watching you sleep. You look so peaceful."

It was the first good night's sleep I had since coming home. "I think you just wore me out last night." But I did feel at peace. I woke up with no regrets, no second thoughts, no guilt, just a feeling of ease and contentment like nothing I'd experienced before. Yeah, I was concealing the truth about my family from her, but that was something she didn't need to know, something that would only get in the way of all that was going to be good in our lives.

"You still love me?" she asked.

"Yes," I said. "That's not going to change."

Her eyes examined mine. I didn't turn away.

"Please don't think I'm perfect. I'm not. I can be bitchy and mean and petty, you know? But I promise you I'm worth it. Just always be honest with me. That's all I ask."

"I will," I said. "I promise." And our life together started off with a lie.

CHAPTER TWENTY

After Elisa left, I washed the dishes and headed for the office. I wasn't in the mood to work. I would rather have stayed home and waited for Elisa, but the thought of Ramona Ortiz's body lying in the mud wouldn't leave me. Instead of going to the office, I drove to the La Bolsa Police Department, hoping to catch Detective Greene. But I wasn't so lucky. Greene was out on a call, but I got his partner, Detective Lombardo, the asshole.

"Yeah, we did find something interesting," he said. Lombardo had kept me waiting for half an hour, before coming out to find me. He looked disappointed that I hadn't left.

"Are you going to tell me, or do you want me to guess?"

Lombardo cracked a smile. "Don't you have anything to share?"

"Not me. You're the cop."

"Jesus, we have to do all the work for you guys, don't we?"

I gave him a shrug and waited.

"We found bits of some torn leaves under her fingernails. We think it's jasmine."

My stomach dropped and my chest felt heavy as I remembered the jasmine at my mother's home.

"We think the suspect used a vine from a jasmine bush to strangle her. We examined the stems and saw there was no clean cut. It looks like they were ripped from the bush as though the victim had clung on to them before being pulled away." Lombardo let out a sigh. "It doesn't tell us much, though. Jasmine is everywhere. But it shows she fought for her life."

I tried to keep steady. Ramona Ortiz's words came back to me when we met at Charlie Moran's office: *The hell with you people.* What did she mean by that? Could Ramona Ortiz have shown up at my mother's house the night of the reception?

"Find anything else?"

"You want a lot, don't you? Greene's out checking on that woman who works on your brother-in-law's campaign." He looked through his notes. "Elisa Vargas, we still need to talk to her."

Beads of sweat trickled down the back of my neck. It was only a business card. It didn't mean a thing. Not a damn thing.

"You think you're going to catch the killer?"

"I don't know," he sighed. "I just wish they'd all go back to where they came from."

"Who?"

"The Mexicans, Chicanos. Whatever you want to call them."

"Most of them came from here, Lombardo."

"It's not Mexico anymore."

"They were born here. They're Americans." I wanted to slam my fist through his front teeth and down his throat. He must have caught my expression.

"What? Don't give me that look. I don't consider you to be Mexican. Not like them, anyway."

Not like them. It wasn't far off from what my father thought. It just sounded a lot different coming from a white guy. Still, I wanted to challenge him, but I knew to never get into an argument with an idiot—especially if they carry a gun and a badge.

Back at the office, my thoughts drifted from jasmine to Elisa and Detective Greene. What was he asking her right now? What was she telling him? I scanned my notes, looking for something that tied together. A connection I hadn't made or a lead I hadn't yet explored.

Some people in this world are good at their jobs; they know what they're doing, but I was lost. There was so much about being a reporter that I still didn't know. All I could do was to poke around and keep asking questions.

The killings began on the street in front of The Alamo. I didn't know what I'd find by going there, but it would make me feel like I was doing something. I peered inside Daniel's office, but he was on the phone. I told Helen at the front desk that I had some follow-up work to do on the Ramona Ortiz murder story.

I drove down Cameron Avenue where I spotted a familiar car parked in front of The Alamo. I found a parking space down the street from the bar. I positioned my side view mirror so I could watch the entrance. I had no intention of going inside, not now. I rolled down the car window to let in some fresh air while Lee Michaels sang "Do You Know What I Mean?" About halfway through the song, Detective Greene emerged from the bar. He looked both ways, then seemed to relax a moment before going to his car. After he drove off, I waited until the song was over and got about halfway through "Draggin' the Line" by Tommy James and the Shondells before venturing into The Alamo. I didn't see that anyone else had left the place, and I wondered who Greene had met there.

The bar seemed darker than usual and I had to blink a few times before my eyes adjusted. April Fairchild stood behind the bar, a blank expression on her face. She glanced toward the rear exit. I dashed to the back door and pushed it open. It led out to an alley dotted with graffiti. Off in the distance, a car engine roared to life, but I couldn't track where it came from.

Back inside, I sat at the bar and turned my gaze to April.

"You just missed him, that Charlie Moran guy you keep meeting here. He left through the back door."

"Was he with a red-haired man?"

She nodded.

"They were at the table. The one you guys always sit at."

"They were together?"

"Yeah. Sit down. Have a drink."

I asked for a bottle of Dos Equis and plopped down on a stool, thoughts spinning around in my head, trying to connect the dots between Greene and Moran.

I took a long drink of the beer. April stood on the other side of the bar, her eyes fixed on me. I figured she was probably a good poker player as her face was impossible to read.

"Have they been here before, together?"

"Twice that I know of."

"Do you have any idea what they were talking about?"

"The guy with the red hair, he's a cop, right?"

"Yes. How do you know that?"

Her mouth twitched. "I could tell. I don't know what they were saying to each other, but the cop, he looks nervous around Moran."

"Who does most of the talking?"

She poured herself a cup of coffee and took a slow sip.

"It was equal, I'd say. Except it appeared the cop was on the defensive. The Moran guy was in command. That's how it looked to me, anyway."

So, Charlie Moran was calling the shots. What did he have on Greene?

"Who is this Charlie Moran guy?"

I ignored her question. "Has anyone come around asking for him?"

April Fairchild blinked a couple of times before responding. "Yeah, a woman came by once. She looked Mexican, but with lighter skin, like yours. What about her?"

"Her name was Ramona Ortiz. She was murdered. The cops found her body along the banks of Sunset Marsh."

She exhaled. "How'd they find her body?"

"Anonymous call. Probably some kids doing drugs or making out in their car."

"That's convenient."

"What is?"

"I don't trust cops."

"Do you trust anyone?"

She let out a good laugh. "Putting your trust in other people is a bad bet, Liam. Watch yourself out there, okay?"

I told her I would. I dropped a couple of bills on the bar, finished off my beer, and headed for the door.

"I'll let you know if either of them comes back."

"Can I trust you on that?"

"Maybe," she said with a straight face.

I walked down to Moran's office, trying to control the urge to kick the shit out of him.

What did he have on Greene? The obvious guess was that the cops were covering up the truth behind the killing of Julio Garza, and Moran found out and was blackmailing Greene. But why kill Catalina and how did Ramona Ortiz figure into all of this? Were Greene and Moran in on something together? I didn't get it. Moran urged me to dig deep into the killings, but Greene was the one who was stonewalling me.

The doors to the Chicano Legal Rights Association were locked. I peered through the window but saw no sign of life. Could Moran have killed Ramona Ortiz? After all, she showed up at his office with a gun, maybe she had a beef with him. I had no answers. Only questions that left me confused.

I needed to talk to Greene. I wanted to see his expression when I told him I knew that he and Charlie Moran were together. The meeting couldn't be at the police station, though. I wasn't about to confront him there. You know the saying, you want to find a cop go to a donut shop, and damn if that wasn't true. I drove up Pacific Coast Highway, the traffic lighter than usual. Most of the schools were still in session, so it was still too early for the tourists to arrive. The beach was active with locals, girls lying out on their towels working on their tans, the boys in the water surfing while the ocean was still theirs, all enjoying the calm before the storm, when the tourists would arrive like Marines storming the beach.

I cruised by Johnny Bob's donuts, but Greene's car wasn't there, though the parking lot was dotted with black-and-whites from La Bolsa, Pacific Harbor, and the CHP. The scent drifting out from Johnny Bob's was enticing, but I needed something better than a donut to tide me over. I drove back to Main and over to The Driftwood for lunch.

The little café was packed, so I ordered my burger, fries, and Coke to go. The customers consisted of a cross-section of those who worked and lived by the water. I remembered coming here with my father, and years later dropping by after surfing. The hamburgers never changed. Good, juicy, and messy, with the right amount of grease. The same old pictures still hung on the wall. Fishermen on the pier with their prized catches, surfers posing with their long, wooden boards, and blushing girls in their modest bathing suits. You couldn't miss the message that the past was a better time and place to live. I wasn't so sure. Some of us were trying like hell to pull away from the past and begin again. But I guess the past never allows anyone to truly start over.

Many of the folks who got to The Driftwood before me were still waiting for their food, so I picked up a copy of The Register and scanned the front page while waiting for my order. Nothing interesting. The Angels lost again, and Nixon searched for peace with honor, while the death count of American soldiers kept rising. I flipped through the local news, pausing when I noticed a picture of James Fordham with Representative Luther Bennett. There was no accompanying article, only a caption that stated they were at a recent Bennett fundraiser. Luther Bennett was the sitting congressman Glenn was trying to unseat. Something else in the picture caught my eye. An unnamed woman stood behind Fordham, her hand resting on his shoulder. Though she was looking away from him in the picture, there was no mistaking the woman. It was Ramona Ortiz.

CHAPTER TWENTY-ONE

Daniels was in his office when I returned. Head down, red pencil in his hand, ripping apart someone's work. I took a seat and pulled out a legal pad and wrote down Charlie Moran, Ramona Ortiz, James Fordham, and Detective Greene's names. I thought for a moment and added Glenn Frost and Luther Bennett to the list. Then at the top of the page, I jotted down Julio and Catalina Garza. I didn't know what good that did, but at least I could see them all together in one place.

I underlined James Fordham's name. I recalled the talk I had with him at my mother's house.

Remember to be careful about surfing strange waters. The water has hidden dangers. You should only go where you know the territory.

I didn't think much of his words then, but after seeing the picture of him with Ramona Ortiz, I wondered if he had been warning me to stay away from digging any deeper into the Garza killings.

I then placed two calls. One to Detective Greene and the other to James Fordham. Greene still wasn't in his office, so I left a message for him to call me. Then I dialed the number for Coastal Shores Oil and Gas and asked to speak with James Fordham. The receptionist asked who was calling.

"Liam Sol of the *La Bolsa Tribune*."

"May I tell him what this is regarding?"

I paused, wondering how best to respond. I could tell her I was a friend of the family, but that would only make me appear weak. I decided to go for the direct approach. "I'm working on a story about the murder of Ramona Ortiz."

"I'm sorry, I don't understand."

"Don't worry. He'll know."

She told me to hold on, but her tone had changed. I knew she didn't want to give Fordham my message, not that I could blame her.

I quickly jotted down a few questions I wanted to ask. A man's voice came on the phone.

"This is Walter Lange. How can I help you?"

Lange had the voice of someone who was too busy to be bothered with.

"I don't think you can. I'm trying to reach James Fordham."

"He's in a meeting. I'm an attorney here at Coastal Shores Oil. You say you're a reporter?"

"With the *La Bolsa Tribune*, yes. Why won't he talk to me?"

"As I said, he's in a meeting. You say you wanted to speak with him regarding a murder?"

"Yes. Ramona Ortiz."

"What is it you think you know, Mr. Sol?"

"I know that James Fordham knew Ramona Ortiz. Her body was found at the marsh near Sunset Beach. I'm wondering—"

"If you're accusing Mr. Fordham of anything associated with the murder of one of his employees, or if you're attempting to halt the proposed development of Sunset Marsh, please know that this company will not hesitate to sue both you and the newspaper that employs you for libel."

"I'm not accusing him of anything." Then it struck me. "Wait, you said Miss Ortiz worked for Fordham?"

There was a pause, Walter Lange knew he had said too much.

"And while he did not know Miss Ortiz personally, you should know that all of us here at Coastal Shores Oil are deeply saddened by her death. I'll give Mr. Fordham your message. But don't forget what I said, Mr. Sol."

And with that, he hung up. Walter Lange talked tough, but Fordham needed to get himself better lawyers. All this guy did was raise more questions. Ortiz worked for James Fordham's company? Why did Lange think I was accusing Fordham of anything? Why were they threatening me? And where did that comment regarding the development of Sunset Marsh come from? I hadn't heard anything about developing the marshland.

I needed to find out more about Ramona Ortiz. I found her address in the police report. No phone number was listed. Maybe she lived with someone. I pulled out the phone book and found an R. Ortiz at the same address. I began dialing her number when I caught a whiff of Daniels's cigar.

He stood over me, a chewed-up red pencil in his mouth. He motioned me to follow him to his office. I hung up and grabbed my notebook, wondering why he wanted to talk to me. He let out a heavy sigh after plopping down in his chair. He pulled the pencil from his mouth and stared at it like it was his enemy.

"What is it?"

"Sit," he said.

I grabbed a stack of newspapers from the only other chair in his office and looked for a place to put them.

"Just toss 'em on the floor, Sol. They won't break."

I dropped them next to the chair and took a seat.

Daniels didn't say anything, but I could read the look of disappointment.

"What is it?"

"I just got a call from a lawyer from Coastal Shores Oil. Then I received another call from James Fordham's private attorney. You know what they wanted?"

They worked fast.

"I don't know," I said.

Daniels rubbed his forehead like he was mad at it. "You called James Fordham, president of Coastal Shores Oil and Gas, and tried to implicate him in a murder?"

"Nothing like that. He knew her. Ramona Ortiz worked at Fordham's company. I wanted to know what he could tell me about her."

"How do you know that he knew her?"

"His lawyer denies it, but I saw a picture of her with James Fordham in *The Register*. She wasn't named, but it was her. She had her hand on his shoulder at a Luther Bennett fundraiser. Someone, either Fordham or her lawyer, is lying."

Daniels went back to work on his forehead. I was expecting to see blood seeping out from it at any moment.

"I'm a ... I'm going to give the Ramona Ortiz story to someone else."

"You can't do that. I'm on to something."

"You're off it." Daniels scanned his desk, grabbed a sheet of paper and handed it to me. "There's a city council meeting tomorrow evening. I want five hundred words. Try not to accuse anyone of murder."

I stood up and headed for the door.

"Oh, Sol," he said. "Are you anywhere with the Garza story?"

I gripped the doorknob. "I'm working on it. There could be a connection—"

"Put it on the backburner. You'll be busy covering municipal services for a while."

I turned to him. "They threatened you, didn't they? Coastal Shores Oil."

Daniels ignored me and went back to marking up someone's story with his red pencil. I left his office without saying a word. My eyes burned as I grabbed my jacket and stormed out of the office. I was embarrassed and pissed off. The message from Fordham was clear: Back off. The message from Daniels was clear, too. James Fordham had gotten to him. Fordham didn't want anyone looking into the death of Ramona Ortiz. He was using his power and influence to distance himself from the murders. Despite what Daniels had told me, I was going after Fordham, no matter what.

Elisa's car was parked in front of my house when I got home. She knew where I kept the spare key, and I was pleased that she felt free to use it. I wasn't going to ask her if Detective Greene had contacted her or if she knew Ortiz. After the day I had, I wanted to fall into arms and let her shelter me from the outside world.

I opened the door and shouted "Honey, I'm home," in my best Ricky Ricardo voice. Elisa came out from the kitchen wearing an apron. She greeted me with a hug and pat on the ass. The house never smelled so good.

I followed her into the kitchen. "What are you cooking?"

Elisa grabbed an extra apron from the counter and tossed it to me. "You mean, what are we cooking?" She pointed to some tomatoes resting on a butcher's block. "Start slicing."

"When did I get aprons and a butcher's block and whatever those things are on the counter?"

"You mean kitchen tools? You're welcome," she said. "And we're having chicken mole with Spanish rice. Sound good?"

It was more than good. She paired the meal with red wine, which we drank out of some old Welch's grape jelly jars that I'd converted to drinking glasses.

Elisa asked me about my day and I proceeded to lie to her by omission. Nothing about Ortiz, nothing about Fordham, nothing about Moran or Greene. Somewhere in the back of my mind I was worried she might somehow be involved.

"How did your day go?"

"Just fine," she said. "Nothing but the usual."

Nothing about being questioned by Detective Greene.

After we did the dishes, she led me into the bedroom where we made love. We started slowly, then moment by moment, the pace increased, to an almost urgent level, almost as if time was our enemy.

CHAPTER TWENTY-TWO

I arrived at the office a little late. I was still pissed off at Daniels, so coming in late served as my little rebellion, one that no one but me would notice. I read through the notes Daniels had given to me about recent city council meetings. I was relieved to see it listed all the council members by name, as I had no idea who most of them were.

I figured they'd give Guy Watson the Ramona Ortiz story. While he had been here a good year longer than me, he wasn't very seasoned. But he'd be a good boy and only report what the police told him.

The phone rang. It was Detective Greene.

"I got your message. What do you want?"

"I have some questions about the Ortiz murder. Can we meet?"

"You can't ask them over the phone?"

"I don't think you'd like that."

"Why?"

"Just take my word for it. How about we meet at eleven at The Alamo? You know the place, right?"

An uncomfortable silence followed.

"Greene, are you there?"

"What is it you think you know, Sol?"

That was the second time in the last two days that someone asked me that question. I had no idea what I thought I knew, but maybe if I pretended that I knew something it would help.

"We can talk there," I said.

"You'd better not be fucking with me."

"See you at eleven."

I hung the phone up before he could respond. My palms were sweaty. I didn't like playing games with cops, but I needed to know what Charlie Moran had on Greene.

I arrived at The Alamo a little before eleven. April Fairchild sat behind the bar, lost in the words of Ralph Ellison's *The Invisible Man*.

"A new reading assignment?"

April cracked a smile and placed the book on the top of the bar.

"What'll it be today?"

"Just coffee."

I took a seat at the bar as she poured the coffee.

"You've got company," she said.

I turned as Greene entered. He waved me over to the table, the Charlie Moran table. April asked him if he wanted anything.

"I'm on duty. Coffee will be fine."

Greene plopped down into his seat, which faced the entrance. I took the chair across from him. April dropped off his coffee, giving me a look I couldn't read, then moved back to the bar.

"What's this about, Sol? I don't have time for your bullshit."

Yet, he still came to our meeting. Greene gave me the tough cop stare-down, but he wasn't quite pulling it off and he knew it. I decided to start with something easy, something that might relax him a little, and something I was curious to know.

"What did you find out from Elisa Vargas about Ramona Ortiz?"

"I haven't gotten around to talking to her yet. Have you?"

No wonder she hadn't mentioned Greene. I was the only liar in the house last night. "No, not sure I will."

"We both know that's not why you called me here," Greene said.

"What do you really want?"

Greene had something to hide, otherwise he wouldn't be so anxious to hear what I knew. I took a deep breath. "How do you know Charlie Moran?"

Greene blinked his eyes, then his gaze shifted to the front door. "I'm working on a case. He's a material witness."

His response was perfectly reasonable and it took me off guard for a moment. Still, from what April had told me about his meetings with Moran, I knew Greene wasn't telling the whole truth. Before I could respond, Greene shot me another question.

"How do you know Charlie Moran?"

"I can't tell you."

Greene leaned forward. "What do you want?"

"What does he have on you, Greene? He may be a witness of yours, but he has something on you. What is it? Maybe I can help."

He sat back in his chair. "You don't know anything, do you? You're just throwing shit out to see how I react, is that it?" Greene looked around, and then he focused on me. "Charlie Moran has nothing to do with anything, got that?" he said, his voice cracking.

He stood up to leave. "Oh, by the way, Guy Watson called me. It seems he's on the Ortiz story, not you."

"So, why did you agree to meet me?"

Greene's jaw tightened, then he marched out of the bar.

April Fairchild came over with a bottle of Dos Equis and placed it on the table in front of me.

"It's on the house."

I thanked her, but my thoughts were focused on Greene's reaction.

"The cop's scared, you know, but I don't get the impression he's a bad guy."

"You don't?" I took a long pull on the beer. It was cold and felt good as it slid down my throat.

"I just wonder why you and the cop are marching to the beat of this Moran guy."

Before I could respond, she said, "Maybe you and Greene should team up."

"I thought you said it was never a good idea to put your trust in other people."

"So, you do listen," she said. "There's an exception to every rule, you know."

I shook my head. "I can't trust him."

"He's probably thinking the same about you."

"I don't know," I said.

"Just think about it. In the meantime, I'll call you if either of them returns, and this time I'll try to listen in. I became pretty good at that in jail." She picked up the coffee cups and headed back to the bar.

The only thing each murder had as a common denominator was Charlie Moran. I didn't know if he was the killer, but if he wasn't, maybe he knew who was. And if so, did he have something on them? And was there a connection between Greene and Ramona Ortiz? I finished off my beer and ordered another one. I thought about my situation and what my next step should be.

Thing was, this wasn't my story anymore. If I walked away now, everything would be fine. Forget Charlie Moran. Forget Detective Greene. Forget my family. I was off the story. I was done with this. I could just get on with my life with Elisa. She was all that mattered to me, anyway. It was as if a huge weight had been lifted from me. I took a sip of my beer and tried not to think about Julio and Catalina Garza. There was nothing else I could do. I had done my best, at least that's what I tried to convince myself.

CHAPTER TWENTY-THREE

Vietnam was hell. My family was hell. But city council meetings were a hell all their own. Getting five hundred words out of this without a hint of sarcasm was going to be the biggest challenge of my journalism career. I sat in the middle of the second row hoping that being close to the action might keep me awake.

In front of an audience of sixteen people, most of them well over sixty, the council members tried in vain to appear interested in whatever subject came up. Mostly, they thanked each other for their support and assistance on various and vague-sounding projects. One councilman, Bob Howard, proposed installing a new traffic light on Main and Marengo. After a little back and forth, the council unanimously voted to delay a decision until a later, yet to be determined, date. Howard appeared pleased with the decision. I guessed that counted as some type of win.

Mayor David Shaw then opened the meeting up for public comments and questions. The council members exchanged knowing looks. It was clear they dreaded this part the most. I could see why. Democracy in action could be pretty tedious. There were complaints about teenagers constantly speeding in their hot rod through town. Mayor Shaw replied that it was a law enforcement matter, but he'd certainly pass along those concerns to the police chief. Others spoke up about their own personal gripes with the city, cracks in the sidewalk, potholes in the road, kids making out in cars in front of their homes, and one thought school should be let out at five o'clock instead of three. The mayor assured them all their situations would be looked into and be given full consideration. Shaw glanced at his watch, trying to mask his expression of obvious relief. "Okay," he said, "if there are no other questions..."

"Hold on. Hold on. I have one."

An old bum wearing a tuxedo jacket over a Hang-Ten T-shirt, with mud-splashed jeans, reeking of body odor and Thunderbird, shuffled up to the lectern. He complained that the waves from the ocean were much too loud at night, causing him sleepless nights. He requested the city build a wall between the beach and the rest of the town, or he'd have to sue. The bum pawed at his unshaven face as if to shoo invisible flies.

The mayor smiled at the bum. "Mr. ..."

"Oh, I'm not telling you my name. You guys have ways of getting rid of people like me. I used to camp out near Sunset Marsh. I saw what happens. People get killed."

It felt as if my heart had stopped beating. Did he see who had killed Ramona Ortiz that night at the marsh?

"Sir," the mayor said, "we can't build a wall around the ocean. I suggest you move inland, away from the ocean. There's a shelter in—"

"Oh, no, those aren't shelters, those are government camps. I saw what they did to the Japs after Pearl Harbor. You stay away from me. Stay away." The bum looked around, his eyes settling on mine. "You can't trust anyone. No one."

He gripped his pants at the waist and stumbled out of the council chamber to the laughs of everyone in the room.

I jumped up and made my way through the row of seats. I cursed myself. I should have taken a seat at the end of the aisle. You never know when you're going to need a quick exit. I hit the aisle and jogged out of the council room. I followed his trail of odor outside, but then lost it in the breeze that blew off the ocean. I ran out to the street, searching in all directions for him, but he was gone.

I checked the grounds of the city hall, hoping he might have hidden there, but to no avail.

City Hall was the most beautiful building in La Bolsa, an odd mixture of Spanish and Moorish architecture, set amidst a garden of plants and trees native to Southern California. I sat next to the stone fountain in the middle of the courtyard. I didn't want to follow any more leads. I was done with this, but I knew I couldn't leave well enough alone. I had to track this guy down and find out what he knew.

I jotted down a few notes about the city council meeting, and decided I needed to follow up with Bob Howard about the traffic light. Who the hell wanted one and why? I knew Daniels would ask me, and I wanted to show him I'd mastered Journalism 101.

I wouldn't have to wait long. As I got to my car, Daniels's pale-yellow Chevy Vega pulled up next to me. He rolled down the window.

"Are you checking up on me?" I asked.

"Get in," he said.

The interior reeked of tobacco, and I spotted remnants of cigarettes past in the overflowing ashtray. I rolled down the window, hoping a good dose of fresh air might soften the odor.

"What's this about?" I asked.

Daniels didn't respond to my question, but instead asked his own.

"Do you know a place outside of this town to get a drink?"

"There's one I like in Pacific Harbor."

"Fine, anywhere but La Bolsa."

Daniels hadn't uttered a word on the short drive to Pacific Harbor. The radio was off and I dared not break the wall of silence that enveloped us. A couple of times I caught him catching a look at himself in the rearview mirror, followed by a deep sigh. Whether it was about his life in general or that he had to deal with me, I didn't know.

A sad and forlorn Irish folk song drifted from the jukebox as we entered The Donegal Man. Daniels gave me the once-over.

"Why'd you pick an Irish bar? I thought you were Mexican."

"I'm half Mexican, half Irish."

"Well, that must be a special kind of hell," he said.

The tables were filled with the after-work crowd, but we found a couple of stools at the bar. We each ordered a pint of Guinness. Daniels grabbed a handful of peanuts from a bowl and tossed them into his mouth. I checked to see if John Wayne had managed to show up, but the Duke must have been working on a film or hanging out in Newport Harbor on his boat.

The Guinness arrived, and Daniels grabbed his glass without giving it a glance and took in a big drink. He looked as if he'd swallowed someone else's vomit.

"You drink this shit?"

"It grows on you, believe me. So, what's the deal? I did what you wanted. I was covering city hall."

Daniels stared blankly into the foam that settled on top of the stout.

"I didn't want to take you off the story. I didn't." Daniels shot me a glance before looking back down at his drink. "I need this job. This is my last stop. No one else is going to hire me. I've made more than a few mistakes in the past and in more ways than you'd think possible."

He shut his eyes, his jaws locked tight as if reliving each transgression that had led him to La Bolsa, the place that could either save him or seal his fate. Maybe I was projecting, maybe that's how I viewed La Bolsa as well.

Daniels took another sip then carefully placed the glass down on the bar. "James Fordham and your family are tight with the papers' owners. I piss them off and I'm out. I can't afford that. I owe alimony to an ex-wife who cheated on me. I don't have savings, not much, anyway. Fordham and your family can squash me like a bug. Small towns have different rules. Big cities are a hell of a lot easier to make waves in, I'll tell you that." He turned to me. "The thing is, I still want to find the truth. We have three dead bodies and the only people who seem to care besides you and me are millionaires. Does that make sense to you? Something's not right and I'm too ... too damn scared to let you go after it."

I should have been relieved that he wasn't going to fire me, but all I'd felt was guilt. The way I had gone after Fordham was stupid. I should have been working with Daniels, letting him guide me. But the fact of the matter was that both of us felt handcuffed. Daniels worried about losing what little he had left, and I wanted to protect my family, a family that through everything, somehow, still meant something to me.

I patted Daniels on the shoulder. "I don't think you have much to worry about. Guy Watson isn't in any danger of stumbling onto Fordham's involvement—if he is involved."

"You're right about that." Daniels downed another sip of the Guinness and winced. "I don't think it was just the potato famine that chased the Irish out of Ireland."

"Why'd you order it?"

"I thought it was a normal beer."

"It is in Ireland."

He shot me a look.

"You get used to it."

"I don't want to get used to it." He pushed the glass away and asked the bartender for a Budweiser. He exhaled and squeezed his hands together. "I don't want to let up. Bowing down to people like James Fordham makes me want to puke."

"Well, I'm not giving up." I said. "I don't want to cause trouble, but I think the Garza and Ortiz killings are related. And I knew Catalina Garza. She trusted me. She believed in me. I have to find out who killed her. I owe her that." The weight that had left me earlier fell back on me with a vengeance. It was too heavy for me, I knew, but Catalina wasn't about to let me go.

Daniels rubbed his face in his hands. "Goddammit. This is why I hate you, Sol." He dropped his hands from his face and exhaled. "It's also why I think you have the makings of a good reporter. You have a hell of a long way to go, though." The bartender placed a frosty glass of beer in front of Daniels. He smiled at it as if it were about to rescue him from certain death. "Okay, you're on the Garza case, but don't, I repeat don't, go anywhere near James Fordham or Luther Bennett, or anyone powerful without checking with me. If the Garza killings are tied to the death of this Ortiz woman, then we'll cross that bridge when we come to it. You understand?"

I told him I did. I thought about telling him what the bum said at the city hall meeting, but I thought I should leave well enough alone for now.

"Good." Daniels downed half his beer in one gulp, but he wasn't happy about it. "Damn you, Sol. That shit you let me drink killed my taste buds."

Elisa met me at my house a little before nine. She'd been working all day on a project for Glenn and appeared to be as wiped out as I was. Since neither of us had had dinner yet, she suggested we set up a fire at the beach. We brought a few cold beers, set out some blankets, and roasted hot dogs over one of the fire pits that dotted the La Bolsa coastline. A few other groups had their fires going, and I hoped the Allegheny girl I had that encounter with wasn't among them.

After we finished eating, we wrapped ourselves in a blanket I'd picked up in San Blas during a surf trip I'd taken shortly after I broke up with Dawn. Getting away was the last thing on my mind now. I wanted to get used to this, this togetherness, this wanting to be with only one person, this image of waking up together every morning. Was I up to it? I hoped so. That was a new thought for me: hope. The thing about hope, though, is that it leaves you vulnerable and if you rely too much on it, it could tear your heart into pieces.

Elisa rested her head on my shoulder and gripped my hand as if her ever letting go wasn't an option. But I knew better. I knew things can change in the blink of an eye, and control is only an illusion.

"What are you thinking?" Elisa asked.

"That I don't want to lose you."

"I don't want to lose you, either."

I kissed her head. Her hair smelled like the sea after a storm, fresh and alive. "I love you," I whispered.

"I love you, too. Is there something you're not telling me?"

I tensed up. "No. Why would you think that?"

"I don't know. It's like you're feeling insecure about us—or me."

"I'm scared of losing you. Part of me wants to run away before you find out that I'm not all that great, that there's less to me than meets the eye."

"You don't think I worry you'll think the same of me? I didn't mean to fall for you, Liam, but now … now I … and I don't mean to scare you, I know we haven't gone out that long, but I don't want to be with anyone else, you got that?"

"I got it."

"You're going to have to try awfully hard to mess this up. I don't think you have that in you. Not with me, okay?"

I felt small tremors race down my body. "You don't have anything to worry about."

Elisa looked up at me and guided me down to the ground. I wrapped another blanket around us to keep out the cold and I held her tight.

"Let's sleep here tonight," she said.

I pulled Elisa closer and felt her drift off, her breaths peaceful, her face secure and content. And me, never wanting this moment to end.

CHAPTER TWENTY-FOUR

I drove to work with a goofy grin on my face. Elisa and I agreed to provide an empty dresser drawer at the other's house and clear up some closet space as well. I didn't know if we were taking turns or what, but she wanted me to stay at her place tonight.

I drove down Pacific Coast Highway, the traffic light, a nice breeze blowing off the ocean. The promise that Elisa and I would be together again tonight made me feel as if anything were possible.

Though I'd whipped up some scrambled eggs for us this morning, I still felt hungry. I stopped by Johnny Bob's to pick up a couple dozen donuts to bring to work. I didn't see Detective Greene there, but the police were well represented, and I noticed Detective Lombardo seated by the door talking to a uniformed cop from Pacific Harbor, but his eyes were fixed on me the entire time.

I dropped the donuts off at Helen's desk and told her to spread the word. I grabbed a glazed old fashioned for myself and took it to my desk. Daniels was in his office, red pencil in his hand, smiling as he marked up someone's copy. We made a lot of jokes about his red pencils, but his corrections were always on target, even if we didn't like to admit it.

"Thanks for the donuts, Liam."

Guy Watson held two maple bars in his hands. He'd taken a big bite out of one of them, speckles of which clung to his lips.

"You're welcome, Guy. Hey, did you find out who owned the marshland where they found Ramona Ortiz's body?"

"Why should I do that?"

"It's where the body was found."

Guy looked at me like I was taking away his donut time.

"You know what? I'll do it for you," I said. "I need to get out of the office anyway."

"Well, thanks, but it's still going to be my byline, right?"

I assured him that it was all his. Still, this information could give me something. The fact that the lawyer for Coastal Shores Oil mentioned the protest of the development raised more than a few questions.

"Can you do me a favor, Guy? Can you keep me updated on what you find on Ramona Ortiz? Who she was, all that stuff."

Watson had just taken a bite of his donut. He didn't look happy.

"I'll have to check with Daniels," Watson said, crumbs bursting from his mouth. "He's my boss, not you."

"Just asking, that's all. I did buy the donuts, you know." I patted him on the back and told him that I appreciated all his help.

Watson looked around as if he were about to reveal a state secret to me and wanted to make sure no one could hear us.

"I did learn one thing. It turns out Ramona Ortiz was six weeks pregnant when she was killed."

"She was pregnant?"

"The coroner confirmed it."

Watson nodded and gave me a smug look before waddling back to his desk.

I thought about Ramona Ortiz showing up at Charlie Moran's office, then the picture of her with Congressman Bennett and James Fordham. Maybe she was at our house the night of the reception. Maybe she came to confront Fordham about her pregnancy. Maybe that's why she was killed.

My phone rang. It was Detective Greene.

"You called?" he asked.

"We need to talk," I said.

"Forget it, Sol. You're off the story, go peddle your bullshit somewhere else."

"I want to talk about our Charlie Moran problem."

"Our problem?"

"We're on the same side. He doesn't own us, Greene. We can't let him own us."

"Us?"

"Yeah, us."

"Okay. I'll meet you at The Driftwood for lunch. Let's get there early, won't be very many people there. Eleven sound good?"

I told him I'd see him then. The Driftwood wasn't very private, but maybe that's what he wanted. It wouldn't look suspicious if anyone saw us. I couldn't sit still. I had an hour and a half until our meeting, and the news of Ramona Ortiz's pregnancy was no small thing. I perused my notes and found her address. I pulled out my Thomas Guide, a spiral-bound book of street maps set out in grids that were cross-referenced which made it easy to find out how to get where you wanted to go. With the rapid growth in both LA and Orange County, new streets and neighborhoods had popped up left and right, so you needed to purchase a new one every year or so. I found Ramona's street in the index and was able to track the route to her apartment, which sat two blocks away from Ocean Street, just a half a mile from the beach.

An Apartment for Rent sign stood on the lawn in front of the building, which to me, looked more like a motel than an apartment building. I wondered if it was Ortiz's apartment that was up for rent. If so, the landlord moved awfully fast.

Time is money, I thought.

She lived in apartment twenty-three on the second floor. I looked for the manager's office first, but there didn't seem to be one. I figured the manager must have lived offsite.

The complex was a two-story rectangular building with a rectangular swimming pool in the middle. I had no idea what I was hoping to find, but maybe she left a note on her front door letting everyone know who killed her.

I knocked on her door and then tried the doorknob, but it was locked. I looked down at the pool, the blue water sparkling in the sun, yet the pool area was empty. I guessed that most people were at work. Directly across from Ramona's apartment I noticed a face peering out from a window. Whoever it was had a direct view of Ramona Ortiz's apartment.

As I walked over to the apartment, I could see it was a woman in the window. She wasn't timid; she watched me the whole time, not caring that I could see her. Though she knew I was at her front door, she waited until I knocked before answering.

When she opened the door, a wave of cigarette smoke surrounded her as if she were a witch appearing before me. Her eyes were bloodshot, but she was an attractive woman, probably in her early thirties. She wore a paisley blouse with white shorts that stopped just above her knee, her hair in curlers, covered by a scarf.

"It's about time. I thought you guys would never get to me."

"You guys?"

"You're a cop, aren't you? It's about the woman across the way, the one who was murdered"

"I'm not from the police. I'm a reporter for the *La Bolsa Tribune*."

She leaned against the doorway.

"The police haven't talked to you?" I asked.

"They haven't talked to anybody."

"You're here all afternoon?"

"I'm a housewife, where else would I be?" Her words had a bitter edge to them.

From what I could see, the apartment was tastefully furnished and immaculate. But I didn't want to know about her life. She clearly had had too much to drink and it wasn't even noon. I wondered if this was a daily occurrence with her.

"I'm Linda, by the way, Linda Bateman."

I told her my name and asked if she knew Ramona Ortiz.

"No, Liam, I never had the pleasure, but she sure was popular, if you know what I mean."

I played dumb. "I'm sorry?"

Linda rolled her eyes at me. "Men. She was very popular with men."

"How many men?"

"Well, I don't sit here all day and stare out this window, you know. I have things to do ... laundry, dishes, vacuuming, dusting, cooking. That's work too, you know."

"Of course it is," I said. I thought of Graciela, the maid we had growing up. She took care of all that for us.

"Anyway, there were at least two men. Both handsome in different ways."

"Can you describe them?"

"I just did. One was about your age, and the other a little older, distinguished, you know. Other than that, I can't really describe them."

"Can you tell me anything else? Did they stay long?"

"You mean were they fucking her?" She smiled.

"How long did they hang around?"

"Beats me. I didn't time them, you know."

"Were the two guys ever here at the same time?"

"Well, that would have been some kind of party, huh, Liam?" She took a long drag on her cigarette, her eyes settling on something in the distance. She blew the smoke out slowly through the side of her mouth, then she looked at me in a way that made me feel uncomfortable, not in a sexual way, but as if she were trying to extend a lifeline to me, something new to break up the monotony of her day.

"Does the owner or manager live on the premises?"

"No, we just phone him if there's ever a problem. If you'd like to come in, I can get his number for you."

"No, it's okay. If you can think of anything else, please give me a call."

I handed her my card, which she buried in the palm of her hand.

"I will," she said. "And if you have any more questions, I'll be here. I'm always here."

She had given me some helpful news, but she also made me depressed. I wondered what she thought being married might bring her. But what did I know? Maybe when her husband came home she became alive and the two had a great life together, but I doubted it.

CHAPTER TWENTY-FIVE

Except for a couple of fishermen drinking coffee at the counter, The Driftwood was empty. This must have been the golden time between breakfast and lunch, when most weren't thinking about having a meal. One of the waitresses, a cute redhead, filled another cup for one of the fishermen, then asked if I was looking for Detective Greene.

"He's out on the back patio. We're in the process of turning it into a dining area." She pointed down the narrow hall.

Greene sat at a small table. He looked as if he had aged overnight. He stared out into space, dark circles sagged under his eyes like anchors. Whatever it was that Charlie Moran had on him, it was beating the life out of him.

There were half a dozen tables outside. Only ours had place settings. The patio was bordered with lattices that stood about four feet high, small honeysuckle plants grew out of planters, the young vines tying themselves onto the lattices. Someday you wouldn't notice the patio was at the edge of a wide alleyway. Across the alley sat an old brick building with small barred windows.

I pointed them out to Greene. "That was the original city jail. It was built back in the twenties, I think. My dad told me they finally had to replace it after World War II because it wasn't big enough. Southern California bloomed after the war. Soldiers who had been stationed here before going overseas wanted to return and live the California dream." For a moment, I thought of Linda Bateman and wondered if she, too, had been taken in by the same dream.

Greene sighed. "And with dreams come nightmares, hence the need for more jail cells."

"There were a lot of jobs available for men who wanted to work in the oil fields. Some of them could be rough customers."

I seated myself across the table from Greene. He eyed me for a moment then he focused on the barred windows. The waitress came out and asked if we were ready to order.

"I'm not very hungry," Greene said. "Just coffee for me."

"I'll have the same, thanks."

"Two coffees it is," she said. She gave a slight twirl and made a show of gently swaying her hips as she made her way inside.

"I think she did that for you," I said.

"She's not my type. What are we doing here, Sol?"

"I'm working the Garza killings and getting nowhere. I know Charlie Moran is somehow connected to both murders, I just don't know how. Were you the lead detective on the Julio Garza hit-and-run or was Lombardo?"

"No, Lombardo wasn't with us yet. He was still with the Orange County Sheriff's Office."

"So, you headed the investigation or was Branch still on the force?"

"Branch was already gone." The waitress came out with the coffee and placed the cups on our table. She smiled at Greene and then repeated both the twirl and the catwalk back to the restaurant. He ignored her, his mind somewhere else.

"There's more to the Garza killings than you're letting on, Greene. What about Catalina's murder, you anywhere with that?"

"We're working on it." He glared at his coffee as if it had betrayed him.

This was the moment. If Greene was going to reveal what Moran had on him, I'd have to tell him what Moran might have on me. This could all blow up in my face, but I had nothing else.

"So I get this call after Catalina Garza's death. It's from Charlie Moran and he asks me to meet him at The Alamo. He, uh, he tells me the police are covering up the murder."

Greene let out a half-hearted laugh. "He told you that, huh? That's rich."

"He also told me that my family might be involved in the murder. He didn't say outright that he was trying to extort me, but I got the gist."

Greene looked up at me. "Why did he think your family was involved in the Garza murders? That doesn't make any sense." I could see his mind racing, trying to put what he knew together with what I had just told him.

"He said Julio Garza learned something bad about an influential family in La Bolsa."

"Your family?"

"Maybe."

"Who did he say—"

"No. It's your turn, Greene. I'm not telling you any more until you let me know what he has on you."

Greene studied the area around us, making sure we were alone. "I'm trusting you, Sol."

"And I'm trusting you, Greene. Come on. Let's get everything out in the open between us. What does he have on you?"

"He doesn't have anything. I don't know what you're talking about."

"I'll find out, Greene. And if I find out what he has on you, I'll print it." I was bluffing, but I could tell it was working.

"Leave it alone."

"Hell, maybe you're the murderer. Moran thinks you guys are covering it up. Maybe that's worth investigating. Who knows what we'll find?"

I didn't like doing this, and I knew I was treading on thin ice, but Greene was holding something back and I needed to know what it was.

"You're on the wrong track, Sol. And let me make this clear, you don't want to mess with me."

"No, you're hiding something. Maybe I can help. Talk to me. Tell me why we shouldn't be investigating you."

He glanced at me and then shook his head.

"Look what it's doing to you. When was the last time you got any sleep?"

"I don't know," he said.

"Don't let that ambulance chaser own you."

Green's face turned red. Tears welled up in his eyes. "I swear to God, Sol …" He covered his face in his hands. When he released them, his face was wet with tears. Once more, he looked around to see if anyone could hear, then he leaned toward me, his voice soft. "I'm so damn tired of being played by him. The hell with it." His voice a whisper now. "If you use this against me, I'll …"

"I won't. You have to trust me."

I'm a … Christ … I'm homosexual, Sol. What you and your surfer buddies like to call a fag."

I flinched. I couldn't help it. It was a reaction I couldn't control. I wasn't proud of it.

"Yeah, I figured as much. Shit. If you breathe a word of this to anyone I will make the world hell for you."

I sat back straight in my chair, my arms folded across my chest. "I'm not going to tell anyone." I couldn't look at him. I didn't want to look at him.

"Don't worry, Sol. You're safe. I'm not attracted to you. I have better taste than that."

He was right. That did cross my mind.

"I think you have something to tell me now."

I swallowed hard, and I found it wasn't easy to say out loud. "Isabelle. My sister Isabelle killed my father, not the pale-faced guy. He killed the others, but not my father."

Greene leaned back in his chair and exhaled. "Christ. We thought there might be more, but it all wrapped up so nicely, and there was nothing to go on. Your family sure is something else. Is there anything you people don't get away with?"

I didn't respond. I just waited for him to continue.

"But Isabelle? I can't believe that she'd be capable of killing anyone." He looked down at his coffee.

"She had every right to do it," I said. "He molested her for years. The strange thing is that she said she did it for me. Isabelle thought she was protecting me from him. It's a long story." A wave of disgust came over me. Or was it shame? I couldn't tell.

"Makes sense now," he said.

"What?"

"I heard she was in a mental institution for a while, but I never knew why."

"Where did you hear that?"

He was about to respond, then paused for a moment. "I'm a cop. We hear things others don't."

We stared at each other for a moment, souls bared, our secrets out, and despite our past conflicts, each of us now forced to trust the other or face mutually assured destruction.

"So," I asked, "how did Moran find out about you?"

"Julio Garza told him. It didn't really matter. I wouldn't have pursued the case. I couldn't."

"Why not."

"I was involved with him. With Julio. We had a ... a relationship. He told Moran. I was caught. If I had let the investigation into his killing proceed, it would ... they might have found out about me, about us, and … and I'd get fired. Or they could have framed me for his murder. Who knows? No one wants a homo on the police force."

"Jesus Christ. You were involved with Julio Garza?"

"He had just turned eighteen when we became involved. He was a good guy, Liam. I wasn't in love with him or anything like that. He was too young. I was just lonely. You don't know what it's like. You don't have to hide your desires. He was sweet and funny, and a little crazy." Greene wiped his face as more tears fell.

"Julio had so much potential. He would have been successful in life, he really would have, but he was so impatient. It was all about shortcuts for him." Greene let out a big sigh. "Oh, hell, maybe I was in love with him, I don't know anymore."

An image of the two of them flashed in front of me. I felt the disgust rise up in me. I didn't want it there.

"You think I'm some kind of freak now? Some kind of pervert?"

"No, Greene, I don't. I'm just surprised. I don't know how I feel, okay?"

There had been a private in our squad during the war who we all thought was a fag. A lot of talk went on behind his back, jokes and such, until his first encounter with the VC. He proved to be a hell of a fighter. After that, no one said a bad thing about Private Moody. He became one of us, a soldier. He never seemed comfortable around us, though, probably scared that if he said too much, something might slip. Something that could get him discharged, or fragged. But still, he re-upped and as far as I knew he was still stationed in Vietnam.

"You know how ashamed I am for not even attempting to find out who killed Julio? You think that's easy to live with? I'm a cop. It's who I am. It's all I ever wanted to be. I betrayed Julio. I betrayed the badge."

Greene balled up his hands into fists and examined them. It must have been hell having to pretend to be straight, to pretend to be someone he wasn't. Jesus Christ, what the fuck did I care about his love life anyway?

"Did Branch know about you?" I recalled how he had defended Greene.

"Yeah, he knew. I didn't tell him, but I guess he saw something. Something I thought I did a good job of hiding. Couldn't believe it, but Branch didn't care. He told me to keep my mouth shut and to be careful. He didn't treat me differently after he knew, either. I know you don't like him, but he's a good man. He taught me a lot. Branch never should have retired. It's hard on him not being a cop anymore. He tries hiding it, but I can tell."

I didn't let on that I had visited Branch and noticed the application on his desk for the Palm Springs Police Department, or the private security uniform that was slung over one of his chairs.

"Now what?" Greene asked. "I mean Moran can still ruin us."

"But he can't play us like before. If it came down to it, it would be his word against ours. We have to find out if he was behind the Garza killings. Or if he's protecting—or extorting—the person who really killed them."

"Nice little business he has going. So, what do we do?"

"I don't know," I said. I was so focused on this meeting, I didn't think about the next step. "But I do know that Ramona Ortiz was looking for him."

"When was this?"

"I dropped by Moran's office. He wasn't there, but she was."

"Ramona Ortiz? Why didn't you say anything?"

"I don't know, but there's something else: James Fordham wanted me off the Ramona Ortiz story."

Greene paused before responding. "You think he's the one who got her pregnant?"

"Maybe she knew more about him and tried to blackmail him."

"Blackmail's a good motive for murder."

"So where does Moran fit in all of this?"

"That's what we need to find out," he said.

"We're together on this?"

"I'm trusting you, Sol." Greene looked tired, but also relieved.

"And I'm trusting you."

We shook hands and agreed to touch base the following day whether we'd heard anything from Charlie Moran or not. I watched as Greene walked to his car. I wiped my hand on the back pocket of my pants for no reason that I could think of, and I felt like an asshole because of it.

When I returned to the office, I worked on the article on the city council meeting, tying in Councilman Howard's request for a vote on the traffic light at Main and Marengo. I spoke to Howard on the phone and he told me that with the city's growth the intersection would need a light there sooner or later, and in his view, the sooner the better.

I asked him if he knew anything about a proposed development at Sunset Marsh.

He paused. "Who told you about that?"

"Word gets around."

"Well, if I had a nickel for every unfounded rumor, why, I'd be a wealthy man."

"Nothing to it, then?"

"Not that I'm aware of." It was a vague answer, one that covered his ass. I thanked him and wrote up the story and dropped it off at the city desk.

On the drive home, I couldn't help but think of Detective Greene. I never had anyone come out and tell me they were queer before. He didn't come off as a fag to me. I wondered how many other men I knew were that way. Some of my lifeguard friends occasionally received complaints about queers hanging out in the public restrooms on the beach. They said I'd be surprised by some of the men they had to chase out of there. They never gave out their names; they just said they felt sorry for them. I couldn't imagine wanting to meet up in a public bathroom. Then again, I'd heard the Pacific Harbor cops would storm into gay bars and throw them all in jail, no questions asked, so I guess they had no other place to go.

I'd heard the pain and quiet desperation in Greene's voice when he revealed to me how lonely he was. I couldn't imagine how hard it must have been for him. All he wanted was to be with someone he cared about and because of that, he was at the mercy of the wrong people.

CHAPTER TWENTY-SIX

We were in Elisa's kitchen. I was chopping up tomatoes on the counter while Elisa strategically seasoned the ground beef as it sizzled on the stove. The scent of the corn tortillas warming in the oven and the fresh cilantro in the bowl next to me filled the air. The Stones' *Sticky Fingers* played on the stereo, and the setting sun splashed out its last rays of the day through her windows. Elisa patted me on the butt and tossed a playful smile my way.

It all felt right. While things had moved fast between us, and at times I thought it might be too fast, I couldn't slow it down. I didn't want to slow it down for fear that if I did, it would all fall apart.

"Have you learned anything more about that woman who was found murdered at the marsh?" Elisa asked.

Her question had come out of nowhere. We had never discussed it.

"You mean Ramona Ortiz?" Detective Greene's words pounding in my head now, telling me they'd found Elisa's business card in her purse. "Why are you asking?"

"Just wondering, that's all." She turned to me. "I read the newspaper, you know. I read what you write. You never talk about your job. I'm actually interested in what you do, Liam."

I didn't know how to respond. All sorts of thoughts dashed through my mind.

"I tell you about my day all the time," she said. "I want to know about yours. You're a great listener, that's one of the things I love about you, but you hardly ever talk about yourself."

"But why are you interested in this story?"

Elisa blinked her eyes a couple of times. "It's a murder, that's why. Maybe it's creepy, but I want to know about it."

"Well, so far, the police don't know anything. In fact, I've been pulled from the story."

"What? Why?"

I knew I should be honest with her and tell her that I'd called James Fordham after seeing the picture of him and Luther Bennett with Ramona Ortiz, but something inside me, something that shamed me, prevented me from doing that. That something was trust. Maybe she was just curious. But odd coincidences kept popping up. Elisa's card was in Ramona Ortiz's purse when they found her body. And now, out of nowhere, she asked me about her murder.

"My boss just wanted someone else to cover it. I don't know why."

"Is that all?"

Could she tell that I was holding something back? "Did you know her? Did you know Ramona Ortiz?"

Elisa took a small step back. "Why are you asking me? You think all us Mexicans know each other?"

"The police found your card in her purse. I saw a picture in *The Register* of Ramona Ortiz with James Fordham and Luther Bennett. Fordham's office confirmed she was working for him. She was swimming with the big fish, so, yeah, maybe you knew her, and why she had your business card."

"I didn't know her or why she'd have my card. I hand them out like candy at campaign events."

And, of course, it all made perfect sense. Her glare came close to searing the eyebrows off my face.

"What are you asking me? You don't think I'm involved in any of this, do you?"

"No, of course not. I thought that once I asked you, you'd be part of it. Then you'd have to have an explanation."

"She had my card, Liam. That's all."

"I know."

"Were you trying to protect me?"

"I don't know what I was doing. I should have asked you as soon as I knew."

Elisa slid up to me and placed her hands on each side of my face. "You can trust me, Liam."

"I'm trying. Trust is a hard thing for me."

"I know."

"You're not angry?" I asked.

Her hands slipped down to my shoulders. "No, I'm a little mad at you. But I understand you, too."

"You do?"

"I do," she said.

"Well, tell me, because I'm not sure that I get me."

Elisa put her arms around me. "Oh, Liam," she said. "If you only knew." Dawn used to tell me the same thing. *If I only knew.*

After coming home from Vietnam, I thought I had developed a new perspective, a new insight that would guide me. But here, back home in La Bolsa, and in the arms of the woman I loved, I discovered that I was still treading water, still guessing, still trying to read and understand the currents that flowed through my life.

A cool breeze drifted through the open window as Elisa and I lay in bed. She was snuggled up next to me, sleeping peacefully. I couldn't sleep. It wasn't one thing that kept me up, it was everything. Greene, my family, James Fordham, a bum who may have seen too much, Ramona Ortiz, the Garzas, Charlie Moran, and yes, even Elisa. The connections to the killings were there, hidden. I could feel them.

I tried putting them together, but it came out looking like a spider web designed by M.C. Escher.

Elisa's blanket had slipped down, leaving her bare back exposed to the chilly night. I kissed her shoulder before covering her with the blanket. I watched as she slept, a serene expression on her face, and the gentle rhythm of her breathing calmed me down. Earlier that evening, she'd handed me a key to her apartment.

"This is a first for me," she said. "I don't take this lightly, Liam."

I knew that giving me the key was an act of trust, that she trusted me and that, in turn, meant that I could trust her. And I wanted to, but doubts crawled into my brain like tarantulas. Elisa made a point of introducing herself to me at Glenn's campaign event at The Beach Club, which was only a few days after the murder of Catalina Garza. Was that just a coincidence, or was there something more to it? I never had a woman be so forward with me before—asking me out on a date, initiating the sex, but I knew the world had changed while I was in 'Nam and Elisa seemed so comfortable in her own skin. Still, Ramona Ortiz had Elisa's business card. And sure, what she said made sense, but where was she the night Ortiz had been murdered? I'd dropped her off at her house, but that was early in the evening, she would have had plenty of time to return to the reception at my mother's house only to find her there. But doing what? Ramona Ortiz may never have been at the house. After all, jasmine wasn't exactly a rare plant in Southern California. Still, how tied up was Elisa into my family's dealings? Or was it me, looking for a way out again?

I woke to the sounds of Elisa singing "Moonlight Mile" to herself. Her voice was dreamy and drifted into my heart like a soft breeze. She gave me a smile.

"Hey, sleepyhead. I have an early appointment. Looks like we'll be getting Senator Tunney's endorsement. See you tonight." She kissed me on the top of my head and told me she loved me, leaving a hint of Chanel No. 5 floating in the air around me.

I stumbled out of bed and into the shower. I put the water on cold, letting it jolt me awake. After drying off and putting on fresh clothes, I headed for the kitchen, but stopped at the doorway. A thought came over me, followed by a wave of shame. I scanned her bedroom searching for I didn't know what. Then my eyes focused on her dresser. I attempted to talk myself out of it. It's an invasion of her privacy. A betrayal ... none of it worked on me. I peered out the window, making sure she hadn't returned. Then I found myself opening her dresser drawers, the top right one first. An ex-cop I served with in Vietnam told me that was one of the first places burglars search as that was where most people put their spare cash. The drawer held her panties and as I began to go through them, I started to feel sick. I stopped what I was doing and shut the drawer.

I made myself a cup of coffee and toast with Knott's strawberry preserves and sat down and read the morning edition of *The Register*. Since becoming a reporter, I found that I had become a regular reader and began following certain reporters, looking not only at their writing style, but how they approached each story. I had a long way to go. I didn't think I was very good yet, but Daniels thought I had potential and I had no idea what else I wanted to do, or what anyone would pay me to do, so I planned on sticking with it for a while. I didn't want to be one of those reporters like Guy Watson. I wanted to matter.

I wrote down a couple of reminders to myself, like finding out who owned the marshland. I didn't know how much that info would help, but I needed some leads. I also made a note to cruise around La Bolsa City Hall every now and then to see if I could spot the bum who spoke up at the city council meeting.

I wandered into her living room and scanned Elisa's bookcase, which overflowed with hardcovers and paperbacks. I'd read some of them, books by John D. MacDonald, Agatha Christie, Kurt Vonnegut, Ken Kesey, but there were more that I hadn't read: *In Cold Blood, The Death of Artemio Cruz, One Hundred Years of Solitude, The Feminine Mystique, Wide Sargasso Sea, I Know Why the Caged*

Bird Sings, The Sensuous Woman, and a host of other books from women authors, many I'd never heard of before.

On the bottom shelf sat a red photo album. I picked it up and brought it to the couch. The first pictures were in black and white. In one photo a smiling Elisa, who looked to be about five at the time, stood next to a man in a police uniform. It must have been her father. He looked handsome and Elisa beamed as it was obvious that she was so proud of him. Another picture showed her with her mother, a beautiful woman about the same age as Elisa was now, along with her father, outside a church in Tijuana. I flipped through the pictures and watched her grow from a cute girl to the stunning woman she was today. I would have to ask her about high school, though. She never told me that she'd been a cheerleader. She didn't seem as if that was something that would have mattered to her, but she looked cute as hell in her powder blue and white uniform.

A few pictures peeked out of a pocket in the back cover of the album, all crinkled as if she'd crumpled them in her hand. I felt my stomach drop. Elisa looked great in her bikini, her arm around a tan and fit James Fordham. They looked to have been taken on his boat as Catalina Island loomed in the background. I flipped through them quickly, but the last one was a punch to the gut. The two of them kissing, her lips on his, her eyes half closed, the setting sun resting behind them. I didn't want to think about what happened between them after the photo was taken.

I shoved the pictures into the back-cover pocket of the album and returned it to the bookcase. I wanted to rip the pictures to shreds, denying her of those images forever, but I knew I couldn't remove the memories. You can never remove the memories, nor could I remove the images of her with James Fordham from my mind.

How involved was she with him? It appeared that she had wanted to destroy the pictures, then thought differently. I didn't get it. Elisa with James Fordham? My thoughts bounced around like a pinball. She'd given me her key. If she had anything to do with all this, why would she let me into her life like this? She was right, it was no small thing for her to give me her key. As usual, nothing made any sense to me.

I had a lot to figure out, but right now there were too many questions for me to handle. I hoped work would grant me a reprieve of sorts, at least until I saw Elisa again.

CHAPTER TWENTY-SEVEN

Guy Watson stood at my desk with a worried look. His shirt had a stain on it that looked to have come from a jelly donut. I wasn't in the mood for playing around. I wanted to dive deeply into my work so I wouldn't have to think about the pictures of Elisa and James Fordham.

"What do you need, Guy?"

"I'm sorry to bother you, but did you find out who owns the marshland? I can do it if you're too busy."

I thought about letting him tackle it. It was a simple enough task, but I still didn't trust him to get it right. "I'll get on it now," I said. "I'll let you know what I find."

The Hall of Records office was in the basement of La Bolsa City Hall. A woman who looked to be in her mid-fifties stood behind the counter. Her beige suit matched the paint that coated everything from the walls to the ceiling, to the stack of shelves behind her. Even her makeup was beige. If it weren't for the lit cigarette in her hand and the red-framed reading glasses, I could have missed her altogether.

She looked up from whatever she had on the counter and greeted me with a big smile. It wasn't faked and it wasn't practiced. She appeared happy to have a visitor. Who could blame her? She worked in a silent, windowless office that attracted few visitors. A placard let me know that her name was Cora Coleman.

"Hello. How are you this fine morning?" Cora asked, peering over her glasses. "What can I help you with?"

I told her I was a reporter searching for anything on who owned the land where Sunset Marsh stood.

Cora cracked a smile and stamped out her cigarette into an empty Marineland ashtray that featured a portrait of Bubbles the whale in the center.

I pulled out my notebook and wrote down the location for her. "Take a seat," she said. "It will be just a few minutes." A twinkle appeared in her eyes as she raised her eyebrows. Cora practically skipped back to the shelves. Whether she loved her work or was just happy to have something to do, I couldn't say.

While I waited, my mind flashed back to the pictures I found of Elisa with James Fordham. Fordham was charismatic. I couldn't deny that. Elisa was single. Why shouldn't they have been a couple? I wondered, too, why they had broken up. Fordham didn't like that I'd been looking into the murder of Ramona Ortiz. His lawyer said she worked for him, but as what? It was obvious from the picture I saw in the paper that he knew who she was. That wasn't a casual hand on the shoulder. Could Elisa have left him because he was seeing someone else, or because of what Fordham was involved in? He knew both Elisa and Ramona Ortiz which only raised more questions.

Cora's voice brought me back to the present. "Found it." She sounded pleased. "One Wyatt Fordham owns the land the marsh sits on."

"Wyatt Fordham?"

"Yes, that surprises you?"

It did. That land had to be worth a lot, and I didn't get how Wyatt came to own it. Nor was it something he'd ever mentioned, to me anyway.

"I can do a little more research if you like, just to see if anything interesting turns up."

"What else could there be?"

"You never know," she said with a smile.

I thanked her and gave her my card. I glanced around the dreary office before leaving. Cora was already searching the shelves. One thing was for sure, Cora Coleman was anything but beige.

CHAPTER TWENTY-EIGHT

The sun had finally broken through the morning clouds, and its warmth felt good on my face. I needed the sunlight. What had kept Cora so cheery working in the gloomy confines of a dark basement office beneath the La Bolsa City Hall, I had no idea, but it was people like her who gave me hope.

Still, I had a lot to process. I walked across the street to a park and sat on a bench under a palm tree, wondering why Wyatt had never mentioned that he owned any land. Maybe it was a gift from his parents. But then the words of James Fordham's lawyer came back to me when he mentioned the proposed development of Sunset Marsh. Why would James Fordham be thinking about developing land that he didn't own?

I noticed a familiar figure sitting Indian style under an oak tree, a bottle of Annie Green Springs at his side. It was the bum who mentioned people getting killed at Sunset Marsh at the city council meeting. His gaze was fixated on something I couldn't see. His breaths were measured and he looked to be at peace. Only here at the beach in Southern California would you find a bum deep in meditation.

He wore the same clothes as at city hall, but his face was freshly washed. He looked younger than I'd thought, probably in his forties, though the mileage had taken its toll. He raised his arms above his head and let out a big yawn.

I slowly walked over to him, careful not to appear hostile or aggressive. He tensed up as I approached, but he didn't move. You don't survive on the streets without developing survival skills.

"Can't I sit here?" I asked, pointing to the ground next to him.

He shrugged but didn't say a word.

I sat a couple of yards away from him. He offered me a sip from his bottle of wine, but I politely declined. He shrugged and took a big gulp from the bottle. I studied him for a moment, recalling what my mother once told me after being approached by a bum on the street. "No child ever dreams of growing up to become a bum, Liam. Remember that." I didn't think much of it then, but now, sitting next to this guy, I wondered what he dreamed of when he was a little boy, what he wanted to be when he grew up, and what he now thought of himself.

"You sure you don't want any?" he asked. "It's strawberry."

"No thanks." I thought back to one drunken night when I downed a couple bottles of Boone's Farm. It wasn't a pretty image.

"My name's Liam."

"You can call me Larry," he said.

He turned his gaze to me. I could tell he was suspicious. Normal people didn't usually want to be anywhere near a bum.

"You from around here?" I asked.

"Cleveland." Larry told me that he'd hopped a freight train and took it all the way to Los Angeles. "I always wanted to see the Pacific Ocean. Now I can see it every day."

"You hopped a freight train?" I always had a romantic notion about riding the rails. "What's it like?" I asked, trying to get him to warm up to me.

"Never jump on a moving train. I've seen some bad shit when people try jumpin' on a moving train." Larry grimaced at the picture that had settled in his brain.

"I'll keep that in mind." I paused a moment before asking my next question. "You were at that city council meeting the other night, right?"

His eyes went blank. "What's it to you?"

"I was there. I like what you said. I was as mad as you were." I wanted him to see that I was on his side. "You said people got, uh, hurt at Sunset Marsh one night. Sounded bad. I'm wondering if you'd tell me about it."

Larry tensed up again. One hand reached into his side pocket. I worried that he might pull out a knife or some makeshift weapon, but his hand rested in his pocket. I decided to keep a closer eye on Larry. He could be dangerous.

"Are you a cop?"

"No, nothing like that. I'm a reporter. The police found a body by the marsh. I think you saw something that night."

"I don't want to talk about it." He started to rise.

"I need your help. I won't put your name in the paper. No one will know who you are. I promise."

He waited a moment, before sitting back down.

"They can't know who I am."

"They?"

"The people who were there that night."

"There were people at the marsh? You saw them?"

He nodded his head. "And the police, or those people at the meeting who run the city, they can't know who I am."

"They won't. I promise." I was still a little sketchy on the whole confidential source thing but felt sure I'd be able to leave his name and any indication of who he was out of the paper.

Larry took another drink from his bottle. "I didn't see much. It was dark. That's why I go there to camp out sometimes. People say the marsh has gators, so sometimes I shake the weeds and bushes around me to scare people away from my camp."

"Let's go back to that night."

Larry's eyes narrowed as if the events of that night had replayed before him. He told me he had set up for the night when a car pulled up to the side of the road. "I wanna take a look. You never know who might show up. I keep my sleep camp pretty well hidden."

"What kind of car?"

Larry ignored my question. "Nothing happens for a while. It's all peaceful. A little while later another car comes. A guy walks out of the second car and he flashes a light around the area, so I duck. Maybe he sees me. I don't know. I stay down."

"Are either of them saying anything?"

"I can't tell, too hard to hear over the noise."

He must have meant the noise from the traffic, but at that time of night there couldn't have been many cars on the road. Larry rubbed his eyes again.

"Did you see anything else?"

"Then the guy has a woman's body in his arms. He walks to the edge of the marsh and just drops her, like it was nothing. Then he flashes the light around and I duck down again. I don't want him to drop me in the water. Then nothing until his car door shuts and then both cars drive away. I wait a while, then sneak over to the body. Her arms are outstretched as if she's holding on to something. But she's dead." He paused for a moment. "I've seen dead before."

"What kind of cars did they drive?"

"It was too dark, but they were just cars you see on the road."

"Anything else come to mind? Anything at all?"

Larry shook his head. "You're making me tired. You need to leave me alone now."

His eyes were unfocused and I knew I had lost him.

"Get some rest."

I handed Larry a ten-dollar bill. He folded it up into a tiny square and carefully placed it in his pocket. "Bless you," he said.

I didn't know if I had enough for a story, but I learned that at least two people were involved in killing Ramona Ortiz. As I walked away,

Larry called out to me. "Hey, I just remembered something."

I stopped and turned to him, wondering if this was a ploy to get more money out of me.

"One of the cars, I don't know which one, but it sounded like it was from outer space."

"What do you mean?"

"Lots of strange sounds and voices coming out of it. I don't know what it was, but it gave me the willies."

"Did you hear anything else?"

"No." He paused for a moment. "I really need to sleep now, okay?"

I handed him another ten. Once again, he folded it up into a tiny square, carefully placing it in his pocket, then he lay down on the grass. His eyes were still open, but he was out like a light.

CHAPTER TWENTY-NINE

Daniels tossed my story on his desk. "Not bad, Sol."

"Thanks." I'd written it up as soon as I'd returned to the office. It was easy to write, the fingers hitting the typewriter almost without thought. It was as close to the high I got from surfing than anything else I'd done.

"We can't run it, of course."

"What do you mean you can't run it? Is it because I'm supposed to be off the Ramona Ortiz story?"

"No. Your anonymous source is a drunken bum whose account of things is highly questionable. You need a lot more. You're getting there, but it's not enough."

I exhaled loudly, showing my frustration. Daniels' eyes bore into me like a hawk.

"What?" I asked.

"The story isn't dead, Sol. Find another source. Keep digging."

The murder of Julio Garza seemed to be the trigger for all that had followed. Did Julio Garza have something on Fordham that got him killed?

"You know, this may all lead back to James Fordham?"

It was Daniels' turn to let out a loud exhale. Then he covered his mouth with his hands and gave me a look. He freed his hands and dropped them down to his lap.

"We'll cross that road when we come to it, but you don't talk to him until you get my go-ahead, understand?"

I assured him that I did and headed out the door.

I contemplated my next move and decided to call Greene. He answered on the first ring, but he sounded exhausted.

"Hey, it's Liam Sol. Can we meet? I want to talk to you about James Fordham."

He didn't respond. All I heard was the hum of distant voices in the background.

"Greene? You still there?"

"I can't do it, Sol. I need this job." His voice turned into a whisper. "Word will get out. No one will hire me."

I was afraid of this. The risk to him was too great.

"We can do this, Greene. We can handle Charlie Moran."

"Do it without me."

"Oh, I'm going to and don't try stopping me."

His breaths were getting short. It sounded like he was doing everything he could to keep from crying.

"I'll do what I can to protect you," I said. "You got that?"

"You do what you have to do and I'll do the same," he mumbled before hanging up the phone.

Charlie Moran wasn't the only thing that owned Greene. The truth did, too. He had convinced himself that his secret life would be exposed if this story came to light. He could only do so much to protect himself. I guessed that every way out of this for Greene looked like a trap. A trap he'd never be able to free himself from.

I thought about trying Detective Lombardo, but now, after talking to Greene, I worried that if I gave Lombardo anything, it could expose Greene's relationship with Julio Garza.

I needed to find Moran. I wanted to know what he could tell me about James Fordham. I called his office, letting it ring at least a dozen times before hanging up. I hadn't heard from April Fairchild, either. She said she'd call if Moran showed up at the bar. But maybe the murder of Ramona Ortiz scared him. I could picture him hiding in the shadows like a sewer rat.

I parked my car in front of The Alamo. On the drive there, I had a lot to think about. The connection to the murders still played in my mind, but now that I was alone, the image of Elisa with James Fordham pushed everything aside. I had told her all about Dawn and she told me about her old boyfriends, though she never mentioned Fordham. I thought back to the party at my mother's house, when Fordham and I were alone. He suggested I bring Elisa along for a ride on his yacht. There was nothing casual about the comment. He was sending me a message, like a dog marking his territory.

At the time I didn't think anything of it, him warning me to avoid going where I didn't belong, but it made me wonder if Fordham was pulling strings I didn't know existed. Whether Elisa was involved in any of this, or if her relationship with him was separate from the other, I had no idea. I didn't want to dwell on that now, but as I'd learned, not thinking about something doesn't make it go away.

I got out of my car, bypassing The Alamo and walked to Moran's office. The front door was locked, so I peeked inside his window. Other than the absence of Ramona Ortiz, it looked the same as when I had last visited.

Johnny Cash's "Sunday Morning Coming Down" streamed out of the jukebox as I entered The Alamo. Two guys sat at opposite ends of the bar, and a middle-aged couple held hands at one of the back tables, a half-dozen empty bottles of beer in front of them. The woman leaned over and kissed him tenderly on the mouth. The man momentarily gazed down at his wedding ring. The woman's hands bore no ring of any kind. I studied them, wondering if the woman saw a future with this guy. Was she fooling herself, or did she even care that he had a wife waiting at home for him? The two of them had sad eyes, focused now on only each other.

April Fairchild drew a beer into a tall, chilled glass. She handed it to the guy at the far end of the bar. He appeared tired, a worn briefcase sat on the stool next to him. He thanked her for the beer and told her to run a tab.

She saw me and smiled.

"Should I be expecting one of your usual guests?" she asked.

"I hope not." I took a seat at the bar and asked for a Carta Blanca.

April grabbed two bottles from the refrigerator. She popped off the caps with a bottle opener and handed me one and kept one for herself.

"What brings you by?"

I took a sip of the beer. "I can't find Charlie Moran. He's not at his office and I haven't heard anything from him."

"I told you I'd call if Moran stopped by. Not that I don't like seeing you, but this isn't really your kind of place." She scanned the room and gave me a knowing look.

"It's growing on me," I said.

I didn't want to go home. I didn't want to face Elisa. I didn't want her to confirm that she had been involved with James Fordham. I didn't know how I would handle the news. I'd been with plenty of women, and I knew she had been with men and that didn't bother me, but Fordham wasn't like anyone I could have ever pictured her with. He wasn't the usual old boyfriend. I knew he was someone who enjoyed making people dance to his tune, when he wanted and how he wanted. The truth was, he sounded a lot like my father. A man you don't mess with. A man who didn't lose. A man who could kill without remorse. And if he was someone I'd have to face down the road, I needed to know which side Elisa was going to be on, his or mine.

I finished off my beer and asked for another. April gave me a look.

"You know, Liam, I've been a bartender for a while. I know what you're doing. Take this for what it's worth. Hiding out here drinking isn't going to solve your problems. It's only going to make them worse."

"Can I have another beer, please?"

She gave me a shrug and placed another cold bottle in front of me. I picked it up and noticed that the guy at the far end of the bar had raised his glass to me in some kind of salute, like we were brothers in arms. The bags under his eyes made it appear as if he'd just lost a long and brutal fight over the choices he had made in his life. I glanced at April Fairchild. It looked like she was studying for one of her classes, classes that would eventually free her from this place. I walked quietly out of The Alamo, a full bottle of beer resting alone on the bar.

CHAPTER THIRTY

We had already arranged for me to stay at her place again tonight. I stopped by my house to pick up some clothes, though I wondered if I'd end up spending the night. I had to ask her about the pictures of her with Fordham and I wasn't looking forward to her response.

I caught the aroma of fried bacon drifting out her window. She once told me how she liked having breakfast for dinner. Before I could put the key in, she opened the door and greeted me with a hug that warmed my entire being.

"I missed you," she said.

Elisa let go of me and kissed me on the lips. Her face radiant, her eyes shining. "You have good timing."

She took my hand and led me to the dining room table. "Sit," she said. "I'm making bacon and eggs for dinner. The bacon's done and I'm about to scramble the eggs."

It all felt so right. We felt so right, but I knew if I didn't ask her about Fordham now, I'd spend the entire evening struggling to act as if everything were normal. I couldn't do that. Elisa started for the kitchen, but I grabbed her hand.

"What is it?" she asked.

"I need to talk to you about something."

Elisa sat down in the chair next to me, a worried expression on her face, her eyes zeroed in on mine.

"I don't like the sound of this. Is everything okay? Are you okay?"

It hurt that her first thought was of me and if I was all right.

"I'm fine." I hadn't given any thought to how I was going to do this and suddenly felt as if I had crossed a line of some kind.

"What is it then?"

I took a breath. "After you left this morning, I made myself at home."

"Good. I want you to do that."

"Well ... I was checking out your bookcase and found your photo album. Well, anyway, I looked through it."

She gave me a confused look.

"There were a few crumbled pictures in the back and—"

Elisa let go of my hands. "And what?" She crossed her arms in front of her chest.

"I saw some pictures of you with James Fordham. It looked like the two of you were a couple at one time."

"There were men before you, Liam. You know that. I have a past. My life didn't begin with you."

"I know that."

"So ...?"

"I think he's a bad guy, Elisa."

"What do you mean?"

I had no idea how much I should reveal to her about Fordham. I had no proof at this point, just hunches.

"You're not seeing him, are you?"

"No, I'm not." Elisa stood up, her arms still crossed. "You still don't trust me, do you? Are you trying to kill our relationship on purpose, or are you just self-destructive?"

"I don't know how you could be with him."

"I was a volunteer for his charity, The James Fordham House for the Blind. He was so proud of it, they did wonderful work. Anyway, we got to talking and a few weeks later he hired me to work for Coastal Shores Oil as part of their legal team."

"Another thing you never told me."

Elisa looked away. "I'm sorry. I'm not perfect, Liam. Far from it. I was attracted to him, and I knew he was attracted to me. I didn't want to marry him. I just wanted to see where it went, that's all." She sighed. "I don't know why I didn't tell you. I guess I was embarrassed, him being older as well as my boss."

"Who broke it off?"

Her gaze found its way back to me. "Is that important to you?"

"Maybe. I don't know."

"I did. I broke up with him. He …" Her voice trailed off.

"What?" I asked.

"I don't know. He wasn't who I thought he was, okay?"

"What do you mean?"

"Liam, I need to know something. Do you really trust me?"

"I do trust you, Elisa." The words felt wrong as they came out of my mouth. I didn't know if I trusted her. "But you never told me you were seeing him. You never told me you worked for him. You haven't been honest with me."

"And you, Liam. Have you been completely honest with me?"

I opened my mouth, but no words followed. I was caught wondering how she was able to read into me so well.

"I know you haven't," she said, "but when you're ready, I'll be here. I'm not going anywhere."

When you hear the truth about my family and me you might, I thought. "I don't want you going anywhere. All I do is think about you. Sometimes I don't understand why you're interested in me. I'm not all that I'm cracked up to be."

"You're a good man. You make me happy. I want to be with you. I've never let any man get this close to me, ever. I look at my future and I see you. I like that. But you need to trust me."

I didn't feel like a good man, not with my past, not with what I'd been covering up. I looked at Elisa and I wanted to see her in my future as well, but that image started to fade, as if someone other than me were erasing it before my eyes.

"Maybe I need some time," I said.

"You walk out that door now, don't bother coming back. I mean it."

I couldn't help but glance at her front door. I felt the tides calling me back to the waves, back to the ocean, away from anything and anyone that wanted something from me.

"You don't like that I know you so well, is that it?" Tears formed in her eyes.

I didn't know what to say. It felt as if I were carving up my own heart with a dull-edged blade.

I'd confronted the pale-faced man. I'd gone through a war I didn't believe in. I'd killed people before they could kill me. I'd witnessed both soldiers and innocents wiped out, obliterated in some cases, but nothing tore into my soul like having someone love me. Nothing made me want to run and hide more. Nothing made me feel more undeserving and more like a fraud than when I looked into her eyes.

I stood there, holding back the urge to run out the door, though I was aware of the outcome. I'd regret leaving Elisa the same way I regretted leaving Dawn. Mistakes that would haunt me, choices I could never take back.

Elisa reached her arms out to me. "Come here, Liam."

She took my hands and pulled me to her. I could feel her tears on my neck and then she whispered in my ear. "You're the one, Liam. You have to believe that. You're the one."

I couldn't describe the emotion that overcame me. It was something more than love. I could only relate the feeling to how the Jesus freaks described being born again, how their hearts raced and their bodies shook, as if a new door inside of them suddenly opened and everything about themselves and the world they had inhabited had changed in an instant.

Elisa pressed her body up against mine, as if trying to burrow inside of me, but then she took a step back from me and began unbuttoning her blouse. Her breaths were short and hard. She pulled off her blouse and quickly unzipped her skirt, letting it drop to her feet. I watched as she unhooked her bra and slipped out of her panties. Elisa stood in front of me, completely naked and completely vulnerable.

"Now you, Liam," she said.

For the first time ever in my life, I was hesitant to be naked in front of a woman. I found myself fumbling with the buttons of my shirt, trembling as I removed the last bit of clothing.

Her eyes searched me as if attempting to find what it was that I had been hiding from her. I folded my arms in front of my chest as if hit by a cold breeze.

"Drop your arms, Liam."

I let them fall to my side. I felt more naked than I'd ever been before.

Elisa shot a quick smile that I was unable to read. She took my hand and led me into her bedroom. She climbed on her bed and lay on her back, leaning on her elbows.

"Turn out the lights, Liam."

I clicked off the switch. The room fell dark, almost pitch black. "I'm right here," she whispered.

I reached out to her in the darkness, knowing she'd be there.

We talked most of the night, at one point we brought our reheated dinner to bed with us. We shared with each other everything about our lives from childhood until now.

Almost everything. I held back the truth about my family's involvement in the deaths and lies that surrounded my father's murder, deciding at that moment that I would never reveal it to her.

Then, when we ran out of words, we lay together in each other's arms and slowly fell asleep.

I awoke around five a.m. Elisa slept softly next to me. I kissed her cheek and climbed out of bed. I walked out to the living room and turned a table lamp. I picked up her photo album. I sat on the couch and removed the pictures of her and James Fordham. She looked happy and almost innocent. But he had a knowing look. Every time I met him he had that look. It was the very definition of a shit-eating grin.

He wasn't who I thought he was.

I placed the pictures back inside the photo album and returned it to the bookcase. I wasn't getting anywhere with finding out who killed the Garzas and Ramona Ortiz. But Fordham knew something about them. If anything was going to happen, I had to make it happen. I wrote Elisa a note telling her that I loved her and that I couldn't wait to see her again tonight.

I placed the note on my pillow and watched her as she slept. I made a promise to never do anything to hurt her, and then I kissed her forehead and headed out to my car.

CHAPTER THIRTY-ONE

A distant light rose from the east, though it was too early for sunrise. I drove north up Pacific Coast Highway, a false dawn behind me—just another lie, this one disguising itself as the beginning of a brand-new day.

There were few cars on PCH, so I hit the pedal and rolled down the window. The cold air felt good on my face. As I approached Pacific Harbor, I pulled off the highway and headed to Bayshore Drive, where Fordham owned a home that overlooked the water. I had no idea what I thought I'd find or what I was even looking for, but I wanted to check out the place where James Fordham lived.

It was still dark as I drove down Bayshore, a rich man's wet dream of a street. Palm trees and thick bushes covered the front of the homes, a tropical feel at the edge of the desert. The backside of the homes, though, that was the big prize. Big glass windows overlooking the bay, docks where you could park your yachts, patios where you could sip your wine and watch as the big boats sailed out to sea. Then there were the tourists in their tiny rented motorboats, the people who couldn't afford to live there, trying to catch a quick glimpse of the wealthy, trying to imagine how it might be to be one of them.

I was one of them. I might be estranged from my family and my inheritance waiting for me to reach thirty, but I was still one of them. I got passes in life because I was one of them. I got laid because I was one of them. I never had to worry about getting what I wanted because I was one of them. But if the average Joe thought superior men lived in these dream homes, they'd be horrified to learn the truth. The rich aren't better, they aren't more refined, and they aren't worth bowing down to. When rich men miss the toilet bowl when taking a pee, they have a maid to clean up after them. When rich men tell bad jokes, everyone laughs, and when rich men kill people, they get away with it.

Fordham's house sat at the end of the street, next to a little private beach. Though it was still dark, I crept along a patch of white sand that sat next to his house. I gazed at Fordham's white yacht, *The Serpent's Dream*. Over a hundred feet long. I could only imagine the guests and the parties that he had hosted.

I returned to the street and made my way to the front of his house. A light was on, but his home was shielded by a wall, behind which stood tall trees with thick branches covered in leaves. I caught the scent of jasmine drifting from his house, which sent a chill down the back of my neck. Could this have been where Ramona Ortiz was murdered?

I could see it. Her confronting him about the pregnancy. Him strangling her as she clung to a jasmine bush, fighting for her life. I got back into my car and drove slowly by Fordham's house, my headlights off. The gate from the driveway began to open and I spotted Glenn's car. I watched as James Fordham came out of the house with Glenn and Isabelle. They didn't look my way. Fordham patted Glenn on the shoulder, and then Glenn stepped into the driver's seat. Fordham took Isabelle into his arms and kissed her on the mouth. She didn't resist. After the kiss, he led Isabelle to the passenger side of the car, opening the door for her. I looked at Glenn, his head down, trying not to witness his wife and James Fordham locked together in another long kiss.

I drove off, the three not noticing my car. I slumped over in pain like I'd been kicked in the gut, the sunrise behind me looking like a lit match head searching for a fuse.

I couldn't begin to process what I had witnessed. Some acts are beyond comprehension, beyond all rational thought, beyond all that you can accept. But you can't ignore them. Though you had to wonder that if there was a God, he must have realized long ago that we were his mistakes, and somewhere in another solar system must lie another planet, a planet where, finally, he could be proud of his creations.

I called Lonnie as soon as I made it home. I hoped a couple hours out on the water might help wash off the stench of what I'd seen. A few other surfers were out on their boards, bobbing up and down in the water. The waves had disappeared for now. We carried our boards to my usual spot away from the pier where we could be alone. We paddled out knowing it might be awhile before any sets came in. The ocean provided only ripples, but it felt good to be out on the water lying on our backs under the bright morning sun.

"Where's Wyatt?" Lonnie asked.

"I don't know. I haven't seen him out here the past couple of days."

"Maybe he found another surf spot."

"Could be," I said, though that didn't sound like Wyatt. He found some strange peace here.

"What's wrong, Liam?"

Lonnie had developed a keen sense of when someone needed help. Whether it was a result of the war, or from his mail-order religious training, I had no idea.

"What do you think God thinks of us?" I asked.

"You believe in God now?"

"Just humor me."

Lonnie didn't answer right away, nor did I push him for a response. After a moment he said, "Maybe the same as we think of ourselves."

"What do you mean?"

"Wars, holocausts, murders, cheating, stealing ... Why do we take part in those things when we know they're wrong? Do things like that make people feel good about themselves?"

"I'm sure there are probably a lot of folks who feel good about those things," I said, thinking of my family. "As long as it benefits them, they can justify it, so they're fine."

"But they don't matter."

"Then who the hell does?"

"The rest of us, the ones who feel God's pain."

Even though Lonnie had a way of talking in circles, I tried to let what he said sink in. I rolled onto my stomach, the water dancing clumsily beneath us.

"Do you ever think about the people you killed over there?" Lonnie asked.

"Over there" meaning Vietnam. Since my return we mostly discussed our war experience in the vaguest terms: the food, the women, platoon leaders, the smell and the dampness of the jungle, the overbearing humidity, but rarely anything about us killing the other side. I didn't know how many I had killed. Sometimes I shot at an unseen enemy, maybe my bullets hit some of them, I wasn't sure. But I remember three, their faces unforgettable. Each one wanted me dead. Each one died because I had acted first. Would they have remembered my face if they had killed me? I don't know. It didn't matter anyway.

"Sometimes," I said, "mostly at night. Something will trigger it, like the wind rattling in the trees, car backfires, stuff like that. What brought this up?"

"I don't know. Dreams mostly. Nightmares, I guess, bad things. Recurring ones."

"Yeah, I've had the dreams. Usually I'm surrounded. I can't see them, but they're there, you know? I'm just waiting for them to open fire on me, but all I hear are their voices. Scary shit." The nightmares had begun to recede, but sometimes they'd creep back in and as hard as I tried to wake myself from them, I could still feel their presence, as if the VC were creeping through my house, setting down landmines for me to trip off.

"I'm glad I'm not alone," he said. "Sometimes it's hard for me to separate the nightmares from the real thing, you know."

"You want to talk about it?"

Lonnie forced a smile. "There's nothing to talk about." Before he paddled back to shore he said, "Hope tomorrow is better than today."

I didn't know if he was referring to the surf or his dreams. I stayed out in the water. I watched Lonnie as he stretched out on the sand, alongside his board, his hands again covering his face, whether to block the sun or to hide from his thoughts, I didn't know.

His question about killing people unsettled me. While in Vietnam I found myself constantly on edge, though some of my nightmares revolved around the pale-faced man. He'd appear in my dreams, not as someone who wanted to kill me, but as a confidant of sorts, whispering to me about how easy it was to kill, and that after your first kill, it only got easier. Everyone I had killed had been in self-defense. But the pale-faced man was right. Each time it had less of an effect on me. I don't know what that meant, nor was it something I wanted to know.

I rolled off my board and into the water. I felt my body constrict as the cold ocean water grabbed me, but after a few strokes, my body opened up and a wave of peace came over me. I swam down about fifteen feet to the bottom, running my hands through the sand. Above me, the blue ocean was lit up from the sun and I could see the sky, bright, clear, and alive. I stayed down under the water and sat in the sand, my eyes closed. I felt no urgency to move. A rush of water suddenly swept by me and pushed me off the bottom. Looking up, I saw the aftermath of a huge wave that had just crashed above me. I swam to the surface, the water around me unsettled. A mixture of groans and cheers came from the surfers down by the pier. Some caught it, some missed it. I examined the horizon, the ocean had begun to settle down, just like that. No sets were forming. It was a rogue wave that came out of nowhere.

My board had washed to shore, waiting for me in the wet sand. I didn't see Lonnie. I guessed he had headed back to his church. I wanted to stay out in the ocean and wait for the next wave, no matter how long it took. But my thoughts had already shifted to what I'd witnessed last night between James Fordham and Isabelle as Glenn stood by and watched, the odor of jasmine as stifling as smog. I knew learning the truth about what happened between them would be another punch to my soul, a soul that staggered forward like a punch-drunk fighter, unable to protect itself from further beatings.

CHAPTER THIRTY-TWO

I stumbled into work an hour late. The predawn spectacle I'd witnessed played in my mind like a bad movie. A few years ago, I experienced the horror of seeing my sister Marie going down on Glenn. Was what I'd seen last night some kind of sick way of Glenn repenting for his sins? I knew that whatever I'd faced in life, Isabelle had confronted much worse—maybe it was her getting back at both our father and Glenn and anyone else in her life who had fucked her over.

The phone rang and I stared at it for a moment, not sure if I wanted to pick it up.

It was April Fairchild. "He's here, Liam. Charlie Moran."

"Is he with anyone?"

"No, it's just him. But he's waiting for someone. He's twitchy, like he's feeling caged in."

I told her I'd be right there. On my way out, I stopped by Helen's desk to let her know I was going out to cover a story.

"He wants to talk to you."

"Who?"

"Mr. Daniels. He wants to talk to you."

"Tell him I'm working on a lead, that I should be back in a couple hours."

Traffic was light, but the other drivers seemed disconnected. Stopping at odd times, drifting into other lanes, it was as if everyone's lives were slightly off balance. It took fifteen minutes to get to The Alamo, though it felt much longer. I parked on the street about a block down and ran to the bar.

I blinked a few times, trying to get my eyes to adjust to the dimness of The Alamo. I scanned the room. No Charlie Moran. No April Fairchild. In fact, the bar was empty except for Patsy Cline on the jukebox singing "Why Can't He Be You?"

I called out April's name and glanced behind the bar. Nothing. The back door that led out to the alley was slightly ajar, casting a blade of sunlight on the floor. I headed to the back exit, when April rushed through the door, blood on her hands, confusion on her face.

"I have to call the police."

I ran out the back door. Charlie Moran lay on the asphalt, his shirt red with blood, his face frozen, and his mouth open as if he'd been shot while trying to talk his way out of death. I stared at him, looking for any sign of life, but he was gone. It took me a full minute to get the strength to walk back inside.

"Was he with anyone?" I asked April.

She took a slug of whiskey. "No. He was alone the whole time and all of a sudden he was gone and then I heard a shot. I ran outside but didn't see anything except for Moran on the ground."

I glanced at my watch, wondering when the police would arrive when I heard the first siren. April nodded her head and I followed her into the alley. Nothing had changed. Charlie Moran didn't pop up like he was faking, nor had his body disappeared like in a cheap movie.

We stayed near the exit. Two black-and-whites pulled up and stopped about ten feet from Moran's body. Greene's unmarked police car came from the other end. When he stepped out of his car, he caught my eyes and then looked away.

"Who found him?" he asked.

"I did," April said. She walked over to Greene and told him what she knew.

I leaned against the wall, trying to figure out who might have killed him. A few officers searched the alley while another drew a white circle around the bullet casing he'd spotted.

The police radios blasted out different voices, giving the whole scene an unearthly feel. My mind jumped to what Larry the bum had told me about the night Ramona Ortiz had died, about hearing voices that sounded like they were from outer space. Was it a police radio he heard? Could the other car at the marsh that might have been a detective's car?

I looked at Greene. I could tell he saw me out of the corner of his eye, then he turned his back to me. My stomach rolled and my breath caught as I stared at the body of Charlie Moran. I didn't know if he'd been playing Greene or not. Maybe they were in it together until ... until what?

I slipped back inside the bar and headed out the front door. I didn't look back. I climbed in my car and drove off, not knowing what I was going to do or where I was headed. I should have stayed and pretended to do my job, ask questions, write up a story, and file it. I couldn't fake it, though. The more I dug into this story, the more people had died. People I knew. People I had talked to. I wondered if Elisa could be in any danger. I didn't think so, but then Dawn shouldn't have been in any danger, either.

I wanted to take Elisa and head down the coast and into Mexico. I still had that small trust fund I hadn't touched. We could rent a little house on the beach. I'd teach her to surf and we could fish the waters, and on the weekends we could drive into town and enjoy a nice dinner under the string lights on an outdoor patio, just the two of us, the waves crashing in the distance. But the killings here would go on. Innocent people would die. And Ramona Ortiz and the Garzas would never get any justice.

I thought about Charlie Moran lying dead in the alley, the expression on Greene's face as he stood over him. I didn't know if it was residual Catholic guilt or a sense of journalistic responsibility, but I stopped at a Richfield gas station and called Helen at *The Tribune*.

"There was a murder at The Alamo bar. Can you get someone over here?"

"Why aren't you covering it?" Helen asked.

"I'm on another story."

"Don't forget, Daniels wants to talk to you."

I told her I wouldn't forget, but before I hung up, Helen said someone from the Hall of Records had called and said I should drop by.

I thanked her and hung up. I stayed inside the phone booth for a moment, relishing the silence. The glass walls kept the sound from seeping inside, but the air was stale and reeked of years-old sweat and tobacco. I opened the door, feeling the ocean air greet me, yet it brought me no relief. Standing out in the open only made me feel exposed and vulnerable.

I found Cora Coleman standing behind the front counter of the records office smoking a cigarette. She wore a navy-blue skirt and a red blouse. A big change from the beige she wore when I first met her. She smiled when she saw me and stamped out her cigarette in the ashtray.

"I heard you called," I said.

"Yes, I did. Something came by my desk today. It may not mean much, but I thought you'd want to know. It's regarding the marshland you asked about."

"What about it?"

"Wyatt Fordham no longer owns it. James Fordham does."

"Wyatt sold it?"

"That's what's interesting. He didn't sell it, but James Fordham is the new owner."

"How can that be?"

"I don't know. Maybe it was a gift to his dad."

After the way Wyatt's father had treated him, I doubted he'd ever give his dad something like that, especially if his dad was planning to develop the land.

"Have you heard anything about it being rezoned?"

"Not a thing."

I didn't get it. According to James Fordham's lawyer, Fordham wanted to develop the marshland. Wyatt Fordham, I knew, was against any development along the coast and was an active protester when it came to protecting the environment. If Wyatt hadn't sold his father the land, then how did James Fordham come to own it?

"Are you okay, Liam?" Cora asked me.

"I don't know."

I didn't know if Charlie Moran's murder had anything to do with the land or not. But the killings had to be related. And now James Fordham's name kept popping up. Somehow, he got his hands on Wyatt's land, and no one had seen Wyatt around lately. Fordham clearly knew Ramona Ortiz and she ended up dead, and then there was that scene with Glenn and my sister last night. A scene I couldn't begin to understand, yet one I felt compelled to piece together.

CHAPTER THIRTY-THREE

I drove up the long driveway that ran up to my parents' home, under a canopy of eucalyptus trees. Next, I was greeted by the sweet scent of oranges that floated down from the groves that surrounded the estate. It brought back memories of a home that had once been a source of peace and happiness, where I had lived a worry-free life oblivious to the horrors that ran through the house.

I knocked on the front door. I had a key and could have gone right in, but doing that would have made me feel as though I belonged in this house and was somehow complicit in all the evil that emanated from its walls. I knocked again, but no one answered. I walked over to the side gate and peered over it. Nothing. A slight breeze came up, rustling the branches of the trees, and pushing the scent of jasmine around me like a straightjacket.

I opened the gate and stepped down to the patio, where I found Isabelle. It was warm in the sun, yet she sat in the cool shade wearing sunglasses and a long black winter coat, an unlit cigarette in her hand. She sat as still as a statue, her stare fixated on an empty sky.

The difference between the Isabelle I knew growing up and the one I saw now were as different as the moon was from the sun.

"Why did you come back to La Bolsa, Liam?" she asked without looking at me. "Why would you do such a thing?"

I told her what I'd kept telling myself. "I had nowhere else to go."

She grimaced and turned to me. "There's always somewhere else, but what do I know? I'm regarded as the crazy one, aren't I?"

"You're not crazy, Isabelle. I think you're the only sane one in the family."

"Wouldn't that be ironic?" she said.

I pulled a chair up next to her and sat down. Isabelle had always treated me as if I were her favorite. She had looked after me in her own way. Marie had always looked upon me as either competition or as a disgrace to the Sol family name and all they had built.

"Are Mom or Marie here?"

"They had business to attend to. They should be back soon."

The hardest part about going to Vietnam had been leaving Isabelle, though at the time I didn't know where she was living, as my mother had placed in her in a mental hospital and wouldn't tell me where it was. Still, part of me felt as if I should have stayed around just in case she needed me.

"I missed you, Isabelle."

Her mouth twitched as if she had tried to smile but didn't have the strength nor the will to pull it off. I wondered what else the treatments had taken from her. If you forget your past, no matter how horrible, would that turn you into someone else? And if she did remember who she once was, did those memories haunt her?

"I missed you, too, Liam. I worried about you over there, especially when you quit writing to me. I thought you had been captured, or worse."

I didn't tell her that our mother had intercepted my letters to her. I didn't want to make things any worse. "I meant to. Things were just crazy over there. I'm sorry."

"Don't be sorry, Liam. I'm just glad you're safe."

"How are Mom and Marie treating you?"

"Treating me? You make me sound like a patient. I'm taking care of myself now, so I'm in good hands." She shook her head. "But I know what they expect from me." *They.* "I know how I'm supposed to act. I can be quite good at it when the need arises."

When it came to public appearances, Isabelle always dug deep to find her stage persona. With Glenn running for Congress, I couldn't imagine how that must have been wearing on her.

"Is everything okay between you and Glenn?" I tried to see through her sunglasses, to see the light in her eyes, but all I saw was my own reflection.

"Define okay. How does he treat me? Like he always has. He doesn't understand how much work it takes for me to make him look good. We all have our roles in the family, don't we? Mother and Marie are the smart ones, you're the prodigal son, I'm the face, and Glenn, Glenn's Pinocchio. My husband desperately wants to believe that he is in control of his own fate but is too vain to realize that he doesn't even own himself."

She turned to me and removed her sunglasses. Her eyes appeared faded, as if someone had tried to erase them. "And that's the secret to life, isn't it? Controlling your own fate. It's something we all have to learn. Something I wish I'd learned earlier."

I thought of what my father had done to her, the years of sexual abuse, and then, years later, what she had done to him. Isabelle placed her sunglasses back on and patted my hand. "You're a good man. I like Elisa, you know. When I met her, I couldn't help but picture her with you."

"I like her."

"Like?"

"Okay, love."

Isabelle smiled, but it disappeared in an instant.

"What brings you by, Liam?"

"I saw you and Glenn at James Fordham's house. What were you doing there?" I asked, trying to push away the image of her kissing Fordham.

Isabelle tilted her head as if trying to recall the moment. "Why would I be at his house?"

"I don't know, but I saw you there."

"What are you talking about, Liam? I despise the man." Her voice as flat as when I arrived, her expression unchanged. I wondered how far gone Isabelle had become. She didn't appear to be lying, but I knew what I had witnessed.

"You were there, Isabelle."

Her mouth quivered for a moment then she stared at her unlit cigarette.

"What are you doing here?" a voice said, and we both flinched at the sound. It was Marie. "Isabelle, is everything all right?"

"She's fine," I said.

Marie regarded me like she always had, with her usual look of disdain. "I was talking to Isabelle," she said.

Isabelle didn't respond. She crushed the unlit cigarette into her hand.

"Liam, can I talk to you?" Marie asked.

I glanced at Isabelle, who turned away from me, her face pointing again at a blank sky. Two tears fell from behind her sunglasses and streamed down her cheek.

"I love you, Isabelle," I whispered.

Isabelle nodded her head, then grabbed my hand.

"It was only a dream, Liam. Just a bad dream." Then she let go of my hand.

I looked at her, confused.

"Can I get you anything?" Marie asked Isabelle.

"I'm fine. I'll be in shortly. The two of you can go on inside."

As we walked back into the house, Marie asked me what Isabelle and I had been talking about.

"Nothing, just old times," I said, not knowing how to respond.

Marie led me into the kitchen.

"Can I get you anything?"

I told her no and took a seat at the kitchen table. Marie poured herself a glass of white wine and sat on the other end of the table.

"Where's Mom?"

"Upstairs, changing clothes."

I breathed a sigh of relief, hoping that Marie didn't hear it.

"What did you want to talk about?" I asked.

"It's Isabelle. She's ... bringing up the past with her is a bad idea."

"Why?"

"There are certain things she shouldn't remember."

Certain things. Marie was good at masking ugly truths like incest and murder.

"She must realize there are missing pieces of her past, that her memory has holes in it. It's must be difficult for her."

"It's better this way," Marie said.

I wondered what kind of life she was living. Isabelle couldn't even remember visiting James Fordham, let alone kissing him.

"Marie, what do you know about James Fordham?"

"Other than he used to sleep with your girlfriend?"

Marie threw the comment at me like a hand grenade. I wondered if she was proud of herself.

"She told me all about it, Marie. Now what do you know about him?"

"Does this have anything to do with that story you're working on? The dead Mexicans?" Marie asked.

I didn't get it. Marie had brown skin and black hair, all from our Mexican father. You could barely see any Irish in her, yet she said *Mexicans* like some people said *criminals*. But her question came out of the blue.

"Why would you think they're related?" I asked.

"Why else would you ask about James Fordham?"

"His name just keeps coming up, that's all."

Marie opened her mouth as if to respond but was interrupted by our mother.

"Well, if it isn't my son. The one who says he can live without us, yet he always returns. I wonder why that is." My stomach constricted. My mother's Irish brogue sounded thicker than usual. She wore a bright emerald green dress, and she made the room smell of hairspray.

She pulled up a chair next to Marie. I kept myself from saying hello to her.

"You were asking about James Fordham?" my mother asked.

I didn't know how much to tell them; I didn't know how close they were to him.

"Just wondering if he's supporting Glenn. I saw a picture of him and Luther Bennett in the paper recently." I decided to go one step further. "And Ramona Ortiz, the woman whose body was found at Sunset Marsh, she was with them."

My mother and Marie exchanged a look of concern.

"Is Isabelle in danger?" I asked.

"What kind of nonsense are you bringing up?" My mother said. "Isabelle is in no danger. And James Fordham is supporting us. I don't know anything about any picture in the newspaper."

My mother rose from her chair. "We must leave soon, Marie." She looked at me. "Liam, I'm sure we'll see you here again."

She left the room, the scent of her hairspray floating above us like a poisoned cloud.

Marie gave me a concerned look. "What aren't you telling us, Liam?"

The last thing I wanted to do was tell Marie about what I'd seen. "Nothing."

"Whatever it is you think you know, stay out of it. We do a lot of work with James Fordham, both in business and in politics. You have a way of bringing trouble to us. That's something we don't need, Liam."

She stormed out without saying another word.

I looked out to the patio. Isabelle hadn't moved from her seat. She still stared off into space as if she were under a spell.

Riding down the driveway, I felt as if my car had taken on unwelcome passengers. I had come to realize the ghosts of my family weren't about to leave me alone.

CHAPTER THIRTY-FOUR

I sat at my desk, trying once again to run through what I knew. I had four victims, all of them of Mexican descent. Julio Garza was killed two years ago by a hit-and-run driver. From what Charlie Moran told me, Julio had some dirt on an influential family in La Bolsa. Two years later, his mother was strangled in her home right after my article on her came out. Ramona Ortiz was also found strangled and her body dumped into Sunset Marsh. The common denominator was Charlie Moran. He knew the Garzas and he knew Detective Greene. Additionally, Ramona Ortiz had been desperately trying to find Moran, but why? And now Charlie Moran ends up shot dead in the alley behind The Alamo bar. So, who could be behind the murders?

James Fordham for one. He was certainly influential, and I had no doubt that he was corrupt. Maybe Julio had dirt on him. Maybe Moran confronted Fordham. Also, Fordham knew Ramona Ortiz and Ortiz was pregnant at the time of her death. Fordham was also the one who had me yanked from covering her murder. And now he owned the land at Sunset Marsh.

Then there's Detective Greene. He'd had an affair with Julio, which, if word got out, would have ruined him. But Julio Garza's death didn't free Greene; in fact, it may have put him in more jeopardy as

Charlie Moran found out about the affair and used that information to pressure Greene. Which meant that Greene did have a motive to kill Moran. Also, Larry the bum heard what might have been a police radio in the background when Ramona Ortiz's body was dumped at the marsh. Did she have something on Greene as well?

There was a reason for each of the murders. And finding those reasons would lead to the killer. The answer was there, but I couldn't tie it together. Or maybe something else was going on, something I couldn't see. While I knew it wasn't my job to solve the crimes, I seemed to be the only one willing to investigate them.

"Sol, get your ass in here. Now!" shouted Daniels.

I dawdled for a moment before heading to his office.

"Sit down," he said.

I removed a pile of newspapers from a chair and sat down.

"If this is about me requesting another reporter to cover The Alamo murder—"

"Sol," he interrupted, "I called you in here. I talk."

He gave me that look again. The one where he wondered which was worse to deal with, me or a hemorrhoid.

"This is hard to say, but this is goodbye."

"You're firing me?" I shouldn't have been surprised. I hadn't written much at all since covering the Catalina Garza murder, and I knew that my questions were ruffling some big feathers.

"I'm not firing you. I'm the one who's leaving."

"I thought you liked it here."

"I do, but the people who own the paper don't like me here. They like me in Brawley."

"That's not a promotion, is it?" Brawley was a dry, dusty agricultural town not far from the Mexican border.

"No, it's not. Listen, these things happen. It's the nature of the business."

"There's more to this."

"People with money and power put pressure on the paper's owner.

They live in a different world than we do. Well, maybe not you."

"I haven't written anything. I'm still working on the story. I have more questions than answers."

"Well, someone's worried."

James Fordham must have seen my car outside of his house when he was with Glenn and Isabelle. He thought I was watching him. That must have been what triggered Daniels's getting fired.

"It's not your fault. Hey, we almost committed journalism. Besides, this isn't my first rodeo, Sol. I'll be fine."

"Why didn't they just get rid of me?"

"I'm sure they didn't want to piss off your family. In any case, you're off the story. That's all they care about."

Daniels smiled and patted my back.

"You were doing good work. Sometimes these stories take more time than we'd like, but that's how it is."

"When's your last day?"

"Today."

I didn't see any boxes in his office.

"I'm leaving my shit here. The next guy can deal with it. He'll be here next week. They didn't tell me his name or anything about him. The newspaper world is a damn funny business," he said, as if the joke was on him.

"When do you start your job?"

"Oh, I'm not going to Brawley. My ex moved up to Idaho. We've been talking. Maybe I can find work at one of the local papers."

Daniels revealed a hint of a smile and shrugged his shoulders. The most cynical man I'd ever met just showed a bit of optimism after getting canned. I had to admire that.

"Everly will be the temp editor until the new guy arrives."

"I'm not done with this," I told him.

"They're not going to run it. They're probably going to drop it altogether."

"They can't do that."

"Of course, they can," he said. "Listen, Sol. I know the editor over at the *Herald Examiner* in LA. If you're looking for a new gig, let me know. I'll put in a good word for you."

"Thanks," I said.

Daniels stood up, indicating the meeting was over. We shook hands.

"You're all right, you know that? Better than I thought you'd be."

"Good luck in Idaho," I said. "You know, with everything."

"Good luck to you as well."

I left his office feeling as if the rules had suddenly changed. The owners of *The Tribune* didn't want one of their wealthy friends investigated. Yet, the rules also changed in a good way. I was no longer beholden to the paper. The rules no longer applied to me. And this wasn't just about journalism. This was about finding the truth. Once I found that, then I'd see about writing it down.

I just didn't have a clue as to what to do next.

As if on cue, Guy Watson walked up to me, red-faced and out of breath.

"Liam, I just got back from The Alamo."

"You're covering the Moran murder?"

"Why shouldn't I be? You're the one who didn't want to cover it."

He had me there. "What did you find out?"

He pulled up a chair. "I've never covered a murder before. I've never seen a dead body."

I knew that could be hard to handle. "Did you do okay?"

He nodded his head. "But this detective ..." Watson thumbed through his notes. "Greene. Detective Greene. He said he wants to talk to you." He looked up from his notes. "He said you shouldn't have left the crime scene."

I'd deal with Greene later. "Anything else?"

Watson scratched his head. "Well, you were there, Liam. Did you see the murder?"

"No. I arrived after it happened. I didn't see anything. Just his body in the back alley."

Watson dutifully wrote it down in his notebook and then gave me a sheepish look.

"Why didn't you stay and do your job?"

Now he wants to be a real reporter. "Conflict of interest," I said, hoping that would satisfy him.

He jotted that down as well.

"Did Greene give you any theories as to what happened?" I asked.

"He said it looked like a robbery gone wrong."

Guy Watson bit one side of his lip and then the other.

"What?"

"This Detective Greene. A bundle of nerves he was. Almost like he was scared of what they'd find."

"What do you mean?"

"Acting really jumpy. And he kept asking me why you left the scene."

I didn't like this. Paranoia was building up inside of me. Greene had a strong motive to kill Charlie Moran. But why did he want to talk to me? What did he think I knew? Then again, maybe Greene had nothing to do with Moran's murder. Maybe Greene was unnerved because the killings were getting too close to him. Still, the image of Moran's dead body lying in the alley formed in my mind. Then I thought of Dawn, and how I had led a cold-blooded killer to her door. I didn't want to get caught unprepared.

I drove home and picked up the Browning from my closet. I checked the magazine. Twelve rounds. Then I headed to Elisa's. I didn't think she was in any danger, but I never thought that Dawn had been in any kind of danger either.

I placed the gun in her nightstand drawer. I knew I was being overly cautious, but Moran's murder left me shaken. On my way to Elisa's I had picked up a couple chicken dinners from Donahoo's along with a big bag of their seasoned fries.

"You cooked dinner!" she said after coming through the front door.

"I almost did," I replied. Elisa slid up to me and kissed me. She hadn't locked the front door. "Go get comfortable. I have some more cooking to do."

"You mean taking the chicken from the box and putting it on a plate?"

"It's not as easy at looks."

Elisa laughed and waltzed into the bedroom to change clothes. I locked the front door. Nothing is going to happen, I told myself, just keep an eye out.

After dinner, we cuddled on her couch and watched *The Odd Couple* and *Room 222* before heading to bed. I held her in my arms until she fell asleep, my eyes wide open, my body flinching at the smallest of sounds.

Elisa had a troubled sleep, often mumbling things I couldn't understand, her head at times shaking back and forth. Perhaps she was feeding off my worries, or perhaps she was having nightmares about her father's death. As bad as my father was, I still found that I missed his presence in my life. I knew, too, he'd do anything to protect me. I wondered if that's how it was with most people, a drive to seek out and find comfort in those who would protect us, no matter if they were good or not. Maybe being protected was all that any us really craved.

Eventually, I dozed off only later to be awakened by Elisa. Her lips on mine, her body on top of me, pressed against me, her hands roaming my body. But it wasn't her. The voice was rough, a tongue scraped against my cheek like sandpaper. I opened my eyes and Greene lay on top of me, our clothes off. "You're going to like this," he whispered. We were in the back of his patrol car. Far-off voices filled the air. Greene's mouth opened, his breath reeking of Sunset Marsh, his tongue pushing through my lips, his hands trying to turn me over onto my stomach. I wasn't sure I had the strength to keep fighting him off. Then he had a smoking gun his hand and jammed the barrel against the side of my head. "You'd better do what I say," he said.

"No," I tried to yell, but I couldn't hear myself over his demands or the voices that spilled out over the police radio.

"Liam, Liam."

"No."

"Liam, it's me, Elisa. Wake up, you're having a nightmare."

I was back in her bedroom. Elisa sat next to me, dressed for work, her face filled with worry. I was out of breath, as if I'd just swum to shore from a long way out.

"Are you okay?" she asked, her hands gripping mine.

I nodded a yes, but I felt disoriented.

"I have to get to work. You sure you're fine?"

"Yeah, it was just a nightmare."

"The war?"

"Yes," I lied.

She kissed my cheek and said that she'd see me tonight. I waited until I heard her drive away and then I pulled the sheets away until I could finally catch my breath. I could count on one hand the number of dreams I'd had that involved other men, though they never went as far as a kiss. This one was different. I'd never had a dream where someone tried to rape me, at gunpoint no less, a dream where I didn't know if I was going to submit to being violated.

I was in no rush to start my day. The effects of the dream still lingered. After showering, I had toast and coffee for breakfast and read the morning edition of *The Register*. On page three was a short article about Charlie Moran's murder. It quoted Detective Greene as saying that it appeared to be a robbery gone wrong. All they said about Moran was that he was a local attorney. Nothing more. The end of his life limited to five paragraphs.

CHAPTER THIRTY-FIVE

If I was going to talk to Greene I wanted to be at the police station. If he had killed Moran, I didn't want to be alone. Ironically, I'd feel safer in the presence of his fellow officers.

"He's not here," the desk sergeant told me, a scowl on his sun-damaged face. His name tag read Sgt. Hanson.

"Do you know when he'll be in?"

Hanson responded with a bitter smile. He didn't like reporters and wasn't about to give me anything.

"Tell him I came by," I said. "He wanted to talk to me about the murder of Charlie Moran."

Hanson shot me his winning smile again.

I drove down Pacific Coast Highway. CCR's "Who'll Stop the Rain?" played on the radio. Though the morning was bright and sunny, the song seeped into my bones, making me feel cold and exposed.

The pure sunlight provided a deceptive tease. May Gray would set in again, and then would be followed by June Gloom, making La Bolsa feel as if it were set in a far-off land, bathed in a dull glow with promises of summer's arrival feeling like a cruel joke.

But overcast or sunny, every late spring and through the summer, kids would find their way to the beach, all part of the annual Southern

California migration process. Pretty girls in their new bikinis, the boys showing off their new muscles that had been worked under weight machines over the winter, both sexes hoping to end their summer with bronzed bodies, tales of love lost and found, until, in a few years' time, when they, too, would be replaced by newer and younger versions of themselves, while they settled down, turning into the kind of people they never thought they'd become, all under an uncaring California sun.

I never thought of becoming anything. I had only cared about the here and now and the eternal rhythm of the ocean. Yet, in Vietnam it was all about survival and hoping to come home in one piece. I came home safely but hadn't given a thought to my life other than I wanted to find a place to live in peace. That changed quickly with the Catalina Garza story. I liked the rush tracking down a story gave me. How what I did mattered. I may have been off the story, but I wasn't going to let that stop me from finding out the truth.

I drove by Johnny Bob's and then The Driftwood. Greene wasn't at his usual hang-outs. La Bolsa was a small town and I knew we'd cross paths soon, I was sure of that. I just wanted to be in control of the when and where.

Back at work, I found a large yellow envelope on my chair, my name written on it along with *Personal and Confidential*, nothing else. I opened the envelope and pulled out a set of black-and-white photographs. I stared at them, my stomach turned in pain as if some creature had reached inside me and clawed out my gut. Each picture more damning than the next. I collapsed into my chair, unable to take my eyes off the images.

Elisa, naked and in the arms of another man. The other man being Glenn. With each consecutive photo, another dull-edged knife twisted and carved its way into my soul: Glenn kissing her breast. Glenn taking her from behind. Glenn on top of her, touching her, tasting her, penetrating her.

I dropped the photos on my desk, then realized they were in

full view of anyone who might pass by. Though my hands trembled, I gathered up the photos and placed them inside the envelope. I grabbed it and marched to Helen's desk.

"Do you know who dropped this off?" I asked.

Helen stared at the envelope, perplexed. "I found it on my desk about an hour ago. I stepped away for a moment to use the ladies' room and when I returned, it was there. It had your name on it. Did I do something wrong?"

"No, Helen, you didn't do anything wrong."

"Are you feeling well, Liam? You look a little pale."

"I'm going home. Let Daniels know for me."

"He's already gone, sweetie. He's not coming back."

"I guess it doesn't matter then."

Helen tilted her head. "Hope you feel better, hon."

I sat in my car with the windows rolled up and scanned the pictures. I was able to force back the waves of nausea that ran through me. I couldn't tell if Elisa was aware of the camera, but Glenn certainly was. One of the photos showed him kissing her nipple as he grinned at the camera. Elisa's face was turned away from the lens.

I recalled the morning after my first night with Elisa, when Glenn had appeared at breakfast, and the way he looked at her, the way he touched her, as if Elisa belonged to him. As if he had marked her place like a dog. Elisa had reassured me that she and Glenn never had a relationship. She didn't tell me about James Fordham, but when I asked her about it, she had told me the truth. Maybe to her it wasn't a relationship. Maybe it was just sex. I felt the dull edges of the knife carve itself deeper into my gut. I thought I could feel the blood leaking from inside of me, spilling down my intestines.

I shoved the pictures back into the envelope. I examined the handwriting, the scrawl appeared as if a child had written it. No note had been included, but the message was clear. Whoever it was, wanted me to back off.

CHAPTER THIRTY-SIX

I sat on her couch, waiting for her to come home. My gut churning. The pictures of her and Glenn were still in the envelope that sat next to me. Sunlight leaked between her blinds, casting shadows on me that resembled the bars of a jail cell.

I heard her key in the door. The click of the lock, the turning of the knob, and that slight cracking sound as the door opened.

"Liam! I didn't expect you." Her smile felt like a sword through my heart. She dropped her purse and briefcase and danced up to me, her arms out, wanting a hug. When she saw my expression and that I hadn't risen to meet her, she stopped.

"What's wrong?" She spotted the photo album on the coffee table. "You're not going to dig that up again, are you?"

I picked up the envelope and handed her to her. She glanced at the writing on the envelope.

"What's this? It has your name on it."

"Just open it," I said.

Elisa sat down next to me on the couch.

I watched her face as she slowly pulled out the pictures. Her eyes veered from curious to confusion to anger.

"What is this?"

"You tell me."

Elisa quickly flipped through the remaining pictures.

"Is this some kind of sick joke?" She tossed the pictures on the coffee table and then stood up.

"Someone faked these pictures, Liam. That's not ..."

"You?"

"I was never with Glenn. Never! Where did you get these?" She balled her hands into fists. "What is this shit, Liam? Tell me."

"Those are pictures of you and Glenn fucking." Hearing me say the words aloud felt like fingernails digging into my heart. "They're not faked. When were these taken?"

"I was never with him. You have to believe me." She grabbed one of the pictures and examined it. Then she dropped the picture and backed into the wall, and slowly slid down to the floor.

"These were taken at James Fordham's house. It's his bedroom," she whispered. Her eyes staring into some far-off place.

"Why would you be there with Glenn?"

Elisa shook her head a couple of times as if in disbelief. "I was never with Glenn!"

Elisa pulled her knees up in front of her and wrapped her arms around them. She closed her eyes for a moment and began shaking her head.

"Oh, God. He was with us one night. Just a casual evening, drinking, cheese and crackers, talking about trips we'd like to take. I remember I felt sleepy and wanted to go to bed. James took me upstairs to his room. He helped me get undressed, but I was too tired to put on pajamas, so I just fell asleep in my bra and underwear. When I woke up, I remember feeling different, I guess. I had a headache. I just thought I had a rough night sleeping ..." Elisa made a choking sound and tears rushed down her face. "How could they do this?"

They, meaning Fordham and Glenn. I sat on the floor next to Elisa and put my arm around her. She buried her face into my shoulder, not wanting me to see her. Her cries were a mix of sadness, horror, and rage. Elisa could stand with anybody in this world. She was strong and good and decent, and it tore my heart out seeing her broken like this. Her body couldn't stop shaking and she seemed to want to shrink down to nothing, so the heartbreak, betrayal, and the shame she felt couldn't find her.

Maybe I shouldn't have shown her the pictures. I didn't do it to protect her or to reveal to her who her enemies were. I did it because seeing them hurt me more than I could bear. By showing her the pictures I could take a self-righteous stand and be superior, and like a good Catholic, a martyr. A symbol of God knows what.

I felt her pain run through me like a surge of electricity, matched only in intensity by the hurt that I had caused her.

"Don't hate me, Liam. Please. I didn't do anything wrong. I love you."

"It's not your fault. It's not your fault," I repeated, but I knew the images would torment me for a long time.

I pulled Elisa closer, her heart pounding against me. I felt like a fraud, pretending to be her protector, when it was me who, after seeing the pictures, had lost faith in her, and now, suddenly, losing faith in myself because I had decided she was guilty before ever confronting her.

I wanted to grab the Browning from her bedroom and hunt down Glenn and then James Fordham and put a bullet in their heads. I had no idea what the two of them had to do with the murders, if anything, but what they had done to Elisa came as close to killing a person as anything I could imagine.

The urge for revenge rose up in me, but I couldn't leave Elisa alone. Her hands gripped me like a vise. After a while, her sobs began to subside, and I felt her body sag against mine. She took in a deep breath and kissed me on the cheek. Elisa rose slowly, her right hand on the wall for support. She wiped her eyes and pushed the hair from her face. She looked as if she had returned from a dark and unforgiving journey.

"I'm okay now, Liam."

Elisa steadied herself, then folded her arms in front of her chest and retreated to the bathroom. I heard the shower turn on and after a few minutes the steam from the hot water slipped under the door like smoke from a fire.

I wanted to see if she was okay, but I knew she needed this moment of privacy. She was singing, her voice broken and almost lost. The words crumbled out in Spanish. Though I didn't understand the language, I knew the song she was attempting to sing. It was the one she used to sing with her father when he was alive, the one that always made her world seem a little better than it was, "De Colores." She struggled to get the words to come out in song, but each time she failed, each time she pounded her fist on the tile, each time she broke down in tears, until finally all I heard was her crying.

Elisa came out of the bathroom, her hair damp and uncombed, wearing a long winter nightgown. She crawled into bed and pulled the covers up just below her chin.

"Can you turn out the lights, please?"

After I turned them off, she asked, "Do you still love me, Liam?"

"Yes," I said, sitting down next to her. "That's never going to change."

I made a promise to myself that I'd do whatever I could to ensure that no one would ever harm Elisa again.

CHAPTER THIRTY-SEVEN

I waited until Elisa had fallen into a deep sleep. I didn't like the idea of leaving her alone, but the rage that had built up inside of me was too great to hold down. I pulled out the gun from the drawer knowing that carrying a loaded weapon in my current state of mind was only asking for trouble. Maybe I should have waited until I had calmed down and then weighed the best course of action. But I was tired of thinking. Thinking wasn't going to settle anything. I didn't plan to use the gun. The gun was there for my own protection. At least that's what I told myself.

Before I left, I took another look at the photographs. I studied Elisa's expression in each picture. In some her face was hidden behind her hands or arms, in a couple of the others she was facing away from the camera or her hair covered her face, and in the rest her eyes were closed. In not one picture did it appear in any way that she was engaged or participating in what was going on. Glenn had no idea what he stole from her, or even worse, maybe he did, and whoever passed me the pictures had turned me into an accomplice to whatever was going to happen next.

I shoved the pictures back into the envelope and thought about ripping them to shreds or burning them in her fireplace. That wasn't my decision to make, though. It seemed cruel to leave them in her apartment, but after what had happened to her I felt she needed to be in control again. I didn't want to take that away from her.

When I was in junior high my friends and I used to talk about the magical properties of Spanish Fly, and how if you slipped it to the most beautiful woman on the planet, she would turn into a nymphomaniac and let you do anything you wanted to her. We all had some out-of-reach girl we said we wanted to give the pill to, whether she was a high school beauty or a movie star. In the back of our minds we all knew there was something wrong with giving a girl a pill like that, though none of us were willing to admit to it as we all wanted to be cool. In the end we wrote it off as a myth, and the whole idea of such a pill had pretty much vanished from our consciousness. I didn't know what drug had been given to her, but I knew Elisa didn't "let" Glenn do those things to her. And wrong was too small a word for it.

Two men, both of whom Elisa had trusted, had to be confronted: James Fordham, her boyfriend at the time, and the man she worked for, Glenn Frost. Then there was me. The man she was in love with. The man who jumped to conclusions and assumed the worst. Instead of being there for her, I had accused her before considering that maybe there was more to the story than what the pictures seemed to tell.

I slipped out the front door and climbed into my car. I turned off the radio. I didn't want any distractions. I turned left onto PCH and drove toward La Bolsa. As I passed Pacific Harbor, something hit me that I should have put together sooner, but through the fog of dealing with Elisa's pain, I missed it completely. The night I went to James Fordham's house, I witnessed Glenn and Fordham escorting Isabelle to the car, as if she were unable to walk by herself. The light in Isabelle's eyes when I visited her the following day reminded me of Elisa's when she tried to recall the night she had been raped by Glenn.

Did Glenn pimp his own wife, my sister, to James Fordham? The thought made my gut burn as if someone had injected acid into my stomach. Glenn had always struck me as a weak and ineffectual man, a man with no anchor, a man whose success was a result of the wishes of those whom he let control him. But this, what he did to Elisa, what he might have done to Isabelle, was beyond anything I could imagine.

I pulled up in front of my mother's house, with the now-familiar feeling of dread and hopelessness. When I got out of my car, I was hit by the suffocating smell of jasmine. The plants seemed to be working overtime to suppress the odor of moral decay that leaked out through the crevices of the house.

I had trouble working the key to the front door, as if the lock and key were at odds. It had been a long while since I used my key. I thought maybe they'd changed the lock, but then I heard the familiar click and I opened the door. I held the Browning in my hand. I didn't plan on shooting him, but Glenn had revealed a new side to me, and I didn't want to be caught empty-handed.

I stood in the entryway and heard the TV. I followed Carol Burnett's voice into the family room, where I stood in the doorway, unnoticed. My mother, Glenn, Isabelle, and Marie all sat on the floor next to the coffee table enjoying fondue. The scene felt like a Norman Rockwell painting reinterpreted by Edvard Munch. I studied Glenn. The way he had his hand on Isabelle's knee, the way he dipped his fork into the fondue pot, the way smugness hung on him like bad cologne. I held my right arm behind my back, hiding the gun. It took everything I had not to run over to him and stick the barrel down his throat.

Glenn glanced up and caught my eye. He showed me his practiced Pepsodent smile. There was no fear in his eyes. If he knew I'd seen the pictures of him and Elisa, he was doing a good job of concealing it.

"What brings you by, Liam?" my mother asked as if I was as welcome as a Fuller Brush salesman.

Marie sensed something, I could tell, but she said nothing.

"Liam," Isabelle said, "sit down with us and have some fondue." Her eyes were clearer than the last time I had seen her.

I didn't move. My eyes bore in on Glenn.

Marie finally spoke, "Liam, what is it?"

I wanted to protect Isabelle. I always wanted to protect Isabelle. But hiding the truth from her wasn't protecting her. And this wasn't only about her. It was about Elisa.

I pulled my arm from behind my back, revealing the gun. "Tell me, Glenn. How is it fucking a drugged-out woman?" The room narrowed as if Glenn and I were now the only ones in it.

I heard my mother gasp, then Marie's voice. "Liam, what's going on?"

"Glenn drugged Elisa and then fucked her while someone took pictures of them. I have them Glenn, the pictures, you can't deny it. Don't try."

"I have no idea what you're talking about."

I raised my arm, pointing the gun at him. I wasn't going to shoot him. The safety was on, but this was the only way that would get him to talk.

"I told you not to deny it."

The gun held steady in my hand.

"Liam, I don't know what game Elisa's playing, but—"

"Don't fucking blame Elisa for this. Who else did you do that to, Glenn? How many women?"

With his smugness wiped away, he looked like a little boy lost in a crowd, searching for his mother.

"I don't know what you're talking about."

My gut was roiling, cold sweat streaked down my back. "What about Isabelle? Did you drug her so James Fordham could rape her? Did you take pictures of that, too?"

Glenn's face turned pale. He searched the room looking for allies, but no one came to his aid. He was backed into a corner with no way out.

"I didn't have a choice," his voice small and feeble.

Isabelle let out a soft groan. Her eyes lost color as she put the pieces together. She looked at Glenn, then stood up and backed away a few steps before letting out a howl that I felt in my bones. Glenn slowly approached her.

"Isabelle, listen to me," he said.

Marie ran to Isabelle and stood guard in front of her, facing Glenn, creating a wall between him and Isabelle, like a lioness protecting her cub. Marie's teeth were clenched, her eyes focused dead on Glenn.

Isabelle could barely stand. The two men in Isabelle's life, her father and her husband, the ones who should have protected her, had betrayed and violated her, casting her into a hell I couldn't begin to imagine.

My mother stood up. "Glenn, tell us this isn't true. Tell us Liam's wrong."

Glenn covered his face. "I'm sorry."

"I said, tell us that Liam is wrong," she demanded.

"I'm sorry. It was James Fordham, he—"

Marie couldn't contain the rage in her voice. "He what Glenn? He made you drug Elisa? And you let him drug Isabelle so he could … tell me you didn't do that!"

"Yes. No. James Fordham knows things." His eyes darted at me, then quickly away. "Things that would kill everything we worked for. He could hurt us all."

"That doesn't explain why you drugged Elisa," I said. My finger pressing the trigger, the safety being the only thing preventing me from killing him.

"He wanted to see her with another man. He said it turned him on."

"And he took pictures of it?"

Glenn nodded his head.

"And you took pictures of Isabelle and him."

"No. No …"

"But you watched them?"

Before he could respond, Marie grabbed a fondue fork off the table and charged at him. Glenn held up his arms for protection, Marie knocked him to the floor, stabbing him repeatedly in the arm and shoulder trying to get at his face.

"How could you, you goddamned piece of shit," she screamed. "You fucking piece of shit!" Glenn's screeching pleas were drowned out by Marie's screams.

"Marie!" my mother yelled. "Liam, do something."

I dropped my gun on a chair and pulled Marie off Glenn. He stayed on the floor in the fetal position, his bloodied arms covering his face. Marie struggled against me, hissing at Glenn as I held her in a bear hug. Glenn remained on the floor, crying, and after a moment, I felt the fight leave Marie. She turned to me, her face buried into my chest. I pulled her close to me. Her body shuddered, but she didn't shed a tear. Whether she was overcome by sisterly love, jealousy, guilt, maybe all three, I didn't know. I had no childhood memories of Marie and me ever hugging. Maybe she hugged me because I was her brother. Maybe it was only because I was there, but all I knew was that I didn't want to let her go.

Then Marie whispered to me: "You know what to do, Liam."

Even in her most vulnerable moments, Marie could always find the ice in her heart.

Glenn had crawled up to his knees, continuing to sob. His hands were clasped together as if in prayer.

"I'm sorry, baby. I'm so, so sorry. We can … I love you, Isabelle. Please believe me. Please. You don't know how sorry I am. None of this was ever supposed to get out. It's him, baby, it's Fordham."

I looked over at my mother, sitting on the couch, a look of despair across her face. Was she blaming herself, or was there something else ticking in that brain of hers?

Then Glenn shouted "No!" followed by gunshots.

Isabelle held my Browning in her hand, pulling the trigger in rapid succession, the muzzle of the gun jerking left and right. Then she stopped, and the room fell silent. The only sound came from the

TV set, the live audience laughing hysterically.

It was a miracle that Glenn hadn't been hit. He had his hands out in front of him as if to block the bullets.

"No!" Isabelle screamed. She pressed the barrel of the gun to her own head. I pushed Marie aside and lunged at Isabelle. I knocked her hand away, just as the gun went off. I wrestled it from her and then cradled Isabelle in my arms.

"No, Liam. I want to die. Please let me die."

Plaster chips fell to the floor around us, the room reeked of gunpowder, the smoke burning my eyes.

"Please let me die," Isabelle whimpered.

Glenn ran past me and into the bathroom, his pants soaked in his own urine, where I heard him throwing up. I held Isabelle close and looked over at Marie, who was kneeling next to my mother.

"We've let him ride our coattails long enough, Brona," she said. "Glenn's the weak link. He always has been. Let's get him and James Fordham out of our lives now. We can deal with this."

My mother rose from the couch and wiped her eyes. "No, we can't do that. We've pressed our luck as far as it can go. We can find a way to work with James. We need him on our side. We can find out what he wants and get back to getting Glenn elected."

"Are you out of your mind, Brona?" Marie asked. "We can find someone else to back."

"No, it's too late for that. We have to think. We have to be clear now. No emotion. Get it out of our system. We're going to be fine now, aren't we?" my mother declared as she had just witnessed a minor family argument.

My mother and Marie huddled up, planning their future. Isabelle's fingernails dug into my arm, as she begged me to let her die. I sat her down on a chair and assured her that I'd be right back. I knocked on the door of the bathroom. "Glenn, get your ass out here."

He opened the door a crack and peered out, his shirt sleeve soaked in blood.

I wanted to inflict more pain on him, make him beg for life, but right now I needed his help.

"The drugs you and Fordham gave Isabelle, do you have any left?"

His expression told me that he did.

"Get one for me and do not fucking ask why."

He stared at me, confused.

"Now, goddamn it."

After Glenn came down with the pill, I escorted Isabelle up to her room.

"Stay the hell away from her!" I said.

Isabelle trusted me enough to take the pill. It made me sick giving her the same drug that had led to her rape, but I had things that needed to get done. I knew the pill would knock her out. A few moments later, Isabelle stared at me with sleepy eyes.

"You should never have come back, Liam."

"I came back for you," I said.

"I'm sorry," she said, then drifted off to sleep.

I watched her for a while. She didn't deserve any of this. The family that was supposed to take care of her only saw her as a means to whatever end they desired. But Isabelle was the one who always looked after me. And right now, all I could do was drug her.

Whatever my family wanted to do about Glenn didn't matter. Fordham was going to have to deal with me now. I walked out of the house, the gun in my hand almost begging me to use it, and me, thinking only about avenging Elisa and Isabelle.

CHAPTER THIRTY-EIGHT

I made a quick pit stop at my house to reload the Browning, then I drove down Pacific Coast Highway and stopped at the light at Main and PCH. Saturday night in downtown La Bolsa: souped-up cars, rock and roll blaring from their radios, teenagers on dates lining the sidewalks along with tribes of boys and girls all laughing, all eyeing each other, all taking in the magic of a Saturday night. It was as if I were peering into a different dimension, one where I no longer belonged. The fog crept up from the ocean, swallowing everyone into a dreamlike mist. In an instant, they all had vanished, even the sounds of a busy Saturday night seemed to have disappeared into the clouds, and all I could see were fragments of my headlights reflecting off the fog bank.

The light changed and as I emerged through the thick blanket of haze, I knew I was about to cross a line, that maybe I was about to do the same thing my father would have done if he were alive. The thought gave me no comfort. It left me cold and scared, but it wasn't about to stop me, either.

I parked about a block away from Fordham's, the entire street shrouded in mist. I snuck up to his home, the Browning firmly in my hand. I felt the same rush of adrenaline I used to get in Vietnam when setting out on an ambush. The gate to the driveway was open, and I crept through the yard. The front door was ajar, as if inviting me inside. I pushed it open and entered, my gun drawn. The inside was pitch black and silent, but I noticed a flickering light near the top of the stairs.

None of this felt right. The hairs on the back of my neck rose, warning me, but I edged up the stairs, my heart pounding against my rib cage.

The flickering came from the last room on the left, splashing dashes of light on the framed newspaper articles that lined the hallway. Each article declaring what a great man Fordham was. Each article picturing a gleaming man trying hard to appear humble. A small humming sound grew louder as I approached the room. The door was open a crack. I opened it the rest of the way with my foot. I stepped inside, my gun ready to fire.

"I've been waiting for you." James Fordham leaned against a large wooden desk. A bottle of bourbon, and two glasses sat next to him on the desk. A film projector stood to his left, perched on a small table. The light from the projector fluttered across his face, making him appear distant though he was only ten feet from me.

"Would you like a drink?"

I ignored the question. "You were expecting me?"

"Glenn called to let me know that you might be dropping by."

I never should have pulled Marie off him. I should have let her kill him.

"You're not surprised by that, are you?"

I shrugged, trying to control my rage. "You know what brought me here then."

"And that wasn't my doing. Those pictures were supposed to be kept private. I'm a very discreet man. I'm sorry you had to see them."

"Sorry? You raped them. Elisa, Isabelle, God knows how many others."

"Liam, I know it's hard, but you need to let this all go. I tried to warn you off."

His overbearing smugness was grating on me.

Fordham nodded toward the screen. "Have a peek, won't you?"

A naked woman lay on a bed. The camera zoomed in close on her face. Her eyes were half-open and there was no mistaking who the woman was. The camera then lingered on Ramona Ortiz's body. Then a pale hand reached down and roughly grabbed one of her breasts.

"You recognize her, I assume?"

I turned away from the screen, disgusted.

"She found out you drugged and raped her. That's why she went to see Charlie Moran. She wanted his help."

"That pathetic little lawyer? Once I saw his office, I knew I had nothing to worry about. How's your jaw feeling?"

Sweat formed around the gun in my hand. He was the one who punched me out at Moran's office. Fordham must have killed them. He killed them all. The prominent family that Julio Garza discovered nasty things about wasn't my family, it was James Fordham's. Fordham killed Julio because he was blackmailing him. He killed Catalina Garza because she must have stumbled on to the truth. Ramona Ortiz found out she was violated and pregnant, and Charlie Moran, he too probably tried to get to Fordham.

"I guess I'm the only one left who knows the truth," I said.

He gave me a puzzled look. "Are you sure you know what the truth is?"

Fordham calmly poured himself a glass. His nonchalant attitude made me nervous, as if he knew something I didn't.

"You sure you don't want one?"

"I'm sure."

"I thought you Irish liked drinking. I thought you Mexicans liked drinking. With that combination in your blood, I would think you'd be incapable of ever turning down a drink."

"I don't think I'd trust taking a drink from you."

"It's damn good bourbon. You don't know what you're missing."

I realized he had taken control, that I was following his lead.

"Observe, Liam." James Fordham pointed to the screen. "This is how one obtains real power."

I took a breath and glanced back at the screen.

A pale, slightly overweight man lay down next to Ramona Ortiz. The expression on his face was both excited and pathetic. Congressmen Luther Bennett shoved his hand between Ramona's thighs. My stomach tightened.

"I know how to find the weakness in people. It's usually sex, but sometimes I get to them in different ways. Whatever their weakness is, I'll find it. I control him now. I don't care who wins the election. Glenn, Luther Bennett ... you see it doesn't matter. I win either way. Possession is good for the soul. The more people you possess, the easier life becomes."

I turned away from the screen. "I don't get it. Why did you send the pictures of Glenn and Elisa to me?"

"I told you, it wasn't me, but I know who did it. I'll deal with that person later." He paused. "How is Elisa? I really liked her. You're lucky to have her." He aimed his conspiratorial grin at me.

The dull-edged knife reappeared and dug its way back deep into my gut.

"Liam, I'm sure we can work something out. I know all about Elisa, what she likes, what she craves, you know, those things that will keep her from straying."

I felt the need to hold on to something as the room felt as if it were bobbing in a rough sea.

"Though I'm not sure you're man enough for her, but perhaps I'm wrong. Am I wrong, Liam?"

We stared at each other. James Fordham looked like the all-American man. Bronze Star in World War II. Star running back for USC. And, like my father, he had grown his dad's business into a powerful force. I wondered if it was something in his family's genetic code that made him who he was, or maybe he was another example of one of nature's fuckups.

"I'm guessing Glenn must have told you about Isabelle. He watched me screw his wife. Can you believe that?" Fordham said it as though it was the worst thing he could ever imagine a person doing. He took another sip of the bourbon. "As I said, Glenn will do anything for me. I know people's weaknesses, Liam."

He read the expression on my face.

"Your mother is coming over for dinner next week. I'm growing fond of her. You never know what might happen."

The gun in my hand seemed to twitch, as if it were nudging me, almost urging me to use it.

"I don't think she'll be joining you."

He let out a small chuckle. He was enjoying himself.

"I'm warning you," I said.

"Liam, you're not going to do anything. You're not going to kill me in cold blood. That would be murder, and you are not a murderer. Nor are you going to risk having pictures of me screwing your sister get out, and believe me, they would. That would kill her, and you would never do that to her. You would do anything and everything in your power to protect Isabelle. She's your weakness."

"There are pictures of you and Isabelle?"

"Of course, there are. Glenn took them."

"He—"

"Said that he didn't take them?" He laughed. "Of course he did. I know people, Liam. I know what makes them tick. I know what they want. I know what they fear, and I know how far they'll go in order to protect themselves."

"You do?"

"Take you for example. You'd fall on your sword to protect your family. But you have a conflict. You have this thing with right and wrong. What's the first thing you do when you come back after Vietnam? You become a reporter. You're like Clark Kent, but without the cape. Your family is your Kryptonite. It's a losing battle, Liam. They're going to drag you down and someday you'll wonder whatever became of yourself."

He was right. They were my weakness. I lowered the gun, letting it rest at my side.

Fordham nodded his head. "That's more like it. You should take my advice and get out of town while you still can, just start over. Don't let them drag you down any further."

"You don't care about me. You just want me gone."

He smiled. "That's true, too. I do want you to leave."

"And if I don't?"

"Let's not go there. I don't want anything bad to happen to you. I think we can find a way to work this all out. If we can make a deal, I'll destroy the pictures along with the negatives. You quit your job at the newspaper, then we'll go our separate ways and no one gets hurt."

"But you'll just keep doing what you're doing. I can't let that go on."

"Yes, you can, Liam. It will no longer be any of your concern."

I glanced down at my gun.

"You should go now before I call the police," he said. "You are trespassing, you know. It might even be considered breaking and entering, but I'll let them sort that out."

He grabbed the phone and picked up the receiver.

"I'm not going anywhere."

"You stay right here then. It will make it easier for the police to arrest you."

"I'll tell them about the pictures."

He laughed. "They won't do anything about them, believe me."

His calm was baffling. How many people did he own? How much power did this guy really have?"

Fordham studied me for a moment. "The color of your eyes match Isabelle's, you know that? Yet your mother tells me that you're much more like your father."

"I'm nothing like him."

"No, no, I can see it."

He was baiting me now, and it was working.

"I told you, I'm nothing like him."

"You don't sound so sure. Have you and Isabelle ever ...?"

"Don't."

The gun twitched in my hand again.

"I wanted her the first time I laid eyes on her," he said. "Isabelle is beautiful. So tender, so soft, so responsive."

"That wasn't really her. You drugged her."

"The body knows what the body wants. And she wanted it."

With my thumb, I gently released the safety. It wasn't a conscious move.

"You're a sick fuck."

"We had a good time together. I swear she was positively glowing."

My throat felt like sandpaper. I couldn't explain it, but I felt both frightened and calm. Part of me was pleading with me to go, just leave and tell the police. But that part was losing out to another side, a side I couldn't control. Or maybe I didn't want to control it.

"You know what I loved best of all?" He smiled, recalling the moment. Then he dialed the phone. 0 for operator.

"I told you to shut the hell up."

"You want to know what we really got me off?"

I gripped the Browning tightly, shaking my head, letting him know he should quit talking.

"Stop," I said.

He put his hand over the receiver. "When I was inside her. When we were fucking. What made me come so fast was when she screamed out, 'No, Daddy. Stop, Daddy,' and then I—"

He didn't finish the sentence. The bullet blew right through his forehead. I didn't even think about it. It was as if someone else had pulled the trigger.

James Fordham teetered in place for a beat and then he slumped to the ground. The phone falling next to him.

A sudden crushing silence shrouded over me. I stared at his lifeless body, then at the gun trembling in my hand, realizing I had just killed a man in cold blood. James Fordham hadn't pulled a gun on me, he just said the wrong thing. Gun smoke hung in the air, stinging my eyes, and seeping into my lungs.

I picked up the phone and held the receiver to my ear. A woman's voice came on.

"Hello? Who's there? Is anyone there?"

I hung up the phone. I didn't know if they'd be able to trace the call or not, but the operator didn't sound alarmed. Maybe the shot went off before she had answered the phone.

Panic worked its way into my nerves. I didn't know what to do. Had the neighbors heard the shot? My heart pounded against my chest as if it were being beaten with a baseball bat. I ran to the window not knowing what I was looking for, but all seemed quiet. No lights from the surrounding homes had come on.

I took another look at Fordham, lying on his back, a single bullet hole in his forehead, his eyes open and staring into a void only he could see.

Every bone and muscle fiber in my body trembled, but I knew from my experience in Vietnam that I had to focus on what needed to be done. And right now, I had to think. The pictures of Elisa, the pictures of Isabelle, he probably kept them here. I needed to get rid of the pictures. I knew I couldn't leave anything that would lead the police back to my family, and ultimately, back to me. Where would he keep them? Closets, drawers, but hopefully not a safe.

I had to worry about fingerprints. I thought of all the cop shows I watched on TV. I pulled a handkerchief from my pocket, so I could wipe down anything I had touched. I examined every door and every drawer until I found them. He kept them in a file cabinet in one of his closets. The pictures were listed alphabetically, neat, tidy, and organized, which made my skin crawl. There must have been dozens of files.

I scanned the file folders and saw both Elisa's and Isabelle's. My hands shook, sweat dripped from my fingers, as I pulled both files and glanced through them, not focusing on any single picture. I was relieved that the files held the negatives as well. I examined the other names, recognized a few. I checked on the off chance that he had pictures of Greene with Julio Garza, but I didn't see either of their names. One name did jump out at me, though, and that was Glenn's. I grabbed the file and looked through them. Most were the pictures of him and Elisa that I'd already seen. But another set caught me by surprise. They were of Glenn and Ramona Ortiz. Christ, Glenn was having an affair with her. These appeared to have been taken in a motel room, and from what I could tell, Ramona Ortiz didn't look as if she were under the influence of any drug. She seemed to be a happy and enthusiastic partner.

If Glenn was having an affair with Ramona Ortiz, could he have been the one who got her pregnant? Judging by what I'd seen, Luther Bennett could also have been the father. Or for that matter, Fordham. In any case, the pictures and the film could ruin both Glenn and Bennett's chances in the election. Fordham owned both of them.

I took one last scan of the closet's contents when I heard a car pull up outside. I ran to the window but couldn't see a thing. It didn't matter. I had to get out. I ran out to the hallway and heard someone coming in through the front door. I didn't want to be found here with Fordham's dead body and my gun.

The window in Fordham's office looked too difficult to climb out of, so I crept across the hallway and snuck into his bedroom. There, like an evil altar, was the bed where he raped Isabelle, where Glenn raped Elisa. A sliding glass door opened to a balcony overlooking the harbor. I unlocked the door and slipped out to the balcony. I put the gun in my pocket, holding the files in one hand, and climbed down to the patio below.

I hid under the balcony, listening for anything that sounded human. The sliding door opened above me. I held my breath, then after a moment, the door closed. I counted to three and then moved quickly and quietly, my Army training coming back to me. I snuck out through the side gate.

Sticking to the night shadows, I ran down the road to my car. I didn't see anyone following me. I started the car and drove away with the lights off until I hit Pacific Coast Highway.

Driving up PCH, I made sure to keep to the speed limit, the highway empty except for the occasional diesel truck. I didn't think I'd left anything behind that would lead the police to my door, but it would have taken only one mistake. I had just killed a man, and in the eyes of the police—and in my own eyes—I was a murderer. James Fordham was a bad man, but did he kill the others? I needed to prove that or otherwise I just killed the wrong person.

I tried to concentrate on what I'd found at Fordham's house: pictures of Glenn with Ramona Ortiz. These were very different than the ones with Glenn and Elisa. It looked as if neither of the two knew they were being photographed. And Ramona looked like a willing partner. Was that what James Fordham had on Glenn? The pictures of him with Elisa and that he was having an affair with Ramona Ortiz? And when Fordham told him he wanted to have sex with Isabelle, was that why Glenn handed her to him so easily?

Glancing at the rearview mirror, I saw a pair of headlights closing in on me. I couldn't tell if it was a police car or not. I checked the speedometer and knew I was going the speed limit. My recently fired Browning sat in the passenger seat. If this was a cop, then I was screwed.

The headlights filled my rearview mirror and then they were gone. I glanced to my left, a black Camaro, filled with teenaged boys all giving me the finger, raced past me. Assholes. Thank God, they were only assholes.

I had to get rid of the gun. The pictures I could burn in my fireplace, but the Browning had to be dumped. Not in the ocean, even at this hour, and even with the fog, it would be too easy to be seen. Then I thought of Sunset Marsh. I drove past my house and parked along the marsh, near where Ramona Ortiz's body had been found.

I stepped out of my car. All was quiet, even the frogs kept silent. The fog hung low, hovering just above the weeds, and the air smelled like a decaying body. I wiped the gun down one last time and then flung it as far as I could. I heard a soft splash and then silence. I waited a moment, listening, then the frogs began to sing, like an all-clear alarm.

CHAPTER THIRTY-NINE

As soon as I made it home, I shoved the pictures into the back of my closet. A lousy hiding place, but since no one followed me home, I thought they'd be safe for the moment.

I collapsed on my bed, feeling as if all the blood had been drained out of me. I lay on the bed exhausted, beaten, and yet wide awake. Sleep, I knew, wouldn't be coming, not now, maybe not for a long time.

I played the scene over again. I felt sure that I'd done a good job of covering my tracks. But who else was in the house and what had they seen? I thought about how I might respond if the police ever questioned me and knew I'd better come up with a ready alibi. Something told me that I wouldn't be able to lie. I'd just admit the truth and hand my life over to the authorities.

After all, I had killed a man, an unarmed one at that. The image of James Fordham's body lying on the floor, a bullet hole in his head, his blood and brains splattered on his desk and on the floor, appeared before me. I shot him without thinking. I didn't know what compelled me to pull the trigger like that, as if he didn't deserve a second thought. I thought of the men I'd killed in Vietnam, and when I killed the pale-faced man—they were killed because it was either them or me. I didn't shoot Fordham in self-defense. I killed him out of rage, and in cold blood.

I felt my stomach turn and begin to rise and this time I couldn't hold it back. I stumbled into the bathroom and made it to the toilet. My body heaving, sweat pouring out of my glands, the contents of my stomach spewing out into the bowl. I lay on the floor of the bathroom until I gathered the strength to stand on my own. I glanced at my reflection in the mirror and looked away in shame. I took a long, hot shower, knowing I would never get as clean as I once was. That what I did last night was now part of me and part of who I was as a man.

I threw on my Levi's and a T-shirt and made my way to the kitchen. The shaking had returned. I needed something strong. I pulled down a bottle of tequila. Perhaps drinking wasn't the best idea, but my body cried out for something strong.

I brought the bottle out to the living room and sat in my leather chair. I took in a few deep breaths, chasing each one with a sip of the tequila. The post-adrenaline rush had begun to pass, so I put the tequila down. Then I just stared out the window, almost as if I were in a trance, until the morning sun peeked above the horizon. On any other day, it would have been a glorious sunrise, but now I felt like I was living on the other side of humanity, as if I had violated the rules of society and had suddenly found myself an outcast. This was the first of many days that I'd have to slog through until I found a way to deal with the new me. I wasn't sure if I was going to be able to handle it.

I sat there alone for another hour or so, then I put on a dress shirt and tucked it into my jeans. I slipped on my desert boots and headed out to my car.

It was Sunday morning and I headed to St. Christopher's Church. I couldn't explain why I felt the need to attend Mass even though I doubted the existence of a God. In my mind, I had committed a mortal sin, though going to church would do nothing for that, but maybe confession would. After I had received my First Communion, my mother tried to impress upon me the importance of confession and what "good for the soul" meant.

"Liam," she said, as she knelt down in front of me, "Every time you commit a sin, no matter how small, your soul gets a little black mark on it. The more sins, the more black marks that darken your soul. When you confess your sins to a priest, your soul becomes pure again. God wants pure souls, Liam. You understand?"

I couldn't remember the last time I'd been to confession; it was probably when I was a teenager and had to tell the priest that I'd lost my virginity. After that encounter, I had been too embarrassed to return.

I parked on the street and walked toward the church, but froze when I saw my mother, Marie, and Isabelle walking arm in arm with Glenn, up the front steps of the church as if last night had never happened. I shouldn't have been surprised. They were bound together by some force I would never understand, a force I wanted no part of, yet a force that repeatedly pulled me back to them.

I drove away from the church and down Pacific Coast Highway. I needed forgiveness. I needed someone's blessing, but I realized it wasn't a priest and it wasn't God I needed to confess my sins to, it was Elisa.

I continued down Coast Highway toward her house. The sun reflected off the ocean, giving it a heavenly glow as surfers slid down deep blue waves, while beautiful girls in bikinis, their skin tanned and glistening in baby oil, cheered them on from the shore. Beach blankets dotted the sand, coolers filled with ice and cold beers waited for the surfers, a reward for pursuing happiness at all costs. The California promise, the promise that life was better here, that we could all start anew, that with each new day we came one step closer to nirvana. It was all a mirage, of course, a beautiful lie, one that we willingly believed, a lie that kept us going, a lie that we held onto as if it were the last bit of hope we had left.

Though I had the key to her apartment, I thought letting myself in would only serve as a reminder that her privacy was no longer hers. I knocked gently on her front door. Elisa opened it, stared at me, sizing me up; she reached her hands out to me. I took them and kissed her. She didn't flinch, but her lips did not linger on mine.

I followed her into the apartment. Elisa wore a long white peasant skirt and a loose-fitting black T-shirt. She moved with a stiff gait; the gentle sway of her hips had disappeared. Then she turned to me, her hands on my shoulders.

"Do you still love me, Liam?"

"I'll always love you," I said.

"No, don't say it because you think you have to. Only say it if you mean it."

She looked me in the eyes as if she were trying to see into me.

"I love you, Elisa. Nothing can change that."

She held my hands in hers. "I need to hear that." She kissed my cheek. "Can I get you anything?"

"I'm fine. Is there anything I can do for you?"

She said no, and took a seat on the sofa, but I couldn't sit. I was too nervous, too shaken.

"Aren't you going to sit down?"

"I have to tell you something, something I've wanted to tell you since we started seeing each other."

Elisa tensed up. I hesitated for a moment, but if I didn't tell her now, I knew I'd never tell her. I spilled out my guts to her. Everything. Every lie, every deceit. I told her that Isabelle killed my father, and what my father had done to Isabelle, about Glenn and Marie, and the truth about the pale-faced man. Then I told her about Glenn sacrificing Isabelle to James Fordham. I told her about last night and how I had killed the man who had infected her own life and Isabelle's. And how I was sure he killed the Garzas, Ramona Ortiz, and Charlie Moran.

When I was done, Elisa looked at me, her face as unreadable as a stone.

"You lied to me."

"I didn't want to. I didn't want to lose you."

"And you didn't trust me."

"All I know is that I should have told you the truth."

"And you killed James Fordham?"

I nodded my head. "Yes."

"You killed a man last night."

"I didn't intend to. It just happened."

"It just happened."

"Elisa, I—"

"And what about Glenn?"

"What do you mean?"

"Glenn raped me, Liam. He raped me. And he might as well have raped your sister. How come he gets to live, how come he gets the get out of jail free card?"

"I ... I ..."

"Because he's part of your family, Liam. That's why. You'll do anything to protect them. Each thing you've told me only makes everything worse. I work for a family of killers, and now, when I finally find a man I can truly love, truly trust, and could picture living the rest of my life with, he turns out to have lied to me about who he is, about what he did, and he turns out to be a killer like the rest of his family."

"Elisa, no, I—"

"Get out, Liam."

"Elisa, no."

I watched as she sized me up, her face reddening.

"I love you, Elisa. Don't do this."

She shot up from the couch. "Get out!"

"Elisa!"

"Jesus Christ, what did I do to deserve this? You don't see it, do you? You don't see that everything you do is about your family. Your family is sick, Liam. You're sick. Get out. Just get out."

"I'm not like my family."

"All evidence to the contrary." Tears rolled down her face. "Just go."

"I'm sorry," I whispered.

"If the police come to me about James Fordham, I'll tell them the truth. I won't lie for you. I won't be like you, Liam. I won't."

She wiped her face in her hands and stared coldly at me, willing away any further tears. I wanted to take her in my arms. I wanted to comfort and protect her. I wanted to take everything back and start fresh, but I knew that all I had to offer was more hurt, more pain, and more lies. I told her I loved her, and I told her again how sorry I was, and then I walked out the door.

CHAPTER FORTY

When I arrived back at my house, I didn't go for a drink. I didn't want to numb the pain. I wanted to feel it, to live in it, I wanted it to run through my veins, and this time I wouldn't hide from it. By the next morning, however, the pain had become too much. I thought of the happiness I had discarded. Dawn, and now Elisa.

I called the paper and told Helen that I wouldn't be in, that I wasn't feeling well.

"Don't worry, hon, it's pretty quiet today."

Did that mean they hadn't found James Fordham's body yet?

I had to press her, just to make sure.

"So, no shoot-outs, kidnappings, or Martian invasions?" I asked, making it all sound like a joke.

"Knock on wood. It's a quiet Monday, Liam. Don't mess it up."

I told her that I'd probably be in tomorrow and hung up.

I felt relieved they hadn't found him yet, as if I'd been given a stay. The police wouldn't be putting me in cuffs, at least not yet.

I couldn't stay inside my house. I wanted Elisa back. I wanted her forgiveness. I wanted to be in the safety of her arms, but I knew she wasn't ready to see me. I also needed to be absolved of my sin. I needed someone to tell me that what I did was right and just.

I walked down PCH toward downtown La Bolsa. The weather had been off lately as if it were suffering from a crisis of identity. Some days the fog and clouds surrounded us and other days, like today, the sun ruled. Nothing was predictable.

I made my way up to Main Street and then to Orange, which led me to The Church of the Innocent Child. Lonnie stood over an old wooden pew, his back bent as he carefully sanded down the ridges ingrained in the wood. Five more were lined up behind him. The smell of wood shavings mixed with burning incense floated in the air around us, gave the church a welcoming scent.

"You like 'em?" he asked. "I found them at a swap meet in Stanton. A strange place to find pews. They were sitting next to half a dozen wood cartons filled with old *Playboy* magazines. It didn't seem right. The pews needed saving. They looked lost and I knew they needed a good home." Lonnie looked around the place. "Someday this will feel like a real house of worship."

"Do you have a moment?"

Lonnie tossed the sandpaper onto the pew he was working on and led me to one of the others that still needed smoothing. The mural of the baby Jesus lying in elephant grass surrounded by three soldiers stared down on us.

"You look lost. What's wrong?"

I told him what I had done. Why I had killed James Fordham. That Elisa had kicked me out over it.

"Are you looking for forgiveness?"

"I think so. James Fordham was an evil man. He deserved what he got, but maybe I'm only trying to convince myself of that. I don't know."

"Did you commit murder or was killing him justifiable?"

"I don't know."

"But you aren't asking about legality, you're asking if it is morally justifiable."

I nodded. I don't know why this mattered to me. This wasn't about what the legal system thought. It was about what was right.

"I don't have an answer to that question. But it wasn't premeditated. You did not lie in wait for him, did you?"

"I came to see him with a loaded gun in my hand."

Lonnie let out a deep sigh. "I don't know, Liam. Which part of the Bible do you want to cling to? Exodus, Leviticus, Matthew, John?" Lonnie suddenly seemed frustrated and upset. "There are lots of opinions there. Do you want to believe in a vengeful God or a forgiving God? I'm new at this. I've been searching for that answer since I came back from 'Nam, and I still don't have one, okay?"

"I'm sorry. I didn't know who else to turn to."

Lonnie rose up from the pew, ran his hands through his hair, and stood there.

"I think what you did was forgivable. You killed an evil man. A man who does that to innocent people deserves to die. Killing an innocent is an unforgivable sin. It's ..."

He looked down at the floor, avoiding eye contact, his mouth agape as if he were witnessing something inhumane, something he couldn't stop.

"Lonnie, what's going on?"

"These dreams I've been having about Vietnam. They weren't just dreams. I did something horrible, Liam."

He sat next to me. I put my hand on his shoulder, trying to comfort him, wondering what had set him off.

"I can't hide anymore. I can't pretend it didn't happen," he said. "I was the devil. I killed the baby."

"What baby? What are you talking about?"

Lonnie lifted his head and nodded at the mural. Then I remembered his story. The one where he said he saw the devil jump into the tall grass. Lonnie followed him only to find the body of a baby boy, an angelic face, but with a bullet hole in his heart.

"I was scared, Liam. We'd gone through two days of firefights, and we'd lost a few men, just boys, still in their teens. We were marching through the jungle and into a clearing. We'd been tracking down some VC troops who'd been torturing the locals, trying to get intel on us. We were closing in on them, we could feel it, but we knew we could be walking into an ambush. And the heat, the damn heat was making me dizzy. I wasn't sure how much longer I could go on.

"At the end of the clearing there was this hamlet. And it was quiet. Just like in the movies, too quiet. It didn't feel right. Then a flock of birds burst from the ground into the air, then a rustling sound came from the tall grass near me, and I just shot at it, Liam. Just one shot and I heard a cry. Then nothing but silence. None of the other men moved, but they had their guns pointed at the tall grass. I ran over, ready to shoot, and that's when I saw the baby, dead. His mother holding him tight, trying to hold back her cries, trying not to make a sound, trying not to die, her face filled with a rage and fear I'd never seen before."

"Oh, Lonnie, I'm so sorry."

"I killed a baby, Liam, an innocent child. I did that."

I didn't know what to say. Shit happened in the war. We shot at shadows, the wind and the faintest of sounds. Each step we took could have landed on a mine or set off some booby trap. We didn't know who we could trust. We followed orders as best we could, even when they didn't make sense, because surely the captains and generals knew best, but they, too, were lost. We had our guns, we had each other, and in the end, we did anything we could to stay alive.

"You didn't know, Lonnie. You didn't know. Charlie could have been in there."

"It wasn't the VC, though. It was a baby." Lonnie wiped his face. "I don't belong here. I'm a fraud."

"You're trying to save people. They need you here." My heart bled for him. He was the finest person I knew. What he told me didn't change that. It was hard for me to imagine a perfect God. If God did exist, I had to wonder if he was sick and deranged, and created life on Earth just so he could play out some awful version of a board game, something to keep him entertained for eternity.

"I failed Him," he said.

I wrapped my arms around Lonnie and placed my head next to his. "It wasn't your fault." And though I wanted to cry, there was nothing left in me. Here we were, two innocent men, two killers, both of us left with permanent black marks on our souls, both of us wondering what the hell we had turned into, trying to figure out how we were going to be able to live with ourselves from here on out.

I spent the rest of the day with Lonnie, helping him sand the pews until they were smooth. He was quiet, but completely focused on the task. Afterward we wiped off the dust, then we stained the wood until it turned to a nice dark brown.

Lonnie examined our work. "It'll do."

"What once was lost has now been found," I said.

Lonnie smiled. "That's right," he replied in almost a whisper. "I was blind, but now I see."

"You feel better?" I asked.

Lonnie shrugged. "No. You?"

"No."

That got a laugh out of him, but we both knew there was a lot we had to sort out.

We shook hands and then I headed for the door.

"Liam?"

"Yeah?"

"Thanks."

I told him any time, and I meant it. I headed back home, mentally exhausted, thinking that a sunset session might be what I needed.

When I arrived home, I changed into my swim trunks, grabbed my board and ran across PCH and hit the water. The waves were head high, the faces steep, the lines clean, the breaks beautiful, but I felt none of it. Some things you can't escape. Sometimes you do things that go against every moral lesson that you ever held close to your heart. Yet you know that they had to be done, because it came down to you or him, but that didn't stop the nightmares that kept you awake at night, that questioned you, that interrogated you and left you wondering if you were just another animal roaming the planet, guided not by morals, but only by the need to survive. But that didn't explain why I had killed James Fordham.

I left the water after a few rides. I sat in the sand and stared at the setting sun. The colors painted across the horizon resembled the aftermath of a bloody ambush.

That night, I received a call from Guy Watson.

"Did you hear what happened?" he asked, huffing and puffing.

They must have found him. "No," I said as calmly I could.

"James Fordham is dead. He's been murdered."

"Really?" was all I'd managed to say.

"The police found his body floating in Sunset Marsh, near where they found that Ortiz lady. Get this, he was shot in the head."

"His body was found at the marsh? Are you sure?"

"Yeah, they gave me the story. I'm gonna need your notes on Ramona Ortiz. The killings might be related."

Shit. Someone moved his body. That didn't make any sense. Who would do that?

"You still there?"

"Yeah, is tomorrow morning okay?"

"I guess so."

I told him I'd bring them in first thing and then hung up.

What the hell was going on? Whoever was in Fordham's house with me that night must have moved the body, but why? I was sure no one had followed me back to La Bolsa. I hadn't seen another car by the marsh when I tossed my gun. While I tried to add it all up in my head, I couldn't escape the thought that maybe James Fordham wasn't the one who killed the Garzas, Ramona Ortiz or Charlie Moran.

Sleep didn't come that night, nor did I expect it to. I tried to block out that Fordham's body had been moved and dumped in the marsh. Instead, I thought about my life, and about what Elisa had said about me putting my family first, despite how evil they may have been. There was truth to her words, but it wasn't the whole picture, or maybe I was lying to myself, who knows? James Fordham was right about one thing, there was something in me that made me want to protect Isabelle at all costs, protect her from my family, from the outside world, and from Glenn, but in truth, I was really protecting my family.

I put the idea of sleep away for the night. I collected the pictures I'd found at Fordham's house, and lit a fire in the fireplace. I flipped through my records, wondering which album might take my mind away from its current state. I settled on an old favorite, Tim Buckley's *Goodbye and Hello,* not exactly a calming choice, but one I could get lost in. I grabbed a Dos Equis from the fridge and opened the windows to let in the night breeze blowing off the ocean. I sat in my leather chair and stared out the window and into the darkness outside, the crashing of waves echoing in the night like a distant storm, Buckley singing, his voice nailing it, asking if the war is inside my mind. *The war is all around me*, I thought. Bullets firing at home, bullets firing in Vietnam, bullets killing babies, bullets burning holes in my thoughts, and even in my prayers.

I threw the pictures of Glenn and Elisa and of James Fordham and Isabelle into the fire. Maybe I should have taken another look at them, maybe clues were buried in the background somewhere, but my soul couldn't take seeing the pictures of Elisa with Glenn again, and I knew I there was no way I could stomach seeing James Fordham abusing my sister. Fordham was dead now, and Isabelle deserved whatever privacy I could give her.

But I did want to examine the pictures of Glenn and Ramona Ortiz one last time. It looked as if someone had been following the two. There was nothing I could find in the pictures other than the two appearing to enjoy each other's company. But Ramona Ortiz was pregnant, and from what I could tell, Glenn, Luther Bennett, or James Fordham could have been the father. If Fordham proved not to be the killer, then perhaps one of the other two did the job. Both had good motives. But it was all speculation. Maybe Columbo might have found something, but if a clue was in the pictures, then it was beyond me. I thought about keeping them as some sort of leverage, but the risk of the cops finding them at my house was too great. I tossed them in the fire and watched them turn and melt in the heat.

I put on a Doors album and grabbed another beer. I stared into the fire and listened as Jim Morrison sang about learning to forget. I decided to have one beer per album. It felt good to have a plan.

There were two questions I couldn't answer. Did the person at the house that night see me there, and why did they take Fordham's body and dump it into the marsh?

I tossed the questions around in my mind through three more beers and through *Let it Bleed* and *Gasoline Alley* before drifting off to sleep as Neil Young sang "Only Love Can Break Your Heart."

I woke up with the sun in my face, and though I had only managed a few hours of sleep, I knew I needed to get back to work. I had to start acting as if everything in my life was normal, that I wasn't the man who killed James Fordham. I stopped off at The Driftwood for a cup of coffee and noticed that none of the morning papers had mentioned Fordham's death. The discovery of his body must have come after the presses had already rolled.

I ordered toast with my coffee and looked over the *L.A. Times,* trying to get my day off to as normal a start as possible, though paranoia ran through my nerve endings like jolts of electricity. Nixon was still cracking down on antiwar protesters, the cost of a stamp jumped up to eight cents, and the Utah Stars and the Kentucky Colonels were battling it out for the ABA championship.

I tried reading the articles, but I couldn't concentrate on the words, as my ears were alert to the conversations going on around me. No one said a thing about the killings, fishermen told new fish tales to one another, surfers were stoked about another day of hitting the waves, and other locals spoke about their plans for the day. I was surprised word hadn't reached anyone. Surely, the police were still searching the marsh for clues, but I knew that later, when word got out, the rumor mill would be working overtime, and I only hoped that somehow that neither me nor my family's name would be brought up.

The office was humming when I arrived. This was a big story for La Bolsa as it wasn't about dead Mexicans. This one had a rich oil man's body found floating in Sunset Marsh. This one people would want to read about. I looked in Daniels' old office and saw Doug Everly, the new acting editor, huddled with Guy Watson and a couple other reporters who must have been on the story. I approached the office, but Everly saw me and waved me off.

As Daniels' predicted, I was out of the picture now. I'd probably be demoted to writing fillers. Part of me wanted to be in there, doing what I could do to keep the story from ever getting near me, but it was out of my hands. I dropped off my notebook on Watson's desk, but then I thought twice about it.

I grabbed it and walked out to the parking lot. I leaned against my car and read over my notes. Other than James Fordham, Ramona Ortiz had three personal links that I knew of: Luther Bennett, Glenn's opponent for Congress, and the man featured in the James Fordham's private movie; Elisa Vargas, whose card was in Ramona's purse; and Glenn, who she had been having an affair with.

Elisa said she didn't know Ramona Ortiz and I believed her. Both Glenn and Bennett had been filmed or photographed in very compromising encounters with her by James Fordham. But neither of them killed him. I did that.

Yet, both Bennett and Glenn had clear motives for killing Fordham and Ortiz. Were either of them in the house that night? And who dumped his body in the marsh? But if Bennett did kill Ramona, then surely the Pacific Harbor police had found the film in the projector of him and Ramona and would have been able to put two and two together.

I didn't want to stand around waiting for news; I wanted to know what was going on. The Pacific Harbor police didn't know I was on the paper's shit list. To them, I was just another reporter covering the crime. I saw no need to go to Sunset Marsh. I wanted to know what the cops were finding at Fordham's house. I grabbed my keys and headed out, with the old police saying ringing loud and clear in my head like an alarm going off: The killer always returns to the scene of the crime.

CHAPTER FORTY-ONE

I parked down the street from Fordham's house, well aware that someone might recognize my car from the night of the killing. Coming here was a risk, but I needed to find out what the police had discovered.

Half a dozen Pacific Harbor police cars were lined up in front of the house. A tall well-tanned cop stood guard on the driveway. He was a good-looking guy who looked as if he'd come off the set of a soap opera.

"Sorry," he said, raising his hand. "You can't get any closer. We're in the middle of a police investigation."

"I'm with the *La Bolsa Tribune*," I said, and showed him my press pass. He looked it over, then waved me through. "You can get in through the front door, but I think everything other than the living room is off limits." He pointed toward the entrance.

I thanked him and almost told him I knew the way. I needed to be careful and reminded myself of a key lie: I had never been here before. I wondered if cops kept a lookout for perpetrators returning to the crime scene and if they could pick up on any telltale clues. But my cover was sound. I was a working newspaper reporter, for now anyway.

The living room was empty except for Scott Waller, a reporter from *The Register,* and an irritated cop who looked as if he'd been demoted and sent to the living room for punishment.

I showed him my press credentials. He sighed and nodded.

"Wait here. They should be answering questions any moment now. Of course, who knows, they don't tell me anything."

"Nice spread," I said, trying to sound as if I'd never been here before. The living room was light and airy, and two big bay windows overlooked the harbor. I noticed there were no pictures of Wyatt to be seen. In fact, the only photographs in the house were portraits saluting James Fordham's accomplishments, and those others which he kept hidden in a file cabinet in his closet. As open as the room was, it all felt claustrophobic to me. I pictured James Fordham's body, I felt the gun in my hand, I felt myself pull the trigger. And now, here, I couldn't help but worry that the cops might uncover something that would tie me to the killing.

"You covering this?" Waller asked. "Some other guy from your paper was here earlier and—"

"I'm filling in for him until he gets here." I wanted to be as vague as possible. "Any updates?"

"They've carried out a few big boxes, but nothing other than that." Waller stretched his arms over his head and let out a yawn.

The pictures of Fordham's victims must have been in the boxes. I paced the room, wondering what else they'd found upstairs, wondering if any of their discoveries implicated me, wondering if I had wiped away every fingerprint.

"Finally," Waller said.

A plainclothes detective sporting a crew-cut made his way down the staircase. I couldn't tell if he was relieved or disappointed that only two reporters showed up. After all, James Fordham was a rich man, but the cop knew that the LA TV stations thought Orange County might as well be in another state, and it would take more than one rich guy getting killed to get them to break through the Orange

Curtain. He introduced himself as Thomas Powell, a detective with the Pacific Harbor Police Department. Powell looked to be in his fifties, but he carried himself like a much older man.

"Okay," he sighed. "We've uncovered evidence that leads us to believe that James Fordham was killed here upstairs in his ... um, office."

"What evidence?" Waller asked.

"Blood and bone fragments, mostly."

Waller followed up. "So, someone went out of their way to dump Fordham's body at Sunset Marsh? Any leads on possible suspects?"

I held my breath, my throat growing ever tighter.

"No. Not yet, but we still have more work to do here and at the marsh."

I let out a silent sigh of relief. They must have found the movie of Luther Bennett with Ramona Ortiz, but I wondered if they'd cover for Bennett. This was a small town and he was an influential man.

"What was in the boxes the police carried out of here?" I asked.

"Possible evidence. We'll let you know more when we ... we'll let you know more soon."

I pushed a little further. "James Fordham was a rich man. He must have had powerful enemies."

He cocked his head. "You know something we don't?"

I felt as if a spotlight had landed on me, but Detective Powell looked unsettled. He was probably wondering how they were going to deal with what they'd found in Fordham's office. He wiped his hands on the side of his pants and then wiped his brow.

"Just seems like a logical question. Someone wanted him dead, unless this was a robbery gone wrong."

"We're looking at all possibilities. We're done for now," he said, and then he lumbered back up the stairs.

"I'll be here," Waller shouted, and then he looked at me. "Cops," was all he said.

I wanted to track down Luther Bennett to see if the police had paid him a visit.

"I have another story I need to get on," I said to Waller. "See you around."

I walked out of the house and saw the cop on guard flirting with a few teenage girls. They seemed to be enjoying his company. I slipped past him.

"Have a nice day," he said.

Jesus, here I was, walking out of a house where a murder had been committed, and the cop tells me to have a nice day.

I headed to my car and ran into Guy Watson.

"What the heck, Liam? You're not covering this, I am."

"I know, I just wanted to give you my notes on Ramona Ortiz. I thought you'd be here. What took you so long? The cops just gave a statement. You're lucky I filled in." I handed my notebook to him. Watson looked confused, which seemed to be his usual state.

"Hey, you'd do the same for me, right?" I said.

I patted him on the back and heard him respond with very weak thank you, but my mind was already focused on how best to approach Congressman Luther Bennett.

Bennett looked like the kind of father figure you'd seen in a TV show: kind, wise, and full of love. But the memory of his sluglike body rolling on top of Ramona Ortiz was another reminder that perhaps we weren't all created in God's image.

Bennett's campaign headquarters was located only a half a mile from Fordham's home, so I decided to stop by on the off chance that he'd be there.

The office was as quiet as a library, and there were only a couple of volunteers working, all silently licking envelopes. One of them, a pretty girl in a red, white and blue knee-length skirt and a "You Can Count on Bennett" button pinned to her blouse, skipped over to me and asked if she could be of any help.

"I'm with the *La Bolsa Tribune*, and I'm working on a feature story about the election."

"You're a reporter?" Her blue eyes lit up, projecting an innocence that I felt in my gut. I couldn't help but wonder if Bennett wanted to drug her as well.

"Congressman Bennett is in his office right now. Let me see if he can make time for you."

She returned a moment later and told me to walk right on in.

Bennett greeted me with a smile he'd been perfecting for years.

"So, you're from *The Tribune*? You caught me on a quiet day. It'll all heat up the closer we get to the election, but once your opponent declares, no matter how early, you need to set up shop."

I glanced at the framed pictures on his desk and on the bookshelf behind him. Some with his wife, some with his kids, and others with what I guessed were his grandchildren.

"Debbie tells me you're working on a story about the election. How can I help?"

He tried to sound calm and collected, but I could sense the tension in his voice.

"First, thanks for seeing me. I'm actually working on another story. I don't know if you heard, but James Fordham was found murdered this morning."

His eyes searched his office as if looking for a way out.

"I did hear. Such a loss to our community."

"I guess." I was playing this all by ear, hoping I could trip him up.

"His body was dumped into Sunset Marsh, near where someone else was found dead a few weeks ago. A Ramona Ortiz? Did you know her?"

"I don't. I mean I didn't know her. I'm sorry, I didn't get your name."

"Liam Sol."

"Sol? I know your family. You're related to Glenn Frost. What do you want? Why are you asking about Ramona Ortiz?"

"I know you knew her. I saw you with her."

Bennett grabbed his phone.

"I'm calling the police."

"You're not going to call them. I saw the film."

Bennett paused, then smiled. I knew I'd just made a big mistake.

"You saw the film? Interesting. I have friends on the force, Mr. Sol. Friends who look after me. There is no film. You understand what I'm saying, don't you?"

I recalled the first time I surfed the Banzai Pipeline in Hawaii. I was still a teenager and had no business taking it on. I remember looking down the face of a giant wave. I'd never seen anything like it. I lost my focus and wiped out, free falling, and crashing into the coral below.

"Nod your head if you understand me, Mr. Sol."

I nodded, feeling the sharp edges of the coral digging into my skin, me not knowing what was up or down, my arms flailing in the water.

"I'm sure the police would like to know what you were doing the night James Fordham was killed, but I'd rather just leave this between you and me. Don't make me have to call the police." Bennett put the receiver down. "Now get the hell out of here."

I walked out of his office trying to maintain some dignity. As I left the building, I heard him scream. "Debbie, get your little ass in here, now!"

I sat in my car, fighting off waves of nausea, trying to figure out what I was trying to accomplish. After killing Fordham, I should have stayed on the sidelines. I should have left everything alone. I didn't know if it was out of a sense of justice or guilt, or the willingness to pay for my sins, but I had to prove that James Fordham killed the Garzas, Ortiz, and Moran, yet all I seemed to be doing was implicating myself in his murder.

I stopped off at work just to show my face, trying to make it look as if all was normal, though I knew nothing would ever be normal again. I saw a note on my desk that Detective Greene had phoned, and he wanted me to return his call. It was marked urgent.

I called him back.

"We need to talk," he said.

CHAPTER FORTY-TWO

April Fairchild gave me a wave as I took a seat on the barstool closest to the front entrance.

"Hey, Liam. Coffee? Beer?"

"Coffee," I said. I wanted to be as sharp as possible in case Greene was planning something.

"I just made a fresh pot."

"You seem happy."

"Just received my first grades. Two As and a B. I know it's only junior college, but I feel good about it, you know?"

"You should feel good."

She smiled again, which was rare for her.

After all the crap I'd been dealing with, her smile, the pride she allowed herself, gave me a glimmer of hope, that maybe for some, at least, redemption was possible. But then a dark expression came across her face as I heard someone enter the bar.

Detective Greene patted me on the back and gave a quick cursory nod to April.

"Let's sit back here," he said. Then to April, "I'll have a beer, whatever you have on tap."

I followed Greene to the back table, forgetting my coffee. He appeared calm, but his eyes scanned the bar. Other than April Fairchild, we were the only two in the room.

"Thanks for coming."

He was about to say more, but April arrived with his beer and my coffee. She gave me a look I couldn't read then made her way back to the bar. Greene waited until she was out of earshot before talking.

He took a sip of his beer, then looked at me like a doctor examining a wound. I felt my body stiffen.

"You heard about James Fordham?"

"I work at a newspaper; we tend to hear about things like murder." I wanted to sound normal but was worried that I was coming off like a politician avoiding a hard question.

"They're looking at Wyatt Fordham as a possible suspect. Do you have any idea where he might be?"

"No. But Wyatt? Why?"

"He had motive. It's no secret the two didn't like each other. That and James Fordham had Wyatt declared him mentally unfit and Fordham was granted total conservatorship. And now Wyatt's missing."

This was news to me. "His dad had him committed?"

"You're surprised? Wyatt's a loon."

That would have been the only way his father would have obtained the land from him. Wyatt loved the environment. He never would have willingly given it to his father.

"He's not that crazy," I said.

"They also found his prints where the body was found, as well as in his dad's office."

"Seems to make sense that his prints would be in his father's house."

"You're right, that would be normal, but his prints were in blood. That's hard to get around. I think there's some other stuff they discovered, but the Pacific Harbor cops are keeping mum about it."

I was sure he was referring to the home movie on Fordham's

projector and the accompanying pictures. Bennett wasn't lying about how influential he was with the police.

Wyatt must have been the one in the house the night I killed his father. Why hadn't he called the cops on me? Why would he have dumped his father's body in the marsh?

I knew I couldn't let Wyatt go to prison for this. Maybe I should turn myself in, give them my theory that James Fordham was the one who killed the others, but I knew I had to prove it first. Maybe then I'd get some kind of leniency.

"I don't think Wyatt has the capacity to kill anyone."

Greene gave me a look. "What makes you say that? You know something I don't?"

"He's harmless, that's why."

"Well, we have two police departments looking for him, along with the sheriff's office. We'll find him."

I had to do something. I had to figure out how all the killings tied together. I thought of Charlie Moran's body lying in the alley behind the bar. The fact that Greene arrived so soon afterward still bothered me.

"Liam? You with me?"

"Yeah," I said. "How were you able to get to the scene so soon after Charlie Moran was killed."

"I was in the neighborhood. What are you implying?"

I recalled the look on his face after Moran had been found dead. It was the same look he had on now, a suddenly pale face aging before my eyes.

"You need to back off and let us do our job," he said. "Let me know if you see Wyatt." Then he hurried out of the door.

The more I thought about it, it was just as likely Greene could have been the killer. It all started to make sense. His affair with Julio Garza. Perhaps Catalina caught him at her house and he killed her. I didn't know how Ramona Ortiz came into the picture, but Charlie Moran certainly could have been moving too hard on Greene, and

Greene, having his back pushed into a corner, saw no way out and came out firing. And if Greene was behind the murders then he certainly would have good reason to want to take me out—or even set me up.

If that all were true, then maybe James Fordham wasn't behind the killings. But I needed him to be the murderer. Because if he was, then maybe I could find a justification for killing an unarmed man. But if Fordham killed the others, then did Greene kill Charlie Moran— or could it have been someone else? I suddenly felt defenseless, and I regretted tossing my gun into Sunset Marsh.

I walked back to the bar and asked April for a bottle of Dos Equis. I sat on the stool next to the front door. I felt edgy, and just knowing the exit was but a few steps away gave me comfort. April came back with my beer and one for herself.

"What's the feeling you get from him?" I asked, meaning Greene. "You think he could have done it?"

April took a long drink from her beer. "Those two got in some heated arguments in here, but the cop wasn't in the day Moran was shot."

"And you've never seen Moran in here with anyone else?"

She thought for a moment. "No, just you and the detective, but he could have met someone here when I was off."

I studied April Fairchild and wondered if she could help me. Her expression indicated she was in deep thought. Thinking of her bright new future maybe, or, perhaps, all that she was trying to leave behind. She caught me looking at her.

"What?"

I didn't want to ask, but I didn't know where else to go. "I think I might have gotten myself into trouble."

"What can I do?"

"You wouldn't ... God damn it ... you wouldn't know where I could get a gun, would you?"

"And I'd know because I'm an ex-con? Is that it?"

"I thought you might know people. I know how it sounds, and I'm sorry, but I think I've pissed off the wrong people."

"I can't believe you asked me that. Even if I did, do you know how much trouble I could get into? I'm on probation. I don't want to go back to prison. I'm getting my life back. I want to help, but God damn you, Liam."

I could tell she was disappointed in me, maybe even hurt. April grabbed her beer and poured it out into the sink.

"I'm sorry, April."

"I'm not a criminal. I was protecting myself from my husband." She stared at the floor for a moment, then locked her eyes on me. "You were the one person who treated me like I was okay, like I wasn't an ex-con. Now ... just leave, okay?" April waved her hand at me in a go-away motion.

I felt like shit. My moral compass, if I did indeed have one, was broken. I told her once more how sorry I was. Outside, the afternoon sun was bright and warm. Its rays felt like hot needles stabbing my skin.

CHAPTER FORTY-THREE

W ell, if it ain't Liam Sol. How the fuck are you?"
Bobby Dix owned a small motorcycle repair shop on Sandy Hook Road, a street that consisted mostly of auto repair shops, including Hector Delgado's, marine supply stores, and a decent taco joint.

But Bobby didn't look like he did when I last saw him a few years ago. Both of his legs had been removed just shy of the trunk of his body. He sat on a flat piece of plywood attached to steel skate wheels. He pushed off the ground with both hands and rolled himself over to greet me. I had to reach down just to shake his hand.

Lonnie told me Dix had stepped on a landmine his first week in country, blowing off his legs. Before the war, Bobby Dix had a mean streak like no one else I knew. He never backed down from a confrontation, though he did start most of them. He liked to surf, fight, and ride his Harley up and down PCH. He rode with many of the toughest outlaw biker gangs in the state but never joined any of them. Yet, out of some sense of duty or honor, he ended up enlisting in the Marines. Still, nothing Lonnie said prepared me for what I saw: a strong, fit man almost literally cut in half, forced to make his way around on a skateboard-type contraption.

"Bobby's Bikes. Not bad, huh?" He waved his arm in a sweeping motion like Carol Merrill showing off what was behind door number one on *Let's Make a Deal*. The garage wasn't large, but about a half-dozen bikes were lined up waiting to be repaired. When I arrived, he was working on an old Triumph motorcycle. His clothes and his face were stained with grease, and for the first time since I'd known him, I actually noticed his eyes. They were light blue and matched the sky.

"I'll give you a few minutes to take it all in," he said, indicating his condition. "You'll get used to it. I have."

"Oh, man, I'm sorry, Bobby. I didn't realize I was staring."

He shrugged. "I'm used to it."

"How are you doing?"

"It was rough at first, man. I'm finding my way. Slowly. But slow is better than nothin'. Shit, I didn't get a chance to shoot any gooks. Didn't even get a chance to serve my country. I just took one wrong step and that was it." He stared off into space for a moment, then caught himself.

"How'd 'Nam treat you? Now don't go thinkin' you didn't have it bad over there just cuz I got it worse. It was a fuckin' shit storm. There are guys, Liam, some of them come in here, who served over there, came back lookin' fit as a fiddle, but they are fucked up, man. I don't know if they'll ever find their way home. You know what I mean?"

I nodded.

"You know your pal, Lonnie? He has it bad. You know that, right?"

"I know, but he'll be okay," I said. But I wondered what Dix had seen in Lonnie that I had missed. I was sure that Lonnie hadn't told him the truth about what he had done over there.

He exhaled loudly. "Yeah, enough of that. So, what brings you here? You looking to buy a bike? I could set you up with a good one. And I know a damn fine mechanic."

The mean streak Bobby Dix once openly displayed to the world seemed to have vanished. It wasn't replaced with peace exactly, but something like acceptance had taken hold.

"I need your help, Bobby. Obviously, you owe me nothing, and I don't want to offend you, but I need a gun. I need a gun quickly."

"A shotgun, rifle, or a handgun?"

"A handgun."

Bobby rubbed his eyes.

"You should do this legally."

"I can't wait five days." A five-day waiting period was required to buy guns in California.

"And I'm sure you don't want the gun traced back to you?"

"When can you get it to me?"

"Come by after closing and bring cash. A couple of hundred should cover it."

I'd have to drop by the bank and withdraw some money.

"You know what you're doin'?" Bobby asked.

I looked down at Bobby, all three feet of him. "I don't know."

Bobby Dix and I shook hands, but he held on to mine.

"See you tonight. But I want you to think this over. You understand what I'm sayin'?"

I told him I did. He nodded his head and skated back to the Triumph, picked up a screwdriver, and stared at the engine.

Truth was, I didn't know what I was doing. But the image of Charlie Moran lying dead in the alley behind The Alamo reminded me that anything could happen, and I should be prepared for whatever might come.

I hadn't eaten all day, so I headed across the street to a Mexican food stand, Taco Paco. I ordered two tacos al pastor and a Coke. I took a seat at one of the outdoor benches. I poured a little salsa verde on the meat and took a bite. Most of the Mexican places in town used hard-shell tacos, but this place had freshly made white corn tortillas.

I felt bad about my encounter with April Fairchild. She was right. It had been thoughtless to ask for her help in acquiring a gun. I'd have to try to make it up to her somehow. April was new ground for me. I thought we could be good friends. I'd never been friends with a girl before, not where sex wasn't in the mix.

"Hey, lookie here, it's a *pocho* eating real Mexican food. Just don't drink the water."

I looked up as Hector Delgado approached me. His shop was only a few blocks away. He had a big grin on his face.

"Hey, Hector."

Hector ambled up to the counter and gave his order. I tried to scarf down my food. I wanted to leave before I had to talk to him, but Hector took a seat at my table.

"They let me have a running tab. Those tacos are good, huh?"

"Well, you know, I'm just a white guy, but yeah, I like 'em a lot."

"Not so white. I hear you're dating a real foxy Chicana. I've seen her. I may have some respect for you after all."

"I'm a lucky man." I wasn't about to tell him that Elisa no longer wanted to have anything to do with me.

"Hey, you know when you asked about The Bad Boogaloo? Well, Freddie Alvarez's little brother, Richard, is driving it now. He just turned sixteen."

I'd never bothered to follow up on the car. It was parked across the street from Catalina Garza's house the day I found her body.

"You listening to me?"

"Do you know where he lives?"

"Yeah, right across the street from where that *loca* bitch was killed."

If he lived there, then it made sense that his car was parked there, but I still needed to follow up. Maybe he'd seen something.

No longer hungry, I tossed my lunch into the trash.

"Thanks for the info, Hector."

"Hey, if your girlfriend ever gets tired of you, let me know. She might like to try it with a real Mexican man."

I made a cash withdrawal at the United California Bank. The teller stared at me as if she knew what I was planning to do with the money. Maybe it just my imagination, or maybe I was giving off a new kind of vibe, the vibe of a killer. After she handed me the cash, I made sure to thank her, but I could tell from her reaction that she still thought I was trouble.

"You sure about this, Liam?"

Particles of dust floated down from the rafters of Bobby's shop, like ashes after a wildfire. Bobby Dix looked up to me, an expression of concern covering his face.

"No," I said. "But if I'm lucky, I'll never have to use it."

I handed him the cash and Bobby handed me the pistol. "Guns have a way of bringing their own kind of luck, Liam, and it's usually bad."

I thought of James Fordham, the bullet hole in his head, his eyes open and staring at me. If I hadn't had a gun, he'd still be alive, my soul wouldn't be stained in black, and maybe I'd still be with Elisa.

"It's a Smith & Wesson 59, 9mm, just came out," he said. "Don't ask me where it came from. You don't want to know." Bobby gave me a quick demonstration on how to operate the gun. I was relieved to see that it handled much like my old Browning. After he had gone over everything, Dix handed me two additional magazines. "I know I don't have to tell you, but you didn't get this stuff from me."

"I know."

"I gotta get back to work. This bike needs to be done by morning."

Bobby Dix patted my knee and rolled his way back to a workbench that sat low to the ground. He sorted through his tools, singing James Taylor's "Fire and Rain," the evening sun drawing deep shadows between us.

CHAPTER FORTY-FOUR

That night I had unwelcome visitors in my sleep. Bobby Dix and Lonnie sat next to my bed examining me like surgeons preparing for a delicate operation. Bobby's legs had returned, but his feet had been replaced by roller skates. Lonnie's T-shirt was covered in Purple Heart medals. They each made the sign of the cross and began to pray in a language I couldn't understand.

Isabelle stood in the doorway, her dress slipping down to her feet, her body covered with scars, my father, Glenn, and James Fordham behind her, naked, their hands groping her body, Isabelle silently screaming, reaching out to me for help. I wanted to free her from them, but I couldn't move. I looked down at my body and saw that my arms and legs had been cut off, leaving only bloody stumps. Then the three dragged Isabelle away as she desperately clung to a jasmine bush, her fingers slowly slipping from the vines, and then she was gone.

The world turned cloudy and cold, and I rolled to my side and into the arms of Elisa, her embrace warming me, her body pressing against mine. "I had the worst dream," I told her. She whispered, "I love you," into my ear, then told me to close my eyes, her fingers running through my hair, as she kept whispering words of love to me, her voice slowly giving way to something that pounded on my front window.

"I'll see what it is," I told her, but when I turned to Elisa, she was gone. Christ. It was all a dream.

I heard myself cuss out loud. I threw on my jeans and grabbed my gun, just in case. There were too many possibilities of who might want me dead. I stumbled out to the living room, wondering if I was still locked in a dream.

"Who's there?"

I peeked out the window, but I couldn't see anyone. I slowly unlocked the door, opening it in one quick motion, my gun pointing straight ahead, my finger on the trigger. But no one was there. I stepped out on my front porch and saw a dead seagull. It must have flown into my window. The reflection must have looked like the ocean, but it was all a mirage and it ended up flying unknowingly into his death. I picked the gull up and gently dropped it into the trash can.

I went back inside, locking the door behind me. I knew digging further into the killings would only make me a bigger target. Maybe I did have a choice in the matter, but finding out the truth was the most important thing to me right now.

I got dressed and drove to Richard Alvarez's home. The Bad Boogaloo was parked in the driveway, gleaming in the morning sun. Catalina Garza's house had a For Rent sign in the yard. The beautiful rose bushes she had planted and maintained wilted in the sun. Everything Catalina Garza took pride in, her son, her roses, her own life, were either dead or dying.

The Alvarez home smelled of new paint and freshly cut grass. As I knocked on the door I could hear Three Dog Night in the background. A handsome boy of about sixteen opened the door. His hair was slicked back, and his crisp white T-shirt was tucked neatly into his pressed black pants. He looked at me, almost startled, as if we'd once had a run-in of some kind. But I had never seen him before in my life.

"I'm looking for Richard Alvarez."

He took a step back.

"I know who you are," he blurted out, his face losing its color. "I didn't see a thing, okay."

His reaction baffled me. I hadn't told him who I was or why I was asking for him. Did he think I was from the police?

"I'm not a cop. I'm a reporter. I just have a couple of questions."

"I don't want to mess with you, man. I didn't see a thing."

He slammed the door and I heard the lock turn.

"Richard," I called out. "I'm not a cop."

He wasn't coming back. Whoever had questioned him had put the fear of God in him. The kind of fear a cop could bring. What exactly had Alvarez witnessed?

I didn't know what else to do, so I spent the rest of the day looking for Wyatt Fordham. I stopped off at the surf breaks he liked to hit, but no one had seen him in the last week. I drove around town and up and down the coast, from Ventura to San Clemente. Wyatt loved the water, and though I knew I was on a failed mission, I had to find him. I had to assure him that I'd turn myself in, that I'd do the right thing, but I needed time to tie everything together before the police found and arrested him.

When I got home, I threw a TV dinner in the oven. Then I sat down at the dining room table and began writing out an apology to April Fairchild. I wrote *I'm sorry* and took a few sips of the beer. I couldn't find the right words, maybe that was all I had, and all that was needed, but it felt too easy.

The phone rang. Though I didn't want to be bothered, I found myself answering it.

"Liam, it's me, Elisa." Her voice formal and without emotion.

Still, my heart jumped and though I tried to fight it, I felt a surge of hope run through me.

"Elisa, I'm so happy you called—"

"The police came by this afternoon to talk to me."

"You? Why you?"

"They're just eliminating suspects, I guess. They wanted to know about you, about where you were that night." She paused. "I told them we were together the entire time. I just want you to know because they'll probably be talking to you."

She lied for me. I couldn't imagine what that must have done to her.

"Elisa, you didn't have to do that."

"I know, but I did it."

"I want to see you."

"No, Liam. I'm leaving."

"Maybe sometime later in the week I can come by and—"

"I'm leaving La Bolsa, Liam. I can't stay here any longer."

"Where are you going? I—"

"Goodbye, Liam." And then she hung up the phone.

I stood there, holding on to the receiver as if letting go would be letting go of her. Forever. After a moment, I hung up and my heart began to crack into tiny broken pieces, the jagged edges cutting into me like rust-stained knives.

CHAPTER FORTY-FIVE

I threw on my swim trunks, the water calling out to me. I left my house in a daze and lumbered across PCH, the sun bleeding into the horizon like an open wound. Pit fires lined the sand with partiers and families preparing for a warm and peaceful night at the beach. Couples held hands as they strolled along the shoreline, the water lapping at their heels. A picture-postcard moment trapped under a burning sky.

I didn't understand why the police asked Elisa about where I was the night James Fordham was murdered. It sounded like they had settled on Wyatt Fordham as the chief suspect. Why hadn't Greene let me know that the Pacific Harbor police might be talking to me? Was he setting me up? Had Luther Bennett put the police on to me? Or maybe I gave away something when I visited Fordham's house yesterday morning. Maybe someone saw me the night I killed him.

I could feel things were coming to a head, but I had no idea how any of it would play out. Either Greene or James Fordham had to be behind the Garza and Ortiz killings. As much as I wanted it to be Fordham, Greene was still a good possibility. Richard Alvarez appeared to fear the police. He thought I was a cop and was terrified that I was coming for him.

Greene had the badge, and he held the cards. Maybe I could bait him into confessing, but I doubted it. However this played out, I knew it would all end in my arrest. I murdered a man and there was no way I could let Wyatt take the hit for it. But I wasn't going down for the other killings. Whoever the killer was, I was going to take them down with me.

I walked onto the pier, past fishermen preparing for their evening catch, and couples getting in their last kisses before the sky turned dark. I made it to the edge of the pier. Catalina Island stood off in the distance slipping beneath a blanket of fog.

I felt the world closing in on me, as if I were in my last moments of freedom. I climbed onto the wooden rail, staring at the ocean below, almost invisible now. I bent my knees and pushed off into the air, free and light, my body bending and then stretching out as I sailed down through space, my arms in front of me forming an arrowhead, my body straight and true, the air rushing past me, as I descended toward the sea, the cool ocean water greeting me, taking me in, returning me to a past life, before consciousness, and into the earth's womb.

I swam to the surface, the sky suddenly dark and starless. I floated on my back and stared into the void, the faint echo of a woman's laugh the only sound breaking the silence. I felt a strong tug in the water as if the earth had shifted, then I headed back to shore, the fog behind me.

I stood on the shoreline, looking out to what I could see of the ocean and listened. I could sense a change in the current of the water. Out of the corner of my eye I saw a teenage girl slowly approach me.

"Are you Liam Sol?"

I told her I was, and she handed me a note.

"Some guy asked me to give you this. He said he was a friend."

I felt a knot form in my gut as I scanned the area, but whoever gave her the note had vanished into the gloom.

"What did he look like?"

She shrugged. "I have to get back to my parents."

I watched as she ran back to a fire pit surrounded by silhouettes huddled next to the flames. I opened the note. It's was a child's scrawl, matching the writing on the envelope that held the pictures of Elisa and Glenn. *I need to see you. Sunset Marsh. Midnight. You know where.*

I knew the place. The dumping ground for Ramona Ortiz and James Fordham. The midnight meeting seemed a little dramatic, and I felt stupid that I was going to walk into something I was unprepared for, but sometimes your worst option is the only one left to play.

Whoever gave the girl the note was probably on his way to Sunset Marsh, whether waiting for me or setting up a trap, I didn't know.

I ran across Coast Highway and back to my house where I dried off, changed, and retrieved my gun. I sat in my living room and tried to think things through, but my brain was muddled. I didn't know who wanted to see me, but the thoughts of my encounter with the pale-faced man lingered in my mind. But he was gone now. I had seen to that. Still, I felt a similar dread.

After a few hours, the sounds of the traffic rushing down Pacific Coast Highway had been drowned out by the sudden crashing of waves. Sometimes the swells seem to come out of nowhere, catching you off guard, unprepared, but I wasn't going to make that mistake tonight. I checked the time, 11:30. Though I knew it would only take me a few minutes to get there, I couldn't wait any longer.

I pulled off to the side of the road about a quarter mile from Sunset Marsh. I knew I wouldn't be sneaking up on anyone, but I didn't want to announce my arrival. The fog, as thick as I'd ever seen, had pushed its way over the ocean and across PCH. I pulled on a jacket and placed my gun in the inside pocket.

I tried to picture the setting, where the marsh water met the shore, where the weeds and bushes lined up, and if a killer were hiding, where he might position himself. Not that any of that mattered. Whoever sent me the note knew I was on my way.

I patted my chest, feeling the gun sitting securely in the interior jacket pocket. A strange and unwelcome realization came over me. I wasn't worried if I'd be able to pull the trigger. No, I knew I was ready to kill someone tonight.

The fog had choked out all the color, turning everything into a swirl of gray and black. A foul smell rose up from the marsh as if the earth were decaying. Something in the water splashed next to me and I pulled the gun from my jacket, letting it rest in my hand.

I approached the spot where Ramona Ortiz's body had been dumped and where James Fordham had been found. I stopped for a moment, and tried to get my eyes to adjust, but still I could only see a few feet in front of me.

A break in the clouds appeared and I saw a source of light glimmering dimly from a car parked just a few yards ahead of me. Then I heard the sounds, weird and otherworldly, and felt my body stiffen.

This was what Larry must have heard the night he witnessed Ramona Ortiz's body being dumped. I wanted to laugh at the absurdity of it. I had jumped to the conclusion that it had been from a police scanner, but it was Pink fucking Floyd. I felt like an idiot, though their music did sound as if it had come from somewhere outside of the universe, so I understood why it had freaked Larry out, especially since his mind was partially gone.

"Liam, is that you?"

Wyatt Fordham sat on the hood of his car. He held a gun in his hand, a bottle of beer next to him. I didn't approach as I tried to gather my thoughts. Wyatt Fordham killing anybody didn't make sense, but if this was the music Larry heard the night Ramona Ortiz's body had been dumped here, then Wyatt, however hard that was to fathom, may indeed be a killer.

I stepped into the clearing. Wisps of fog swirled around his car, his body shrouded in mist, and with Pink Floyd playing in the background, I felt as if I had been pushed into someone else's nightmare.

"Hey, Wyatt," I said, making my voice as calm as I could.

Wyatt took a swig from his bottle. "I was hoping you'd show up."

"Why did you call me out here?" I kept my eyes focused on his gun, which looked loose in his hand.

"I need to confess something to you."

"Me? What for?"

"I made you kill my father."

"What are you talking about?"

"Isabelle told me all about why she killed your dad and how you protected her, and how you protect the ones you love. I figured that once you saw the photographs you'd go after both of them. I don't know why you didn't kill Glenn, too. He's not good for Isabelle."

Both of them. His father and Glenn. "You sent me the pictures."

Wyatt looked as if he was about to break down and cry. "My dad was with Isabelle, but you know that now. I couldn't find those pictures. I wanted to destroy them, but he must have hidden them somewhere."

"I destroyed them, Wyatt. No one will ever see them."

"She was right, you protect the ones you love."

Wyatt's fingernails dug into his arm, breaking the skin. "He knew I was in love with her. He didn't care. Then he stole the land from me. He kept taking bits of my soul, tossing them away like garbage, like I was garbage."

"You were the one in your father's house that night."

"I followed you from your mom's. I knew once you saw the pictures you'd show up there. When I heard the gunshots, I panicked and ran to my car. I didn't know what to do, but when I saw you leaving the house I decided to follow you."

"Why did you dump his body into Sunset Marsh?"

Wyatt let out a mean little laugh. "That's where he belonged. He made the state say that I was crazy. His own son. I wanted to save this place and leave it untouched forever, as it had always been, wild, innocent. You know how few places like this are left? He wanted the land that bad, I thought he should rot there. I only wish I'd done a better job of hiding his body."

For a moment Wyatt was completely shrouded by the fog. When the clouds cleared, he looked lost and alone, his fingernails digging into the arm that held his gun.

"But now I'm scared, Liam. The police want to arrest me because they think I killed him. They should be on their way. You need to tell them the truth."

A jolt of panic ran through my nervous system. This could be it for me, but I needed more answers before I could let them arrest me.

"Wyatt, you killed Ramona Ortiz, you remember that, right?"

"No, I didn't do that."

"But you were here, someone saw you."

"I dumped her body here, but I didn't kill her."

"I don't understand?"

"She called me. Said she needed my help."

"What do you mean she?"

"Isabelle. She knew I'd loved her, that I'd be there for her."

I felt my heart stop. "Isabelle killed Ramona Ortiz? Why?"

Wyatt nodded his head. "That woman threatened her. Isabelle told me she had no choice. She killed the others, you know."

"What others?"

"Some kid who was trying to blackmail her. Then she killed his mother."

Damn it, the pieces were beginning to fit now. We *were* the prominent family that Julio had dirt on. Isabelle ran him down because of it, and then when my article was published, she murdered Catalina Garza. But why Julio's mother?

Suddenly I understood Richard Alvarez's reaction to me. He had either seen Isabelle kill Catalina, or she threatened him because of what he might have seen. When I came to the door, he saw the family resemblance. He knew I was related to Isabelle and that scared him. He was scared of the Sol family, not the police.

It was all Isabelle. "Jesus Christ," I muttered to myself.

Wyatt looked at me, his fingernails cutting into his skin, drawing blood.

My mind raced ahead of me. There was a lot more to the puzzle, but I was having trouble keeping anything straight.

"Wyatt, do you know where Isabelle is now?"

"She's with Glenn."

Isabelle had already tried to kill Glenn once, she might try again. "Where are they?"

"I don't know. She didn't tell me. I think she used me, Liam."

Of course, she did. Using people was a family trait. "Did she say anything else?"

"She just said she was going to take him someplace special. She wants to be with him, not me."

I thought of the pier, the place where Isabelle had killed my father.

"Wyatt, stay here. I have to get Isabelle."

Wyatt raised the gun and pointed it at me. "You can't go anywhere."

"No, Wyatt." Possible scenarios played through my mind as if I were watching a dozen movies on the same screen simultaneously. "I'm going to find Isabelle. You need to trust me. Can you do that?"

Wyatt nodded his head and dropped the gun into the mud below.

"I'll do right by you, Wyatt. I promise."

"I'm sorry, Liam. I shouldn't have done any of this. I shouldn't have made you kill him." He examined his arms, as his fingernails clawed ever deeper into his flesh, his blood dripping freely into the marsh.

I didn't know where the cops were. Maybe they were on their way, or maybe Wyatt had been talking nonsense about having called them. It didn't matter. I had to stop Isabelle before she killed again.

CHAPTER FORTY-SIX

The Karmann Ghia sputtered its way through the mist as I drove to the pier, as if it wanted me to reconsider what I was doing. I couldn't shake what Wyatt had confessed to me. How he knew he could turn me into a killer. And Isabelle again. Maybe murder was a family trait.

I parked on the highway just in front of the pier. The waves pounded hard against the sand, but the ocean was all but invisible. The fog had dug itself in and seemed to be making a stand for the night.

I stood at the foot of the pier. The waves crashing now with more frequency, crashing hard, the wood pillars of the pier creaking in their wake. For a brief moment, a break in the fog appeared and the pier looked as if it were a bridge leading to purgatory.

The clouds filled the air again and I could only see a few yards in front of me. I heard screams coming from the waves as surfers rode blindly through the dark wall of fog. It wasn't going to end well for them.

I had no idea where Isabelle and Glenn were, so I kept my pace slow and deliberate, the knot in my stomach winding ever tighter.

The pier reeked of dead fish, something the clean salt air couldn't sanitize.

I was at the halfway point, the spot where I had killed the pale-faced man. I hadn't seen anyone, no fishermen, no lovers kissing in the mist, nothing. The La Bolsa police were strict about keeping curfew. I kept moving forward, my pace quickening the closer I got to the end of the pier. Then silence, a break between sets kept the ocean and the surfers quiet. Then I heard a man pleading and begging.

"I'm sorry, I'll never—"

It proved to be a short lull, the waves came crashing back, breaking louder than before, and I heard a gunshot that faded into the roar of the waves. I sprinted toward the sound of the gunfire.

It was just the two of them, Glenn on the ground, bleeding, and Isabelle sitting down, her back against the rail, a smoking gun in her hand, tears streaming down her face. I stood frozen, taking in the scene as if watching a play. Glenn struggled to his knees and reached his hand out to her.

"Isabelle, don't, Isabelle. You know I love you."

She pulled the trigger and Glenn slumped to the ground.

Isabelle looked at me. "Liam," she said, as if she were happy to see me.

I ran over to Glenn and rolled him onto his back. His chest painted red, his mouth agape as if he were still trying to call out Isabelle's name. I checked for any sign of life, but he was gone.

I felt his blood on my hands, sticky and warm. I looked at Isabelle, her gun now pointed at me.

"Isabelle, are Marie and Mom okay?"

"Of course. Why wouldn't they be?"

I glanced back at Glenn's body. "Why did you kill him?"

"Why? How can you ask that? Look at me!" she screamed. "This, he did this to me! They all did!"

The gun in her hand held steady, a far cry from when she had tried to shoot Glenn at the house.

322

"Isabelle, give me the gun."

"Stay there, Liam."

I wasn't about to approach her. She appeared calm, yet also apart from reality, as if she were in her own world, one where I was only a visitor.

"Did you kill Julio Garza?"

"I was only trying to protect myself, Liam. He wanted money; he knew I'd been locked up in that asylum. He was going to tell everyone. I couldn't let that happen. People laughing at me behind my back. Whispering lies about me."

"You killed his mother?"

"I wished you'd never written that article," she said. "I didn't want to kill her. You have to believe me. She liked you. I told her I was your sister and she let me in. Such a sweet woman. After she went into the kitchen to make us coffee, I searched his bedroom to see if he had left anything that could implicate me. She caught me going through his stuff and ran to the phone to call the police. I tried reasoning with her, but ..." She let out a sigh and shrugged. "She gave me no choice."

"You have a choice now."

"No, Liam. I never had a choice." Her eyes were void of light now.

"What about Ramona Ortiz?"

"I had to. She wanted to take Glenn. She was pregnant with his child," she said, pointing at Glenn's dead body. "Did you know that? She came to the house the night of Glenn's reception, demanding to see him. Everyone had gone home by then, and it was just the two of us. I did what I had to do. I called Wyatt Fordham and he helped me dump the body. He'll do anything for me."

"Charlie Moran, what about him?"

"Who?"

"Charlie Moran, you shot him in the alley behind The Alamo."

"I don't know what you're talking about. Are you accusing me of murder?"

"You didn't know him?"

323

"Stop trying to confuse me." Isabelle shook her head.

Maybe James Fordham did kill Moran, but I couldn't think about that now. I had to help Isabelle.

"Please put the gun down, Isabelle."

The waves were relentless now, the fog and mist swirling all around us made Isabelle look like the angel of death.

"I didn't want this, Liam. All I ever wanted was to be left alone."

"I know."

"Daddy, Glenn, Fordham ... why, Liam? They hurt me. I didn't do anything to them." Isabelle gritted her teeth, her face turning red. "They hurt me!" she screamed. "They hurt me!"

I took a couple of small steps toward her.

"Isabelle ..."

She aimed the gun at me. "Stop, Liam. Please."

I did as she asked. She was tearing me apart. I wanted to hold her. I wanted to help her, but I didn't know how. "Let's go, Isabelle. Let's get in my car and go someplace where no one can find us."

Isabelle tilted her head. "Oh, Liam. I can't let you do that. I need to free you from me. I'm sorry for what I've put you through. I'm the one who turned you into a killer."

"No, you didn't."

"Don't lie, Liam. You killed James Fordham because of me. You're the sweetest brother I could ask for, but look what I've done to you."

"I'll be okay," I said, trying to reassure her.

"No. Don't lie, Liam. You've changed. I can see it. I did that to you."

She turned the gun on herself, placing the barrel right above her right temple, tears streaming down her face. "No one will ever hurt me again."

I was getting desperate. "Don't Isabelle, please, please put the gun down."

I took a couple of steps toward her. I needed to get a few feet closer if I was going to have any chance of taking her gun. My heart pounded rapidly to an offbeat rhythm, my breaths rapid and shallow.

"I can't do this anymore," she said. "I can't. I just want to go home now, Okay? I just want to go home."

I edged closer to her.

"Don't do this, Isabelle. I love you, you know that."

"I know that. I've always known that. I love you, too, Liam."

She pushed the gun hard against her temple and closed her eyes.

"Isabelle!"

And then she pulled the trigger.

The breaking waves drowned out my screams, drowned out the gunshot, but they couldn't block out what I had witnessed. It was as if I could see it all in slow motion. The bullet coming out of the barrel. Isabelle's face, never lovelier, as if she had finally found the peace that had always eluded her. The bullet burrowing into her skull. An explosion of blood. And Isabelle falling to her side, her eyes closed, her pain forever gone.

Then I was holding her in my arms, shaking, crying like a baby, begging and praying to God to save her soul. I didn't know how long I sat with her in my arms.

Detective Greene walked out of the mist and into the scene, his police revolver firmly in his hand.

I pulled the gun from my jacket and pointed it at him. "I'll do it, Greene. I have nothing left to lose, you know that."

Greene raised his gun and aimed it at me. It was the third time tonight someone pointed their gun at me.

"What the hell happened?" he asked.

Greene placed his gun back into his holster and checked on Glenn.

He knelt down next to Glenn's body and exhaled. He looked at Isabelle then averted his eyes.

"Why are you here?" I asked, lowering my gun.

"We picked up Wyatt Fordham on PCH. We're arresting him for the murder of his father. He's really fucked up. He started babbling about you being here and that something bad was going to happen. I rushed over as fast as I could, but I'm obviously too late." He let out a sigh.

"So was I."

Greene rubbed his face with both hands.

"You can't arrest Wyatt Fordham. He didn't ..."

"Didn't what?"

"He's innocent. I'm the one who killed James Fordham." I couldn't keep the lies going anymore. Nor could I protect Isabelle any longer. I told him everything.

Greene rubbed his forehead. "You killed Fordham? Christ."

I looked down at Isabelle, wishing I could have prevented all this.

"She killed Julio Garza. I'm sorry. I know how you felt about him, but he was blackmailing her about being locked up in a mental asylum and she didn't see any other way out."

Greene shut his eyes, a look of anguish across his face. "Fucking Julio," he said. He turned away from me and put his hands on his knees. "I told him about Isabelle, Liam. He was in awe of your family, drove me crazy. I told him you guys weren't perfect, that Isabelle had once been put in a mental hospital. I was trying to make him feel better. Jesus. I didn't know he'd try blackmailing her. I didn't ... Goddammit."

I didn't know what to feel. Anger, sadness? I couldn't tell. It was an innocent comment, but it triggered so much death. Yet I couldn't ignore what I knew I knew to be true, what I'd seen with my own eyes.

"Isabelle's a killer, Greene. She didn't just kill Julio and Glenn. She also killed Catalina Garza and Ramona Ortiz. But not Moran. She didn't even know who he was."

He turned back to me. His eyes red. "I'm sorry," he said.

"What do we do now?"

Greene worked over the scene before him as if attempting to put together a puzzle.

"We don't have much time, Liam. Give me your gun."

"No way."

"You need to trust me."

I let Isabelle down to the ground gently and kissed her cheek. I struggled to my feet and handed him the weapon.

"You don't want to be found with this," he said.

He pulled out a handkerchief, wiped the gun down, and threw it into the ocean. I was about to tell him that it wasn't the gun that I shot James Fordham with, but then he pulled out another gun from his jacket pocket. I tensed up thinking I'd just made a grave mistake.

He held it in his handkerchief and placed the gun in Glenn's hand. He wrapped Glenn's index finger around the trigger and pointed the gun at the rail near Isabelle's body, and he pulled the trigger. Shards of wood exploded around her. The shot drowned out by the crashing waves. He let Glenn's hand drop to the ground, the gun falling next to the body.

"It's a crude job," he said, "but maybe we can make it look like Isabelle shot him in self-defense."

"What the hell are you doing?"

Greene gave me a look that told me everything I needed to know.

"It wasn't Fordham," I said. "You did it, didn't you? You killed Charlie Moran with that gun. He was done threatening you. He was going to let everyone know about you and Julio. You couldn't let him do that to you. Now you want to make it look like Glenn killed Moran."

He rubbed his eyes and let out a long sigh.

"I had to. Moran kept pushing me, he wouldn't let up." Greene shook his head. "I hated having to bow down to him. I hated what he could do to me, that he could ruin my life."

The waves pounded harder, shaking the pier. I didn't say anything. He killed Charlie Moran for the same reason Isabelle killed the others. They were tired of being used and controlled.

"Do you think we can trust each other?" he asked. "If we stick together, this might work."

A dark thought crossed my mind. "You were hoping to frame me, weren't you? You didn't know what you were going to find here. But you knew I was here. That's why you brought the gun, the gun you shot Charlie Moran with."

"I wasn't hoping for anything, certainly not this."

"What about Wyatt? He's innocent. I killed his father."

"We won't file any charges, I'll make sure of that."

"Are you going to arrest me?"

He didn't respond.

"We need to make this work to our advantage," he said. "We know your brother-in-law had a lot to hide. Let's say Glenn was the one being blackmailed, first by Julio Garza and then by James Fordham. It'll be tough, but I think we can make it stick. Isabelle won't be remembered as a murderer, and Glenn will take the fall for all of the killings, the Garzas, Moran, Ramona Ortiz, and James Fordham."

"I can't do this," I said. "I can't."

"You have an alibi for the night James Fordham was murdered. That guy was the scum of the earth, Liam. Don't go to jail for that guy. He's not worth it."

"Wyatt knows what I did."

"He was a babbling mess when I left him. He's not a credible witness."

"I don't have an alibi."

Greene placed his hand on my shoulder. "Yes, you do."

Elisa, I thought. Why had she lied for me? I looked back at Isabelle, then at my jacket and shirt, and they were covered in her blood. I felt my gut churn, as if I'd just downed something vile. I leaned over the rail, retching and heaving into the ocean below. Then I crumbled to the ground, my body shaking and covered in cold sweat.

Greene crouched down in front of me. "I know this is hard, but if we're going to get out of this, we need to get our story straight."

And that was it. Glenn had taken Isabelle out for a walk and tried to kill her because she had discovered the truth, that he was the killer, but she beat him to it and then took her own life. I was the lone witness.

Though you could drive a truck through the holes in the story, it was the only story that made any kind of sense. With Greene leading the investigation, and me being a trusted and reliable witness, I thought maybe the two of us could make it work.

Yet, something nagged at me, something I couldn't ignore. I had made a promise to myself that I would find justice for Julio and Catalina. Glenn being blamed for killing them wasn't giving them the justice I had promised. I met Catalina Garza. I saw the hurt in her eyes. I saw, too, that she believed in me, that she trusted me to do the right thing. I wasn't going to let her be anyone's pawn. The truth was the only way to get her and her son any justice. It couldn't be any other way.

"No, Greene."

"No, what?"

"I can't protect Isabelle any longer. It's not right. We have to tell the truth."

"The whole truth?"

I knew what he was asking.

"I'm not going down for Charlie Moran's murder," he said, "and you shouldn't have to go down for the murder of James Fordham. He was a sick fuck who deserved what he got."

"Isabelle killed Julio and Catalina Garza. Then she killed Ramona Ortiz. I can't lie about that."

The waves began to crash harder, spraying saltwater over the pier. Greene closed his eyes and took in a deep breath. "Okay, but then we need to pin Moran and Fordham's death on Glenn."

"I don't know. Where does it stop?"

"It stops here." Greene came up to me. "You want to go to prison for this? Don't be an idiot. Glenn had plenty of reasons to kill Fordham. He's dead now, and you don't need to go to prison for something Fordham put into play."

It all sounded like a sick version of Monopoly, except we weren't trading properties, we were trading our morals. Everything was for sale, everything could be bartered, not exactly what I learned in church, but why should I go to jail for killing a piece of shit? Greene made sense, or maybe I was once again lying to myself. I was in no mood to contemplate it any further. Glenn put his fate into play by raping Elisa and then letting James Fordham rape Isabelle.

"I'll think about it. But why did Glenn kill Moran then?"

"Let me worry about that."

"I will."

Was I betraying Isabelle by coming forward with the truth? Part of me felt like it, but maybe she would want everyone to know that she was nobody's patsy.

Everyone believed that Glenn and Isabelle were the perfect couple. JFK and Jackie reborn, a West Coast Camelot in the making. Now they were going to look like Bonnie and Clyde, and my mother and Marie would do everything to fight back, even if it meant sacrificing me to the wolves in the process.

"Are we good, Liam? I need to get back to my car and call this in."

I looked over at Isabelle. Her body lying alone, wisps of fog hovering around her. I knew what was going to happen. The leering, the jokes, the insults, her lying naked at the coroner's office where I'm sure officials would find a reason to stop by, each one wanting to take a good look at the woman they had all lusted after, the beautiful Isabelle Sol. Seeing her now, she was so vulnerable, such easy prey. I had to do something for her. I couldn't leave her like this. I marched back to her.

"Sol, where are you going?"

I didn't answer, I kept going. I knelt down next to her and said a prayer. Then I scooped her up in my arms.

"Damn it, Sol, what are you doing? Don't fuck this up."

I knew that what I was about to do could ruin everything, but I didn't care. I held her in my arms, her body somehow lighter in death. I kissed her forehead. "I love you, Isabelle," I whispered. I held her over the railing and gently let her go, her body disappearing into the fog and falling into the raging sea below.

"God damn it!" Greene yelled. "God damn it!"

Yes, there was a good chance her body would wash to shore, but I couldn't leave her here, and maybe the ocean could somehow cleanse her of her sins, leaving her soul clean and unmarked.

"Now what are we going to do?" he asked.

"You'll think of something."

"Shit," was all he said.

"I have to check on my mom and Marie." Isabelle had alluded that they were alive, but I had to see for myself. And if they were alive, I'd have to tell them about Glenn and Isabelle.

"You can't go anywhere, Sol. You need to be here!"

I ignored him and drove home. There, I washed off and put on a clean shirt. I called my mom's house. With each unanswered ring, it felt as if someone had slapped me. What had Isabelle done to them?

Marie finally answered the phone, her voice groggy from sleep. A wave of relief washed over me.

"It's Liam. I'm coming over."

"What do you want?" Her voice gruff and on edge.

"Wake Mom. I'm on my way."

"Liam?"

"Just wake her up. I'll be there soon."

I hung up the phone and stared outside. I saw my reflection in the window. With the fog swirling outside, I looked like an image from a horror film. And then, suddenly, I started crying again, and I couldn't stop. I got back into my car, tears rushing down my face, my body heaving uncontrollably.

CHAPTER FORTY-SEVEN

Isabelle is what?" Marie asked, her face as pale as death. She gripped her robe and collapsed on the couch as if someone had pushed her.

"What have you done, Liam?" my mother hissed. "You can't leave us alone, can you? All of your holier than thou bullshit. Tell me, how many people have died because of your interference?"

Too many, I thought. We were in the living room. I had no idea how this was going to play out. On the drive over, I'd thought about telling them the lie that Greene and I had concocted, but they knew Glenn was incapable of killing anyone. He was too weak to pull a trigger, too weak to strangle another person to death. I told them the truth instead.

"Isabelle wasn't acting strange? You didn't know?" I asked.

"Of course, we didn't know! We don't keep track of her. We thought she'd been fixed. She could come and go as she pleased. If we had known we would have put her back in that place." *That place*, that's how my mother referred to the mental hospital where Isabelle had been committed. "Glenn could have been the governor, maybe senator. Who knows how far he could have gone?"

"Glenn was a piece of shit."

"At least he was ambitious. He wanted something out of life. My own son, who could have had the world at his feet, would rather play in the water like a child."

I held back from responding. I couldn't get us off track.

"What about Felix's death?" Marie asked, referring to our father. "And the others from before?" Her expression still one of disbelief.

"The pale-faced man killed them, that story stays the same."

"It's over," my mother said. "We're ruined, you know."

And there it was. No tears for Isabelle, her own daughter, the daughter that her husband chose over her. Something for which she could never forgive Isabelle. No, all that mattered was that the family's image would be shattered. The political ambitions of obtaining even more power were about to vanish. And, of course, the shame, that's the dagger that my mother feared the most, the shame.

"When will they release her body?"

"They won't." Then I told them what I had done.

"Jesus, Liam." Marie looked broken, something I thought I'd never see in her.

"You did what?" my mother cried out. "How could you?"

"I don't want their hands on her. I don't want anyone to touch her. I don't want anyone looking at her. I want her to be left alone."

"So, because of you, we can't even give her a proper goodbye. Who gave you that right? Who do you think you are?" My mother stepped toward me, her hands clenched. I thought for a moment that she was going to hit me. Then she stopped. "I can't hold her in my arms one last time. Not ever again. How could you?"

"He was only trying to protect her, Brona. I don't like it any better than you, but maybe Liam did the right thing."

"I want her back. I want ..." My mother broke down, unable to complete the sentence. She staggered over to the window and stared at the darkness outside, contemplating God knows what.

We stood in silence for a moment, each in our own world.

Marie finally spoke, "I can't believe Isabelle could do such a thing."

"She killed before," I said. "I don't know why we thought she was

334

incapable of doing it again. Isabelle got back at the those who ruined her, the ones who destroyed her life, and those she thought were trying to ruin her. She couldn't take it anymore. Can you blame her for that?"

My mother turned around, her face cold as a stone. "But you, Liam, you killed James Fordham and you want us to lie for you now. And this detective, we have to lie for him as well. Tell them Glenn was the killer?"

"It's the only way."

"And why should we lie for him?"

"Because he knows the truth about our own cover-up. And we're all implicated in that."

"Why is he helping us? Maybe he wants something he can hold over us, is that it?"

I wasn't about to tell them about Greene's sexuality, but I wasn't going to leave him in the clear, either. Too much was at stake. "No, he killed Charlie Moran. And Moran was digging into our family's history." Which was a lie, but one I knew they'd believe.

"This is going to be horrible, isn't it?" Marie asked. "The police, the press, they'll never stop asking questions, will they?"

"Greene will help us on the police side, but no, it won't be easy."

My mother turned to me. "Why should we lie for you, Liam? You're the one who killed James Fordham, not Glenn. You're the one who should go to jail."

Marie stepped in before I could reply.

"Listen to me, Brona. What Glenn and James Fordham did to Isabelle, they deserved to die. I'm glad Liam killed Fordham, and Glenn can burn in hell for all I care." Marie let out a sigh. "Why can't we frame Glenn for all of the murders? Keep Isabelle in the clear?"

"There would be too much to cover up. Too many ways we could get caught lying. Look, if you want me to confess, I will."

"No one is touching you, Liam," Marie said. I didn't know where her sudden regard for me came from, and I wasn't sure I could trust it. She put her arms around me. Her tears soaked through my shirt. She began whispering to herself, almost chanting,

"No, not Isabelle. Not Isabelle. God, not Isabelle."

Guttural cries then came from her, as if all the masks, all the protective shields she had been wearing for all the years of her life had been stripped away and there was nothing that could protect her from the pain and the hurt and the loss. The realization that her only sister had died, and everything she had resented Isabelle for seemed trivial, a waste, and she felt her own heart shatter into pieces. Or maybe that was what I'd hoped she was feeling. It was just as likely that she realized her hopes had all gone up in smoke and there was no backup plan, and for the first time in her life, she felt alone and afraid.

She let go of me and wiped her face and left the room without saying a word.

My mother stepped toward me. "And this is all because of you, Liam. Everything. But we'll do it, we'll lie for you."

She grabbed me by the collar with her left hand and reared back her right hand and slapped me across the face. I felt the sting, along with all the bitterness and anger that she'd felt toward me. My eyes watered from the slap, then she slapped me two more times before I stopped her. She fell to her knees and began to cry, for whom or what I couldn't begin to guess.

A couple of moments later her tears subsided.

"Help your mother up, Liam."

I pulled her to her feet, then she pushed me away and staggered to the kitchen where I guessed she'd start hitting the whiskey. I don't know why, but I followed her. Maybe I needed a shot as well.

She pulled out a pair of glasses and filled them to the brim. She took a long swallow, her eyes settled on the bottle. We stood in silence until she finished her drink. She refilled her glass and turned her gaze to me.

"Do you think it's a sin, Liam? Resenting your own daughter?"

"I think we all have more than enough sins to go around."

She finished off her drink, then grabbed the bottle and once more filled her glass.

"Everybody loved Isabelle, but I never could. Not even when she was a baby, as beautiful as she was." My mother cast her eyes downward. "She never fussed, you know, and rarely did she ever cry." She took another shot of the whiskey. "Isabelle was always the most beautiful girl in the room. I don't think she ever truly realized that, you know? Your father would come back to our bed after being with her. I'd lie awake next to the man as he slept soundly, hating him, hating her, but never doing anything about it, just praying that someday it would be over and he would come back to me. Eventually, he stopped. He came back to me and it was wonderful, until someone else came along. The times when he was mine were magical, glorious, but I knew that soon there'd be someone else, and there always was, you know."

I knew I should try to comfort her, to make her feel better, but it wasn't in me.

"Why did you kill James, Liam? Were you seeking revenge? Was that it?"

"He deserved to die." I didn't say what else I was feeling, because now, suddenly, I wished I had taken my time with him and killed him slowly and deliberately, making him suffer, making him beg for his life. Would that have been worse than what I'd done to him, taking him out quickly and without thought? I didn't know. The concept of good and evil was lost on me. I just knew that Isabelle didn't deserve any of what came her way. Maybe if God did exist he'd be able to figure it all out, but for now I was at a loss. I looked over at my mother, her eyes dry, but vacant.

"You're a lot like your father, you know."

"Don't say that."

"He would have done the same thing."

"I'm not like him."

"Keep telling yourself that, Liam. As much as you try to pull away from us, you keep coming back. You're part of the family. You're one of us."

I didn't respond. I finished off the whiskey, wondering what kind of deal I had made for myself.

"So," she said, "we all get our stories straight and then we move on, is that it?"

"Yeah," I said. "That's it."

She turned to me and smiled.

"Welcome back to the family, Liam." Then she left the kitchen, leaving me alone with my thoughts, my gut churning, my chest on fire as if someone had branded my heart with red burning coal.

CHAPTER FORTY-EIGHT

And so we moved on, or tried to. We went through the motions, we all stuck to the same story, the same lies, all bound together by our own self interests.

Isabelle's body never washed to shore. We held a private funeral service for her, just the family. Glenn's family had his body driven down to his childhood hometown of La Jolla. His parents were bewildered and confused over what had driven their son to such madness. They deserved the truth, but instead they became unwitting accomplices in our charade. That's how it had to be. I questioned whether Glenn deserved his fate, but after what he did to Isabelle, I could shed no tears for him. His parents, though, were victims of a crime they knew nothing about.

I quit my job at the *La Bolsa Tribune* and began to live off my savings and my trust fund. I did some surfing, and I wrote a couple of freelance articles for *Surf's Up!*, a local surf magazine, just to fill up some time. Other than that, I hung out at The Alamo. April Fairchild and I were on good terms again. She accepted my apology with grace, and that meant a lot to me.

The midafternoon July sun peeked through the cracks of the front the door of The Alamo, casting slivers of light which appeared like slash marks on the floor. I was in the middle of *The Death of Artemio Cruz*. I couldn't exactly explain why, but I found myself reading every book I could recall that had sat on Elisa's bookshelf.

"What are you doing?" April shot me a look. She didn't look happy.

"What do you mean?"

"Come on, Liam. You're here most every afternoon, have a few cups of coffee, and read. Don't you have anything else to do?"

This is what my life was now, surfing, hanging out here at The Alamo, and occasionally sitting in on different philosophy classes at Long Beach State.

"What's your point?"

"You sit here by yourself in a dark bar, reading all of the books she owned. You look miserable and alone. Do the math."

I wasn't happy. She was right. I tried to forget what I could about the killings, and about Isabelle, but that turned out to be a doomed effort. I could never forget about Isabelle. At the same time, I was trying to remember every moment that Elisa and I spent together. Another doomed effort, because the most lasting memory I had of Elisa was when I broke her heart.

"I don't know where she lives."

"Figure it out. You used to be a reporter."

"I've caused her enough pain."

"So that's it, huh?" She leaned close to me. "Liam, I want you to take this in the way it's meant. You're as bad as the drunks who come in here every night, full of regret and self-pity. Just because you're not drinking alcohol doesn't mean you're not wasting your life. You've gone through a lot lately, you don't talk about it, but I read the papers, the whole thing was god awful, but how long are you going to hide out?"

She grabbed my coffee cup and emptied it into the sink.

"Go ahead and sit there for all I care, but I'm done serving you."

April moved to the other side of the bar and began sorting through a stack of receipts.

I moved to a table in the back and returned to my book, but I found it hard to concentrate. The more books of hers I read, the more I wanted Elisa back. I had only cracked the surface of who she was and knew there was so much more to her, and that knowledge had carved a hole in my heart.

I had lost all direction. I didn't like who I saw in the mirror. I knew I needed to do something. I'd been contemplating re-upping with the Army and going back to Vietnam, but I knew that would mean embracing the darkness that was growing in my soul, something I'd been trying to fight off. I held the book in my hands, though it wasn't her copy, I felt her presence. Maybe April was right, maybe it was time to do the math.

CHAPTER FORTY-NINE

Detective Greene and I were at The Driftwood, sitting outside on the back patio, our meals untouched. Greene had dark circles under his eyes, heavy like wet sandbags. He had kept his word and did yeoman's work guiding the investigation away from us. But he looked haggard and worn, not because of his lies, or our lies, but because he had killed a man in cold blood, and he too, found that hard to live with. Detective Greene was okay in my book. I could never condone what he did, but I understood why he had killed Charlie Moran. Moran was holding Greene hostage with a ransom he couldn't afford to pay, so Greene did what he had to do, or thought he had to do. We both did. But I also knew that killers could always find ways to justify their crimes.

"I'm leaving the department."

"What are you going to do?"

"I'm still going to be a cop. That's who I am. There was an opening in San Diego. Looks like a good place to live. I have to get out of La Bolsa. It's not good for me here." He paused for a moment. "It's a pretty little town though, isn't it? At least from the outside."

"Everything looks better from the outside."

Greene nodded his head. "This is for you." He reached into his shirt pocket and pulled out a slip of paper and handed it to me.

"Thanks, I appreciate it." I placed the paper into my pocket without looking at it.

"You know what you're going to do?"

"Hopefully, the right thing."

"Yeah, knowing what the right thing is isn't always that easy."

"No, it isn't," I said.

"I should probably get going. I have a lot to get done before I leave, packing mostly." Greene stood up and we shook hands, but we avoided eye contact. We were two compromised men, trying to get back what we'd lost, or at least trying to learn to live with what we'd lost.

But life, I learned, was all about making choices and I was choosing to try to move on.

I sold my Karmann Ghia and bought a used VW van. I secured my surfboards on the roof rack and removed the interior seats and replaced them with a small raised bed, with storage for my clothes underneath. Lonnie built a table and a small bench seat for eating and writing, as well as a tiny bookshelf.

Lonnie had considered shutting down his church because of what he did in Vietnam, but people kept showing up, knocking on the door, seeking his advice and the comfort they received from his sermons.

"I don't think I'm worthy of their trust, Liam."

"They aren't looking for perfection, Lonnie."

"I know." He looked away for a moment. "Hey, thanks for the chair. I know it means a lot to you."

There was no one else I'd have rather handed off my old leather chair to.

"I put the sign in the van for you," he said.

"Thanks."

"You're doing a good thing."

I put my hand on his shoulder and then we hugged, his arms tight around me.

"We need to forgive ourselves, Liam," he whispered.

"I'm trying."

We broke free from the hug and shook hands one more time, each of us wondering if forgiveness was really possible.

CHAPTER FIFTY

I drove up Pacific Coast Highway, past Main, then slowed up to a vacant lot where my house once sat. It was gone now, nothing left but dirt and memories. A large sign had been constructed on the corner of the lot. *Coming Soon! Luxury Apartments Overlooking the Pacific Ocean ... Live, Play, and Relax in One of California's Most Desirable Beach Cities!* The sign showed a painting of a young, good-looking couple in their bathing suits, full of smiles and promise. If they only knew.

The two oil wells that sat next to my house had been dismantled, the oil now gone, soon to be replaced by luxury real estate. Even with the scandal still fresh in everyone's mind, money kept pumping into the Sol family.

Marie had called me up last week and asked if I could join her for dinner. She and I had only spoken a few times since Isabelle's death, but never in person. We met at Rosa's Cantina and sat in a booth next to a window overlooking the ocean. Neither of us felt at ease and we struggled with small talk. Marie and I were never good at the kind of chitchat that most families can pretend to engage in.

"Are you and Mom holding up okay?" I asked.

"Brona's been good," she said. "It's hard for her, for us, I mean the shame and all. She hasn't left the house once since … you know. But it's time to move on, and that's why I wanted to meet tonight."

Marie had never asked how the aftermath had affected me or if I was still mourning the death of Isabelle, something I had witnessed firsthand, an image I could never shake. I still missed Isabelle, and I always would.

Marie reached into her purse and pulled out a sheet of paper and handed it to me.

"It's an eviction notice," she said.

No matter how prepared I thought I was, when it came to Marie she still found a way to blindside me. And this was just one more in a long line of punches to my gut that she seemed to administer without thought or feeling.

"It's business, Liam. The wells have dried up and we're losing money on the land. We can build a beautiful apartment complex there. We'll be getting an outstanding return on this."

"I'm sure you will."

Marie caught the tone of my voice. "It doesn't have to be like this, you know."

"It seems natural to me."

"You've never wanted to be part of the family, Liam, yet you always found a way to take advantage of it. Don't look at me like that. You know it's true." She paused a moment before continuing. "Brona and I have been talking. It's just the three of us now. If you want to be part of the family business, the door's open."

I was the last person on Earth Marie wanted to work with. I was tempted to call her bluff just to see her reaction, but I wasn't in the mood to play games.

"I think I'll pass."

"Of course you will. I told Brona you wouldn't do it." Her voice sharp and biting. "She thought that with everything that has happened you'd want to come back and be part of the family, but no, same old Liam."

"Same old Marie."

She leaned back in her chair, a hint of a smile on her lips. "I heard you quit your job at the paper. You're just going to go on surfing and keep taking money from us, is that the plan?"

"It's my trust fund. I can do what I like."

"I don't care about the trust fund. It isn't that much money anyway. It's the inheritance that's coming to you. You didn't earn it. You haven't contributed anything to the family."

Thirty was the magic number. That was when my inheritance was going to kick in and it was about a year away. I don't know why my dad put that date on it. Perhaps he thought I'd be all grown up by then. And yet, as much money that was coming to me—and it was a mind-boggling number—I didn't want it. I wanted nothing to do with them or their imagined legacy. Yet, I didn't want to let Marie off so easily. Then it came to me, something I had wanted to do, but hadn't figured out a way to get it done, until now.

"I have a proposal for you."

"Of course you do. You always want something, what is it?"

"I want you to buy Sunset Marsh for me."

The land was in probate now since the death of James Fordham, and Wyatt had been moved to a mental asylum, legally declared mentally unfit, and, it seemed, he was going to be there for a long time. He was left out of his father's will, though he did have a trust fund his mother left him that was now going to his mental care.

Marie laughed. "For you? You want me to buy it for you? We're already in the process of getting the land, and we have plans for it."

I started doing calculations in my head.

"What if I let you and Mom have all of the inheritance?"

"What are you talking about?"

"My inheritance. I don't want it. It's yours." I knew I could have waited until my next birthday and the money would be mine, and I could buy the land then. Yet, much to my shame, I worried that once I had that money, I'd have a hard time parting with it.

"You're not serious, Liam. This is the dumbest thing I've ever heard."

"I'll trade it for the land. Yes or no? It's one hell of a bargain. You'll get a great return on it."

"Why do you want it so badly?"

"That's my business."

Marie flashed me a suspicious smile. "You really want to do this?"

"Yes."

"Why, Liam?"

"It's personal. And getting out of my inheritance frees me."

"From us?"

"Yes. The money, the inheritance, I don't want any of it." What I didn't tell her was another lasting fear of mine, that if I kept my inheritance, or if I came to work for the family, I'd be in danger of becoming like my father, something Isabelle had warned me about.

Marie's face clouded over. "Go to hell, Liam. You think you're superior to us, don't you? Keep lying to yourself. You're no better than any of us. At least we haven't killed anyone."

Marie liked to throw punches that connected. She knew that one stung.

She paused, then nodded her head. "Okay, we'll do it. You can have the land in exchange for your inheritance." Her eyes bored into mine. "You have a month to get out of your little house. We're going to bulldoze that place into the ground whether you're there or not. You don't like the terms, hire a lawyer. Oh, that's right, you can't afford one now. And, Liam, if you ever want money from us in the future, no matter how badly you may need it, you can forget about it. You made the deal, not me. Our attorneys will draw up the contract." She stared at me, her eyes edged with tears. Her mouth opened as if she had one more thing to say, but nothing came out. She threw her napkin at me and stormed out of the restaurant.

I thought I'd feel relieved, but part of me felt that I had betrayed my family. You never know how deep blood runs in a family until you

350

make a clean break.

The waitress arrived with our order and set the plates down. She asked me if there was anything else she could get.

"No, thank you," I said.

"Is your dinner companion returning?"

"No," I said. "It's just me."

The waitress gave me a confused look and then scurried off to another table

I sat there by myself, feeling more alone than I ever had. I thought of Elisa and wished that things had turned out differently, that she was here with me now, her hand gently touching mine. I recalled a moment, the two of us bathed in the morning light, Elisa lying next to me, her head resting on my chest, just the two of us, together, doing nothing. I'd give anything to have that moment back.

I pulled up along Sunset Marsh and grabbed the sign Lonnie had made for me. I dug a hole and planted the signpost into the ground. Lonnie had carved the sign out of driftwood.

Welcome to The Wyatt Fordham Marshlands.

While I still owned the land, I was in the process of trying to donate it as a preserve to the State of California, which I thought would be an easy transition, but had turned out to be a rather complicated process. Ironically, it was easier to develop land in California than it was to give it away.

I snapped a few pictures of the sign with my Pentax camera that I'd purchased while on R&R in Sydney. Bangkok or Hawaii proved to be more popular choices for soldiers on R&R, depending on what they were looking for. I wasn't interested in renting women or going back to the US. I'd never surfed Australia and since fewer soldiers chose Sydney, I thought it'd be a better place for me to get away. It was a beautiful country, and the surf, while a little too close to the sharks, was invigorating. Yet, somehow, Australia made me long for home. I didn't know why, but for better or worse, I realized I was a California son and that was where I belonged.

But not here, not La Bolsa, not anymore.

I pulled out the piece of paper Greene gave me when we said our goodbyes. His handwriting resembled a doctor's scribble when writing out a prescription. Hell, maybe it was a prescription. I folded the note up neatly and put it back in my pocket.

A lone car sped by me, heading north on the highway, the sound of its engine slowly eclipsed by the pounding surf. For a moment I thought I'd heard Isabelle's voice whispering to me from somewhere deep in the ocean, urging me to pursue what I'd lost. I took in one last breath of the fresh salt air that I'd grown up with. I felt a strong undertow pulling me back, and for a moment I wondered if I was doing the right thing, but the time had come for me to swim against the familiar yet deadly currents that flowed through my family's bloodstream, and finally find out what I was made of.

CHAPTER FIFTY-ONE

The drive up the coast gave me a lot of time to think, too much time maybe, or maybe not enough, I don't know. I'd been camping along the roadside, in no rush to get to my destination, if in fact, that would end up being my destination.

I surfed a few times, wrote up a couple of articles on my Royal Mercury typewriter to submit to *Surf's Up!*. The little desk Lonnie made for me turned out to be pretty handy.

The further north I'd gone, I began to sense the subtle and the not-so-subtle changes in place. The smell of the breeze coming off the ocean, the water temperature, the rhythm and pull of the waves, the vegetation, all new, yet somehow all familiar. The ocean crashing against the land, as ancient as the planet, yet each place had a different story to tell.

I had just finished *The Death of Artemio Cruz*. I wasn't a fast reader, and the novel proved difficult for me to get through. I thought of California, how it had passed through the hands of the Indians that had first settled here, to the Spaniards, then on to the Mexican government, and now to America. The past living with the present, the tensions, the raw beauty, the exploitation, each generation trying to stake their claim, yet knowing that, in the end, the land would never truly be owned by anyone. In the end, none of us are free, we are owned, whether by those more powerful than us, whether by blood relations, whom we love, or the whims of chance, we are not free, and maybe we shouldn't be. Perhaps freedom isn't all it's cracked up to be. Maybe we ought to define ourselves by the people we choose to be held accountable by. Maybe Kris Kristofferson got it right in "Me and Bobby McGee."

We all know who we want to be, and we try to wear that face every day, believing that if we act the part, then we will become that person, that good person whom we strive to be. Then we'll be able to sleep through the night and be able to face ourselves each morning. But life doesn't work that way. Things happen in our lives, things we can't control, that we can't foresee. Something will hit us, slowly, or suddenly and without warning, forcing us to face who we truly are. And if you can, you move on, struggling to be the person you want to see in the mirror, that vision of yourself you can never truly be. But still you keep working on it, because the alternative is living your life in a type of purgatory that will eat at you and eventually consume you, leaving you soulless, bitter, and resentful.

When Lonnie returned from Vietnam he tried to put on a new face, and he tried doing God's work, and maybe he had been succeeding in that, but eventually the never-ending nightmares had caught up to him, leaving him to question if man ever had been guided by God. Perhaps man was just another animal, and like all the other creatures who evolved onto this earth, he wasn't driven by goodness or faith or leaving the world a better place, but surviving as best he could in a hostile world where survival of the fittest wasn't just an evolutionary theory. Somehow, through it all, Lonnie found a way to hold on to his belief in God. "We all have to have faith in something greater than us," he said. "I can't imagine life without it."

I envied his belief. Yet, when I look out and see the ocean, and the land, and the people who I love, I can't help but wonder if there isn't more to this world, and more to us, that we are more than primordial beings thirsting for food, and that there is purpose and meaning for us in this world, and just because we may never find it, doesn't mean it doesn't exist. But if we are lucky enough to find it, we owe it to ourselves to honor it, and not let it slip away.

As I said, I had too much time to think.

I had driven most of the day. Darkness had begun to fall, and the fog was settling in, but I didn't want to stop for the night. I needed to keep moving on. I glanced in the rearview mirror. The face I saw wasn't perfect. It was flawed as all hell. Yet, it was the face of someone I wanted to be, of someone I thought I could be. It was a strange sensation looking in the mirror and liking who I saw.

I entered Santa Cruz just past midnight. I pulled out the piece of paper Detective Greene had given me and studied the map I'd picked up at a Richfield station just outside of town. Almost there.

Elisa lived in a tiny cottage. The lights to the house were out, but her car was parked in the driveway. I climbed out of my van and leaned against it, staring at her home. The beats of my heart increasing, my breath getting short. She didn't know I'd found out where she lived, and I had no idea how she'd react when she saw me. But all I knew was that I couldn't wait to see her.

I made my way across the street, my stomach tying itself into a tangle of knots. A light came on from inside of her home, as if she had sensed my presence. I could just make out her silhouette in the window. She was watching me, daring me to come forward, which caused me to pause, but only for a moment. No, I wasn't about to stop. After all, I hadn't come this far to turn around now. Because I wasn't about to run away. Not me. Not now. Not ever again.

ACKNOWLEDGEMENTS

I'm proud of *California Son*. It took me places I never intended to go and sometimes to places I wasn't sure I wanted to go, but in the end, the journey was worth it. It was not an easy process, though. This book confounded me, confused me, taunted me, and whispered despicable things to me in the dead of night, and it would have defeated me if not for my family and friends.

So, a big thank you to:

My wife, Karen, who patiently listened to my whining and complaining, then lovingly encouraged me to get back to it. She gets to read my stuff first, and her wisdom and keen observations helped keep me sane. She'll always be my rock and the love of my life.

My brother, John, who combed through countless manuscript revisions without losing any enthusiasm. I relied a lot on his story/ editorial judgment, and I'm thankful he was always willing and eager to bounce ideas around with me. He went way above and beyond the call of duty.

Fellow author, Keith Tittle, whose sound insights and advice were greatly welcomed.

Ellen Snortland and her wonderful Writers' Workout group—Gail Libman, Justin Chapman, Alaine Lowell, Teri Ortt, Jefferson Black,

Cynthia Frederick, and Maeve McGrath Harkness.

JaBari Brown, Tony Perez, Guy Margedant, Debra Ono, James Vasquez, Miles Corwin, Jennifer Taw, Andrea Jarrell, David Alfaro, Tommy Robinson, Therese Bagsit, Gigi Herbert, Charles Garcia, Phil Bonney, Steve Bailey, Stella Lopez, Paul Kikuchi, Carol Woodcliff, Lisa Gaeta, Diane O'Connell, Brianna Flaherty, Donna McCrohan Rosenthal, Iram Shahzadi (Aaniyah Ahmed at 99designs), and Crystal Watanabe.

My mom, Anne Burgess; my father, John Burgess Sr. (I miss you, Dad); my sister, Barbara Shaw; and to my funny kick-ass daughters, Hayley and Kinsey. You guys are the best!